THE LOST SWORDS: ENDGAME

THE LOST SWORDS: ENDGAME

WAYFINDER'S STORY
SHIELDBREAKER'S STORY

Fred Saberhagen

Contents

Contents

THE SEVENTH BOOK OF
LOST SWORDS:
WAYFINDER'S STORY

1

His huge, work-roughened hands shaking with excitement, young Valdemar turned up the sleeves of his farmer's shirt. Squatting on the earth floor of his solitary hut, peering intently by firelight and fading daylight, he reached for the long, heavy bundle that lay near the fire and began very gradually to undo its wrappings of gray cloth. The bundle was neatly made, tied with strong cord. As Valdemar worked to undo the knots, he did his best to keep himself from thinking of what he might expect to find within. He told himself he had no right to expect anything at all. But it was as if he wished to shield himself from an enormous disappointment . . .

The wrappings loosened and began to fall away. As soon as an area of unrelieved blackness came into view, unmistakably part of the hilt of an edged weapon, the young man's fingers ceased to move. Like many other people, he had a sensitivity to the presence of powerful magic, and he was already beginning to realize just what kind of weapon he had been given.

Valdemar thought that he could feel the blood drain from his face. Leaning his enormous weight back on his heels, he did his unpracticed best to formulate a prayer to beneficent Ardneh.

Whatever prayer he at last managed to say went up in silence. Outside, spring wind howled fiercely, shoving against the rough stone walls of his lonely hut, rattling the crude, ill-fitting door, spattering rain through the hole in the roof that served as chimney, so that the small fire, fueled mostly by last year's dried vines, hissed as if in pain.

He had a serious mystery to contemplate.

An unknown visitor, working alone in pursuit of some unguessable purpose, who had come and gone before Valdemar had been able to catch more than a glimpse of him—or her—had just made the young grape-grower a present of one of the Twelve Swords. The recipient felt overwhelmed by the discovery. And yet—even in this tremendous moment when Valdemar first glimpsed the ebon hilt, he found himself thinking that he ought to be more surprised at the nature of this gift than he really was.

He had the strange feeling that he had always known, had never doubted, that something like this—something truly great—was fated to happen to him sooner or later.

Well, here it was. And whatever unconscious anticipation might be keeping him from being properly astonished, he was certainly beginning to be afraid.

Scant minutes ago, the unexpected shadow and the silent form of the mysterious caller had moved almost simultaneously, and with a swiftness almost magical, past the door of Valdemar's isolated dwelling, interrupting the young man in the midst of preparing his evening meal. The door had been left slightly ajar for more light, and to let the smoke-hole draw.

Until that moment, Valdemar had had no suspicion that any other human being was anywhere within a couple of kilometers. By the time he had jumped up and run outdoors, the figure of his anonymous visitor was already almost out of sight in mist and rain. Valdemar had caught only a single glimpse of a human shape, so muffled in gray garments that it might have been either man or woman.

The gigantic youth had started in pursuit, swiftly bounding up one, two, three of the narrow cultivated terraces that rose above his hut. But by the time he had reached the third terrace, his caller had already disappeared into the wet twilight shrouding the domesticated vines, the scant wild bushes, and the granite outcroppings of the lonely mountainside.

Shouting for his vanished visitor to stop, Valdemar had continued the chase a little farther, almost to the boundary of his cultivated land, but without success. Returning to his hut a couple of minutes later, the young man had picked up the bundle which had been so mysteriously deposited at his door. He had paused to reassure himself that at least it was not alive (he had heard stories of babies being left at the doors of lonely huts) and carried it in by the fire. After closing the ill-fitting door again, and shaking his garments dry as best he could, Valdemar had hesitantly begun to unwrap his present—a process which came, moments later, to a shocked halt.

Though he was scarcely past the age of twenty, and for most of the past year had dwelt in this lonely place, Valdemar could not claim complete innocence or ignorance regarding the affairs of the great world.

Like every other thinking person, he knew something of the history of the Twelve Swords, magical weapons created almost forty years ago by the gods themselves. Valdemar knew also that two of the Swords had been destroyed not long after they were made. This black hilt partially visible before him, if it were genuine, might belong to any of the remaining Ten. And though like most people he had never seen, much less handled, any of the Twelve, Valdemar could not doubt the authenticity of this one. A heavy elegance of magic flowed into his fingertips the instant they brushed against it; and to magic he was not a total stranger.

It was common knowledge in the world that four Swords—Shieldbreaker, Dragonslicer, Stonecutter, and Sightblinder—had for some years been gathered in the royal armory of Tasavalta, under control of that realm's powerful and unfortunate Prince Mark. Among the six others now lost to public knowledge were the two Valdemar considered the most abominable of the god-forged weapons, Soulcutter and the Mindsword.

No one, as he understood the case, could ever be sure of the whereabouts of Coinspinner, a tricky blade given to randomly moving itself about. Nor was there any way to guess the whereabouts of Farslayer, Wayfinder, or Woundhealer. That last was the only one of the surviving ten that Valdemar would have rejoiced to find in his own possession.

Crouching near the fire, alone with his mysterious gift, the youth hesitated for a long time before continuing the process of unwrapping. His irresolution was grounded in the fact that he feared certain of the gods' Swords more than others, and at this point it was still at least theoretically possible for him to refuse the knowledge of which one he had been given. At this point he would still be able, if he chose, to tie up the gray cloth again, carry the whole still-mysterious bundle back out into the rain, and drop it, lose it, deep in some rocky crevice among the nearby crags, hoping that no one else would ever discover the presence of the thing of power, or be able to come near it.

For what seemed to Valdemar a long time he sat there on his heels. The wind battering at his door seemed to mock his fearful hesitancy, while outside the clouded daylight slowly faded. Still, enough light remained inside the hut, around his dying fire, for him to see whatever white mark might be emblazoned on the Sword's hilt, when his next tug at the gray cloth should reveal it.

Of course, one Sword had no white symbol at all. If that was what he found, it would mean fate had put into his hands Soulcutter, the Tyrant's Blade.

The young giant's eyes closed briefly. His strong, almost-handsome face was troubled. Awkwardly he uttered words aloud: "Ardneh, let it not be that one. I do not want the responsibility of trying to hide that demon's Blade. Or of trying to destroy it." He understood full well that breaking any Sword, or otherwise rendering it ineffective, would be far beyond his powers.

"Therefore let it be any of them, except Soulcutter, or . . ."

Valdemar's prayer stumbled to a halt, as he realized that for him the second most fearful of the Blades would probably not, after all, be that called the Mindsword. Given that one, he could simply refrain from drawing it; for him, he thought, the power to bend others to his will would pose no great temptation. Farslayer would be far more likely to be his downfall. There were certain people in the world, oppressors of humanity, for whom—though he had never met them—the youth felt a dislike that threatened always to spill over into personal hatred; and if the life of one of those persons, wherever they might be, should be so helplessly delivered into his hands, Valdemar feared his own latent capacity for violence.

Yes, it would be better if he got rid of this unknown Sword at once, not tempting himself by looking for the symbol which it must bear upon the hilt . . .

Valdemar's hands quivered. Because he might, for all he knew, be holding Woundhealer, the Sword of Mercy. That glorious possibility was enough to eliminate any thought of plunging the mysterious gift into a crevasse before he had identified it.

After minutes of immobility, the youth with a sudden jerk stripped back the gray cloth completely from the black hilt.

A small white arrow-symbol, pointing upward to the pommel, leapt into view. Neither the best nor the worst of possibilities had been realized. The weapon in Valdemar's hands was Wayfinder. The Sword of Wisdom, it was also called—Ardneh grant it bring him that!

Valdemar breathed somewhat more easily. Toward Wayfinder he felt timidity and awe, but no overwhelming fear. Gently he peeled away the remaining wrappings, exposing a plain leather sheath. Without pausing for further thought, he clasped the hilt and drew forth a full meter of incomparable double-edged Blade. The faint light of fading day and dying fire gleamed softly on steel smoother and sharper than any human armorer had ever crafted, at least since the lost civilization of the Old World. Beneath the surface of the metal a lovely mottled pattern was perceptible.

Valdemar ran a tremulous finger along the flat side of the tremendous Blade. No, despite his youth, he was no stranger to the touch of magic. But he had never in his life felt anything the like of this.

A happy thought struck suddenly. Some of the new strain and worry vanished from his youthful face.

"Powers who rule this Sword," he said, self-consciously—then paused for a deep breath, and started over. "Powers of this Sword, whoever or whatever you may be—I understand that giving guidance is your function. Guide me, therefore—guide me to the person—to her—to the woman I have—I have almost despaired of ever finding. The one who is most fit, most suitable, to share my life."

Though he was utterly alone, the young man could feel his cheeks warming. Frowning suddenly, he quickly amended: "Let all be done in accordance with the will of Ardneh."

Having concluded this awkward speech, Valdemar arose, gripping the black hilt firmly in both of his great hands, fingers overlapping. Tentatively he moved the great Blade in a horizontal circle. One direction alone, almost straight east, set the Sword's tip quivering. At the surge of magic he cried out, wordlessly. For just a moment the movement had become so violent that the weapon had almost leaped free of his grip.

On a warm spring afternoon, seven days after the day when Valdemar had unwrapped the Sword, and more than a hundred kilometers distant from his hut, two pilgrims were making their way across a heavily wooded hillside that formed one flank of a deep ravine.

The first of these gray-clad travelers was a woman, apparently about sixty years of age, but still vigorous and hearty. There was nothing feeble in the way she moved across the steep slope, among the thickly-spaced, narrow trunks. Her silver hair was long, but bound up closely. The strains of a long life showed in the woman's face, but no burden that seemed too much for her present determination. Like many other female pilgrims or travelers, she wore boots, trousers and a loose jacket, and was armed for self-defense with a short sword.

The crowded treetrunks made it all but impossible for two to travel side by side. The woman's companion, who walked three or four paces behind her and carried a similarly serviceable but somewhat more impressive weapon at his belt, was a man in his early twenties, sturdily built, of average size. The young man's appearance, like the woman's, suggested both the weariness of long travel and a remaining capacity to deal with formidable difficulties.

The woman halted suddenly. She frowned and squinted at the sun, which shone brightly from beyond the canopy of the tall trees' small spring leaves. Then she inspected the terrain, as well as she could in the midst of a forest.

"This hill curves round," she announced to her fellow traveler at last. "And I see no end to the curve ahead. It carries us farther and farther to the east."

"And that, my lady, is not the direction in which we want to go," the young man responded. "Well, then. Shall we try climbing to the top of the ridge again? Or going down into the ravine?"

The lady sighed. "Zoltan, we are well and truly lost. No reason to think the bottom of this ravine will be more hospitable than any of the others we've struggled through during the past two days." In those dark gorges, the ubiquitous thin-trunked trees had grown more closely and ever more closely together, until it became impossible for adult humans to force a passage anywhere between them. An army of men with axes would have earned their pay clearing a road.

"And no reason either," replied Zoltan, "to suppose that the leather-wings are going to let us alone this time if we come out of the trees up on the hilltop." He rubbed at his left arm, which was still bandaged—though fortunately not disabled—from their last encounter with flying reptiles, two days ago.

"I suppose we might risk trying the hilltop just before sunset," the woman said thoughtfully. "If we were able to see far enough to get our bearings—" She broke off abruptly, holding herself motionless. Above the high canopy of leaves a silent, broad-winged form drifted; a half-intelligent enemy, cruel-clawed and implacably hostile.

When the wind-borne reptile had drifted out of sight and hearing, Zoltan spoke again, his voice cautiously low. "Anyway, we're soon going to need water." Each was carrying a single small canteen. "We'll have to go down into the ravines for that, of course. This one may be dry, but the next—" He fell silent at the woman's imperious gesture. Her face had abruptly turned away from him, and she was listening intently for the repetition of a small sound just detected from ahead.

In a moment Zoltan, looking over his companion's shoulder, could see a tall human shape, garbed in dull colors, moving among the dun-colored trunks, still fifty meters off, approaching along the hillside.

Both travelers watched in ready silence, hands on swordhilts. The single figure approaching seemed to be making no effort at stealth. The towering, broadshouldered man was clad in what appeared to be a farmer's rough shirt and trousers and woolen vest. In both hands he gripped a long-bladed sword with which he steadily swept the air before him. Zoltan, watching, felt the hair stir on the back of his neck. This could be a Sword indeed!

The stranger continued moving along the slope directly toward the pilgrim pair, though as yet he had given no indication that he was aware of their presence.

Zoltan, staring at the approaching figure with intense, frowning concentration, whispered: "Is that—?"

"Shh. We'll see."

Amid the dun trunks the seeker so superbly armed had approached within ten meters of the two motionless travelers in dull gray before he saw them. When he did, he stopped in his tracks, startled, continuing to hold the Sword leveled in their direction. Then, looking somewhat flustered, he grounded the bright point.

For a long moment all three remained silent.

At last the young farmer—for so his clothing made him appear to be—said: "Greetings." His voice was soft, but the pair who heard him got the impression that only a conscious effort made it so. "Greetings, in Ardneh's name." He was peering closely at the lady, and appeared to be trying to conceal growing disappointment and confusion.

"And to you," replied the lady. "May you find peace and truth." Zoltan at her elbow murmured similar sentiments.

"My object is entirely peaceful," the other assured them, gesturing with an enormous hand. He seemed now to be recovering from his initial shock, whatever might have been its cause. He was a head taller than most men, and of massive build, his body carrying a minimum of fat. His clothing, particularly his boots, gave evidence of an extended journey. He carried pack and canteen, as any traveler most likely would. A long, plain, leather sheath belted at his waist, of a size to hold his Sword, looked vaguely as if it should belong to someone else.

He added: "I am called Valdemar."

"I am Yambu," the woman told him simply. "This is Zoltan, who has chosen to travel with me. We are both pilgrims, of a sort."

The young farmer nodded and smiled, acknowledging the information. His hair was dark and curly, his blue eyes mild, flanking an interestingly bent nose. The more one looked at him, the bigger and stronger he appeared.

"Yambu," he repeated. "Yes, ma'am." His eyes moved on. "And you are Zoltan." Then some memory visibly caught at Valdemar, so that his gaze went back to the silver-haired woman. "An unusual name, ma'am." he remarked.

"Mine? Oh yes. And an unusual weapon that you are carrying today, young sir."

Perhaps Valdemar flushed slightly; in his weathered face it was hard to be sure. "Lady, in my hands I hope this Sword is something other than a weapon. It has guided me here—to you. Your pardon, lady, if I aim the blade at you again; I promise you I mean no harm."

Taking care to remain at a distance well out of thrusting range, Valdemar lifted his Sword's point again. All three could see distinctly how the fine blade quivered when it was leveled straight toward Yambu.

The lady did not seem much surprised. "And what desire of yours," she asked, "does Wayfinder expect me to satisfy?"

This time there was no doubt that Valdemar was blushing. "I see you know this Sword's name. So I suppose you know what it is. That should— that ought to—make it easier for me to explain. As I said, my goal is peaceful. I . . ."

"Yes?"

"I am a farmer, lady. Actually I have a vineyard, which I have left untended. And I am looking for a wife."

There was a pause.

"Ah," said Yambu at last. A thin smile curved her lips. "And you confided this wish to the Sword of Wisdom?"

"Yes ma'am."

"And the Sword has brought you to me."

"Yes ma'am."

"And I am not quite the bride you have been imagining. Well, rest easy in your mind, young man. Were you to make me a proposal of marriage, I would not accept it."

"Yes ma'am," repeated Valdemar. He looked partly relieved and partly chagrined.

"We must discuss this," said the lady, "but just now my companion and I face problems of greater urgency. Have you experienced any particular difficulty along the way, in the last day or two of your journey?"

Valdemar blinked at her. "Difficulty? No. What sort of difficulty? Oh, do you mean bandits?" The young giant smiled faintly. "I never worry much about that sort of thing. And if there were any who saw me, no doubt they kept clear when they saw how I was armed."

Zoltan cleared his throat. "No trouble in finding your way through this forest, perhaps? Or in dealing with flying reptiles?"

Valdemar looked up, concerned; at the moment the sky was free of drifting shadows. "No trouble finding my way; I simply walked the way Wayfinder told me to go. And no reptiles of any kind; I've never seen one that could fly."

"*Any* kind of trouble?"

"None. Well, several times, for no good cause that I could see, the Sword counseled me to change direction. And once, when I saw no reason not to move on, it kept me walking in a tight circle for an hour, so in effect I was held in one location. But nothing that I would call trouble. Why?"

"Then would you now ask your Sword," put in Yambu gently, "to put aside for the moment the matter of your bride-to-be, and lead us all three safely out of this damned wildwood?"

Openmouthed, Valdemar gazed at her for a long moment. Then he nodded.

Less than an hour later all three travelers were resting comfortably at the bottom of another ravine, where a spring of clear water bubbled gently out of a crevice between rocks, and the trees grew just closely enough together to keep all sizable airborne creatures at a safe distance. Yambu and Zoltan had already satisfied their thirst at the spring, and were now refilling their canteens. Valdemar meanwhile had sheathed his elegant weapon and was bringing out generous portions of dried meat and hard bread from his pack.

Far upslope, too far to be of immediate concern, an ominous, silent shadow drifted overhead, above the canopy of leaves; drifted and came back and went away again, as if it were no longer certain of where its prey might be.

"Those creatures hunt us, young man," said Yambu, almost in a whisper. "Leather-wings—and sometimes worse than that. You say you have never seen them before?"

"I know them only by reputation." The youthful giant looked vaguely horrified, and at the same time fascinated. But not particularly afraid. "Why do they hunt you?"

"I believe they are in the service of some much more formidable enemy. Serving as his scouts. Then, too, it is my belief that any of the Twelve Swords tends to draw trouble to itself. And that one you are carrying in particular."

"And yet I have asked this Sword only to help me find a bride. And now to guide all three of us to safety." Valdemar seemed more disappointed, and gently puzzled, than alarmed by Yambu's reading of their situation.

"You've heard the Song of Swords? You remember how the verse about this one goes?" Zoltan asked him, and without waiting for an answer proceeded to recite in a low voice:

"Who holds Wayfinder finds good roads
Its master's step is brisk.
The Sword of Wisdom lightens loads—"

" '—but adds unto their risk,' " Valdemar concluded. "Yes, I've heard that song since I was a child. Never thinking . . ."

The gigantic youth let the matter drop. Then he looked at the silver-haired woman again. His gaze was timid, but resolute. "I can remember hearing, long ago," he remarked, "of a lady named Yambu, who was once known as the Silver Queen."

She who bore that name ignored the invitation to discuss her past. Having finished filling her canteen, she sat at ease on the mossy bank beside the spring.

"Zoltan and I thank you for your help, young man," she said graciously. "Where will you ask your Sword to point you next? And may I ask you just where and how Wayfinder came into your possession?"

Valdemar looked up at the treetops. "I still seek a wife," he declared stubbornly. "Why this Sword has led me to you, lady, I confess I do not understand."

"There may be an easy explanation. When the object sought is otherwise impossible, or very difficult, to obtain directly, Wayfinder leads its master first to the necessary means to bring the goal within reach. You may be sure the Sword of Wisdom is not suggesting that you propose marriage to me, who could be your grandmother. At least let us hope not. Sword or no, that would be far from wise. Besides, I have no wish to spend my last years growing grapes."

"Why, then, has Wayfinder brought me to you?"

Yambu shook her head. "It would seem that, somehow—I do not know how—I can help you to achieve your goal."

Valdemar sighed. More to himself than to the others he murmured: "I will now repeat my first request. I want this Sword to lead me to the woman, of all the women on earth, who will be the perfect, the ideal wife for me. Nothing more and nothing less."

And he drew Wayfinder from its sheath and held it out again in his great hands.

Once more the point reacted, quivering, only when it was aimed precisely at the lady.

Without comment the young giant re-sheathed the Sword of Wisdom at his waist. Giving up the puzzle for the moment, he recounted to his new companions the story of his enigmatic visitor, seven days past.

He concluded with a question. "Has either of you any idea who my strange caller might have been? It was someone who wore gray, even as you do. That's all I could really see."

Zoltan and Yambu looked at each other. Zoltan shrugged. The lady said: "A number of ideas; but no reason to take any of them seriously."

Her young companion nodded. "Certainly it was neither of us, if you are thinking that. A week ago we were nowhere near the region where you say you live. As for wearing gray, uncountable thousands of folk do that. Your own garments have acquired something of that tinge from travel."

The bigger young man nodded ruefully. "Then can either of you guess why this Sword should have led me to you?"

Zoltan only shook his head.

"I think," Yambu told Valdemar, "you will have to be patient if you want an answer to that question. It may be that the answer will never become clear, even if you do find your wife."

Valdemar took thought, running long fingers through his dark curly hair. A sparse beard was beginning to sprout on his youthful cheeks. Then almost shyly he inquired: "Might it have anything to do with the fact that . . . as I said before, a lady with your name was once the Silver Queen? But I had thought . . ."

Yambu nodded impatiently. "Very well, my history is no great secret. That was once my title. But I don't know why my past, good or bad, should have anything much to do with a young man who raises grapes and seeks a bride. You would have expected the Silver Queen to be a somewhat younger woman? Hold Soulcutter in your hands, my friend, throughout a day of battle, and you will be fortunate indeed if you do not look worse than I do."

Now young Valdemar indeed looked awed. "I apologize, my lady, for what must seem unwarranted curiosity."

"No apology is necessary."

The peasant-looking youth frowned for a while at the weapon hanging from his belt. Then he said: "Perhaps I must take the Sword's bringing me to you to mean that I should stay with you until it tells me otherwise. Perhaps it even means that I should turn over Wayfinder and its powers to you."

Yambu was frowning too.

Impulsively Valdemar said: "Let us try that!" In a moment he had unbelted his Sword, and was gallantly proffering the black hilt in her direction, the sheathed Blade balanced flat across his forearm.

Quietly she responded: "I do not know that you have hit on the right interpretation, young man. But . . . on the other hand, why should I fear this Sword?"

Her lips moved again, almost silently. Only Zoltan, who was close beside her, could hear her very low whisper: "Yet I do."

A moment later, she was reaching out to firmly grasp Wayfinder's hilt. Having accepted the weapon, and drawn it from its sheath, Yambu stood up straight, her voice becoming a little louder. "It is a long time since I have felt the power of any Sword in my hands. Well, Sword of Wisdom, here you are, and here am I. If you can read my heart, show me the way which I must go to satisfy it."

The Silver Queen held out the blade in a strong two-handed grip, then swept it around the horizon, in unconscious imitation of Valdemar's first gesticulation with the weapon, seven days ago.

In her hands, Wayfinder's keen point quivered at one point of the compass only—almost straight east.

Yambu let the tip of the heavy blade sag to the earth. She said to Valdemar: "I am favored with a definite reply. Now, do you want me to give you this weapon back?"

To the surprise of both the others, the giant youth put both his hands behind him, as if to make things difficult for anyone who meant to thrust the black hilt back into his possession. He said: "My lady, I wonder . . ."

"Yes?"

"Might the Sword's response to me mean that I am to stay with you, at least for a time? Travel with you?"

Yambu thought about it. "It brought you all this way to me. I suppose it might mean something of the sort," she conceded at length, as if reluctantly.

"And just now, in your hands, Wayfinder pointed east. Do you know what lies in that direction?"

Yambu smiled. "Half of the world," she said.

Zoltan, with his head tipped back, was leaning alternately to right and left, trying to peer upward through the canopy of leaves. He said: "Some days ago, we two were discussing the question of our destination, the true object of our pilgrimage, in philosophical terms. Then we began to be hunted. Being hunted limits one's time for philosophical discussion. In the process of trying to escape from the reptiles we became lost. Valdemar, you've helped us now to temporary safety. But as a practical matter, I must say that our next goal, whether east or west, ought to be some place of greater security. Somewhere completely out of the ken of those whose creatures stalk and harry us."

Valdemar looked from one to the other of his new companions, trying to assess the situation. There was no doubting the reality of those drifting shadows that kept reappearing no very great distance up the hill.

"And who might your enemies be?" he asked with concern.

"There are a number of possibilities," said Yambu drily. Again she took up the Sword in both hands. "But let us not become obsessed with safety. We are going east."

2

"HURLED to the ends of the earth, you say? Astride a demon?" The speaker, a startlingly handsome and apparently very youthful man, gave every indication that he found the prospect hugely amusing.

"Yes, to the ends of the earth, or farther for all I know. That was months ago, of course, and neither the Dark King nor his demonic steed have been heard from since." The youthful-looking man's informant, a short, blond woman or girl who appeared even younger than he, flashed a bright grin of her own. "Is it not entertaining, Master Wood?"

The two who spoke with such apparent carelessness of sorcerer's and demon's fate were standing casually just outside the massive outer wall of the world headquarters of the Blue Temple. The man was actually leaning against the building's stones. Squat granite columns, each thicker than the length of a man's body, and broad stone steps leading up to doors worthy of a fortress made the establishment an archetype of the substantial, or perhaps even a parody of such. The two appeared to be waiting for something; but what that might be, or why they had chosen this spot to hold their talk, was not immediately obvious.

The handsome young man nodded. His large, athletic-looking body was well dressed in tunic and cloak of rich fabric, though of no outstanding elegance. He might have been a prosperous merchant, or perhaps a physician. Surely not a warrior, for no trace of any material weapon was visible about his person.

He said: "Entertaining, yes. The demon was hurled away, I suppose, by the Emperor's name in the mouth of the Emperor's bastard, and that poor pretender of a magician, who likes to ride on demons, was whisked away helplessly with his mount—"

The young man laughed again, louder than before, and this time his companion laughed with him. She was garbed in a tight-fitting outfit of silver and blue that showed off her fine figure to advantage; the clothing suggested an expensive courtesan. The heads of passers-by turned in their direction; such merriment was uncommon here in the Blue Temple precincts.

Both parties to the conversation ignored the passers-by, even as they appeared to be ignoring the Blue Temple itself. But he who had been addressed as Master Wood soon sobered from his laughter. He stroked his chin in thought.

Almost wistfully he said: "And yet, Tigris—an alliance with Vilkata might well have been to our benefit."

Tigris had already assumed a more thoughtful expression too. She responded: "He may be able to return, Master, sooner or later. Or, if he cannot come back unaided, we might help him. That may still be possible. Yet, I fear that the Dark King was—or is—something of a bungler. Considerable skill in handling demons, one must admit that."

"Considerable. But finally insufficient," amended the other.

"Yes, Master, as I say—finally insufficient." The shapely young woman nodded soberly.

"And one of the Swords went with Vilkata."

"Yes, Master. The Mindsword, as you well know."

Wood allowed his displeasure at that accident to show. He had particularly coveted that weapon for his own. Then he brightened slightly. "Well, none of that can be helped now. Today we face other problems, quite sufficient to claim our full attention for a time."

"As you so accurately say, my lord."

In the bustle of the populous city, even a pair of such striking appearance did not draw a great deal of attention. Once or twice a beggar started to approach them, then, as if warned by some instinct, veered away.

Once a sedan chair, guarded on both sides by a file of mounted men, passed very close to them, entering the Blue Temple headquarters through a nearby gate.

The man called Wood appeared equally indifferent to potentate and mendicants. "So," he mused, "our erstwhile rival Vilkata, the Dark King, is probably not going to be available in the foreseeable future to discuss alliances. Nor is the demon who bore him away into—ought we to say into eternity? Nor, I suppose, can we hope to recruit any other demons from the Dark King's retinue." Wood's voice became abstracted. "That's all right, though—I can summon powers enough of my own whenever there's a need."

"Yes, Master, certainly you can." Impish little Tigris nodded violently.

Squinting at her, her master thought to himself that she was almost certain to prove something of a distraction in the staid Blue Temple offices, into which he planned to bring her very soon. Very likely, Wood considered, he would have to dismiss Tigris—or else effect a drastic

though temporary change in her appearance—before the conference got
very far. But that decision did not have to be made now.

The girl began to fidget, as if rendered uncomfortable by an overabun-
dance of energy. She moved a step away, and with a dancing glide came
back again. "If it is permitted to ask, Master, why are we waiting? Are
those moneybags in the Blue Temple expecting us at a particular time?"

The young man grinned. He was not really a young man, for even now
his eyes looked very old. "My dear Tigris, they are not expecting us at all.
I expect that an unannounced arrival will produce a more co-operative
attitude on their part, once they have recovered from their initial . . .
yes?"

This last word was not addressed to Tigris, but to a sudden blurring of
the atmosphere approximately a meter above her blond head. Out of this
miniature aerial vortex proceeded a tiny inhuman voice, speaking to
Wood in squeaky, deferential tones:

"The man Hyrcanus is now alone, Master, inside his private office. Do
you wish me to accompany you inside the building?"

"Yes, but see that you remain invisible and impalpable in there. Unless, of course, you hear me suggest otherwise." Wood was standing erect
now, the air of indolence having fallen from him like a shed cloak. "Tigris?"

The disturbance was already gone from the air above her head.
"Ready, as always, Master."

Wood gestured, and their two human bodies instantaneously disappeared.

The locus of their reappearance a moment later was a tall, narrow,
dimly lighted chamber deep in the bowels of Blue Temple headquarters.
Though the room was obviously only an anteroom of some sort, the
visitors found it elegantly furnished, with a thick carpet underfoot. The
walls were paneled in exotic wood, subtly lighted by Old World lamps
that burned inside their glassy shells with a cold and practically inex-
haustible secret fire.

Wood and Tigris came into existence standing side by side and almost
hand in hand, before a cluttered desk behind which a male clerk or
secretary looked up in petrifaction at their unanticipated presence.

The thin man in a tunic of blue and gold stared at them uncomprehendingly, his eyes watering as if from long perusal of crabbed hand-
writing and columned numbers. Even now, in what must have been a
state of shock, the words that fell from his lips were trite; perhaps it had
been a long, long time since he had spoken any words that were not.

Clearing his throat, the clerk said in a cracked voice: "Er—you have an appointment?"

Wood smiled impishly. "I have just made one, yes."

"Er—the name, sir? Er—madam?"

"I'm hardly that." And Tigris giggled.

The assured, undeniable presence of the pair seemed to place them beyond the scope of any fundamental challenge.

"I will see . . . I will . . . er . . ." Almost choking in confusion, the clerk bowed himself away through a door leading to an inner office. The two visitors exchanged looks of amusement. A few moments later the thin man was back, ushering Wood and Tigris into the next room. There they confronted the Chairman of the Blue Temple himself, a man known to the world by the single name of Hyrcanus.

Here, in the inner sanctum of power, the furnishings were more sumptuous, though still restrained, their every detail tastefully thought out. Wood had expected nothing more or less, but Tigris was somewhat surprised.

"I thought to see more gold and jewels," she murmured. Wood shook his head slightly. He understood that splendor here would have been out of place; the finest appointments could have done no more than hint at the immensity of the temple's wealth.

The Chairman was small, rubicund, and bald, with a round ageless face and a jovial expression belied by his ice-blue eyes. He was seated, flanked by ivory statues of Midas and Croesus, behind an enormous desk, engaged in counting up some kind of tiles or tokens. A large abacus, of colored wood in several shades, stood at the Chairman's elbow. The walls of the chamber were lined with account books and other records, some of them visibly dusty. Spiders had established themselves in at least two of the room's upper corners. The windows were barred, and were so high and dark that it was impossible for ordinary human eyes to see outside.

Raising his gaze from his desk, Hyrcanus stared at Wood in utter blankness for a long moment. His eyebrows rose when he looked at Tigris. Then he snapped irritably at his visitors: "Who are you? What are you doing here? I have made no appointment for this hour."

"But I," Wood retorted, "have made one to see you."

Such a response, from an utter stranger, evidently could not be made to fit into the Chairman's view of life's possibilities. Hyrcanus fixed a stern gaze upon his shaken underling, the thin clerk who still hovered near. "What possessed you to schedule an appointment at this time?"

The man's fingers fumbled with imaginary knots in the air before him.

"Sir, I—I have scheduled no appointment. I thought perhaps that you had done so privately. I have no idea who these people are."

"My name is Wood," said the male visitor in a languid voice, speaking directly to Hyrcanus. "I should think it almost impossible that you have not heard of me."

The name took a moment to sink in. Then, with a slight movement of one foot beneath his desk, a gesture quite imperceptible to ordinary visitors (but noted at once by these two callers, and dismissed as harmless), the Chairman sent a signal.

Wood made a generous, open-handed gesture. "By all means," he encouraged, with a slight nod. "Summon whatever help will make you feel secure." Tigris, at her master's elbow, giggled. It was a small sound, almost shy.

In response to the Chairman's urgent signal, there ensued a subtle interplay of powers within the chamber's dusty air, much of it beyond the reach of the Chairman's senses, or those of his secretary. Powers charged with the magical defense of this room and edifice clashed briefly, trying immaterial lances, with the invisible escort of the two human visitors. The trial was brief but quite conclusive: the defenders of the Temple retreated, cowed.

Moments later came sounds of hurried human movement in an adjoining room. A door, not the one through which the callers had come in, opened quietly, and another bald man, this one obviously elderly, looked in with a wary expression.

"I assume," Tigris said to him, smiling brightly, "that you must be the Director of Security?" She almost curtsied.

The newcomer glanced at her, frowned, and kept silent, looking to his chief for orders.

"I would like to know," Hyrcanus grated at him, "how these two got in here."

The man in the doorway cleared his throat. "Sir, I recognize this man as the well-known wizard, Wood. The woman with him—"

"He has already told me his *name,*" Hyrcanus interrupted. "What I want to know is how—"

"And someday perhaps I will tell you how we got in," said Wood, interrupting the interrupter. "But there are other matters I wish to discuss first."

The Director of Security, seemingly unimpressed, stared at his fellow magician. "I know your name, and I warn you that you had better leave. At once."

"You? *Warn me?*"

The elder nodded impressively. His face had become lugubrious. "I am indeed the Director of Security here. We here do not fear your powers." Wood's eyes were twinkling dangerously. "Only because you do not comprehend them."

"I believe," the Director remarked drily, "that you are the same Wood who about two years ago visited Sha's Casino, a Red Temple establishment in the city of Bihari."

"And so?"

"On that occasion—correct me, sir, if I am wrong—you encountered certain enemies and were forced to make a swift retreat. It has further come to my attention that you entered Sha's Casino armed with the Sword Shieldbreaker, and that you left without that weapon—and lacking any compensation for it." The elderly man in the doorway smirked faintly.

Tigris, looking at her master, paled a trifle.

Wood put his fists on his hips. His voice was ice. "On that occasion, my man, I was opposed by forces well beyond your ability—let alone that of your money-grubbing masters here—to understand, much less to deal with."

A moment of silence followed. It was plain from their expressions that Wood's current hearers—except for Tigris, of course—remained unconvinced.

The wizard nodded briskly. "Very well, then. I see that a demonstration will be necessary."

The Director's expression became uncertain.

Hyrcanus behind his desk started to say something, then remained quiet.

Silence held for a long moment.

Wood's eyes closed. His left hand extended slightly in front of him, palm upward. The long fingers quivered. Then the hand moved, and the forearm, slowly, made a gentle lifting gesture. Near the high ceiling an almost imperceptible turmoil in the air grew briefly, lightly sharper.

In moments this gentle disturbance was answered by a much heavier vibration. An inhuman groaning and thudding seemed to start in the roots of the huge building and progress slowly upward. Soon distant frightened yells could be heard, rising from somewhere below the thickly carpeted office floor.

Tigris was smiling faintly now, watching the Blue Temple men for their reaction. Neither of them had moved, though the eyes of the Chairman seemed about to pop.

Wood's face, his eyes still closed, had hardened into an implacable mask.

The door to the secretary's anteroom burst open, to frame the large form of an armed guard officer. "Sir! The gold—" The man had trouble finishing his sentence.

Hyrcanus snapped: "What of the gold?"

The guard turned halfway round, gesturing over one beefy shoulder. "It's—coming—up the stairs—"

The Chairman leapt up from his chair, trying to see out past him.

The deepest rumbling, which had begun down around the massive, vaulted foundations of this Mother Temple, was now gradually shaping itself into a heavy, metallic rhythm. It sounded like a company, perhaps a regiment, of heavy infantry, clad in armor, marching upstairs in close formation.

There were continued cries of alarm, and more security people came pressing up behind the officer in the doorway.

Hyrcanus started to come around from behind his desk, and then went back.

The guards now crowding the doorway were pushed aside. But not by human force.

Bursting past them, into the Chairman's private office, came moving gold, coins and bars and works of art, all moving as if alive. The yellow treasure had somehow been conglomerated, magically held together, into the shape of a huge and heavy many-legged creature, a gigantic centipede. At intervals this animation broke apart into separate marching figures, all headless, some in the shape of men and some of beasts. Whether in the form of many bodies or only one, the gold tramped upward and forward, the several shapes enlivened by Wood's magic all glowing dull yellow in this chamber's parsimonious light.

The Director of Security, jabbering incantations, avoided the score of trampling golden legs. Gesturing, he intensified his magical efforts to undo what Wood was doing.

But it was obvious to all that the Director's attempted counterspells were failing miserably. Losing his temper, he rushed at his rival.

That was a serious mistake.

Halfway toward the object of his wrath, the Director slowed, then staggered to a halt. It was as if he had forgotten where he was going. Worse than that, it was as if he had almost forgotten how to walk.

Turning now to Hyrcanus, and then to all the others in the room, a smile of infantile imbecility, the Director of Security sank slowly into the nearest chair. Simpering vacuously at nothing, he appeared ready to be entertained by whatever might happen next.

His eyes lighted on the inexorably marching metal. "Gold," the old man whispered, obviously delighted. "Pretty, pretty."

Meanwhile Wood, his arms folded, had turned away from the Director and sat down on the edge of Hyrcanus's desk. He was watching the proceedings with an abstracted look, as if he were not personally very much involved. Tigris, taking her cue from her master, was now seated also, in a leather chair. From a purse that had appeared as if from nowhere she had actually brought out some knitting, with which she appeared to be fully occupied.

With the intrusion of the marching gold, and the ruthless disabling of his first assistant, Hyrcanus abandoned all pretense of calm control.

He jumped up onto his desk. With screams he rebuked his Security forces.

Then he turned to Wood, pleading: "Put the gold back! Send it back at once!"

"And you will listen to me if I do?"

"Of course, of course. And this fool here"—the Chairman indicated his chief aide, now smiling as he counted up his fingers—"can you restore him to what ordinarily serves him as his right mind?"

"If you will listen."

"I will. I swear it, by Croesus and Midas. What was it you wanted to discuss?"

Accepting this surrender graciously, Wood slid off the desk and with a few gestures quickly restored Blue Temple headquarters more or less to normality. The weird upward progress of long-hidden treasure ceased. The marching golden centipede and all its fragments, immediately obedient to Wood's most subtle command, reversed direction, and headed docilely downstairs. And at the same time the Director lost his carefree interest in his own fingers; his eyes closed and his head sank slumberously upon his chest.

Within moments after the tramping treasure had retreated, the building ceased to vibrate. Inside the Chairman's office only the shouts of guards, somewhere in the middle distance, remained as evidence that something remarkable had occurred.

Slowly, shakily, Chairman Hyrcanus resumed his seat behind his desk. He wiped his brow. With a gesture and a few muttered words, he offered Wood and Tigris chairs. The three were now alone.

With the opposition satisfactorily crushed, Wood was calm and reassuring. He glanced at the Director, who was snoring faintly. "He will regain his wits—such as they were." Then Wood focused an intense look on the Chairman. "Hyrcanus, understand me. Your wealth is safe, for the time being—safe from me, at least. Every coin is now back where it was. I do not crave Blue Temple gold, or any other treasure you may possess."

Hyrcanus, smiling glassily, murmured an excuse. Then, turning away momentarily, he beckoned the clerk to him from the next room, and dispatched the man with orders to take a complete inventory of the wealth down below.

Wood shook his head impatiently at this interruption. "Depend upon it, Hyrcanus, not a gram of your metal will be missing. I am not your enemy. Rather we have enemies in common, and therefore should be allies."

The Chairman brightened a trifle. "Yes. Enemies in common. Certainly we do."

Tigris had put aside her knitting, and was now sitting with folded hands, paying close attention to the men.

Her master said to Hyrcanus: "I am thinking in particular of Prince Mark of Tasavalta. I suppose you may rejoice almost as much as I do over his recent misfortunes."

The Chairman, relaxing just a little, nodded heartily.

His formidable visitor said: "I am told that Mark is making every possible effort—so far to no avail—to heal his wife of the injuries she sustained last year."

"A pity," said Hyrcanus, and uttered a dry sound intended for a laugh.

"Indeed. My agents assure me that Princess Kristin is hopelessly crippled, and in continual pain. The only real hope of ever helping her lies in the Sword Woundhealer."

Mention of the Sword concentrated the attention of the red-faced man behind the desk. "Ah. And where is Woundhealer now?"

Wood's eyes twinkled again. "Your question brings us to the very point of my visit. The best hope of anyone's getting Woundhealer in hand lies in the Sword Wayfinder—would you not agree?"

Hyrcanus responded cautiously. "It is said that Wayfinder can guide its holder to any goal he wishes."

"Even, as has happened at least once in the past, into the deepest Blue Temple vaults of all . . . but I have no wish to remind you and your associates of past sufferings and embarrassments. Hyrcanus, I have come here to offer you a partnership."

"What sort of partnership?"

"The details can be worked out later, if you will agree with me now in principle. You were already Chairman of the Blue Temple nineteen years ago, at the time of the great robbery. I believe I am correct in thinking that you and other insiders still consider that the worst disaster that your Temple has ever suffered?"

The Chairman's face grew somewhat redder. "Let us say, for the sake of argument, that you are right—what then?"

Wood put on a sympathetic expression. "And Ben of Purkinje, the wretch who was chiefly responsible for that calamity, still lives and prospers, as the right-hand man of our mutual enemy Mark of Tasavalta."

The Chairman nodded gloomily. Ever since Mark had become Prince of that generally prosperous domain, there had been no new Blue Temple installations at all in Tasavalta—the organization maintained in that land only a single banking facility, relatively unprofitable, in the capital city of Sarykam.

Tigris so far had been maintaining a demure demeanor, so it had not become necessary for Wood to banish her, or take any steps to alter her appearance. Brightly and alertly she continued to pay attention to everything that was said and done between her master and their reluctant host.

Genial-sounding Wood now inquired after the health of legendary Old Benambra, founder an age ago of the Blue Temple.

Hyrcanus assured his guests that the Founder ("our Chairman Emeritus, in retirement") was still very much alive—more or less alive, by most people's standards, since he was now turned completely into a Whitehands, and lived underground somewhere, jealously counting up the bulk of his remaining treasure. Then the current Chairman, supremely stingy unless he made an effort not to be, belatedly ordered some refreshment to be served.

Presently—while the Director of Security by stirrings and mumblings gave indications that he might soon awaken—Wood smoothly returned to the subject of the Sword of Wisdom. "You, the Blue Temple authorities, have certainly known for a long time that Wayfinder was used by those daring thieves to despoil your hoard."

"Well . . . yes."

"For years you have been keeping a jealous watch for that Sword in every quarter of the world, ready to try to seize it as soon as it should appear again."

The Director of Security, had by now risen and stretched and finally re-settled himself in a chair at a little distance, much chastened in his manner. Whether he was aware of what had just happened to him or not, he was evidently grimly determined to keep an eye on Wood as long as the intruder remained.

Now the Director said: "Wayfinder's vanishing, as you probably know, was utterly mysterious. The only report we have—admittedly unconfirmed—says that the Sword of Wisdom was stolen, by some unknown agent, from the belt of the God Hermes, after he had been struck down by Farslayer."

Everyone in the room was silent for a moment, no doubt meditating on that unlikely-sounding but undeniable event.

"Yes. I know," Wood answered patiently. Though he had not been personally present at the fall of Hermes, he stood ready to accept that story as confirmed.

The slight jowls of the Chairman of the Blue Temple were quivering. "The treasure we lost at that time, including three Swords, has never been recovered."

"I know that too." The handsome, youthful-looking Wood was now doing his best to soothe his hosts. Tigris looked sympathetic too. Wood continued: "How unjust, how odious, that the robbers should have been able to prosper as they have."

"Odious is an inadequate word," said Hyrcanus fervently. "But let us get down to business."

Wood, with a smile and gesture, indicated that he was perfectly ready to do just that.

The official inquired: "What exactly do you want from the Blue Temple, that you have taken these, uh, drastic steps to bring about this conference?"

Wood smiled. His answer was straightforward, or at least it seemed to be: "I want no more than I have already indicated. A chance to use Wayfinder for my own purposes, which will in no way conflict with yours. A league of mutual assistance against Tasavalta. And against the Emperor."

Blank looks on the faces of the Blue Temple functionaries greeted Wood's last assertion. He was silently contemptuous of their ignorance, but not really surprised. The Blue Temple evidently knew little about the Emperor, and seemed to care less. Or perhaps their lack of interest was only feigned. Like the Ancient One himself, they must be aware of certain recurrent rumors, concerning the enormous treasure that potentate was reported to have stashed away.

But the problems posed by the Emperor could wait. Spelling out his proposal in a straightforward way, the wizard confirmed that he wanted to be informed as soon as any of the Blue Temple people had any knowledge, or even a clue, concerning the whereabouts of the Sword of Wisdom.

"I am aware that you have had your people on the alert, everywhere around the world, or at least across this continent, for years now, for any evidence concerning that Sword. No matter what kind of defences you devise for your vast remaining treasure, Wayfinder can probably find a way to let another bold and clever robber in."

Hyrcanus groaned audibly.

Less than half an hour later the meeting concluded, with Wood and Hyrcanus shaking hands, while their respective aides looked on watchfully. Both leaders pronounced their satisfaction with the agreement they had reached.

Outside Blue Temple Headquarters again, their removal having been effected without the use of any mundane door, Wood and Tigris strolled the streets in silence, until they were rejoined by the demon Dactylartha.

"Noble masters!" hissed the tiny voice, coming out of the barely visible disturbance in the air. "Was my performance satisfactory?"

"At least you will not be punished for it." Wood spoke abstractedly, his main thought already elsewhere.

"Madam Tigris!" Dactylartha pleaded softly. "Did I not do well?"

"As our Master has said," she responded curtly. "Did your old rulers recognize you, do you suppose, Dactylartha?"

This terrible creature, she remembered, had once been Blue Temple property, involved in the famous robbery, on which occasion the demon had failed as dismally as all the other layers of defense of the main hoard. That did not mean, of course, that Dactylartha was weak or ineffective. Against any one of the Swords, only failure could generally be expected—unless, of course, one was armed with another Sword.

A dangerous being to recruit; Tigris, though her own skills in enchantment were great, was not sure she could have controlled the thing without her Master's help.

Wood, now giving the thing its new orders, curtly dismissed it, and in a moment it was gone.

"What are you thinking about, my dear?" the Ancient One inquired. "You look pensive."

"About demons, Master."

"Ah yes—demons. Well, as a rule, one kills them, or has some firm means of control—or is as nice to them as possible. That is about all there is to know on the subject." And Wood laughed, a hissing sound that might have come from the throat of one of the very creatures he was contemplating.

Tigris changed the subject. "Which of the Twelve Swords would you most like to possess, Master?"

"Ah. Now that—that—is indeed a question." The Ancient One mused in silence for a few paces. Then he said to Tigris: "There's Soulcutter, of course. I certainly wouldn't want to draw that little toy with my own hands—having heard what has happened to others—the trick of course would be to get someone else to draw it, under the proper circumstances."

"I understand perfectly, my lord."

"Do you? Good. As for the Sword of Wisdom, I confess to you, my dear, that I nourish a certain hope—that on coming into possession of that weapon I will be able to use it to lead me to the Emperor."

Tigris wondered briefly whether she ought to pretend to be surprised. In the end she decided not to do so. She asked, instead: "What Swords does the Emperor have?"

"None, that I can determine with any certainty."

Tigris, flattering: "Then of the two greatest magicians in the world, neither now has any Sword."

It was true that her Master, Wood, at the moment had not a single Sword to call his own—while Prince Mark of Tasavalta, gallingly, had no less than four.

Tigris was taking great care not to remind her Master directly of this latter fact.

He grunted something, for the moment sounding completely human—a mode of existence he did not always appear to favor.

"Where to now, Master?"

"To a place where I trust we will not be interrupted, Tigris. We have work to do."

3

MORNING had arrived, and Ben of Purkinje was enduring an enormous headache.

He sat up slowly, further tormented by a fierce itching. Particles of the hay in which he had been sleeping had worked their way into his clothing. According to the feeling in his head, the hour ought not to be much past midnight, but the exterior world ruthlessly assured him that a new day had indeed begun. The cavernous interior of the barn in which he had sought shelter was now becoming faintly visible, venerable rough-hewn beams and gray wall planks bathed in an illumination that could only be that of dawn. Intermittent crowing noises now issuing from the adjacent barnyard offered confirming evidence.

The noises were there, but Ben was reasonably sure that they had not awakened him; they were completely routine, and he had been too deeply asleep to be roused by anything so ordinary.

Too deeply asleep indeed. Unconscious, he thought, would be a better word for it. Recalling some of last night's adventures in the local tavern, he wondered if the second or third girl to sit on his lap might have put something unfriendly in his ale. The first, as Ben recalled, had been almost unconscious herself at the time, and he thought he could exclude her from the list of suspects.

He doubted that any of last night's girls would have played a dirty trick like that on her own accord. Someone would have put her up to it.

Ben clenched his eyelids shut again. His memories of last night were somewhat hazed. He went prowling through that fog, in search of his newly-met drinking companions. They had been three or four youngish men, who had had the look of bandits—or, if not bandits, of people who had no higher moral standard than they found absolutely necessary for survival. A couple of them, perhaps not realizing what a formidable opponent they had encountered, had challenged Ben to a drinking contest. Before that had been carried to a conclusion, the tavern girls had taken a notion to sit on his lap, first in sequence, then together . . . or had that been his own suggestion?

. . . but of course nothing could be done about any of that now. If in fact someone had tried to drug his drink, he had survived the effort. This was morning, and at least it wasn't raining—he would have heard that on the barn roof. Trouble was, the first subtle indications of this fine spring morning were that things were not going to go well today for Ben of Purkinje, known in recent years as Ben of Sarykam. Right now he feared that his headache might be the least of today's problems, because certain sounds outside this borrowed barn were like those of no ordinary farmyard in the early morning. These were the noises, he now felt sure, which had awakened him.

These ominous mutterings and footfalls evoked for Ben the presence of a number of men, maybe half a dozen or even more, clumsily exchanging low-voiced words with undertones of urgency. Muttering, and then separating, spreading out, moving quickly but quietly as if they meant to get the barn surrounded.

That was not at all a reassuring image.

Getting off to a bad start as he seemed to be this morning, Ben hoped that no one today was going to call him by any name that mentioned either Purkinje or Sarykam. As soon as anyone did that, he would know that the false identity under which he was currently traveling had been penetrated. Not that he had much hope for the false identity anyway. It had been a resort of desperation, conceived on the spur of the moment several days ago, when other plans had at last gone desperately and completely wrong. A man who weighed close to a hundred and forty kilos, and looked capable—and was—of twisting a riding-beast's iron shoe into scrap with his bare hands, tended to attract attention. For such a man, ordinary disguises were seldom of much avail.

Ben's worst suspicions were presently nourished by new evidence. If he had been in the least danger of drifting back to sleep—and with a start he realized that he just might have been—that peril was destroyed by a loud call in a hoarse male voice, coming from somewhere not far outside the barn. The words were meant for him. The man outside was threatening to fire the wooden structure if he didn't immediately come out and surrender.

The bass roar was almost instantly repeated: "Ben of Purkinje! We know yer in there!"

Despite the beseiged man's huge size, he came up to his feet softly and promptly amid the hay, the wooden floor of the hayloft creaking under the shift of weight. At the same time he took a quick inventory of assets. Through recent misfortunes his personal weaponry, apart from his own mind and body, had been reduced to one middle-sized dagger. Leaving the dagger at his belt, he caught sight of a pitchfork not far away, and swiftly and softly took possession of it.

A certain urgency within his bladder next demanded his attention, all the more so with impending combat probable. Relieving himself quietly into the hay, regretting the lack of heroic capacity that might have served to put out a fire, Ben listened for more shouts but for the moment could hear only the throbbing of his aching head.

Doing his best to give the situation careful thought, he decided that allowing or encouraging the barn to burn down around him would be a waste of time for all concerned, and a waste of some perhaps innocent farmer's property as well. Ben had no real idea how many of last night's companions and their friends might be outside. What sounded like the clumsy muttering of six or eight might instead be a much cleverer attempt by two or three men to suggest greater numbers.

Well, he would soon find out how many men were outside, and whether they were bluffing. He would go out and see. But he would do so without announcing his real intention first.

Ready for action now, he bellowed a defiant challenge, to the effect that if they wanted him, they were going to have to come in and get him.

Then, as quietly as possible, he slid down the ladder from the hayloft to the dirt floor of the barn. And then, pitchfork in hand, he came out fighting.

Ben's youth was behind him, but he could still run faster than anyone would be likely to expect from a man of his size. He went out, moving fast and hard, through a small door in what he would have called the rear of the barn. The suggestion of numbers, he saw with a sinking feeling, had been no bluff. At least five armed men were waiting for him among the manure piles at the back, but at first they recoiled from him and his pitchfork, yelling.

The bass voice that had commanded Ben to give up now shouted orders meant for other ears, screaming hoarsely that if they wanted to survive this day themselves, they had better take this fellow alive. These commands and threats were issuing from a squat oaken hogshead of a man, somewhat shorter than Ben himself, but apparently little if any lighter. Not one of last night's tavern companions. Ben would have remembered this one.

Ben now had his back against the barn wall, hemmed in by a semicircle of lesser men, most of them fierce-looking enough to inspire some measure of respect. They kept him at bay, turning this way and that. While feints came at Ben from right and left at the same time, one of them got almost behind him with a clever rope. A moment later Ben's pitchfork had been lassoed, and a few moments after that several strong hands had fastened on him, and his dagger was plucked from his belt.

"We got him, Sarge!"

But in the next instant Ben proved to those who grasped his arms and legs that they really hadn't. Not quite, not yet. He used his arms to crack a pair of heads together with great energy.

The blade of a very keen-looking knife, coming up under his throat, stopped this effort.

One of the Sarge's wrists, prodigiously thick and hairy, came into Ben's field of vision. The enemy leader, striking out at his own knife-wielding man, seemed to have suddenly become Ben's ally. "*Alive*, I says! He's the one Blue Temple wants!"

That name made Ben redouble his efforts to break loose. It was useless, though. He might have been able to fight off two or three of the ill-clad, ill-equipped bandits at a time, and the remainder of them might have been poorly coordinated or plain cowardly enough to stay at a safe distance. But when the Sarge himself jumped in and grabbed him, using the biggest hands that Ben had ever seen or felt, while two of his more stubborn minions still clung on, Ben no longer had any chance of wrestling free.

This time he was down flat on his back. Raising his head as well as he was able, he peered through a drifting haze of dust and barnyard chaff to take a count. There were six or eight of them altogether, and two of them at least, the ones whose heads he'd banged, were just as flat as he was. He hadn't done so badly at that.

Now, though, four or five held Ben more or less in position, and another was commencing operations with a coil of thin rope brought from the barn, tying his wrists skillfully behind his back.

Ben, looking at the world through a reddish haze of exhaustion, his chest heaving, his pulse thudding in his ears, had the sudden notion that at forty-two, give or take a year or so, he was definitely getting too old for this kind of thing.

Now, Ben's arms immobilized, a couple of his stronger captors took him by the arms and heaved him to his feet.

It seemed there were going to be formal introductions.

"Sergeant Brod," growled the walking hogshead, standing directly in front of Ben, and extending one enormous hand as if Ben ought to be able to snap free of his bonds and shake it. "Better known to some of me own followers as the Sarge. I am the leader of this small but efficient band."

"Pleased to meet you," said Ben. Squinting at Brod and the men who surrounded him, Ben decided that Brod's men all appeared to be more or less afraid of him, and with some cause.

Brod's coloring was fair, right now still red-faced from his recent efforts. His features were fairly regular except for a nose that approached the size to qualify as a disfiguring defect.

Fancy tattoos adorned the Sarge's massive shoulders, which bulged out of a sleeveless leather vest. His dirty hair, some indeterminate shade between blond and red, was tied in long pigtails.

From inside his vault of a chest, his bass voice rasped out what sounded like an accusation: "You're Ben of Purkinje."

Ben blew a tickle of straw free of his upper lip. Trying to get his breathing back to normal, he replied as nonchalantly as he could: "You have the wrong man. My name is Charles, and I'm a blacksmith."

The Sarge had a good laugh. He really enjoyed that one.

"Aye, and my name's really Buttercup, and I sell cobwebs for a living!" Fists on hips, he sized up his prisoner's size and shape, and appeared delighted with what he saw. He clouted Ben a friendly buffet on the shoulder, rocking him on his planted feet.

In another minute the little gang was on the march, away from barn and farmyard. Ben, arms bound, marched in the middle of the group. No one bothered to grip his arms now; he wasn't going to run away. From snatches of conversation between Sergeant Brod and his followers, he gathered that he was being held for delivery to certain representatives of the Blue Temple, who had a standing offer of a great reward for the live body of Ben of Purkinje, or some lesser amount for that body dead. To Ben the proposed transaction sounded all too convincing.

That the Blue Temple wanted him was easy to believe. But that those notorious skinflints would consider paying any reward at all was frightening. It showed how badly they craved getting their hands on him.

The little band of freebooters, Ben still with his arms tied in their midst, were angling downhill, approaching the good-sized river which ran only a couple of hundred meters from the barn. On the near bank Ben saw a flatboat tied up. It was a crudely constructed craft, a score of paces long, half that distance wide, fashioned mostly of unpeeled logs.

As soon as it became obvious that he was being escorted right to the boat, Ben stumbled. Then he dug in his feet. Or gave the impression of trying to do so.

"Where are we going?" he demanded.

"Just a little cruise." Roughly he was pushed along.

On being taken aboard the flatboat, the prisoner gave every indication of trying to disguise a deep distrust of water, edging reflexively toward the center of the crude plank deck.

One of the gang, watching him with shrewd malice, probing for a weakness, smiling slyly, asked him: "Don't care for the water?"

Ben, a nervous expression on his ugly face, turned to his questioner. "Not much of a swimmer," he admitted.

They were willing to let him sit down approximately amidships. There was a little freight on board as well, a couple of barrow-loads of unidentifiable cargo tied down under a tarpaulin. From where Ben was sitting, he could see one small rowboat, stowed bottom-up on the broad deck. It looked serviceable. He couldn't see any oars.

Ben considered making a serious effort to break his bonds. Having got a look at the old rope before they used it, he thought that doing so would not be completely beyond the bounds of possibility. But any such effort would have to wait until he was unwatched.

While the men began what seemed an unfamiliar process of casting off, the Sarge, as if he wanted to talk, came to sit on a small box facing Ben.

Any effort at breaking ropes would have to be postponed. Ben, ready to try a different tactic, announced: "If I *were* this fellow from Purkinje, or wherever, why my friends might pay a better price for me even than my enemies."

"Maybe." Brod sounded doubtful of that proposition, to say the least.

"Did you ever try to get money for *anything* out of the Blue Temple?"

The other looked at his prisoner thoughtfully. "I know what you mean, friend. But they'll pay this time, in advance, or they won't get you. 'Sides, we've contracted to do another little job for them."

"What's that?"

The answer had to be postponed. Brod rose to supervise his unskilled crew's efforts to get the boat free of the shore.

By dint of much poling, and the blaspheming of many gods, along with energetic sweeps of the four long steering oars, the flatboat was at last dislodged from the riverbank and under way downstream. Ben was no great expert in these matters, but in his judgment the men manning the sweeps and poles were being pretty clumsy about it. The difficulty wasn't entirely their fault, though. Obviously this craft had been designed for use somewhere upriver, maybe for ferrying livestock about, and had somehow been taken over by these goons, who were riding it downriver into waters somewhat rougher than those for which it had been built.

* * *

At about this time Ben noticed a distracting presence, one he certainly didn't need just now, maneuvering on the outskirts of the scene. This was a large, gray-feathered bird, and with a sinking feeling he recognized it as a winged messenger from Sarykam. At any other time he would have been pleased to get some word from home, and to have an opportunity to send word back. Just now, though, the hovering presence of the courier threatened the last faint credibility of his pose as Charles the Smith.

Perhaps the creature was bright enough to understand this in some dim way; as if unable to make up its small mind whether or not to communicate with Ben, the bird came no nearer than the bottom of the upended rowboat, where it perched uncertainly and cocked its small-brained head at him. Presently one of the bandits threw a chip of wood at it, causing it to take wing for the shore. But after being driven from the boat, the messenger just flew along the shore from tree to tree, at a little distance.

Brod had noted the bird's presence, and was evidently shrewd enough to understand what it signified.

"Reckon maybe it wants some blacksmithin' done? New shoes, maybe, so it can run like a ridin'-beast?" The Sarge enjoyed another laugh.

Ben did his best to pretend he didn't know what bird Brod was talking about.

Several hours passed in uneventful voyaging, with the current bearing the clumsy craft downstream at a good pace. A tributary came in on the east bank, and the river—Ben had never learned its name—broadened appreciably. Rocky hills on the horizon ahead suggested that the water might get rougher there, when this river became narrower and swifter, forcing itself between them.

Still the gray-feathered messenger effortlessly kept pace, darting from tree to tree along the shore. Trying to put that problem out of his thoughts for the time being, Ben considered Sergeant Brod. The brawny Sergeant was still smiling at his prisoner from time to time, nodding, appraising him. He seemed to have a more than commercial interest in the famous—well, semi-famous—Ben of Purkinje as well. Ben was vaguely aware that he enjoyed an almost legendary reputation for strength, among people who were interested in keeping track of such things.

The Sarge came to stand in front of Ben. This time he put his foot on the box. At length he remarked: "They say you're a pretty good wrestler."

"Me? No. This Ben of Purkinje maybe is. I don't bother with that kind of thing."

"Don't bother with it?" Brod screwed his eyes almost shut in puzzlement.

"No." Ben shook his head. "What's there to know about wrestling? It all comes down to who is stronger, and there I always have the edge. Nothing like blacksmithing to build the muscles. Lucky for you you had six men to help you tie me up."

The redness of the Sarge's face seemed to be deepening. "Lucky for me? What by all the gods' elbows can you mean?"

Ben shrugged.

By now a couple of Brod's followers were starting to take an interest. Obviously they were fascinated by the prospect of watching a wrestling match between these two titans.

Afterward, Ben was never quite sure just how the first specific proposal had been made, or by whom.

"Think you could take him, Sarge?"

"Gwan! Sure, our Sarge could take 'im. Could take anyone!"

"Wrestling on a boat?" Ben, glancing nervously at the surface of the river so perilously near at hand, displayed apprehension at the mere idea.

Either Brod was supremely confident in his own strength and skill or he was shrewd enough to realize that his authority might be adversely affected if he failed to meet this adversary fairly. For whatever reason, he made no objection when someone started to untie the old rope with which Ben's arms were bound.

Someone else suggested they tie a rope around Ben before the bout, so they could pull back their valuable prisoner in case he tried to swim away. Ben for a moment considered seconding the request for such a safety measure, confident that it would be denied. And sure enough the scheme was hooted down. No one could wrestle with a rope tied round them, could they?

The rocky hills ahead were somewhat closer now, and the river was gradually becoming swifter and rougher here, with traces of white water ahead. Just a few such traces, along both banks, which were growing steeper, so that the passage between increasingly rocky shores, Ben thought, might at some point require careful steering. Better steering than even skilled boatmen could manage with these sweeps.

The ropes were off.

Brod was considerably younger than Ben. Ben, sizing his opponent up, was struck for the first time by the fact that this fellow was young enough to be his son.

But he couldn't *really* be . . . could he?

Ben found that an ugly suggestion, but not one that was going to cause him a whole lot of worry. Besides bulk and apparent strength, there was very little resemblance.

Ben moved out to the middle of the crude plank deck, rubbing his arms, stamping his feet to get the circulation going. Actually the blood was flowing pretty well already, but he wanted another chance to look around, getting a good view now of the stern of the boat, which had been behind him when he was tied.

Brod, doing his own muscle-flexing, was grinning at him. "You were really a good wrestler once, hey pop?"

"Did a lot better after I got my full growth." Ben considered. "You probably will, too."

There was really no problem about room. A central space was quickly cleared of a litter of odd personal possessions and miscellaneous garbage. Basically the arena was a deck of rough planks, covering the central two-thirds of the craft. The crew grinning and making almost-secret wagers—no one wanted to offend the chief by betting openly against him—arranged themselves around the rectangle, while with a minimum of preparation the two contestants moved to diagonally opposite corners of the space.

There rose a minor chorus of cheers, incoherent enough that Ben could not tell who they were meant to encourage.

The two contestants began circling, stalking each other.

Ben noted from the corners of his eyes that two of the gang who were currently supposed to be on watch, manning a couple of the large sweep oars, had abandoned their duties, preferring to keep an eye on the contest. The drifting raft was turning this way and that.

Brod growled, shuffled his feet and flexed his muscles. Both feet and muscles were really enormous.

Ben stood in one place, swaying slightly with the motion of the planks underfoot, doing his best to appear hesitant and uncertain, yet gamely determined. This was a clumsy blacksmith, wondering what to do. He looked wide-eyed, innocent in an ugly sort of way.

Brod, quicker than he looked, lunged at him. The two men grappled, grunting and straining, coming to no immediate conclusion, each testing the other's strength and skill. The watchers yelled incoherently. Ben felt sure that some of them at least were cheering for him. Not that he gave a damn.

Ben and Brod broke apart, each backing up a step or two. "Don't know no wrestling, huh?" The Sarge shook his pigtails in what might have been admiration. Ben's fingers had left red and white imprints on his hairy arms. Ben seemed to be wondering what all the excitement was about. "Anybody can do this." The Sarge's face stiffened. He charged again. At the impact, a cheer went up from the onlookers; Ben, bracing his booted feet, took the charge without being driven back.

"Don't like the water, huh? 'Spect me to believe that?" Brod gasped between exertions.

Ben said nothing, saving his breath. He had the feeling he was going to need as much of it as he could get; the Sarge was just about as strong as he looked.

After the pair of them had made the round of the little arena a couple of times, struggling from fore to aft and port to starboard, Ben nodded to himself. He thought he now had his opponent pretty well figured out. Unfortunately, a real win in this situation was going to require more than putting Brod down on his back.

Before Ben could plan his next move, Brod took the initiative again, coming in a screaming, all-or-nothing charge. Ben, trying his best to sidestep, could get only partially out of the way. The two big men, arms momentarily linked like those of whirling dancers, spun out of the arranged arena, toward the edge of the raft-like deck, almost under one of the stern sweeps.

The watchers were screaming themselves hoarse. The long, unwieldy steering oars were bouncing in their locks, unmanned. The two wrestlers had come to a stop only a step from the water. Brod's wide, astonished eyes, half a dozen centimeters from Ben's stared at the unmanned oars. The little crowd of onlookers was sending up a greater roar than ever.

There came a crash, a great shuddering impact. The raftlike craft had struck a glancing blow against a rock.

Feet planted solidly, Ben kept his balance. He gulped his lungs full of air, held his breath, and strained his muscles. Lifting his opponent clean off his feet, he took him overboard. Brod's scream had something in it of the tones of a delighted child.

Cold water smote them both, the fierce current twisting their bodies even as they sank. The Sarge's grip loosened immediately as they hit the water. Ben pushed his opponent away, and let himself plummet as deep as the river would take him, trying to swim upstream. He rejoiced to find that right here, at least, the cold torrent was deep enough to offer concealment and protection.

When he had to come up for air, Ben looked back in the direction of the boat and was glad to see that half the people aboard had been knocked off their feet. No one at the moment was even thinking about pursuing Ben.

Right beside him, as in several other places in the vicinity, some rocks rose well above the surface, offering the fugitive a solid refuge while he caught his breath.

Many of the raftsmen looked terrified. Maybe they couldn't swim. They clung desperately to whatever portion of the boat they could get their hands on. Some, shrieking and cursing, went sliding helplessly overboard.

Ben couldn't wait around all day, watching the fun. Orienting himself toward the west bank, which looked to him a little more hospitable, he plunged under water again and started swimming.

Swimming with boots on was difficult indeed, but there hadn't been time to take them off. Besides, he expected that he was going to need footgear when he came ashore.

Though the river was perhaps a hundred meters broad at this point, most of its depth was concentrated in a single narrow channel. Striking for the west bank, trying to angle upstream to put more distance between himself and the flatboat, Ben soon found he could once more plant his feet on the bottom and still get his face high enough to breathe.

Fortunately the majority of his former captors still had their hands full with other problems. But a few had recovered. A few missiles—one arrow, a slung stone or two—hurtled inaccurately after him. Ben saw the arrow pierce only the current, the rocks go banging and breaking on bigger rocks.

If he lingered in the neighborhood, the next step would probably be a determined swimmer or two, blade-armed, coming after him.

Ben decided not to wait. A couple of additional missiles landed in the general neighborhood. He thought he could hear Brod, surfaced and clinging to another rock, or back on the boat, bellowing in rage. Gulping a breath, Ben went under water again, striking once more for the west bank, swimming powerfully, staying under as long as he could.

Briefly he worried that the bandits might find oars for the rowboat, and launch it successfully. But in the continuing confusion that threat now looked increasingly unlikely.

Currents and rocks grew tricky, and he endured a struggle in rough water to reach shore—but, being an excellent swimmer, he made it safely. Definitely he was ready for a rest. But now was not the time. Stamping and squishing, he moved inland, getting Brod and all his people thoroughly out of sight and sound.

4

GETTING away from the river as expeditiously as possible, Ben struggled to put distance and obstacles between himself and the bandits. Their angry yells—concerned more, he was sure, with their own plight than with his escape—were drowned by the water raging at the rocks; and then all sounds coming from the river faded altogether.

Unfortunately the messenger-bird from Sarykam had now disappeared as well. For the next half hour he concentrated on making strides inland, staying on the hardest ground he could find, just in case anyone should attempt to trail him. No doubt the Blue Temple had promised a good reward.

After half an hour it was necessary to pause for a brief rest. Once he had squeezed some residual water from his clothing, he continued west at a steady pace.

The landscape ahead of Ben spread itself out in a rugged, arid, and uninviting prospect. In several places he could observe distant hills approaching the size of mountains. There were no roads, fences, or houses to be seen. In another half hour his steady pace became hesitant. Then he began to angle to the north. Lacking anything in the way of food, or even a canteen, he was reluctant to go straight out into what looked like utter desolation.

Ben spent the night in the open, having encountered no one, and seen few signs of settlement. He lay down in the chill of early night, grateful that at least by now his clothing had dried completely, and wishing for last night's itchy hay. He breakfasted on a couple of juicy roots, and kept on going.

A full day after his escape from the flatboat, now walking almost straight north, he caught sight of three people on foot in the distance. They were approaching him from the northwest, on a course that seemed calculated to intercept his own. Ben halted, squinting with a hand raised to shade his eyes. Even at a distance it was obvious that these three were not members of Brod's cutthroat gang.

Shrugging his shoulders, he resumed his advance. As the distance between them diminished, he observed that there was something familiar about two of the approaching figures; and one of those two was holding in both hands a gleaming thing, like a long sword. Or, rather, like a very different kind of weapon. Something much more than any ordinary sword.

A minute after making that discovery, Ben was exchanging enthusiastic greetings with two of the travelers he had so fortunately—as he thought —encountered.

One of these two old acquaintances, she who had once been the Silver Queen, was saying to Ben: "So, you are my gate to peace and truth, you man of blood? It seems unlikely. And yet the Sword of Wisdom has fastened me upon your trail."

Ben looked at the Sword, and at the woman who held it. He said: "I think I must hear some explanation."

As soon as the greetings between old friends had been concluded, Valdemar and Ben were introduced. Valdemar was certainly the taller of the two gigantic men, but Zoltan, watching, thought it hard to judge which was the more massive. The two clasped hands, and sized each other up with quick appraising glances.

Presently Ben heard what Valdemar's request to the Sword of Wisdom had been: to be guided to some woman who would match his image of an ideal wife.

The older man sighed wearily. "Maybe I should have asked that oracle the same question, years ago."

The day had been gray ever since sunrise, and now a threat of rain was materializing. Casting about for a place of safety and reasonable comfort, the party of four took shelter from a shower under an overhang of cliff. From here it was possible to look back in the direction Ben had come from the river, so any bandits who might be after him ought to become visible in time to be avoided.

The three old friends naturally had much to talk about. Zoltan demanded of Ben: "Tell us how things are going back in Sarykam. How long ago did you leave there?"

Some of the cheerfulness so recently restored now faded swiftly from Ben's eyes. He said softly: "They are not going well."

Yambu, like Zoltan, was strongly interested in what news of Tasavalta Ben might provide. "Then tell us," she urged.

Ben drew a deep breath. "I'll try to put the worst of it in a nutshell. There was an attack on the palace last year; all of the royal family survived, but Princess Kristin was badly crippled in a fall from the roof. For a time everyone feared that she would die. Now—some say death is the happiest result that can be expected."

All of them were quick with more questions. Ben's answers offered them little or no comfort. The stones of a Palace courtyard had badly damaged Kristin's spine, had broken other bones, and crushed internal organs. Her mind, spirit, and body had all been badly damaged.

Zoltan, who was Prince Mark's nephew, muttered blasphemies in a low voice. Yambu frowned in silence.

Valdemar, who knew next to nothing of Tasavalta or its rulers, still expressed his indignation, and his loathing of villains who could cause such pain. He then demanded to know who was guilty of launching the attack.

Ben shrugged. "Chiefly Vilkata and his demons, along with a certain Culmian prince. We're rid of them all now. Good riddance. But—too late to help our Princess."

Yambu was looking closely at her old associate. "And you, Ben? How are you, apart from this evil that has befallen those you love? How are your own wife and daughter—Barbara and Beth are their names, are they not?"

"As far as I know, my daughter and my wife are well enough in body," Ben answered shortly. "Let me put it this way. My life at home has recently been such that I do not mind spending most of my days and nights away from home."

Yambu was sympathetic. "How old is the girl?"

"Seventeen."

"That can be an age of difficulty."

Ben made a sound somewhere between a grunt and a laugh. "When I myself arrive at some age that fails to bring its troubles, lady, I will make a note of it."

Zoltan gave Ben one sympathetic look, but then the young man's thoughts quickly turned to the difficulties his aunt and uncle, and all their realm, must be experiencing.

He asked: "Tell us of my Uncle Mark."

Ben seemed glad to leave the talk of his personal affairs. "Your uncle is unhappy," he answered shortly, "as one might expect."

At that point he fell silent, staring past the lady's head. When the others turned to see what he was looking at, they saw, and Yambu and Zoltan recognized, one of the half-intelligent messenger birds of Tasavalta, sitting on a branch of the only sizable tree in the immediate vicinity.

Getting to his feet, Ben addressed the bird: "I had given you up, messenger. Well, now I am here, free to talk with you. What word have you for Ben?"

Spreading soft wings, gliding from its branch to a nearby rock, the creature chirped in its inhuman voice: "Ben, the Prince asks you for news. The Prince asks you for news."

"Well, when you reach the Prince again, tell him the news could be a lot worse; because here I am, still alive, and I have met friends who are armed with a Sword. But it could be better, because I am no closer to finding the Sword we want."

"Say message again. Say message again."

"I will, messenger, I will. But later. There's no hurry about this one." Ben spoke slowly and distinctly, as if to a child. "Rest now. Message later. Rest now."

The bird flew back to its higher perch, where it settled itself as if to rest.

"The Prince is at home, then," Zoltan commented.

Ben nodded. "Since Kristin's crippling, he's spent more time in Sarykam than he did in the past two or three years put together. No more roaming the world, trying to look out for the Emperor's business."

"And what of their sons?" Yambu wanted to know. "How old are the two princelings now?"

Ben considered. "Stephen must be twelve. He has a temper. He'll be a dangerous man in a few years."

"And Prince Adrian?"

"Two years older. Secluded, somewhere well away from home, I don't know where, perfecting his wizardry. I expect we'll not see much of him for a year or two to come." It was common for serious apprentices in the arts of magic to withdraw from the mundane world for a time of preparation.

"And nothing can be done for Kristin?"

"In the ordinary ways of healing and of magic, nothing. There is only one real hope, of course," Ben concluded shortly.

"The Sword Woundhealer." Yambu nodded, and sighed.

Ben nodded too. "Of course we had the keeping of it there in Sarykam for years, but . . . there's no use worrying over that now. Mark nowadays thinks of little else but somehow getting Woundhealer back. He stays in Sarykam himself, but he sees to it that every clue, every hint we can obtain—whether reasonable or not, I sometimes think—is followed to the end.

"That is why I am here now. There was one rumor, one hint, about

Woundhealer, that we thought especially promising. It put the Sword somewhere in this area."

"And you came alone to track down this hint?" asked Valdemar, who until now had been largely silent.

Thunder grumbled overhead, and more rain was starting to come down. Ben looked at his questioner. "I was not alone when I set out. Six other people and three of the great birds came with me. I can give you the unpleasant details later, but at this point only I, out of seven humans, am still alive; as for the birds, they no longer travel with me, but one of them finds me from time to time, as you have seen. Thus I am kept somewhat in touch with Sarykam."

Ben related to Yambu, Zoltan, and Valdemar additional details of his struggle with the band of river bandits, and his escape.

Zoltan asked: "Are they seeking the Sword of Mercy too?"

"Perhaps. They had something going with the Blue Temple, besides selling me to them—or they thought they did."

In turn, the Silver Queen and Zoltan told Ben the tale of their recent harassment by the leatherwings, of their fortunate encounter with Valdemar and the Sword he had been so strangely given, and how during the last few days the three of them, with Wayfinder's help, had managed to avoid the flying reptiles.

Ben gestured toward the Sword of Wisdom. "Speaking of your treasure there, I suppose you'll have no objection to my borrowing its powers for a while?"

Yambu smiled faintly. "I have been expecting you to ask. Let me see if I can guess for what purpose."

"No doubt a single guess will be all you'll need. I want first to locate the Sword of Healing, and then to get my hands on it."

"Have you no more selfish wants than that, big man?"

"That will do for the time being."

In unconsciously queenly fashion, Yambu raised Wayfinder in her own hands and apostrophized the Sword: "I asked you, Sword, for peace, and you have led me to this man of blood."

Zoltan saw Ben frown slightly at that.

Yambu continued: "I see my own quest must give way to one of greater urgency. But before I hand you over to him, Sword, what else do you have to tell me? Is it possible that by following him I will discover the peace that has eluded me for so long?"

The other three, watching closely, could see plainly how the Sword tugged, slowly twisting in her hands until it bent her wrists, aiming itself at the huge man.

Without further comment the Silver Queen reversed her grip on the black hilt, and handed Wayfinder over to Ben.

Reaching for the weapon eagerly, he murmured thanks. Once Wayfinder was in his grasp he wasted no time, but at once demanded of it bluntly: "Sword, lead me where I want to go!"

The Sword of Wisdom in his hands at once twisted around sharply; Zoltan, though no stranger to the Swords and their powers, felt his scalp prickle. The weapon reminded him of some intelligent animal, responding differently as soon as it came under the control of a different master, perhaps a warbeast roused from sleep and scenting blood. Zoltan thought that this time he saw the blade actually bend, until the tip pointed somewhere to the northeast. That direction, he thought, was close to, though it did not exactly coincide with, the bearing of Sarykam.

Still holding the Sword leveled, Ben shuffled his feet, as if getting his weary legs ready to move again. He asked his companions: "Are all of you ready to move?" It did not appear to have entered his thoughts that any of the three might choose not to accompany him.

Valdemar stood up, towering over everyone else. He said slowly: "I began my journey holding in my hands that Sword you now have, and with my own goal, not yours, in mind. And so now I have my doubts about going with you."

At that Zoltan turned on him sharply: "I suppose you think your quest is more important than this one?"

Valdemar raised his eyebrows. He said mildly: "It is important to me."

The two young men were of the same age, or very nearly so; but Valdemar—only partially because of his size—generally gave the impression of being older.

"Well, perhaps you can manage to locate a wife without the help of Wayfinder," said Zoltan. "Or—who knows?—if you come with us you might discover one to your liking in Sarykam."

The other shrugged. "Perhaps, friend Zoltan. Anyway, you should remember that I am not ready to abandon my purpose. But I have already given the Sword to Lady Yambu, given it freely, and so I have no claim on it any longer."

"You are welcome to take it back, long enough to ask a question," the lady assured him.

Ben nodded. "Just don't be all day about it."

The lady paused in the act of handing Wayfinder back to Valdemar. Frowning, she said to him: "You are something of a magician, are you not?"

The tall youth blinked at her as if the question had surprised him. "I have a certain knack for doing tricks with light, and mirrors, and sand and water," he admitted. "No more than that. Depending on the company in which I find myself, I sometimes claim to know a little magic. But how did you know?"

"I have known another magician or two in my time. The art is wont to leave its traces." Yambu shrugged. "In this company you may freely claim competence," she told Valdemar. "I doubt that any of us are able to surpass you, in whatever it is you do with light and mirrors."

Valdemar received the Sword from her, and held it steadily. "I ask—" he began firmly, then hesitated, looking at the others. "I suppose there is no preferred formula of words?"

"None I know of," said Ben impatiently. "Just ask your question." The rain was falling harder now, though so far the overhang of cliff had kept them almost dry.

"Then I ask," said Valdemar, with perhaps a hint of embarrassment in his voice, "the same question as before. When I spoke to this Sword in my own house."

Wayfinder pointed straight in the direction of the Silver Queen.

The rain slackened somewhat. Ben, though tired, was eager to get moving, and none of the others insisted on a chance to rest. All four set out together, in the direction indicated by Wayfinder.

Ben, who walked with Zoltan in the lead, now wore the Sword of Wisdom at his belt—drawing and using it occasionally, to confirm that they remained on the proper course—while Lady Yambu walked at Valdemar's side.

They had been hiking for a quarter of an hour when Valdemar asked: "What lies ahead of us?"

"Not much but desert," Ben returned shortly. "And somewhere in it, I suppose, the river I went boating on yesterday."

"A wasteland," said Yambu. "One that will take us days to cross."

5

O NCE Wood decided to depart the city where he and Tigris had visited the Blue Temple headquarters, he summoned up his preferred
form of rapid transportation. He and his young lieutenant were soon
mounted upon a griffin, riding the wind a kilometer above the land. The
Ancient One's chosen destination was one of his remoter strongholds.
He and Tigris were bringing with them only a few assistants, chosen from
those of his people he least mistrusted, who rode clinging for their lives
on the backs of similar steeds.

As soon as the Ancient One and his party had reached their goal, all of
his helpers, including Tigris, were promptly assigned their tasks of magic,
and set to work.

Some hours later, laboring inside a stone-vaulted chamber enclosed by
many barriers of matter and of magic, the master of the establishment
raised his head over a massive wooden workbench lighted by Old World
globes and marked with an intricacy of carven diagrams.

He asked: "Tigris, are we completely secure against unfriendly observation?"

"Master?" Across the room the young woman, startled, looked up
from her own work.

"I mean observation from outside. Are there spies, human or otherwise, anywhere in sight of our walls? Do you make sure that there are
none. I would attend to the matter myself, but I am otherwise engaged at
the moment."

"Now, Master?"

"Now."

Suffering in silence the interruption of her own work, the young
woman methodically disengaged herself from her current task. Then she
employed her considerable powers to satisfy her Master's latest wish,
sending her perception outwards, while her body remained standing beside the bench.

Outside the stronghold, not many meters distant and yet a world away, behind grim walls of heavy rock and curtains of dark magic, some trees and other vegetation grew naturally. There a handful of birds were singing. Not messengers, these. These birds were wild and small and totally unintelligent.

Of unfriendly observation there was not a trace. Unless the small birds could be counted as unfriendly to the Master and his cause.

For another moment, a moment longer than was really necessary, Tigris harkened carefully. Her body standing indoors did not move, except that her red lips parted.

"Well?"

The young woman returned fully to her body. "Nothing, Master. Nothing and no one out there now."

"You sense nothing?"

Again Tigris employed the full range of her trained perceptions. Again she came back. "Only songbirds."

The Ancient One grunted something, a sound of grudging satisfaction, and returned to his powerful ritual, whose goal, his assistant knew, was the discovery of information about certain of Wood's enemies, notably the Emperor, and the Emperor's son, Mark of Tasavalta.

Tigris, aware of a strange reluctance to do so, firmly put from her thoughts her memory of the outside world. She also returned, but more slowly, to her tasks.

At odd moments during the next few hours, she pondered her own reactions. She had been somewhat surprised—though not entirely—to find herself prolonging the reconnaissance unnecessarily, simply to harken to the songbirds for one moment more.

The hours passed. Lesser aides, bringing messages, were intercepted by Tigris, so that her Master should not be disturbed. The great magician had been isolated at his workbench for some time with certain half-material, semi-animate powers, and his own thoughts.

At length, when it seemed a safe moment to interrupt her lord, Tigris approached him.

His eyes, coming back from a great distance, at length focused on hers. "Well?"

"Master, a reptile scout has just arrived at the stronghold, carrying intelligence." She named a region that was many kilometers away.

"So? What word, then?"

"Sire, some Blue Temple people in that area have very recently acquired the Sword of Mercy."

Now the man's beautiful blue eyes were truly focused. "Woundhealer."

He breathed the name in a hoarse whisper. "We know just where it is? There is no mistake?"

"The location is only approximate. But I believe the report."

In excitement he seized her arm. His grip for some reason felt icy cold. "Tigris, my plans bear fruit!"

"Master, we all expected nothing less."

Wood paused in thought, clasping his hands in front of him, smiling and nodding with satisfaction. "Woundhealer, my dear," he remarked to his young associate, "is perhaps the only Sword that I would be willing to trust in the hands of a subordinate.

"Therefore I am not rushing out into the field to take it away from those Blue Temple fools—I may decide to send you. When you have completed your present tasks."

The blond head bowed deeply. "I will of course be honored, Master."

"We shall see. As usual, I have other important tasks to perform. Though I must admit that, in a way, there is no other Sword that I am more anxious to possess."

Tigris allowed herself a display of mild surprise. "Master, the Sword of Mercy is certainly a tool of great value. We are, any and all of us, subject to injury sooner or later."

"Obviously. But I think you miss my point."

"Master?"

"Certainly, when one is badly hurt, healing is priceless. But surely you cannot fail to see that Woundhealer will also be of exquisite value in the torture chamber."

"Ah."

"Yes, 'Ah' indeed. Just consider the possibilities, when the occupant of the rack or of the boot can be revived over and over, times without number. When one is entertaining one's enemy under such favorable conditions, one always hates to say a permanent goodbye. Imagine the guest, just as final unconsciousness is about to overtake him—or her— being restored to perfect physical health and strength, every nerve and every blood vessel intact again. And restored quickly, almost instantly! No need even to remove him—or her—from the rack for a period of recuperation."

Wood sighed faintly. "I tell you, Tigris, I would give a great deal to be able to take the Sword of Love—and a few well-chosen guests, of course —and retire to one of my fortresses for a few years of well-earned rest and entertainment."

"My Master, I look forward to making such a retreat with you. What pleasures could we not devise?" The blond young woman giggled, a delicious sound.

"Yes." Wood stroked her hair, and his features softened momentarily. "You are a beautiful creature."

"Thank you."

"And loyal to me."

"Naturally, Master."

"Naturally." The stroking hand moved on. "Really beautiful. And, of course, still really young. That is a rare quality among my close associates, and one I value. Yes my dear, you are precious to me."

The head of yellow curls bowed humbly.

But Wood's expression was hardening again. His fondling hand fell to his side. "Unfortunately, we can spare no time for any prolonged diversion now."

"No, Master."

Standing with hands braced on his workbench, issuing brisk commands, the Ancient One dictated the reply he wanted sent back to his people in the field.

The necessary materials were readily at hand. Tigris wrote what she was ordered to write. The message was short and to the point; the written words glowed briefly, then disappeared from the thin parchment, not to regain their visibility until the proper spell should be recited over them.

Now the wizard paced as he completed the dictation. "Tell my people that they are graciously granted permission to use Woundhealer to cure whatever wounds they may have suffered."

"Yes, Master."

"As for healing anyone else, if the question should come up . . . I think not." The handsome man smiled his youthful smile.

A few minutes later, standing on the battlements to make sure that the winged messenger was properly dispatched, she gazed upon the open sky, and heard birdsong again.

This time, as she listened, the faint crease of a frown appeared above her eyes. There was something she did not understand. Something that bothered her.

Something those cheerful voices not only symbolized, but actively conveyed. A plea, or a warning, that she ought to, but still did not, understand.

The singers of course were only birds, nothing more than they seemed to be, she was very sure of that. And that point perhaps had meaning.

Small and mindless and meaningless animals. Perhaps, though, simplicity, an absence of trickery, was not altogether meaningless.

Tigris had the irrational feeling that, years ago, when she was only a child, she might have been able to comprehend the birds . . . though the child she had been of course had not begun to understand the world as it really was.

Yet recently—today was not the first experience—she had been nagged by the notion that in childhood she must have known something of great importance, something essential, which she had since utterly forgotten. Recently there came moments when it seemed to her that the thing forgotten had once been, might still be, of overriding importance in her life.

It was unsettling.

Tigris closed her eyes, long enough to draw a breath and let it go. For no longer than that did she allow herself to waste the Master's time. Here in the stronghold of the Ancient One, one had to guard one's very thoughts with extreme care.

At that same hour, the Sword of Wisdom gripped in the huge right hand of Ben of Sarykam was guiding four people across an extensive wasteland.

They were making good time for travelers on foot, and Zoltan, the most impetuous of the four if not precisely the youngest, did a good job of restraining his impatience with the comparative slowness of his elders. But he kept wanting to hurry them along. As soon as Zoltan had heard of his Aunt Kristin's horrible injury and desperate need, he had become wholeheartedly committed, perhaps even more than Ben, to the search for Woundhealer.

Their march across what was basically an uninhabited plain had gone on for two days now. In the afternoons the spring sun grew uncomfortably warm. Shade was scarce in this wasteland, and the walkers were all thankful that summer was yet to come.

Now and then Ben grumbled that if they kept on much longer in this direction, they were bound to come back to the river on which he had left the bandit boat, though at a point considerably downstream from that where he had made his escape.

"You are reluctant to reach a river?" Valdemar asked him. "I think it would be a refreshing change."

"This one has bandits on it. I'll tell them you're the real Ben of Purkinje."

* * *

As the day drew toward its close, the four, led to water by the sight of thriving vegetation, came upon a small stream that issued from a spring at the root of a rocky outcrop. Ben consulted with the lady, and by agreement they called a halt for food and rest.

Shrugging out of his small pack, Valdemar remarked: "I have no doubt that we are being led toward Woundhealer. But I wonder how far we have to go."

Zoltan, shedding his own pack, answered: "No telling. We may not even be going straight toward the Sword itself."

"Ah. It has already been explained to me that I may not be going directly toward my bride. Whoever she may be."

"Right," Ben grunted abstractedly.

"My purpose then may well be twice delayed." For the first time since he had joined the others, the young vineyardist sounded faintly discouraged.

As the simple process of making camp got under way, Ben began to reminisce about another journey once taken under the guidance of the Sword of Wisdom. That had been nineteen years ago, and Wayfinder had been then in the hands of the vengeful Baron Doon, who had used the powers of the Sword to guide himself and his band of plunderers to the main hoard of the Blue Temple's treasure.

"You speak as if you were there," commented Valdemar.

"I was," Ben answered shortly.

"I have heard some version of the story."

"Would you like to hear the truth?"

"Of course."

"Maybe one of these nights, when we are resting."

The four had pooled their food supplies, but the total was quickly becoming ominously low. Zoltan expressed a hope of being able to find game in this country, despite its barrenness. He had with him a sling, a weapon with which he had gained some proficiency over the last few years. Zoltan went away to hunt.

At least two kinds of wild spring berries were ripening in this otherwise harsh land. And edible mushrooms were also coming up after recent heavy showers. Yambu and Valdemar were able to gather a useful amount of food within a short distance of the camp.

Meanwhile Ben was building a fire of dried brush and twigs. In anticipation of making a stew of small game and vegetables, he also cut a large gourd from a last year's groundvine. This receptacle he hollowed out

with a skillful knife, to serve as a cooking pot. A couple of hot stones
dropped in would boil the water nicely.

Once darkness had fallen, and the rabbit stew had been cooked and
consumed, Ben and Yambu drifted into serious talk beside the small
campfire.

Their conversation acquired an earnest tone when Ben began to reminisce about that last time, nineteen years ago, he had taken part in an
expedition guided by Wayfinder.

"Oh, I trust our guide, all right." He patted the black hilt as if it might
have been a favorite riding-beast. "As some of you well know, this is not
the first time I have held this Sword, and followed it."

Zoltan and Yambu nodded.

Ben was coming to the point now. He turned his ugly face toward
Yambu. "Ariane too was a member of that party."

She returned his meaningful gaze with an intent look of her own. "I
know that."

Valdemar, looking from one of the two older people to the other,
asked innocently and idly: "Who is Ariane?" There was not much hope
in his voice; doubtless he thought it unlikely that any woman who had
been robbing the Blue Temple nineteen years ago would qualify now as a
good wife for a man of twenty.

Yambu answered without looking at him. "She was my daughter, and
the Emperor's. And she died, nineteen years ago, in that damned Blue
Temple treasure-dungeon."

"I am sorry to hear it," said Valdemar after a moment. He sounded as
if he truly was.

Keeping his gaze fixed on Ariane's mother, Ben said: "Four years ago,
you and I had a chance to discuss what happened in that treasure-dungeon, as you aptly call it. Four years ago we started to talk of Ariane, but
it seems to me that, for whatever reason, we said nothing important. Now
I want to talk with you about her, whom we both loved. And about the
Emperor."

Silence held. Yambu was not looking at Ben, but no one doubted that
she was listening.

"Because there is something I did not tell you when we met four years
ago," Ben continued, frowning.

"Yes?" Yambu's tone was noncommittal. She tossed a handful of fresh
fuel on the fire.

"A few years before our last meeting I encountered Ariane's father.

The Emperor told me that she was still alive. That she had been living with him."

Ben's words hung in the air. Meanwhile the small campfire went on about its business, snapping with brisk hunger at its latest allotment of twigs. In the infinite darkness beyond the firelight wild creatures prowled, not always silent. Yambu was looking at Ben now. She stared at him in silence for what seemed a long time.

At last she asked: "Where, under what circumstances, did you have this conversation with the Emperor?"

"On the shore of Lake Alkmaar. I was pretending to be a carnival strongman, he was pretending to be a clown. You, as I recall, were not far away, nor was Zoltan; you must both remember our situation."

Zoltan nodded thoughtfully.

Ben went on: "Understand, at the time my mind was on other things entirely. I was afraid Mark might be dead, and I said something about that. He said no, Mark was alive, it was hard to kill one of his—the Emperor's—children. And then he said to me something I have never forgotten: 'My daughter Ariane lives also. You may see her one day.' At the time I could not even begin to think about Ariane again. But her father's words have kept—coming back to me. Though I've never allowed myself to believe them."

"How . . . strange." Yambu was staring into some distance where none of her companions' thoughts or even imaginations were able to follow.

Ben's eyes remained fixed on the Silver Queen. His voice was urgent: "You know him better than I do. You tell me how likely he is to be truthful in such a matter."

"I, know him?" The Silver Queen, shaking her head, gave a kind of laugh. "I've shared his bed, and borne his child. But I don't even know his true name—assuming that he has one. Know him? You'll have to seek out someone else for that."

"But does he tell the truth?"

The gray-haired woman was silent for what seemed to Ben a long time. At last she said: "More than anyone else I've ever known, I think. One reason, perhaps, why he's so impossible to live with."

No one said anything for a time. Then Valdemar, yawning, announced that he intended to get some sleep.

Conversation immediately turned to the practical business of standing guard—whoever was standing watch would of course be armed for the job with the Sword of Wisdom.

* * *

Zoltan, having by lot been given the honor of standing the first watch, paced in random fashion for a time, his worn boots making little sound in the sandy soil. Slowly he looped round the still-smoldering fire in an irregular pattern, remaining at a considerate distance from the three blanket-wrapped forms of his companions.

Now and again the young man, his face vaguely troubled, stopped to gaze at the naked weapon he was carrying. Then he silently and deliberately paced on.

During one of these pauses, as Zoltan stared at the Sword of Wisdom, his lips moved, as if he might be silently formulating a new question.

Even in the night's near-silence, the words were far too soft for anyone else to hear: "If I were—*if* I, like Valdemar, were seeking the right woman for myself—which way would I go?"

If the Sword reacted at all to this hypothetical new command, the turning of its point, the twisting of its black hilt in Zoltan's grasp, must surely have been very subtle, a movement right at the limit of his perception.

But probably, he thought, the Sword would not answer such a conditional question at all.

Ought he to make the query definite? No, That part of his life he ought to be able to manage for himself.

But it did cross Zoltan's mind that perhaps it would be wise for him to ask, now when the Lady Yambu could not hear him, whether he should remain with the Lady Yambu any longer or not.

In response to this question—if it was indeed a real question—the reactions of Wayfinder in Zoltan's hands were very tentative, indicating first one direction and then another.

Or was he only imagining now that the Sword responded at all?

Frowning with dissatisfaction, Zoltan sat down for a time, his back to the dying fire, the weight of the drawn Sword resting on the sand in front of him, faint stars and sparks of firelight reflecting in the blade.

When the stars in their turning informed the young man that his watch had passed, he crawled softly to Valdemar's side and woke him with a gentle shaking.

"All quiet?"

"All quiet."

Moments later, Zoltan was wrapped in his own blanket and snoring faintly.

*   *   *

Now Valdemar was the one holding Wayfinder, and pacing. Presently, like Zoltan, he sat down for a time, and like the smaller youth he found another question to whisper to the oracle.

"Sword, how soon will you bring me to the goal I have asked for? Another day? A month? A year?"

There was no reply.

Softly he pounded his great fist on the ground. He breathed: "But of course, how can you answer such a question? It is only *Where* that you must tell, never When or Why or How—or Who. So *Where* must be enough for me."

Ben's turn on watch followed in due course. The older man did little pacing—his legs felt that they had accomplished quite enough of that during the day just past. But he moved around enough to be an effective sentry. And he stayed creditably alert.

Ben too, found some serious personal thoughts and questions that he wished to put to the Sword. But none of these queries were voiced loudly enough for anyone else to hear.

He did not fail to keep track of time, or neglect to wake the Lady Yambu when her turn came around, well before the sky had begun seriously to lighten in the east.

Yambu took advantage of the opportunity to have a word or two with Ben.

"What do you think of him?" she whispered, nodding in the direction of the sleeping Valdemar.

Ben shrugged. "Nothing in particular. I doubt he's much more than he seems to be. What I do wonder . . ."

"Yes?"

"How it is that the Sword will satisfy his wish, and yours, and mine, by leading us all together in the same direction."

If the Silver Queen nursed private thoughts during the hours she spent alone with Wayfinder she was not inclined to share them, even with the Sword. Her watch passed uneventfully.

When the sun was up the party of four adventurers broke camp and moved on, following the guidance of the Sword of Wisdom, once more in the hands of Ben.

For another day or two the Sword continued to lead them steadily northeast. Foraging and hunting kept them tolerably well fed. At night they camped by water when it was available, and made dry camps when it was not, and in either case stood watch in turn, in turn armed with the Sword of Wisdom.

Still there was no sign of the river Ben said they must inevitably encounter; evidently its winding course was carrying it also farther to the east.

Progressively the country surrounding the four seekers became more and more a desert. And then one day the river, of which Ben had been so wary, was again in sight.

6

THE course of the rediscovered river, as indicated by the vegetation growing thickly along its banks, ran ahead of the travelers and somewhat to the east. A kilometer or so after slicing its way into view between hills to the north, the watercourse emerged from a rocky gorge onto relatively flat land. Becoming visible at approximately the same time was a faint road or track, the first sign of human endeavor the travelers had seen for days. This came gently curving toward the river from the west, with a directness suggesting that the point of intersection would provide a ford.

Shortly after this road came into their view, the sight of half a dozen scavenger birds, circling low in several places above the near bank of the river, alerted the four travelers to the presence of death. The number and position of the gliding birds suggested that destruction of animal or human life might recently have occurred on a substantial scale.

Less than an hour after first sighting the birds, the four seekers, advancing steadily but cautiously, their afternoon shadows now gliding far ahead of them, reached the place where the sketchy road descended a shallow bank to ford the river.

Mounting a slight rise, Ben, who was a little ahead of the others, came to a stop, grunting. The bandits' flatboat had survived, substantially intact, its encounter with the rapids. It now lay run aground several hundred meters away, a little downstream from the ford.

Ben pointed, and said to his three companions: "That's the boat I swam away from."

The flatboat's sweeps and poles, or most of them, were missing, as was the covered cargo, whatever that had been. There was no human presence, living or dead, on the boat or near it.

Some small four-legged scavengers, whose presence had evidently been keeping the hungry birds aloft, slunk away along the shoreline as the four humans approached. One of the scampering little beasts turned to bare its fangs, until Zoltan slung a stone at it, scoring only a near miss, the missile kicking up a spurt of sand.

"I think I see a dead man," said Valdemar in a strained voice, standing as tall as he could and squinting ahead from his great height. "There. Just upstream from the ford."

The four advanced, still cautiously, the three who were armed with hands on weapons. It was soon possible to confirm Valdemar's sighting. Then almost at once they came in sight of another fallen body, lying nearer to them, motionless beside a slaughtered riding-beast. And then a third man, this one obviously dead, his skull crushed in.

"No more than a day ago," Zoltan muttered, looking closely at the handiest corpse and sniffing.

Soon the total of human dead discovered had reached approximately a dozen, all within a stone's throw of the ford.

Ben, peering closely now at the bodies, announced that he could recognize some of the bandits from whom he had so recently escaped. He confirmed that this definitely was—or had been—Brod's band, though the Sarge himself had not yet been found.

"Some of them are wearing blue and gold," Valdemar commented in a subdued voice. "That has to mean Blue Temple, doesn't it?"

Ben nodded. "Brod kept his rendezvous with them," he mused. "Can't say I'm surprised that a fight started—but over what?" He drew Wayfinder, which he had momentarily put away, muttered over the Sword, turned it this way and that.

Signs on the ground indicated that riding-beasts, and perhaps loadbeasts too, had galloped here, had run in panicked circles on the flat land where the stream widened and smoothed into the ford. All this could be read according to the tracks, which were quite plain in the moist sand of the riverbank. The imprints were a day old, or not much more than that, drying and crumbling around the edges. But no running animals were now in evidence; whatever mounts and loadbeasts might have survived the fight had evidently scattered.

Zoltan, darting about on the field of combat more energetically than any of his companions, was seeking among bushes and boulders, bending over bodies, examining one after another in rapid succession.

The four, exchanging comments, reached a consensus: One side, either Blue Temple or bandits, had tried to cheat the other. Or perhaps both had simultaneously attempted some kind of treachery. Then they had efficiently killed each other off.

Ben was still leveling his Sword, turning it this way and that, frowning, trying to interpret what the bright blade told him now. Wayfinder's point was twitching.

Violent death was nothing new to any of the travelers, except perhaps to Valdemar.

"Have you seen this kind of thing before?" the Silver Queen inquired of him.

The towering youth replied with a shake of his head. He appeared to be repelled, and somewhat upset by the unpleasant sights.

He muttered: "Foolishness, foolishness. Why are folk determined to kill each other? It's as if they looked forward to their own dying."

"I have no doubt some do," Yambu assured him.

Now Zoltan, who with a veteran's callous practicality had begun rifling the packs of the fallen, announced with a cheerful cry the discovery of food.

The provisions were mostly dried meat and hard biscuit. He began to share them out with his companions. He came upon spare clothing, too, and announced the welcome find.

Zoltan compared his own right foot with that of a corpse. "I think this one's shoes may fit me. Just in time, mine are wearing through."

There was a cry—really more a grunt—of excitement, from Ben. Not long distracted from his quest by a mere battlefield, he had been guided by Wayfinder to a wounded loadbeast.

The others saw him pointing the Sword at the animal where it stood amid some scrubby bushes, which until now had screened it from their observation. The loadbeast's harness was marked with the Blue Temple insignia of gold and blue, and it carried a full load on its back. The beast was favoring its right foreleg, streaked with dried blood. There was water here, and some good grazing along the river, so the animal must have been disinclined to wander far.

No doubt, thought Zoltan, the scavengers had so far let the loadbeast live because there was easier meat on hand for the taking.

In Ben's hands the Sword of Wisdom was pointing straight at the trembling, braying animal.

Valdemar said: "Put the poor creature out of its misery, at least."

But Ben had already sheathed the Sword of Wisdom, seized the animal by its bridle, and pulled it out of the bushes so he could get at its burdens more easily. In another moment Ben was unfastening panniers from the loadbeast's back and dumping their contents on the ground.

His companions, alerted now, scarcely breathing, were all watching him in silence.

Of all the bundles that had been strapped to the back of the burdened animal, only one was long and narrow enough.

When the coverings of this package were ripped away by Ben's powerful hands, it proved indeed to contain a Sword, black-hilted and elegantly sheathed.

"Wait! Before you draw. That could be Soulcutter . . ." Valdemar fell silent.

Ben was holding the sheathed and belted Sword up for the others to see. A single look at the white symbol on the hilt, depicting an open human hand, allayed whatever fears they might have had. Here was Woundhealer, the very Sword they had come looking for.

Ben, with grim satisfaction, strapped on the Sword of Mercy. Then he turned, his eyes sweeping the horizon, warily ready for someone to challenge him for his prize.

Valdemar studied him for a moment, then turned away, once more examining the fallen on the field.

"What are you looking for?" asked Yambu.

"I want to see if any of them are still alive."

Indeed one of the fallen, and only one, still breathed. Evidently he had managed to drag himself under a bush, and so lay relatively protected from the sun, the scavengers, and discovery.

Ben on getting a look at the fallen man at once recognized Sergeant Brod. "This is the very one I wrestled with."

The squat leader of the bandits, his chest rising and falling laboriously under his leather vest, lay in a welter of his own dried blood, dagger still clutched in his right hand, not many meters from the treasure the two armed factions must have been struggling to possess. Either he had not known Woundhealer was there, or he had been too badly hurt to reach it.

Valdemar cried out suddenly, his voice for no apparent reason argumentative: "Ben! If that's really the Sword of Healing, you'd better use it!"

Ben, faintly puzzled, looked at the young giant in wary silence.

"Use it, I say!" Valdemar sounded angry. "The man is dying. Even if he was your enemy."

"Did you think I wouldn't use it?" Ben asked mildly. Stooping, he grabbed Sergeant Brod by both ankles and pulled his inert weight roughly straight out from under the bush, evoking a noisy breath that might have been a gasp of pain, had the victim been fully conscious.

Valdemar looked slightly surprised and vaguely disappointed, as if he had been ready for a confrontation with Ben.

Bending over the fallen man once more, Ben pulled the dagger from Brod's hand, and took the added precaution of kicking out of his reach another weapon which had fallen nearby.

"Just in case," he muttered. "Actually, I look forward to speaking with an eyewitness of this skirmish. Might be a help, even if we can't believe much of what he says."

Once more Ben delayed briefly, this time to search the pockets of the fallen man, and his belt pouch. Evidently the search turned up nothing of any particular interest.

Then Ben, who was no stranger to the Sword of Mercy and its powers, postponed the act no longer, but employed Woundhealer boldly, thrusting the broad blade squarely and deeply into the victim's chest.

Valdemar flinched involuntarily at the sight. Zoltan and Yambu, more experienced observers of Swords' powers, watched calmly.

The bright Sword's entry into flesh was bloodless—though it cut a broad hole in the Sarge's leather vest, which Ben had not bothered to open—and the application of healing power was accompanied by a sound like soft human breath.

Recovery, as usual when accomplished through the agency of Woundhealer, was miraculously speedy and complete. The man, his color and energy restored, sat up a moment after the Sword had been withdrawn from his body. He looked down at his pierced and bloodied garments, then thrust a huge hand inside his vest and shirt and felt of his own skin, whole again.

A moment later Brod, now staring suspiciously at Ben, got his legs under him and sprang to his feet with an oath. "What in all the hells do ye think yer doing?"

Ben stared at him with distaste. "What *am* I doing?" he rumbled. "I may have just made a serious mistake."

The Sarge was scowling now at the Sword in the other's hand. "Reckon you know that's my proppity you got there?"

No one answered him. Ben slowly resheathed Woundhealer at his belt. He grunted: "You might express your thanks."

Brod turned slowly, confronting each of his four rescuers in turn. When he found himself facing the lady, he introduced himself to her, using some extravagant gestures and words.

Yambu was neither much impressed nor much amused. "I am not the one who healed you, fellow."

Brod finally, reluctantly, awkwardly, thanked Ben.

"I had a reason." Ben gestured at the field of death by which they were surrounded. "Now entertain us with a story about your little skirmish here. And you might as well tell the truth for once."

"You think I'd *lie?*"

"The possibility had crossed my mind."

Protesting his invariable truthfulness, Brod began to talk. He told his rescuers that his worst problem had been surviving the scavengers, having half a dozen times come close, he thought, to being eaten alive. He said that whenever he had regained consciousness he had waved his dagger at the predators, and by that means managed to keep them at bay.

Moving about a little, surveying the field, he grimaced at the sight of his fallen comrades, their bodies stabbed by Blue Temple blades and gnawed by scavengers. But the Sarge was able to be philosophical about their loss. "The magic hasn't been made yet that'll do any of these a bit of good."

Meanwhile Zoltan had quietly borrowed the Sword of Mercy from Ben, approached the injured loadbeast, and tried Woundhealer on the leg which it kept favoring, listening meanwhile to Ben's ongoing interrogation of Sergeant Brod. It did not sound like Ben was managing to learn anything of importance.

Almost at the Sword's first touch, the animal's braying ceased, and the wound disappeared from its leg. It looked at Zoltan in mild satisfaction, accepting with inhuman complacency its miraculous return to health. The young man rubbed its head before it turned aside to graze along the riverbank.

By now the Sarge, in response to insistent, probing questions from Ben and the Silver Queen, had launched upon a rambling and at least generally plausible explanation of just how the fight for Woundhealer had come about between his gang and the Blue Temple people. The latter, Brod said, had been in the process of escorting the Sword of Healing back to their headquarters, and had hoped to engage the bandits—at a ridiculously low fee, according to Brod—as additional guards.

He complained bitterly about Blue Temple stinginess, which he said he was sure lay at the root of their treacherous behavior.

Zoltan, his cynical amusement growing as he listened, thought that this Sarge was not so much a dedicated enemy of truth and Tasavalta, as a complete opportunist.

Brod, his imagination now warmed by the fact that his audience so far seemed to believe him, began to stretch his story. Now, it seemed, the Sarge had been trying for some time to get the Sword of Healing for the noble Prince Mark of Tasavalta.

Ben and Zoltan exchanged glances in which amusement and outrage were mingled.

Yambu appeared to share their sentiments. But by now she had moved a little apart from the others, and, sitting on a rock in deep thought, did not seem to be giving much thought to the Sarge and his tall tales.

Valdemar now was looking with distrust and disgust at the man whose rescue he had insisted upon.

Brod returned Valdemar's gaze with some curiosity, and demanded to know this young giant's name. When he had been told, his next question was: "Ever do any wrestling?"

"Some."

"Ah. Aha! Maybe you and I should try a fall or two one day."

"I don't know why." Valdemar did not appear at all interested in the challenge.

Brod shrugged. "Have it your way." He squinted once more at Ben and Zoltan. "Atmosphere's a little chilly in these parts. Guess maybe I'll be on my way."

"An excellent idea," said Ben shortly, standing with his powerful arms folded.

Brod made a casual move to rearm himself, bending as if to pick up a fallen weapon or two from the field, but this action was cut short by a sharp "No" from Ben.

Brod straightened. "What?"

"Don't pick up any tools. Just start walking." Zoltan too was watching Brod closely, and Zoltan's hand was on the hilt of his own serviceable sword.

The bandit leader, all injured innocence, loudly protested, "You'd send me away as nekkid as a babe? Man's got a right to protect himself, don't he? There's wild animals in these parts." He paused, as if gathering breath to deliver the ultimate argument, then spat: "There's *bandits!*"

"Get walking," said Ben quietly. "Before I change my mind."

Brod turned. "Lady Yambu? A high-born lady like you wouldn't . . ." His voice died, withered by the expression on Yambu's face.

Ben, his right hand on the hilt of one of his two belted Swords—the one devoid of healing power—continued to consider the Sergeant thoughtfully.

Brod fidgeted uncomfortably under this inspection. He glowered, but then with an obvious effort, he smiled, achieving at least a pretense of gratitude and co-operation. "All right. All right. Maybe you're right. I'm going, just the way you want."

The others, remaining more or less suspicious, watched him walk a semicircle, first, as if completely undecided as to which way he wanted to go. Then the Sarge moved in the direction of the ford, and went downstream along the near bank of the river. On reaching the grounded flat-boat, a hundred meters or so from where his watchers stood, Brod waded to it and climbed aboard. There he helped himself to the small boat that still was lashed to the deck, loosing the lashings, and manhandling the small craft into the water.

Zoltan, idly pulling the long thongs of his hunting sling through his free hand, commented: "Might be some weapons there."

Ben shrugged. "Let him help himself; as long as he keeps moving, away from us."

Now that Ben had the Sword of Healing securely at his belt, he had only one thought: to be done with worrying about Brod and other unimportant matters, and convey his new treasure quickly back to Sarykam.

Another gray Tasavaltan messenger-bird arrived at this point, as if it had been waiting for the Sarge, antagonistic as he was to Ben, to take himself away. Ben made welcome use of the opportunity to dispatch a written note to Mark, informing the Prince that his friends had now acquired the long-desired Sword.

Then Ben, Valdemar, Yambu, and Zoltan all availed themselves of Woundhealer, clearing up all of their own hurts, old and new; the most recent of these being a couple of minor injuries sustained by Ben in the course of his wrestling bout and subsequent escape from the flatboat.

Accepting the Sword of Mercy, Yambu murmured: "This knee is wont to give me problems . . ." And with a surgeon's steady hand, she pulled up one leg of her gray trousers, and thrust the hurtless Blade straight into the pale skin . . .

There was no pain, and of course she had not thought there would be any. But the shock was unexpected, and tremendous, far greater than she had anticipated. In the instant when Woundhealer entered Yambu's body the world changed, subtly but powerfully. Her chronically sore knee was healed, but the nagging pain and its relief were alike forgotten, in the simultaneous curing of a greater, deeper anguish, so long endured that the Silver Queen had ceased to be consciously aware of it at all.

So long endured . . . ever since that day of evil memory, almost a score of years ago, when she had overcome the Dark King's army with Soulcutter in her hands.

"Ah . . ." said she who had once been the Silver Queen, and let the black hilt of this far different blade slide from her grip. The Sword of Love fell to the earth. She stood for a moment with head thrown back, a woman overtaken by some sudden fundamental pain, or ecstasy—no human, watching, could have said, in that first moment, which . . .

The paroxysm shook her for no more than a handful of heartbeats. Then Yambu could move again.

There were no mirrors at hand, and for long moments she could only marvel silently at the way her companions, open-mouthed, were staring at her now.

And even more strongly did the Silver Queen wonder at her own internal sensations, when she paused to savor them. This, this, she could remember now, was what it felt like to be fully alive.

At last she demanded: "What is it? Why do you all stare at me?" But in her heart she thought that she already knew the important part of the answer.

"My lady . . ." This was Zoltan, her traveling companion for several years, now suddenly hushed and reverent. "My lady, you have grown young again."

Ben, his ugly countenance a study in awe, was nodding soberly. Valdemar stood gaping.

"Young again? Nonsense!" And to confirm that it was nonsense the Silver Queen could see strands of her own long hair, still gray, drifting before her eyes. She could clearly see her own hands, weathered and worn, not at all the hands of a young girl.

Yet even as Yambu contradicted Zoltan, she felt that he must be speaking some fundamental truth.

"You are all looking at me so . . . has anyone a mirror?"

What had seemed almost a spell was broken. Zoltan's thought was that there might possibly be a mirror in one of the Blue Temple or bandit packs that now lay scattered about. He went to look.

Ben agreed, and joined the search. But he failed to prosecute this effort vigorously, stopping every few seconds to turn and look back at the Silver Queen.

Valdemar was in this case the most practical of the four. He said nothing, but went a little apart to squat on the very shoreline of the river, where he scooped up sand with his huge hands, and splashed and puddled water into a concave excavation, muttering the while. When his efforts at magic had born fruit, he lifted from the bank a kind of reflective glass, as broad as a human countenance, formed by the solidification of warm river water.

The object he handed to Yambu was as heavy as liquid water but no heavier or colder, flat and mirror-smooth on one face, rough as stone on its round edge and convex back. "My lady, be assured that the glass as I give it to you is completely honest."

Accepting the gift, Lady Yambu stared into the brilliant surface. There was no denying it, she now looked forty again, or even slightly younger, instead of the sixty she had appeared to be before Woundhealer touched her—or her true age of fifty-one.

Her hair was still white, or nearly so; but this alteration in color now appeared premature. Lines of tension and weariness, so long-engraved she had forgotten they were there, had been expunged from the face which now looked back at her, in which a long-vanished light and beauty had now been re-established. This was the countenance of no mere girl, but neither was it any longer old.

Zoltan, who had been her fellow pilgrim for several years, continued to stare at Yambu in timid awe, as if she were a stranger.

It was time now for the others to enjoy their turns at gaining what benefit they might from the Sword of Mercy's power. None of the three underwent any visible transformation. Ben stretched and groaned with the enjoyment of having several minor aches and pains removed, as a tired man might luxuriate in a massage. Valdemar was silent and thoughtful as Woundhealer's blade searched his flesh for damage; the youth had evidently not accumulated much.

When Zoltan had had his turn, it was time to make camp for the night. Even freshly healed, they were tired enough to camp where they were, right by the ford, with water readily available. But the dozen dead still held that field, and none of the four were minded to spend their own time and energy as a burial or cremation detail.

Another problem with this location lay in the fact that Brod would be able to find them easily should he return with some mischief in mind. But these were minor considerations beside the counsel of the Sword of Wisdom.

It was Yambu who at last put the question directly to Wayfinder: "Where is our safest place to camp tonight?" And the Sword promptly pointed them across the ford, away from the field of death.

Before leaving the battlefield, Valdemar did as Brod had been forbidden to do. He armed himself with two of the many weapons, now ownerless, that lay about for the taking.

From one fallen soldier Valdemar chose a battle-hatchet, and from another one a dagger, with its sheath. He had to unbuckle this last tool from its owner's stiffened corpse. The business was unpleasant, but still he did it without hesitating.

He muttered to himself: "If I am to be a warrior, I am going to need a warrior's tools."

Zoltan asked him: "Have you any skill with those?"

"Not with weapons. But knives and hatchets are familiar implements enough."

"Then I suppose you've chosen well."

Having forded the river, the four headed northeast by north, still following the Sword of Wisdom in Ben's hands.

Following them, for a short distance only, came the healed loadbeast. The creature paused, watching them depart. Then it shook its head and went back to where grass grew along the river.

7

ATOP the highest tower of the sprawling white stone Palace in Sarykam, standing on a paved rooftop that overlooked the red-roofed city, the placid harbor, and the Eastern Sea red-rimmed with dawn, Prince Mark of Tasavalta, wearing nightshirt and slippers, wrapped in a robe against the morning chill, was leaning on a railing, gazing to the south and west, waiting and hoping for the arrival of one of his numerous winged messengers or scouts.

Dawn was a good time, the most likely time in all the day, for certain birds, the night-flying class of owl-like scouts and messengers, to come home.

The Prince of Tasavalta was a tall man, strongly built, his face worn by weather and by care, his age just under forty, his hair and eyes brown, his manner distracted.

The semi-intelligent creature whose arrival Mark was anticipating presently became visible in the dawn sky as a faraway dot that in time grew into a pair of laboring wings.

Twelve-year-old Stephen, Mark's younger son, already fully dressed, joined his father on the rooftop, as he did on many mornings, to see whether any messengers might arrive.

The boy was sturdily built, his hair darkening to the medium-brown of his father's. The facial resemblance between father and son was growing stronger year by year.

The beastmaster attending the eyrie this morning was a man of exceptionally keen vision. He was the first to confirm the distant wings, now laboring in from the southwest, as those of a particular messenger-bird, whose arrival had been expected for more than a day.

The beastmaster climbed up on a perch to meet and care for the animal, which on landing turned out to have suffered some slight injury from the claws of a leatherwing. The Prince and his son, climbing also, were first to touch the large owl-like creature. Mark gently took from around its neck the small flat pouch of thin leather.

The great bird, its huge eyes narrowed to slits against the early daylight, hooted and whistled out a few words indicating that it had been delayed for some hours by storms as well as reptiles. Leaving the bird to the beastmaster's professional care, Mark carried the pouch down from the perch. After hastily performing a magical test for safety, he snapped open the container and extracted the single piece of paper which lay inside.

Unfolding the note, Mark read, silently the first time through. The message had been sent by Ben of Purkinje.

"Is it from Ben, Father?"

"Yes. He's several days away from Sarykam, or he was when he wrote this . . ." The Prince read on, skimming bad news, not wishing to contemplate any more of that than absolutely necessary.

"Ben's coming home?"

Mark's face altered. He stared at the note, his mind almost numbed by the two code words that leapt out at him from near the end. Almost he feared to allow himself to hope, let alone to triumph.

Putting down the paper for the moment, he looked around to make sure that no one but his son was close enough to hear him.

"Ben mentions an earlier message," he announced softly, "and repeats it here, to the effect that he has found Wayfinder. We never got that message. Some are bound to go astray."

"Dad! That means—if we've got Wayfinder—that means we can use it to find Woundhealer. Doesn't it?"

Mark held up the note. "We could, but there's more. He already has Woundhealer too."

"Dad!"

"He also says here that he's encountered old friends, your cousin Zoltan, and the Lady Yambu. I don't know if you remember her."

"What are we going to do?"

Mark grinned. "What would you do if you were in command?"

"Go get those Swords at once!"

"Not a very difficult decision, hey?"

But there was a considerably harder choice to be made immediately: Whether to let the news of Ben's evident success spread through the Palace, and thence inevitably, before long, into the ears of enemy agents. The boost in home morale that this news should produce would be welcome, but if the effort to bring Woundhealer home came to nothing, a corresponding letdown would ensue.

Stephen was staring anxiously at his father. Mark commanded the boy to tell no one else the content of Ben's message for the time being. The Sword was not yet safely home.

When Stephen had been given a chance to read the note for himself, father and son, teasing and challenging each other like two twelve-year-olds, went skipping and jumping down a set of ladders to the next lowest level of the tower, and thence down several levels to the broader roof of the keep below.

There, moving decisively, the Prince quietly began to set in motion preparations for an expedition to reclaim Woundhealer.

Stephen, as his father had expected, wanted to come along.

"Father, will you be leaving right away?"

"Within a few hours."

"Can I come with you?"

Mark made quick calculations. "No, you'll be needed here."

The refusal sent Stephen into a silent rage; he asked no questions, said nothing at all, but his face reddened and his jaw set.

Mark sighed; knowing his son, he was not surprised. He had no reason to expect or hope that this boy might be sheltered from danger all his life, and every reason to believe that the lad had better be hardened to it. The Prince would probably have acceded to his son's request to join the expedition but for one fact: Stephen seemed to be the only person capable of brightening his mother's countenance or manner in the least.

Mark explained this point. Then he repeated his refusal, couching it this time in terms of military orders, which made the pill somewhat easier to swallow.

When Stephen choked on another protest, his father ordered briskly: "Get control of yourself and speak coherently."

"Yes, Father." And the boy managed. He was learning.

"Now. This is an order . . ."

With Stephen under control, for the time being at least, the Prince's next impulse was to rush to Kristin with the good news.

But then on thinking the matter over, he was not sure how much he ought to tell his wife.

Catching sight of a junior officer going about some other errand, Mark hailed the man and dispatched him to find General Rostov.

Proceeding in the direction of his wife's room, Mark encountered the chief physician of the Palace, a tall woman with a dark, forbidding, age-less face and kindly voice.

This lady inquired: "Good news, Highness?"

"Yes. Or the possibility of good news, at least. I will be making an announcement presently." Yet Mark hesitated; it would be terrible, he thought again, to raise hopes that might in a few days be dashed.

Since Kristin's fall, neither physicians nor wizards had ever been sanguine about her prospects for recovery. None of the experts saw any real hope, unless the Sword of Healing could somehow be obtained.

The physician said: "I have just come from Her Highness's room."

"What word today?"

She bowed slightly. "Your Highness, I have no good words to say to you."

Mark interrupted the doctor at that point, and dispatched Stephen to look for Uncle Karel. "And when you have found him, I expect it will be time you are about your regular morning tasks."

"Yes, Father."

When Prince and physician were alone, the healer went on gloomily to explain that she had quietly alerted the attendants to maintain a watch against a possible suicide attempt on the part of the long-suffering patient.

"As bad as that." Mark was not really surprised; but no mental preparation could shield him from the chill brought by those words.

"I fear so, Prince."

"Well, well." He could still force his voice to be calm. "Carry on. We will do what we can."

The doctor bowed again, and moved away.

Mark had not progressed a dozen paces farther in the direction of his wife's room before he encountered General Rostov, who seemed already to have learned somehow that important matters were to be decided.

Rostov was as tall as Mark, but the general's barrel-chested frame was even broader. He had black skin, with an old scar on the right cheek. His curly hair had once been black, but was now almost entirely gray.

Drawing Rostov aside, Mark quietly outlined for him the expedition he wanted to lead out to gain possession of both Swords.

"Karel will be going with you?" Rostov asked.

"He will." Mark considered that Kristin's uncle, the chief wizard of the royal family and of the nation, would be indispensable on such an expedition. "Therefore you will be left in charge here at the Palace."

After providing the Prince with requested advice on several points, and receiving a few detailed orders, Rostov saluted and moved away, going about his business with his usual efficiency.

The Prince at last reached his wife's room and entered.

The Princess was occupying the same chamber as before her injury, though now the room was even more brightly decorated. Cheerful paintings, some of Kristin's favorites in her days of health, hung on the walls, and her favorite flowers stood in vases, or grew in pots. Everything about the place was joyous, airy, lightsome, and pleasant—everything except for its occupant, who lay garbed in a plain white gown, her countenance like a mask of clay.

Originally the nurses and other attendants assigned to care for the crippled Princess had been chosen as much for their cheerful attitude as for their professional ability. But those people had been replaced, when Kristin, complaining bitterly to her husband, had said she could not stand having such laughing fools around her.

This morning Kristin was in her bed as usual. She was capable of leaving it only seldom and briefly. Her body, always slender, was twisted now by broken bones that had healed only poorly, and by spasmed muscles. Her face, once beautiful, had been eroded from within by pain and loss of weight. Indoor pallor had replaced her tan.

Other than to utter an occasional grim comment on her own future, or lack of one, Kristin now rarely spoke.

Pulling a chair close to the bed, Mark sat down and gave his wife a partial report on the information that had just arrived by courier. Mark said only that there was new hope now, and that he would soon be leaving town in search of Woundhealer.

The Prince took this precaution against raising hopes that might be dashed, though in the bleak silence of his own thoughts he felt sure that the problem with Kristin was really the absence of any hope at all.

Mark took his wife's hand, but then let it go when the touch seemed to cause her some new discomfort.

Kristin appeared to listen to what her husband had to say, but she made no comment. Obviously her attitude regarding the news was one of bitter pessimism.

Her husband was saddened but not surprised by this reaction. That, he had learned, was consistently the disposition of his wife's mind whatever news he brought, or when, as was more usual, he had none to bring.

After leaving the sickroom, Mark found the old wizard Karel waiting for him, a fat old man with puffing breath and a rich, soft voice.

Karel, on learning of the morning's message, was in a hopeful mood.

"I might suggest, Prince, that you send a strong flying squadron to pick up the prize and carry it back to us, as we ride south. If this plan is successful, it would speed up your gaining possession of the Sword by a day or two at least."

Mark was impressed favorably by the old man's suggestion, but he postponed making a final decision on it. If he were eventually to decide in favor of such a maneuver, there would be no need to tell Ben about it in advance. So the Prince omitted any mention of the scheme in the message he now began drafting to be carried back to Ben.

As Mark considered it, strong arguments took shape in his mind against sending such a flying squad. Chief among these was the fact that any such half-intelligent flying force would run the risk of being detected, and then ambushed, by enemy magic, flying reptiles, or griffins. No birds were strong enough to stand against such an attack.

Wood himself, who Mark loathed as one of his great antagonists, was known to travel airborne on a griffin, or sometimes even on a demon's back.

The danger presented by the possibility of ambush eventually came to seem too great. By the time he had dispatched the message to Ben, Mark had all but finally decided not to take the risk.

Shortly after sunset the Lady Yambu, her new reserves of energy not fully depleted by a long day's hike, was pacing restlessly about the simple camp she shared with her three companions. The conversation that had begun a quarter of an hour ago had gradually died out, and the three were now all watching her in vague apprehension.

Suddenly she stopped her pacing, and declared: "I think I must consult our Sword again. I grow doubtful that the road I must follow to the truth lies through Tasavalta."

Ben looked at her, grunted, then wordlessly detached Wayfinder in its sheath from his belt, and held the weapon out to her.

Valdemar's expression suggested that he was surprised. He said to Yambu: "If you are having doubts, then I must have doubts also."

For several days now, the four had been slogging steadily northeast, in the general direction of Tasavalta. The land through which they traveled had gradually grown more rugged, and their progress had become correspondingly slower.

Now and then the Sword they followed decreed some slight variation in their course toward Sarykam. When this happened, the four travelers sometimes speculated about the possible cause of this deflection. But none of the three who had considerable experience with the awesome power of Swords suggested doing anything but going along with Wayfinder. And the detours, whatever their cause, had proven short. At the moment the four were once more, as nearly as they could estimate in this almost roadless waste, on or near a straight-line path toward the Tasavaltan capital.

Over the last few days and hours, Yambu had started several times to ask Ben more about what the Emperor had said to him regarding Ariane. But Ben, who had suggested such a conversation, no longer seemed to know what else he wanted to say, or hear, on that subject.

The lady was about to raise the matter with Ben again. But before she could do so, the travelers were excited by the arrival of a winged messenger.

Eagerly Ben unfastened the pouch from the great bird, and fumbled it open. Intently he scanned the note inside.

Zoltan read it over his shoulder. "Nothing of importance," the young man complained.

"Better than it looks," Ben assured him. "There are a couple of code words. First, congratulations—that'll be for our getting Woundhealer. And second, help is on the way."

Their spirits considerably lightened, the four pushed on.

Within an hour, they had became aware that someone was following them, maintaining a careful distance.

"Your old friend Brod," Zoltan decided, squinting at the distant, barely visible man who doubtless thought himself adequately concealed. "We should have finished him when we had the chance. I suppose he went off in the little boat just to be deceptive."

"Why should he be following us?" Valdemar wondered.

Ben shrugged. "His gang's been wiped out, and he's going to have to find some other way to make a living."

The Silver Queen had no comment; her thoughts were evidently elsewhere.

That evening, she spoke confidingly to her old friends Ben and Zoltan, and her new follower Valdemar.

"I am almost a girl again . . . no, I don't mean that. What foolishness! I am fifty-one years old, and healing will not turn back the years; age in itself is not an illness or an injury. But in a way I *feel* like a girl. The horrible burden that Soulcutter put on me so many years ago has at last been lifted. Can you understand what that means? No, there is no way you could understand."

And in her emotion the lady laughed and cried, in a mixture of joy and confusion; the emotional reaction which had come upon her when she was healed was now repeated, even more strongly than before.

"Can you understand? I can no longer be certain what my purpose in life is, or ought to be."

"I think I can understand, my lady." Ben's large hand pulled the Sword she had given them out of its sheath; he held the black hilt out toward her.

Zoltan nodded; it was a slow, uncertain gesture, as if he had trouble comprehending the Lady's difficulty, but considered that Wayfinder's powerful medicine ought to be worth a try in any case.

Once more gripping Wayfinder, Lady Yambu posed a new question.

"Blade, once more I seek your guidance. Was I speaking only foolishness when I asked you to find eternal truth for me? You answered me, I know, but . . . I am no longer sure what I was thinking two days ago. It is almost as if I have been reborn."

The Sword of Wisdom hung inert in her grasp. Of course. The question she had just asked, as Yambu understood full well, was not the kind Wayfinder could be expected to answer.

"Take your time, my lady." Ben was respectfully concerned.

The trouble, Yambu was discovering, was that she now found herself unable to formulate any inquiry to her own satisfaction. Indecisively she raised the Sword, and lowered it, and raised it up again.

At last, words burst forth: "Was my healing the only truth I needed? I have been granted the touch of the Sword of Mercy . . . but again, that is not the kind of question any Sword can answer for me, is it?"

Even as she spoke, Yambu was wishing that she had gone off by herself to so apostrophize Wayfinder. Certainly the others were watching and listening with intense interest. But now, as if he were embarrassed, Ben motioned to the two younger men, and all of them moved away, leaving the Lady alone with Wayfinder.

The mute Sword only quivered uncertainly, in response to the questioner's uncertainty.

"Changeable, are you? At least you are a silent counselor, and there's wisdom to be found in that."

Rejoining the others, she sought out Valdemar, and held out the black hilt of the sheathed Sword. Yambu said: "I am having but poor success. Will you try it for yourself once more?"

The young man in farmer's clothing hesitated, then shook his head doggedly. "No, I have already used Wayfinder more than once, and each time it has led me to you. My purpose has not changed. So, for now, let me continue as I am."

"Even if I have changed? If I no longer know where I am going?"

The young man smiled faintly. "Very well then, let me try the Sword once more."

As steadily as ever, the Sword of Wisdom with its black hilt once more in the huge hands of Valdemar, pointed straight toward the Silver Queen.

He returned the weapon to her hilt-first, making an almost courtly flourish. He said: "I am content to follow, Lady, whatever you decide to do."

She sighed. "Then let your fate be on your own head."

8

This night it was Valdemar's turn to stand the last watch, the hours just before dawn.

At the proper time Ben woke him, and silently held out to him the black hilt of the Sword of Wisdom, with which his comrades were to be protected as they slept.

The young man sat up, the folds of his blanket falling from around his massive shoulders, and held both hands to his head for a long moment before he accepted Wayfinder.

"Bad dreams?" Ben inquired in a low voice.

"No. Yes, I think so, but I don't remember." Valdemar shook his head. "I keep worrying about my vineyard."

"Once upon a time," said Ben, "when I was very young, all I wanted out of life was to be a minstrel. I really thought that I could be one, too. Carried a lute around with me everywhere. Can you believe that?"

"Yes, I can," said the other after a moment's thought. "Were you any good?" he asked with interest.

Ben appeared to consider the question seriously. "No," he said at last, and turned away. "Me for my own blanket."

Valdemar began his watch in routine fashion, by asking the Sword of Wisdom a question concerning the safety of the camp. Testing the limits on the kind of question the Sword would answer, he tended to keep trying new variations. Tonight's first variant was: "Will we be safer if we move?"

To this query the Sword in Valdemar's hands returned him no detectable answer; he presumed that Wayfinder would have pointed in the proper direction had its powers decided that the camp would indeed be more secure somewhere else.

The general safety assured, for the moment at least, to the sentry's satisfaction, he asked his second question of this watch. This one was whispered so softly that he could not hear his own words. "Where is the nearest person present whose advice I should be following?"

The Sword of Wisdom indicated Yambu, who appeared to be fast asleep.

Valdemar nodded. Carrying Wayfinder drawn and ready, he paced the vicinity of the small camp, applying the good sentry's technique he had learned from his new friends. He varied his route and pace, turning sharply at irregular intervals, eyes and ears alert to the surrounding darkness. He kept his eyes averted from the small fire's brightness to preserve their sensitivity in the dark.

Meanwhile his routine worries returned. Counting the days he had already been away from home, confirming his estimate of the advancing season by the current phase of the Moon, Valdemar knew with certainty that his vines would soon be leafing out, and would need care. He had done all he could for the plants before he left, but they would soon be growing wild, and insects would attack them.

He lacked the skills of magic necessary to do anything effective about these problems at a distance, though of course he could try. Valdemar doubted whether he could project any potent spells against insects, at least not over more than a few meters. He'd make the effort, of course, but not now. Right now he had to concentrate upon his duties as a guard.

Once more he put a safety question to the Sword, on the chance that circumstances had changed adversely in the past few minutes. Once more Wayfinder seemed to assure him that all was well.

Time continued to pass uneventfully. Ben had hardly hit the ground before falling fast asleep, as a faint rumble of snoring testified. The night wind ghosted past Valdemar's ears, and the moon and the familiar stars, though only intermittently visible through a patchwork of clouds, moved in their familiar paths above his head.

Where, he wondered suddenly, was Woundhealer resting at this moment? He tried to remember who had been carrying the Sword of Mercy. Then, in the course of his next sharp turn as he patrolled, the young man, peering intently by the vague light of stars and moon, caught a glimpse of the black hilt. The Sword was currently in Zoltan's custody, its shape unmistakable within its wrappings, lying in contact with his sleeping body.

All was well, then. Valdemar relaxed though he reminded himself sternly to remain alert. But as his watch dragged on, he strayed into asking Wayfinder one private question after another, only to realize guiltily once more that long moments had passed in which the Sword of Wisdom was no longer really charged with protecting the camp.

Tonight he was not only worried about his vineyard, but also bothered by particular concerns about his bride-to-be. As pictured in his imagination, she was a creature of unsurpassed loveliness. But her existence, as anything but a creation of his own imagination, he had begun to doubt.

Lost intermittently in these problems, Valdemar continued his pacing, circling the small campfire on an irregular path, the Sword of Wisdom naked in his right hand, a battle-hatchet belonging to some fallen warrior stuck in his farmer's belt.

At the moment his half-distracted mind presented Wayfinder with a new inquiry for the benefit of himself and the sleeping three: "Which way to go to foil our enemies? Which way to go—"

This time the Sword returned him a firm answer; generally northeast, the direction of their daytime travel.

Then Valdemar stopped, listening to himself. Actually, of course, neither he nor any of his three companions wanted to *go* anywhere at the moment—right now they all wanted to get some rest.

But how hard it was, thought Valdemar as he paced on again, for a man to know consistently what, beyond the physical necessities of the moment, he really wanted to do, to achieve. The world held so many kinds of things to want.

Anticipating the first rays of dawn, the young man found it impossible to keep his mind with absolute consistency upon the camp's defense. Then he would silently upbraid himself, and once more stalk about in his random pattern holding the Sword, and murmur: "I seek the safety of this camp. I seek the safety of this—"

Receiving no answer to what was not really a question, he would shake his head and mutter: "No need to keep repeating things like that. No need to keep repeating things . . ."

An hour passed. All continued quiet, and nothing untoward occurred.

And, as nothing in particular seemed to be happening, other questions, other urges, drifted as subtly as growing vines into control of Valdemar's mind.

Thus it was that the pacing, dreaming sentry was granted no warning whatsoever. One moment he and his sleeping companions were, as far as he knew, all safe, all at peace, save for the faint animal noises of the nocturnal wasteland, sounds more reassuring than disturbing.

And in the next moment they were being overwhelmed.

The onslaught, as Valdemar came later to understand, was well-coordinated, and consisted of an airborne magical component as well as a force of more mundane attackers on the ground. Somewhere over the young man's head there came a beating of great unseen wings, sounding far larger than those of any flying creature Valdemar had ever seen or heard before; simultaneously he heard a prosaic thunder of approaching hoof-beats on the ground.

Letting out a hoarse cry Valdemar whirled about, brandishing his Sword, unable for the first moment of the attack to see anything out of the ordinary at all. Then suddenly the sentry found himself confronted by a live man standing where a moment earlier there had been no one at all. The figure was that of a warrior, sword upraised, garbed in the same Blue Temple colors worn by half of yesterday's fallen.

For just a moment Valdemar was frozen by his own imagination, by the terrible image of all those bodies he had helped to rob of food and shoes and weapons, of those dead risen now to claim some kind of vengeance . . .

For a moment only. Then a second swordsman and a third material-ized behind the first out of darkness and the desert, and the young man understood that his attackers were only too full of mundane life. He let out a hoarse shout of alarm, realizing even as he did so that his warning must now be too late.

But his companions were reacting very quickly. Around him, friends and foes were scrambling in the darkness.

The first attacker recoiled from the camp's sentry, out of respect for the Sword that Valdemar was holding, if not for his gigantic figure. But now others were coming at him from the sides—and now a gossamer net, more magic than material, came dropping softly toward him from a great blurred form in the softly moonlit sky.

Barely in time he twisted out from under the net, sensing its enchant-ment. Drawn steel, Valdemar had heard, was the most effective counter-measure an ordinary man could take against a wizard's onslaught, and perhaps the Sword in his right hand, the battle-hatchet now drawn in his left, exerted some measure of protection.

The Lady Yambu, who had been the closest of the other three to Valdemar when the enemy appeared, now rose up at his side, hands spread in a magician's gesture, joining him in his hopeless though spir-ited defense of the camp.

Part of his mind noted that the Lady did not have Woundhealer—of course, that Sword had been with Zoltan.

"Fight!" she snapped at Valdemar. "We must not let ourselves be taken alive! Not by these—"

Valdemar, with no time to think, only grunted something in return. Brandishing the battle-hatchet in one hand and Wayfinder in the other, and confident in his own strength though mindful of his lack of skill, he

faced the enemy soldiers as what looked like a crowd of them came at
him.

The young giant wielded both hatchet and Sword with ferocious energy, and by sheer strength he succeeded in chopping down at least one
of his attackers.

To his surprise, the others fell back momentarily. The Silver Queen
had become a shadow gliding at Valdemar's side, and afforded him some
unexpected but very welcome magical assistance.

Still, the odds in favor of the enemy were overwhelming, and they were
returning to the attack.

Zoltan had come wide awake, alerted by some subliminal perception,
two or three heartbeats before the attack actually fell on the camp. He
was fully conscious and active in an instant, and aware of Ben beside him
also springing to his feet. Both were veterans, who needed only a momentary glimpse of the assailants surrounding Yambu and Valdemar, the
latter fighting with the Sword of Wisdom, to convince them that the odds
were hopeless. But so far Zoltan and Ben were not surrounded; rather,
they were at one side of the struggle, and escape appeared to be still
possible.

Getting the Sword of Mercy back to Tasavalta came ahead of everything else. Zoltan, with Woundhealer already in his hands, unsheathed
the Blade and without hesitation plunged it deep into his own body,
holding himself transfixed with a hand on the black hilt. With his other
hand he pulled his own short sword from its scabbard, and used it to run
through the first enemy trooper to come at him in the dimness of the
fading night. The trooper's dying counterstroke cut down on Zoltan's left
shoulder, and might have nearly taken off his arm, had not Woundhealer's overwhelmingly benign force prevailed. The enemy's sword fell
free, Zoltan's wound closing behind it so quickly that he lost no blood.

Ben, who had been unarmed except for a short knife and Wayfinder,
grabbed up the fallen weapon, and killed two men with it in the next few
moments of confusion.

Zoltan was running now, with Ben beside him, away from the belea-
guered Yambu and her young ally. Zoltan struck down another attacker,
receiving another harmless sword-slash in the process and Ben smashed
another foe aside. Both of them kept on running, their backs to the noise
and turmoil surrounding Valdemar and the Silver Queen.

A flying reptile came lowering out of the sky at Zoltan, talons biting
harmlessly, almost painlessly, into his head and face, which were still
protected by the magic of the gods. One claw bit through his eye and did

no harm, his vision clearing once more with a blink. He could hear, below the harsh gasping of his own lungs, the softly breathing sound made by the Sword of Mercy, mending this new damage to his body as quickly as it happened.

Even as his eyesight cleared, Zoltan's killing sword bit into the airborne reptile's guts. He heard the beast scream, and then fall heavily to earth behind him as he ran on.

Ben kept pounding along beside him, so far managing to keep up. But now a net of magic fell about them both, a gossamer interference with thought and movement that would have stretched them both out on the ground, had not Zoltan been protected from all injury. His senses and his thought remained clear, and he felt the evil magic only as he might have felt a cobweb tear across his face.

Beside him, Ben staggered and stumbled in his run, and would have fallen headlong had not Zoltan managed to sheath his own killing blade and catch the huge man under one arm, pulling and hauling him through torn cobwebs. Grunting with the effort, Zoltan kept Ben on his feet until the last shreds of the magic net had been left behind them.

Still the young man had trouble believing that the two of them were really going to get away; glancing back when they had run another fifty meters, he decided that he and Ben were being greatly helped in their escape by the fact that the attackers were concentrating so thoroughly on getting the Sword of Wisdom into their hands.

Valdemar kept hearing someone in command of the Blue Temple forces shouting orders to take that man alive. He knew the order referred to him. There was nothing to do but fight on, Yambu's warning fresh in his mind, and the Sword in his hands making it substantially harder for the enemy to do what they wanted. If only, Valdemar prayed fervently, this Sword were Shieldbreaker . . .

A rough ring of enemies kept forming around him and Yambu. But he kept muttering rapidly at Wayfinder, asking the Sword of Wisdom to show him the best way to escape. Then, keeping up as best he could with the Sword's rapidly changing instructions, he charged bravely at one Blue Temple weak point after another. The trouble was that soon there were no weak points in the rapidly closing ring.

Yambu meanwhile stayed on her feet, moving with agility to remain at Valdemar's back. She kept doing magical things, things he could not comprehend, but that must be serving to keep the attackers at least temporarily off balance.

But the odds were too great, their resistance could not last. The enemy magic was stronger than the Silver Queen's if not than Wayfinder's. At last Valdemar, the Sword in his hands notwithstanding, felt himself overwhelmed by swirling powers, by rampaging physical forms. Gold and blue faintly visible in moonlight, were everywhere around him. Whether the force that finally overcame him was material or occult he could not have said, and anyway it seemed to make no difference.

Dimly aware that the Lady Yambu was still nearby and shared his fate, he was knocked down, disarmed, made prisoner. Then, with her limp and evidently unconscious body being dragged beside Valdemar, both of them were removed a short distance from their place of capture, to a place where a strange bright light was shone on their faces, and their captors puzzled in mumbling voices over their identity.

That question having been answered to the winners' satisfaction—or else determined to be not quickly answerable, Valdemar could not tell which—the pair were moved another short distance. There they were left on the ground, seemingly temporarily abandoned.

Quickly Valdemar discovered that his arms and legs had been efficiently paralyzed by magic. But within moments after those who threw him down had turned away, he managed to shake free of some kind of cover, evidently a material one, which had been thrown over his head.

His first use of this limited power of movement was to look for Zoltan and Ben, wondering if they were still alive, and what had happened to Woundhealer. Three or four meters away lay the dim, inert form of the Silver Queen. The young man spoke to the lady quietly, but received no answer.

The attack, as Valdemar saw when he once more began to obtain a clear view of his surroundings, had been carried out by a small but powerful force of Blue Temple troops, magicians, and inhuman creatures. A few reptiles had already come down out of the clouded, slowly brightening sky. Larger forms were looming there.

Even as he watched, a pair of the giant wings he had earlier sensed overhead came closer. A creature landed. Valdemar, harking back to stories heard in childhood, realized that it must be a griffin. He could only gaze in wonder.

This was a large creature, much bigger than a riding-beast, with eagle's head and beak and wings, and legs and talons of a gigantic lion. Across its back was strapped a kind of saddle, flanked on each side by a kind of hanging woven basket, a sidecar or howdah. One or two men—Valdemar could not get a clear look at first—were riding on the beast. There would have been room for three, with a driver in the central saddle.

On the ground, the four-legged monster knelt, then crouched. The first of the passengers to disembark was a well-dressed man, short, redfaced and bald, who made an awkward dismount from one of the sidecars.

Moments later, a second elderly Blue Temple official came into Valdemar's field of vision. He was older and less ruddy of countenance than the first. Valdemar could not be sure whether this man had disembarked from the same mount, or from a slightly smaller griffin which had landed close behind the first.

It was soon evident that the attacking force was commanded by the rather short, red-faced man. Valdemar now heard this individual addressed as Chairman Hyrcanus. The elder, obviously second in importance, was called the Director.

Valdemar, with some difficulty raising his head a little farther against the bonds of magic that still held him down, was able to watch and listen as the Chairman expressed his satisfaction at having the solid ground under his feet again.

Now from among the mixed group of Blue Temple military and irregulars who had gathered there emerged a face, and a voice, that Valdemar to his surprise could recognize. Chairman Hyrcanus was greeted by Sergeant Brod, who came pushing forward from amidst the latest detachment of cavalry to reach the scene.

At least the Sarge, having somehow attached himself to the attackers, made an attempt to offer the Chairman such a greeting.

But the official, scowling at this interloper, would not listen. "Who're you?" Hyrcanus demanded; and then, before the man could possibly have answered, turned irritably to his cavalry officer. "Who's this?"

The officer seemed to shrink under his leader's glare. "The man is a local guide we have signed on, Your Opulence. He's been useful—"

"Another expense, I suppose." The Chairman turned away with an impatient gesture. "Get my pavilion up."

Thus brusquely rebuffed, Brod looked about. Catching sight of Valdemar and Lady Yambu, he came to stand over them, an expression of satisfaction gradually replacing the scowl on his ugly face.

"Reckon I've met you folks before. Good mornin' to ye."

"Good morning," said Valdemar, thinking he had nothing to lose thereby. Yambu did not answer; the Lady's eyes were closed, her face relaxed as if in sleep.

While Brod hovered nearby, evidently wondering what to do next, Valdemar saw and heard the officer in command of the small Blue Temple cavalry force, standing at attention before Hyrcanus, respectfully ask the Chairman if there were any further orders? If not, his men had been riding all night and were in need of rest.

Hyrcanus, abstractedly seeing to the careful unloading of a trunk from one of the griffins' cargo baskets, gave the troops permission to rest, once camp was properly established and a guard posted.

Then Hyrcanus, stretching and twisting his body as if he might be cramped from a long ride, exchanged some words with his Director of Security. Both men complained about the weariness and nervous strain brought on by this regrettably necessary means of travel.

The Chairman also congratulated his Director of Security on the fact that that gentleman's wits, such as they were, seemed to have been fully restored.

The Director chuckled, dutifully and drily, at the little joke—if such it was.

Then both of the Blue Temple executives, the Chairman in the lead, came to gaze sourly at their prisoners.

Staring at the supine youth, Hyrcanus demanded: "Who are you, fellow?"

"My name is Valdemar."

"That means nothing to me."

"You—are Chairman of the whole Blue Temple?" Valdemar didn't know much about how such great organizations were managed, or, really, what he would have expected their managers to be like—but certainly he would have anticipated someone more impressive than this dumpy, commonplace figure.

Brod, evidently still determined to gain points with the greatest celebrity he had probably ever encountered, had edged his way forward, and now took the opportunity to kick Valdemar energetically in the ribs.

"Show some respect to Chairman Hyrcanus!" the Sarge barked.

Someone else, in the middle distance, called: "We have the property ready for your inspection, sir."

Hyrcanus, readily allowing both kicker and victim to drop below the horizon of his attention, turned away. Valdemar got the impression that this man cared little for anyone's respect; the property, whatever that might be, was of much greater interest.

Valdemar supposed that the interesting property ready for inspection was the Sword of Wisdom. He stretched his neck, but couldn't quite make out the object on the ground that Hyrcanus and the others gathered round to look at.

Whatever it was, after a short conference, Hyrcanus was back, looming over Valdemar.

"Fellow, they tell me that you were standing watch, sentry duty, at the time of our arrival." The Chairman had the look of a man who was perpetually suspicious.

"Yes, I was." Valdemar's bitterness at having failed in that duty came through. "What of it?"

Brod, having moved into the background again, was not in sight at the moment. It was an ordinary soldier who kicked Valdemar this time, though Valdemar really hadn't been trying to be insolent. These people, he thought, were really difficult to deal with.

Hyrcanus asked him impatiently: "And you were holding the Sword called Wayfinder as you stood guard?"

The youth saw no reason not to admit that fact.

The red-faced man nodded. "No doubt it looked an excellent weapon —and it is. But perhaps you did not understand its real value?"

"Perhaps I did not."

To Valdemar it seemed no more than a reasonable answer, but there must have been something wrong with his tone of voice, for he was awarded another kick. Soon his ribs were going to get sore.

"Perhaps you were not using the Sword properly? Not engaging its full powers?"

"Perhaps I was not."

Chairman and Director turned away and walked a little distance, to put their heads together for some more mumbling. Then the latter emerged from the huddle to announce: "We'll question him more thoroughly later. What about the woman?"

Soon both officials were bending over Yambu. Magical assistance was called for, and provided. Soon the Director admitted: "She seems to have put herself into some kind of trance. We'll soon have her out of it when we're ready to talk."

Hyrcanus, squinting and frowning, taking a closer look at the woman, ordered someone to bring him a better light. When a magically-enhanced torch, so bright it almost hurt to look at it, was held over the sleeping face, Hyrcanus said in a low voice that she reminded him of the Silver Queen, but that seemed improbable, and in any case this woman appeared too young.

Another subordinate approached the Chairman deferentially, to inquire of him exactly where he wanted his pavilion put up; some soldiers and a minor magician were ready to get to work on that task now.

Hyrcanus considered, and told him. Then he and his Director continued their discussions, with Valdemar still able to hear most of what was said. One of the soldiers had pointed out that curiously three or four of his comrades had been killed at some little distance from the spot where the two prisoners were taken.

"Killed by whom?"

"That's it, sir. We don't know."

The Director of Security demanded: "Are we sure there were four of these people on the scene before we attacked?"

"Yes sir."

"Then it is obvious that two have somehow managed to get away. You should not have allowed that!"

The military officer's only defense was that orders had been to make sure the Sword was captured, no matter what else happened.

The two high officials moved a little farther off. From what Valdemar could overhear, they were remarking how strange it seemed that the Sword of Wisdom had not only failed to save the camp, but failed to guide its wielder to some means of avoiding death or capture.

The Chairman was coming back. "I wonder if this could be in fact the Lady Yambu."

Sergeant Brod, presented at last with a chance to be useful, did not allow it to go to waste. "Sir! Master Chairman. It is in fact the lady herself that we are looking at. I have seen her before, and I can swear to it!"

"You? Again?" Hyrcanus, frowning, looked around at his subordinates, appealing silently for someone to take this fellow away.

A small squad of soldiers moved to do the job; Valdemar, hearing only a mutter and a scuffle, thought philosophically that he would not be surprised to see Brod back again.

"If she is Yambu," Hyrcanus was brooding to himself, gazing once more upon that silent face, "if she *is* . . . then she at least would have realized the value of the Sword with which her little group was traveling."

"That is certainly the case, Your Opulence," agreed the Director.

Then he raised his eyes to meet Valdemar's. "Well, fellow? Who do you say she is?"

9

UNTIL Zoltan was sure that he and Ben had left the enemy behind, he continued running with Woundhealer transfixing his own body, his left hand gripping the hilt to hold the Sword in place. So far he and Ben were managing to stay together, though this required Zoltan to slow down. The young man calculated that Ben's presence would be a mighty advantage toward their goal of getting Woundhealer home.

The continued presence of the Sword of Healing inside his rib cage engendered in Zoltan a very strange sensation, neither pleasure nor pain, but rather a sense that some tremendous experience, whether good or bad, must be about to overwhelm him. The feeling was mentally though not physically uncomfortable.

Both men ran on, without speaking, under the gradually brightening sky of early morning. As soon as Zoltan could be reasonably sure that no enemies were in close pursuit, or ahead of them, he paused and released Woundhealer's hilt; there was no need to pull in order to extract the Blade. Instead it slid itself smoothly and gently out of his heart and lungs, away from his torso. Once more a sighing sound came from the Sword; then it was once more inert.

Zoltan felt physically fine. Taking a quick inventory of his body, he could discover no residual harm or damage at all from the several deadly blows he had recently sustained.

His giant comrade, swaying and groaning at his side, was in considerably worse shape, and in need of Woundhealer's immediate help.

Ben, completely out of breath, indicated with a silent gesture that he wanted Zoltan to hand over the Sword to him. The younger man complied.

A quick application of Woundhealer abolished Ben's injuries as if they had never been. Now the voice of the older man was clear and strong. "Ah, that's better. Much better."

With Ben retaining the Sword of Mercy, the men moved on together, at the best pace the older man could manage. Their running flight had already put several low rolling, almost barren hills between them and the site where the Blue Temple attack had fallen.

Zoltan, beginning to chafe and fret with the need to accommodate his slower partner, now suggested: "I might take it and run on ahead."

"No." The answer was definite, though made brief to conserve breath.

Making himself be patient, Zoltan allowed his more experienced companion to set their course. The sky continued brightening, but only gradually and sullenly; more spring rain appeared to be on the way. Ben was not heading directly toward Sarykam, but somewhat to the west, where a few trees grew along a ravine that held a trickle of muddy water at its bottom.

Trudging toward the ravine, Ben and Zoltan made plans as best they could.

Both were eagerly anticipating the help promised from Mark, but neither could see any way to guess when such assistance might be expected to arrive.

"No hope for the lady back there, or the young man either," said Ben, pausing momentarily to look over his shoulder toward the place where their camp had been. All was silent in that direction, but Zoltan thought he could see, beyond a series of intervening hills, the glow of bright, unnatural lights, contending against the slowly brightening sky of morning.

"No. It seems a miracle that we got away." Zoltan shook his head. "They looked like Blue Temple."

Ben grunted. "So they did. That means it's probably not a miracle. Whatever a job may be, if it's nothing to do with counting money, they're as like as not to botch it up."

"I take it we're pushing straight on to Tasavalta."

"More or less straight. I mean to get there," Ben said grimly. "With Woundhealer."

Daylight was coming on in earnest now. The sky continued overcast, now and then dropping a spatter of rain, or lowering patches of drifting fog. The fugitives welcomed this weather, certain to render more difficult the task of any airborne searchers.

"We have to assume there'll be more reptiles."

"Of course. And maybe worse than that."

The few trees along the ravine offered only scanty cover. On a sunny day the Tasavaltans might have been forced to look for somewhere to remain hidden during the day. Clouds, rain, and fog offered some hope, but weather was subject to change.

Continuing their conversation as they hiked, Zoltan and Ben discussed the question of whether or not the Blue Temple attackers would know that they had got away. It seemed almost certain that they would.

"We hacked down a few people as we left."

Zoltan nodded. "And if they know we've got this Sword—they'll certainly be after us."

"Unless they're so distracted by having Wayfinder—and Yambu and Valdemar, perhaps alive—that they're not interested in us."

"Depends what they do with Wayfinder. If they're going to use the Sword of Wisdom to hunt us down, or hunt this Sword we're carrying, we've got no chance."

Ben grunted stoically. "All we can do is move ahead. Keep trying."

But the day wore on, and still no pursuit appeared, in the air or overland. Pleasantly surprised at their luck, Zoltan and Ben could only pray that it would hold.

"They must have discovered some better use for Wayfinder than tracking us."

"Better than hunting down another Sword?—it sounds strange, but the truth must be that they don't realize that we have Woundhealer. Possibly they don't even know that it was in our camp."

The day passed in hiking, scanning the skies, which fortunately remained clouded, and foraging for berries. When dusk came on, Ben changed course, now leading the way generally north and east, in the direction from which they could expect the approach of Prince Mark and his people.

Half an hour after the Blue Temple attack, morning was brightening slowly and sullenly as Chairman Hyrcanus was establishing himself in an organized field office.

In intervals between his other tasks, Hyrcanus kept coming back to look at the supine figure of the captive woman. Each time he looked, and shook his head, and went away again. He said: "If this is indeed the Silver Queen, it would seem that she has somehow grown young again."

"Magic," offered the Director succinctly.

Another Blue Temple wizard, evidently some kind of specialist brought in for a consultation, sighed uncertainly. "No mere ordinary youth-spell, I can vouch for that." He glanced toward Valdemar, still lying under magical paralysis. "What does her companion say?"

"He says that she might be anyone, for all he knows. We'll conduct some serious questioning presently."

But Hyrcanus and his aides were giving the Silver Queen and Valdemar only a small part of their attention. Much more of their time was spent in gloating over their captured Sword, and getting the field office organized.

A swarm of hustling soldiers heaving poles and fabric, aided by some minor magic, had needed only a few minutes to complete the task of erecting the Chairman's pavilion.

This large tent was put up very near the place where Valdemar still lay, with a light rain falling on his face. From the moment when the pavilion started to take form, he had a good view in through its open doorway. New lights, even stranger than the magically augmented torch, were somehow kindled inside it, to augment the morning's feeble daylight.

Valdemar kept looking toward Yambu. He could see her face rather more clearly now, still unconscious, or submerged in some kind of self-inflicted trance.

A bustle of blue and gold activity continued around the pavilion and inside it. Gradually the movements became more orderly. As soon as the work was finished, the Director ordered that the two captives be brought into the big tent, with a view to beginning their formal questioning.

Valdemar was hauled roughly to his feet, and words muttered over him, giving him movement in his legs, and some degree of control. Then he was marched in through the fabric doorway. Chairman Hyrcanus himself, redfaced and puffing as if the labor of erecting the tent had fallen to him personally, still garbed in heavy winter garments despite the relative warmth of spring, was seated behind a folding table near the center of the pavilion, still grumbling in an almost despairing tone about the sacrifices he had had to make to venture personally into the field on this operation so vital for the Blue Temple's future.

The Director, seated at the Chairman's side, tried to soothe him with expressions of sympathy.

Standing before the central table, Valdemar heard once more, somewhere behind him, the voice of Sergeant Brod. Turning his head, he saw that the Sarge had reappeared, evidently still trying to make himself useful to the Chairman and his people. But Brod had been forced to remain outside the tent.

Hyrcanus himself was wasting no time, but not hurrying particularly either, shuffling papers about in front of him, methodically getting ready to undertake, in his own good time, whatever business might be required.

Behind the Chairman, piled inconspicuously in the shadows toward the rear of the tent, Valdemar could see what appeared to be certain metal tools, looking too complicated to be simple weapons. Vaguely he wondered what they were.

The Chairman cleared his throat. He made an announcement, something to the effect that this session was going to be only preliminary.

Looking sternly at his clerks, seated at another table along one wall, he added: "The fact that we must conduct, in the field, operations more properly performed at headquarters, is no excuse for inefficiency. Everything must be done in a businesslike fashion."

Yambu, having somehow been restored to at least partial consciousness, was now being brought into the pavilion too, and made to stand beside Valdemar. They exchanged looks; neither said anything. Valdemar thought that probably there were no useful words to be said at the moment.

Rain and wind surged against the blue and gold tent, as if in a fruitless endeavor to get at the papers inside.

Several folding chairs, enough—as Valdemar thought he heard someone remark—for the absolute necessary minimum of meetings, were disposed about within the tent. Two or three of the strange Old World lights had been placed on the tables, and another mounted on a folding metal stand. Valdemar got the impression that there was some kind of heating device as well, Old World or magical, giving off a gentle invisible glow of warmth around the Chairman's feet.

Hyrcanus, mumbling almost inaudibly to himself, was busily extracting more sheaves of paperwork from a dispatch case of dull leather, and laying the stuff out upon his table under the bright, efficient light. Valdemar, watching, assumed that this array of written records must be intended to serve some magical purpose. He could not picture any mundane necessity for it.

At a nod from the Chairman, one of his subordinates gave the order for the prisoners to be moved, one at a time, somewhat closer to the central table.

Before getting down to serious questioning, the Chairman, acting in the tradition of his organization, saw to it that his captives' names and descriptions were noted down, and that they were methodically robbed. Hands went dipping into Valdemar's pockets, and his clothing was patted and probed, by means both physical and magical.

Valdemar realized to his surprise that these people were more concerned with him than with the Silver Queen. The only reason he could imagine for this was that he had happened to be holding the Sword when they arrived.

An exact inventory was taken of all valuables confiscated from the two prisoners. Actually these were very few, and of disappointingly little value.

Valdemar noted that the high officials of the Temple took very seriously this business of accounting for items of trivial financial value.

"Money?"

"Practically none, sir." But the clerk, under the Chairman's cold stare, went on to itemize the few small coins which had been taken from Valdemar and Yambu. This painstaking listing, accomplished in the meticulous Blue Temple fashion, occupied what seemed to Valdemar an inordinate amount of time.

Though Valdemar had never before had any direct dealings with the Blue Temple, he like everyone else had heard a thousand stories exemplifying its legendary greed and stinginess. While the young man had no liking for the picture painted by those stories, the tales inspired in him not terror so much as contempt and wariness. He was now waiting impatiently for a chance to argue that he should be considered a non-combatant here and allowed to go on about his business.

But the Chairman was in no hurry, nor were his clerks, who evidently understood exactly the attitude toward work that was required of them. While Hyrcanus sat shuffling and rearranging his papers at one folding table they were busy writing and calculating at another. Among their other tasks, Valdemar gathered as he listened to their clerkly murmurs, was that of keeping a precise expense account—how much was this mission costing the corporation?

In the background, two or three meters behind and above the droning clerks, a small window high in the rear wall of the pavilion afforded Valdemar an occasional sight of one of the griffins, or perhaps two—he could not be sure whether it was really the same huge, nightmarish head and neck that now and then loomed up in the morning's gloom, as if the beast were curious about what was happening inside the tent. The griffin, or griffins, had evidently been tethered close behind the pavilion.

The griffin or griffins, Valdemar realized at a second look, were eating something out there. Lion-jaws dripped with a dark liquid in the uncertain, cloudy light. Suddenly he had the horrible feeling that the creatures were tearing some animal—or human—body to pieces for a snack.

The Chairman coughed drily. But then, just when Valdemar thought Hyrcanus might at last be ready to get down to business, the Chairman delayed again, turning to his Director of Security to lament the cost to the Temple in time and money of this journey. He had spent some days in getting here, traveling from the unnamed city of his headquarters, and he considered the expense of shipping his necessary equipment to have been almost ruinous.

Talking to his Director of Headquarters Security, upon whose bald head the Old World light gleamed brightly—and who, here in the bright light, looked even older than he had outside—now and then looking up to glare at his new prisoner or prisoners as if he considered them to blame—the Chairman deigned to give them all several reasons why he had felt it necessary to take charge personally of this expedition:

"One, because I feared that Master Wood, on once getting the Sword of Wisdom into his hands, would never relinquish it." Hyrcanus paused thoughtfully. "Of course I suppose Wayfinder is one Sword Wood might be induced to give up—for a price."

The Director, to no one's surprise, expressed agreement.

Now a long strongbox was carried into the tent by a couple of soldiers in blue and gold, who handled the prize warily. After depositing the strongbox at the Chairman's feet, they opened it, lifted out the Sword of Wisdom, and placed it carefully in front of Hyrcanus upon the table, after a blue satin cloth had been meticulously folded and positioned for a cushion.

One of the clerks, moving fussily and nervously, slightly adjusted the Old World lights to provide Hyrcanus with the best illumination.

Only at this point was Valdemar struck by the conspicuous absence of the Sword of Mercy. Since he had been taken prisoner, no one in his hearing had even mentioned Woundhealer—that could only mean, he thought, that either Ben or Zoltan had managed to get away with the Sword of Healing.

At this thought, Valdemar shot the Lady Yambu a sharp glance. And she, as if she somehow knew just what idea had just occurred to him, responded with a glance urging caution.

Yes, Valdemar thought, it must be true. Hyrcanus and his people gave no indication of realizing how close they had come to capturing the Sword of Healing. Had they been aware of how narrowly that prize had just escaped them, they would already have launched an intensive search for it, and not be dawdling through this leisurely preparation for an interrogation.

Of course Wayfinder by itself was treasure indeed. Treasure enough, as Valdemar was beginning to realize, to dazzle at least slightly even the Chairman of the Blue Temple himself. When the soldiers put the Sword of Wisdom down in front of Hyrcanus, his eyes came alight. He touched the black hilt with a tentative forefinger, then stroked it greedily.

Confronted with the reality of Wayfinder, Chairman and Director both appeared to speedily lose interest in their prisoners. Evidently any serious questioning would be allowed to wait.

The Director of Security rubbed his bald head nervously as he stared at the Sword. He said: "Sir, we must get this property to a place of safety as soon as possible."

"Of course." Hyrcanus leaned forward on the table. "But surely we would be at fault, derelict in our duty to the Temple Stockholders, if we did not find one other duty even more pressing, and perform that one first?"

"Sir?"

"We must delay carrying this treasure away to safety, just long enough to make our first use of it."

The Director hesitated. "May I ask what use Your Opulence has in mind?"

"You may ask. Though I suppose it should be obvious." The Chairman, his face displaying a look of satisfaction, paused as if for emphasis. "I intend to require this Sword to indicate to us the location of the greatest treasure in the world."

For a moment there was silence in the pavilion.

Valdemar was suddenly struck by what he considered an ominous indication. Neither Chairman nor Director was displaying the least concern about the fact that their prisoners were listening to this discussion. It was, the young man thought, as if the Blue Temple officials considered their captives already dead.

At last Hyrcanus, standing up, moving carefully, drew Wayfinder from its sheath. The blade caught bright gleams from the Old World lights as the Chairman gripped the hilt in his two soft hands, making the Sword's powers for the moment his own.

"Now, how shall I phrase this request exactly?" This preliminary question seemed to be addressed more to himself than to anyone else, or to the Sword itself.

The worried Director answered with a murmured suggestion that the first care be for safety.

But Hyrcanus stubbornly shook his head. "We have," he said, "had direct assurances regarding our present security from our cavalry commander, and also from your powers, magician. True?"

"True, Your Opulence, but—"

"Tell me, do you believe that our encampment here is now secure, or is it not?"

"At the moment, sir, it is secure enough," the other murmured unhappily.

"Then there you are. Would breaking camp right now make the Sword any safer? Besides, our men and beasts are tired. They are all in need of rest before we undertake another march."

"True enough, Your Opulence."

"While they rest, we at the executive level can best make use of our time by pursuing our further duties to the stockholders."

Now for the first time Hyrcanus addressed the Sword directly. In his dry voice he phrased a simple demand: "Where is the greatest treasure in the world?"

Valdemar, watching with a dozen others, thought that the Sword did not react; or it reacted only slightly, and in an uncertain way.

"What in the world now?" the Chairman demanded, suddenly querulous. Obviously he had been expecting a more dramatic response of some kind. Letting the Blade rest on the table, he rubbed his left hand, the one free of the Sword's hilt, over his bald head.

After a little silence, the Director cleared his throat. "Do you think, Chairman, there might possibly have been some ambiguity in your phrasing of the question?"

"Ambiguity? You mean, some uncertainty as to which of the world's treasures is actually the greatest? Ah, the question of determining the best measure of determined value. Authorities do disagree on that, it's true." Hyrcanus cleared his throat again. "Perhaps I should rephrase my inquiry."

Valdemar hoped that if Hyrcanus did receive from the Sword a plain unequivocal answer to any of his urgent questions regarding treasure, the Chairman would not feel it necessary to break camp at once, tired men and beasts or not, and follow the direction indicated.

Because what might he do with his prisoners then?

Hyrcanus was now interrupting himself to raise another point: "I wonder whether we ought not to approach Prince Mark—or any successful monarch might do, I suppose—with the idea of making some kind of trade for this lovely piece of magic, or offering it for sale—*after*, of course, we have used it to the best advantage for the Temple."

"Prince Mark," mused the Director, in a non-committal tone.

"I am assuming Mark can raise sufficient treasure to make such a purchase—indeed such a powerful Prince ought to be able to do so."

A brief debate on this point followed, between Hyrcanus and his Director of Security. Finally the latter brought the discussion back to considerations of safety.

Valdemar, listening attentively, gathered that neither the Chairman nor the Director believed Mark had been able to retain any appreciable amount of booty from the fabulous, infamous Great Raid. Both officials seemed to be saying that comparatively little Blue Temple wealth had actually been lost on that occasion.

But neither of the Blue Temple leaders seemed able to believe that Mark had not spent his years in power in Tasavalta amassing more wealth for himself.

Eventually they came back to the business at hand—getting the best possible quick advantage from Wayfinder.

"The more I think about it, Director, the more it seems to me that you are right. To assure that we obtain an unequivocal, useful answer, we must be clear in our own minds about the nature of the specific treasure we are seeking." Hyrcanus toyed meditatively with the Sword.

The Director said: "I should think, Your Opulence, that the most likely site for a truly unsurpassable treasure might well be in one of the Blue Temple's own vaults."

"What do you say?"

"I wonder, sir, if we will know whether this Sword is pointing at our own gold. Do you, personally, know the locations, and certified values, of each and every one of our own hoards? Their bearings from this spot?"

Hyrcanus hesitated fractionally before insisting: "Of course I do! Don't you?"

"Of course—sir."

Valdemar, listening, marveled at the indications suggesting that neither of these men was really sure of the matter.

The young man could see the fires of cupidity beginning to burn out of control in the eyes of the new masters of the Sword of Wisdom, as they huddled close over their prize. It looked as if the Director was beginning to be won over from his concerns of safety by his master's all-powerful greed. They were both staring at Wayfinder obsessively now. Perhaps, Valdemar thought, they were coming to terms with the condition all users of this weapon had to face—that the so-called Sword of Wisdom would never tell anyone Why, or What, or How, or When—or Whether—regarding any thing—but only, with seeming infallibility, exactly Where.

Hyrcanus murmured: "You are right. If our own treasure be not the greatest—then whose?"

Hyrcanus's chief aide said to him: "Possibly some Old World trove that for all our searching we have never been able to discover?"

"Possibly." The Chairman sank back into his chair. "Or possibly it is some property of the Emperor's, to which access is restricted by some tremendous enchantment?"

The Director, who had risen when his leader did, was not really listening. Instead he now waved his arms in the excitement of an inspiration of his own. "Wait! I have it! The Sword's answer to your original question was hard to interpret, ambiguous, for a very good reason—because it was self-referential!"

"Aha!"

"Yes, Your Opulence, the Swords themselves are the world's greatest treasure. And this Sword in particular must be valued above all the others—*Wayfinder itself may be*—no, *must be*—*the greatest treasure in the world!* And why? *Because it is the key to all the rest!*"

"Ahh." Hyrcanus, his eyes suddenly gone wide, let out a breath of satisfaction.

He had no need to ponder the Director's claim for very long before giving it his approval. "This very weapon before us, my good Director. Yes, what could be more valuable? I will see to it that you receive a bonus of shares. Perhaps even—a seat on the Board."

Valdemar was thinking that it made sense. Very possibly they were right—from their point of view the Sword of Wisdom had a transcendent value, because it was capable of leading them to all the other Swords, or to any other treasure that they cared to specify.

"Having made that identification," the Director remarked, "are we any further in deciding how best to use our greatest treasure?"

"I think," said the Chairman, "that we must be somewhat more specific, and somewhat more modest, in our next inquiry."

"Indeed. Yes."

"Very well then." He addressed Wayfinder again. "Sword, I adjure you to show us . . . to show me . . . the way to the Emperor's most magnificent treasure." Hyrcanus hesitated, then gave a little nod of satisfaction and plunged on. "I mean, to that thing, or collection of things, that *I* would consider most magnificent were I to see them all."

Valdemar, and Yambu standing beside him, watched and listened, the young man at least hardly daring to breathe. But he was somewhat puzzled. The Emperor? The name evoked only the vague image of a hapless clown, of a legendary figure out of childhood fables, who, even if he really lived, would be far less real and less important than any of the now-vanished gods.

Wayfinder twitched visibly in the Chairman's hands, but that was all. Evidently it was still giving only an ambiguous indication at best.

Hyrcanus evidently found this behavior unacceptable. "Surely you can respond more definitely, Sword. If I said I wanted to find the Emperor, how would you answer me?"

This question was so obviously hypothetical that Hyrcanus scarcely paused before recasting it, with firm Blue Temple legalism.

"Sword, I bid you guide me to meet the Emperor."

But again the Sword only demonstrated uncertainty.

The Chairman set his treasure gently down upon the table, and drummed his fingers next to it. "Well, Director, how are we to interpret this? That we are only to wait here, to meet the Emperor? That does not seem to make much sense—unless he is coming to call upon us." He added drily: "An unprecedented event, surely."

"I agree, Your Opulence."

In the following silence, Yambu's voice sounded quite unexpectedly, so that everyone turned to look at her. "Perhaps the Emperor *is* on his way here, to meet you." Her face wore what Valdemar thought an odd expression, even considering her situation.

Her statement was received with mixed reactions by the men in power. These were knowledgeable, worldly leaders. They were constitutionally wary of the unknown in all its aspects, and whatever knowledge they possessed about the Great Clown, beyond what ordinary people knew, they did not particularly fear him.

Hyrcanus looked with interest at Yambu. "You know him, then?"

"I am indeed the Silver Queen. I suppose I know him if anyone does. I have borne his child."

"If he is coming here now," said the elderly Director after a time, "do you suppose he will be bringing his greatest treasure with him?"

The Silver Queen said, "I do not know."

Hyrcanus, letting Wayfinder lie on the table but rubbing the hilt as if for luck, stood up, pushing back his chair as if he wished to stretch.

He raised his eyes to find his male prisoner watching him intently. "Well, fellow? Had you any experience similar to this when Wayfinder was yours?"

Valdemar nodded slowly. "I admit it puzzled me a time or two. If that is what you mean."

No one asked him to elaborate, and he did not try.

Standing awkwardly beside him, Yambu was gradually growing more perturbed, as if she found the prospect of an Imperial visit somehow unsettling.

Time passed, very slowly in Valdemar's perception. Outside the pavilion, the Blue Temple's military people were stolidly going about their routine business of guard duty and camp making. Nothing of consequence seemed to be happening.

Not that the two high officials were going to be content simply to wait for the Emperor. No, people kept coming to the door of their tent with practical questions, matters that required answers. The commander of the cavalry, still awake himself though (as Valdemar thought) most of his troops—who had evidently ridden all night—were probably asleep, came in respectfully asking to be informed: Would they be breaking camp first thing the next morning? Would they spend the remainder of the day and night interrogating their fresh-caught prisoners?

Hyrcanus had excused himself, Valdemar supposed probably for a latrine break, and the question was left to his second-in-command to answer.

"Oh, I doubt that." The Director, stretching, allowed himself a smothered yawn. "You might as well haul that stuff away and pack it up again." He gestured toward the rear of the tent; and only now did Valdemar realize what the piled instruments of torture were, as a pair of soldiers packed them up again, and bore them out.

When the Chairman returned, a few minutes later, rubbing his hands together, the Director questioned him about the prisoners too: Was there really any point in dragging the wretches all the way back to headquarters?

"Perhaps, perhaps not. How can we know at this stage? Let us see if my question brings any result within the next few hours."

The morning hours dragged on. Hyrcanus and his Director were, as they thought, being their usual practical, businesslike selves when the clouded sky outside the tent seemed to split in half, and the gold and blue pavilion was torn away from above their heads.

Valdemar closed his eyes and yelled, momentarily certain that the last instant of his life had come.

10

IT was still morning, on that cloudy, rainy day, when the young woman commonly known as Tigris, accompanied by ferocious (though not very numerous) supporting forces—including one demon of more than ordinary power—and riding her own griffin, came crashing in with a murderous assault upon the newly established Blue Temple camp.

The Blue Temple griffins, being the cowardly creatures that they were, rose into the air, breaking their tethers, and took flight immediately. At the moment of the attack, Hyrcanus's people were doing their best to be alert, but they were simply overmatched, and the attack was a complete success.

Valdemar had never seen Tigris before, nor had he any means of identifying any of Wood's other people or creatures. The result was that while the fighting raged around him the young man had not the faintest idea of the true nature of this fresh batch of invaders.

On finding himself unhurt after the first few moments of the attack, Valdemar began to hope that he might after all be able to survive. By this time a heartening explanation had suggested itself, namely that these conquerors were the friendly Tasavaltans of whom he had heard so much from his traveling companions; Valdemar's spirits rose sharply with the prospect.

Had the youth been aware that a demon was among the attacking force, this would have dashed his risen hopes. But although the proximity of the foul thing soon began to make him physically ill, the young man was unable to either see or identify the source of his symptoms.

Valdemar's companion in captivity, the Silver Queen, was considerably more experienced and knowledgeable. Quickly recognizing the nature of the latest onslaught, Yambu felt her heart sink. Almost instantly she was able to recognize Tigris, and the presence of a demon as well.

The Silver Queen would have made some effort to enlighten her fellow prisoner, but she could neither talk to him effectively nor help him at the moment.

* * *

As had been the case in the previous assault, the struggle in magical and physical terms was intense but brief. Too late, one after another, the pair of high Blue Temple officials tried to grab up the Sword of Wisdom. But the neat tables full of paperwork had already been knocked over, and the top of the pavilion ripped away before either of the Executives could get his hands on Wayfinder. The Sword fell to the ground, and was covered in folds of collapsing fabric. The clerks ran in panic, or writhed in pain as enemy weapons struck them down.

At this point the magical bonds constricting Valdemar's movements began to slacken, and the youth enjoyed a few moments' hope that he would be able to escape. As he looked, Hyrcanus himself was slain. Valdemar, watching, could not have named the cause of death; one moment the Chairman was grimacing in alarm, and the next he was slumping inertly to the earth.

A moment later Valdemar himself was buried under the folds of collapsed fabric. Struggling ineffectually, the youth could tell by the sounds reaching his ears that more swordfighting was taking place. He could see nothing of the conflict.

With some strength and feeling coming back into his tingling limbs, Valdemar struggled against the enveloping folds that were keeping him a prisoner. He could only hope that Yambu, luckier or more skillful in the arts of magic, or perhaps both, might be able to get free in the confusion.

During the few moments in which the Director and the Blue Temple troops continued to make a fight of it, all local Blue Temple spells were shattered; and Yambu, given such an opportunity, did what she could to make the best of it.

Valdemar at last managed to crawl partially out from under the folds of the collapsed pavilion.

Before him the latest attackers, as they came slicing their way in, led by a woman, concentrated their efforts on getting control of the Sword of Wisdom.

And these attackers, in blue and silver livery, were ruthlessly successful.

In a few minutes at the most, the female leader and her forces had stunned, scattered, or killed all Blue Temple opposition. The warrior woman had fairly got Wayfinder into her pretty white little hands.

At the last moment, the Director of Security, emerging from some obscure hiding place, attempted to escape. Valdemar saw him first, scuttling on all fours, then slowly trying to crawl away, and finally trying to play dead—but he was discovered and pounced on, captured alive.

And what of the Silver Queen? Valdemar, looking in all directions, realized with a faint dawning of hope that he could no longer see Yambu anywhere.

The young woman who had led the attack took a moment to examine the Chairman's body.

She then complained to some of her subordinates; evidently she was dismayed to find this eminent person dead.

Her anger flared at those who had killed him, and Valdemar thought she would have been angrier had she not been distracted by the discovery of Wayfinder.

Someone asked her whether the body of such a leader could be put to any use magically. No, she said that it was worthless—perhaps she did not want to divert her time and effort from a greater opportunity. "Might as well feed him to my griffin."

And now Tigris, annoyed at having been forced to waste even a few moments on other problems, was picking up Wayfinder, claiming the great Sword for herself.

She looked at the Sword of Wisdom with great satisfaction, and, thought Valdemar, considerable surprise. It seemed to him as if this lady warrior had not been expecting this Sword at all. Again he wondered about Zoltan and Ben, and prayed to Ardneh that one of them at least might be able to keep Woundhealer safely away.

The Director, somewhat dazed, was being brought before his conqueror. He managed a slight bow. "Lady Tigris," was all he said.

She was still absorbed in the contemplation of her new treasure. The prisoner being held before her would have fallen had not the grips on his arms held him up. Now he looked about him as if uncertain of where he was.

At last giving him some attention, Tigris remarked: "You're not looking well, my friend."

The Director only stared at her wanly.

She added, speculatively: "You know, sometimes people never completely get over the kind of treatment that you received from my Master in your Temple."

The elderly man smiled, as if that idea pleased him. The smile, in the circumstances, made him look like the village idiot.

But now Valdemar's opportunity of leisurely observation was coming to a sudden end. A soldier had discovered him, and in moments he had been disentangled from the wreckage of the pavilion. Soldiers in mixed dress, looking like a gang of peasants, were dragging him before the Lady Tigris.

Gesturing for the Director to be taken away, she frowned at Valdemar. Her free hand moved in a subtle gesture, and her blue eyes narrowed as she stared at the gigantic young man.

"You are not Blue Temple," Tigris said. It was not a question.

"No ma'am. I was their prisoner."

Tigris adjusted the swordbelt she had so recently fastened around her slender waist. Meanwhile her gaze at Valdemar did not waver in its intensity.

"I more or less expected to take a few prisoners," she murmured to herself. "One can always find good use for prisoners. But . . ."

She raised the Sword she was still holding in her right hand, so that for a moment Valdemar thought she was going to kill him right away with Wayfinder.

Then, to his immeasurable relief, he realized that she was only going to ask the Sword a question.

"Sword," she whispered again, "where am I to turn to win—that which I most desire?"

Valdemar at the moment was physically closer to the enchantress than any other person. No one else, perhaps, except the stolid soldiers who were holding his arms, was near enough to have heard the question. No one else, perhaps, observed the look of sheer surprise in her eyes when Wayfinder, in response, swung up in the enchantress's grip to point directly at Valdemar.

He was at least as astonished as the young woman holding the Sword of Wisdom.

"This one?" she muttered, in slightly louder tones. "And what am I supposed to do with him—sacrifice him?"

But that kind of question, as the questioner herself appeared to understand full well, was not the kind to which Wayfinder could be expected to reply.

Meanwhile other matters began intruding, frustrating her evident wish to concentrate on the Sword. The blue and gold pavilion had been thoroughly wrecked in the skirmishing, and one of the young woman's aides was wondering what to do about it. She commanded him to see that the wreckage was got out of the way and searched for whatever of value it might contain.

"And are we to camp here, Lady Tigris?" the soldier asked.

The lady, seemingly indifferent to the rain which darkened and plastered her blond hair, muttered some kind of an answer that Valdemar did not really hear.

In Valdemar's eyes the young woman's face was so hard and ruthless that he felt morally certain she could not really be as young as she appeared.

Now she came a few steps closer, pointing Wayfinder deliberately at his midsection, so that momentarily he once more felt in danger of being skewered. From the steady way she held the heavy Sword, it was apparent that her slender wrists must be stronger than they looked.

Fiercely she demanded of Valdemar: "You . . . very well, what is important about you? There must be something. What are you good for, what use am I to make of you?"

The only response that came to the lips of the dazed youth was: "Well, you are certainly not the Emperor."

One of the lady's eyebrows rose. "I should hope not." It was a wary, calculating answer. "Were you expecting him?"

She sounded as if she thought the Emperor's arrival not a totally ridiculous idea. Why, Valdemar wondered, were all these knowledgeable people apparently taking the Great Clown so seriously?

To his captor he replied: "Someone just moments ago—I mean the Chairman—was asking that Sword about the location of the Emperor's treasure."

"I see." Again what he said was being taken seriously.

Meanwhile, Tigris was evaluating her young captive as impressively arrogant. At first glance he was only a peasant, but of course there had to be something special about him, for the Sword of Wisdom to pick him out as her ticket to freedom.

He was continuing to stare at her in what she considered to be a very insolent way—allowing for the fact that men did tend to stare at her. The look had some fear in it, as might be expected of anyone but a madman in his situation. But it contained a measure of haughty defiance too.

Just as Tigris was about to speak again, a small bird, unperturbed by drizzling rain and sullen cloud, began singing somewhere nearby. Her reaction, the way she turned to get a look at the bird, made Valdemar turn his head too. Yes, there was the little feathered thing, looking quite ordinary, perched in the branches of a tree not far from the destroyed pavilion.

The diminutive songster, seemingly indifferent to the affairs of humans and the weapons of the gods, produced a few more notes, then flew away, as if suddenly frightened by something beyond the range of Valdemar's senses.

Tigris turned her attention to her prisoner again.

Valdemar felt a sudden return of the physical sickness. Still he was unable to assign a cause.

The lovely young woman regarded him in silence a little longer. Then she said: "I am still trying to fathom why the Sword of Wisdom should have pointed you out to me. Have you any idea why?"

Before Valdemar could attempt a reply, one of the lady's human subordinates came up to request orders, interrupting her train of thought. Turning aside, she commanded this man to dispatch a message to Master Wood. "Inform the Master that we have had great success."

"Shall I tell him, my lady, that the Sword we have taken here is not the one we were expecting to find?"

"No, fool! The Master will know of that already. Use just the words I have just spoken: 'great success.' Nothing more and nothing less."

"Yes, my lady." The soldier bowed himself away.

Tigris returned her full attention to Valdemar.

"Where is the Sword of Healing?" she demanded abruptly.

"I don't know."

Tigris stared at him. If she was really determined to find Woundhealer, he thought, all she had to do was put to work the Sword she had just captured. But he was sure that she had had some other goal in mind when she put her first question to Wayfinder. And she had been quite as surprised as he was at Wayfinder's answer.

In another moment Tigris, still with the Sword of Wisdom in hand, was giving orders that the camp be guarded well. She herself, she proclaimed to her subordinates, was about to go apart from them, because she needed solitude to work a certain special spell.

With that accomplished, a new word and a gesture from the sorceress sufficed to grant Valdemar another degree of freedom from the magical restrictions on his movement. Suddenly he felt he could walk normally; he wondered what would happen should he attempt to run. Brusquely ordering him to follow, her eyes on Wayfinder, which she held in front of her, Tigris led the way out of what had been the Blue Temple camp.

Stiffly Valdemar followed. His legs still moved only slowly, his powerful arms hung almost useless at his sides. Maybe, he thought, he could use both arms and legs effectively if he really tried. But probably that thought was delusion. The confident small woman who had just turned her back on him did not seem to be worried about anything that he might do.

She continued to carry the Sword extended horizontally ahead of her, and he thought she was muttering to it again, though he could not make out her words. As if she might be asking Wayfinder for the best place to take Valdemar—for what purpose? He supposed that he was going to find out soon.

As they paced on across the sandy wasteland, Lady Tigris still in the lead, the rain continued, a sullen dripping from a lowering, overcast sky. The birds were silent now, or absent, having taken flight from the ominous presence of the demon.

This stalwart, healthy-looking youth, as far as Tigris could tell, was a damned unlikely candidate to be of any magical or political prowess or importance whatsoever.

Physically, of course, he was impressive. It occurred to her to wonder whether he might have been someone's personal bodyguard. Not Hyrcanus's or the Director's, because he was not Blue Temple. But then who . . . ?

"Who are you, fellow?" she demanded, turning to stare at him again, but almost as if asking the question of herself.

He shook his shaggy head, perhaps to rid his eyes of rain. Looking down at her from his great height, he answered simply: "My name is Valdemar, lady."

"That tells me almost nothing."

"I am a grower of vines and grapes."

For a moment Tigris regarded this reply as brave mockery indeed, and was on the brink of administering punishment. Then, reconsidering the tone of the answer, she came to the belief that it had been sincere.

She shook her own wet blond curls, impatient but wary, pondering, ready to kill or to bless, as might be required. "I can smell some kind of magic about you, I believe . . . though not, I think, any impressive power of your own. What have you to do with the Swords?"

Again the towering youth shook his head. "Nothing at all. Except that the one you now hold, lady, was once given to me."

That surprised her. "Given to you? Why?"

The young giant sighed. "I wish someone could tell me why."

"Who gave it?"

"I don't know that either."

Tigris made a disgusted sound. "I fear that getting at the truth about you is going to take time, and my time just now is in extremely short supply. If I thought you were being wilfully stubborn . . . but of course that may not be the case at all. You may in fact know nothing, and still be vitally important—somehow."

When Valdemar's feet slowed, and his shoulders moved as if he wanted to wave his arms and argue, Tigris with a gesture of her own increased the paralytic restriction on the movement of his arms. "Keep moving, and be quiet!"

Then she once more consulted the Sword, murmuring: "Guide us to the safest place within a hundred meters."

Following Wayfinder's indication, she continued to march her prisoner quickly along until after another forty meters or so they reached a place where the Sword indicated that they should stop.

Here Valdemar thought at first that the two of them were now entirely alone. But when he looked and listened carefully, calling into play such sense of magic as he did possess, he became aware of a faint disturbance in the air, just at the limit of his perception. They were in fact being attended by certain immaterial powers, of which his human captor evidently was well aware.

And in another moment these magical attendants were gone, dismissed by a wave of a small white hand.

Their mistress looked steadily at Valdemar. "When Hyrcanus had this Sword," she asked, "what question or questions did he put to it?"

"As I have already mentioned, lady, he spoke chiefly of the Emperor, and the Emperor's treasure. Why the Chairman of the Blue Temple should do that I do not know—I have always thought that the Emperor, if he really existed, was no more than a clown."

The lady was not interested in Valdemar's opinions. "And what exactly did Hyrcanus ask of this Sword?"

"I don't remember the exact words. He wanted to be shown the way to the Emperor's greatest treasure."

"And what answer was he given?"

"Nothing very definite. The Chairman discussed this with his colleague —the man you were just talking to back there—and they thought the ambiguity might mean the Emperor was actually approaching. But . . . you arrived instead."

The red lips smiled faintly. "Perhaps the real answer was that the Great Clown has no treasure." The smile vanished. "But you and I, grape-grower, we have no time to worry about that now."

"What are we to worry about instead?"

Tigris did not reply.

Her one overriding worry was Wood, escape from whose domination was the single thing in the world which she most desired. Now she caught herself instinctively looking over her shoulder. A useless gesture, of course, and she was irritated to catch herself doing it more than once.

Valdemar took note of this quirk of behavior, and of the expression on the young woman's face when she looked back toward the encampment where her troops were busy with the tasks she had assigned them. He wondered silently who or what it was that this mighty sorceress feared so much.

He asked: "You are very powerful in magic. Also you have just won a victory, and captured one of the gods' own weapons, which you now hold in your hands. What are you afraid of?"

She raised the Sword a little, as if she wanted to pretend that she would strike him with it. "Yes, this is indeed one of the gods' own weapons—but remember that the gods are dead. Or did you know that, grape-grower?"

"I think the gods are not all dead, my lady. I still pray to Ardneh. Ardneh of the White Temple, who never allowed himself to be caught up with the other deities in their games—"

"Ah yes—well, grape-grower, it may surprise you, but I could wish sometimes that Ardneh still lived, and still ruled the world—not that I believe he ever really did."

"Why should such a wish surprise me? I could share it. I was once," continued Valdemar, not really knowing why he chose this moment for his revelation, "a novice monk in a White Temple."

"So? And did those fat Brothers in their Temple warn you, when you abandoned safety for the great world, that you should choose to stay instead?"

Without waiting for an answer, Tigris once more raised the Sword of Wisdom.

Careless of the fact that Valdemar watched and listened, she couched her next question in clear terms: "Hear me, Sword! Show me the way to gain freedom from the one I fear above all others! I do not mean my own death; that road to freedom I could find without your help. I want a long life, in safety from any harm that he may try to do to me."

And again Wayfinder pointed, immediately and steadily, straight at Valdemar.

"Just who," he asked the enchantress, "is this one you fear above all others?"

She ignored him. She gave the impression of a woman fighting back panic, trying to remain patient. There was a faint tremor in her voice. "Very well, Sword. I now have firmly under my control this great clod of farmyard mud that you keep pointing at. You are able to perceive that, I suppose? Well, what do you expect me to do with him next? Sacrifice him, eat him alive, lie with him? You will have to give me some further sign."

The Sword, of course, was not to be commanded thus, and it said nothing in reply. It still pointed where it had been pointing—straight at Valdemar—and that was all.

Valdemar cleared his throat. "I have noticed, that this Sword's way of conveying meaning can sometimes be rather hard to interpret." Though his voice was calm enough, he could feel how his ears had reddened, oh so foolishly, with the echoing in them of those three words: *Lie with him.* Odd, that now, with his very life at stake, he should be so affected by that suggestion.

Tigris did not notice Valdemar's reaction. She cared nothing for her captive's ears, or for his whole head, come to that. Her trained senses, contemplating the Sword whose hilt she gripped so hard in both her hands, could perceive the intricate knots of magic interpenetrating the hard steel, strands invisible to ordinary vision, stretching forth and fading away in all directions, becoming lost in bewildering complexities of power. . . . Even she, long accustomed to the tremendous capabilities of Wood, was awfully impressed by this, forced to an attitude that had in it much of reverence.

And this enigmatic Sword, each time she questioned it, only kept reinforcing the importance of her captive, this otherwise inconsequential youth who called himself Valdemar.

Letting Wayfinder's point sag to the ground, looking keenly at the bold and ignorant fellow, Tigris was totally convinced that there must be something more to him than he admitted. Whether he himself realized what his peculiarity was or not.

Haughtily she insisted: "Who *are* you, fellow? What are you holding back? I must somehow determine your importance to me."

The giant shrugged. "I have told you my name, and who I am. Tell me who you are. Perhaps a meaningful connection can be established. Maybe I have heard of you."

"You have a kind of serene insolence about you, unusual in a peasant. Very well. My name is Tigris."

That much he had already heard. He blinked rain from his eyes. "The name means nothing to me. I don't suppose you are from Tasavalta?"

"I am not—are you?"

"No, I have never been near the place."

"And have you," Tigris asked her captive, "any connection with Prince Mark of that land?"

Valdemar answered as usual with the truth: no, he had never seen Prince Mark, and knew very little about him. He volunteered no information about having made contact recently with Prince Mark's friends.

Tigris next asked him if he knew anything of a magician called Wood. "He has other names as well."

"I have heard," said Valdemar, "that that one is a powerful and evil man."

Tigris muttered under her breath: "This is getting me nowhere." She tried another tack in her interrogation. "When I arrived, you were a prisoner of the Blue Temple."

"Yes ma'am, I certainly did spend an uncomfortable hour or two in that condition. It seemed like days. I thank you for putting an end to that. I believe they would have killed me."

"How polite he is. That's good. Yes, certainly the late Hyrcanus and his associates would have killed you, if they thought there was any profit to be made that way—making your hide into parchment perhaps—but they did not. What did they actually want of you?"

"Actually it was only the Sword Wayfinder they wanted. And when they got it, they were so busy worrying about what to do with it that they never got around to wanting anything much from me . . . except to ask me where I had got Wayfinder, and from whom."

"And what did you tell them?"

"Lady—Lady Tigris—I could give them only the same poor answers I have given you."

With every heartbeat of time that fled, she could feel her brief allotment of opportunity rapidly running out. Every moment Tigris spent asking questions, puzzling over the answers, and yearning to rend this poor fool to bloody ribbons with her nails, the inevitable end was drawing steadily nearer. Her end would come when Wood learned that she had taken the Sword of Wisdom, and was keeping the discovery from him. At that moment her gamble for freedom would turn out to have been a catastrophic blunder.

Valdemar, in the moments when her attention faltered, had begun to tell her the story of his life. The existence of a grape-grower sounded extremely dull.

Still she forced herself to listen patiently, hoping to gain the clue she needed, even though the timekeeper in her head was running, as regularly as her speeding pulse.

Now the first real suspicion has been born in his mind. Now he is considering sending out a demon to check up on me . . .

"Cease babbling about grapes!" she shrieked at her captive. "Why are you here? Why were you in the camp of Hyrcanus?"

Valdemar, with an effort maintaining his own calm, revealed to his questioner his purpose in setting out on the journey which had brought him first in contact with the Silver Queen, and then afoul of the Blue Temple.

He did not say anything to Tigris about the Sword of Healing, and she did not raise the subject.

All this seemed to Tigris to be bringing her no closer to understanding what she ought to do next. It was maddening to think that the Sword on which she had abruptly decided to risk her life was giving her the answer she had to have, but she was unable to interpret it. Her anger flared at this babbling fool of a peasant, at the Sword, at the whole world and her life in it. And then her rage began to settle, to congeal into a deadly calm that tasted bitterly of despair.

She said: "All very fine . . . for a grower of grapes. But I don't see how any of that helps me." She raised the Sword of Wisdom again, glaring at it. "All right! Powers of the Sword, I have accepted that for some reason you want me to make this grower of grapes my own. What-ever happens, I intend to keep him, until you deign to show me what his usefulness may be. And when are you going to get around to that?"

Valdemar shook his head. He offered mildly: "Wayfinder will never answer a question of that type. But it occurs to me that, being a sorceress yourself—no offense intended—you may be making too much of the idea of sacrifice and magic."

"What do you mean?"

"I mean the Sword might simply be indicating that you are to take me with you somewhere."

Her blue eyes widened. "Is that it, Sword? Am I now to travel to another place, taking this peasant along?"

At once, to the young woman's immense relief, the Sword responded strongly. The tip moved away from Valdemar, and now pointed almost straight west.

"You do know something, fellow, after all." Her spirits rising abruptly, Tigris half-jokingly remarked: "Perhaps your function is going to be that of counselor, interpreter of Swords for me."

Valdemar shrugged his enormous shoulders. "It is only that I have had that Sword, and tried to use it, longer than you have. And you appear somewhat distracted at the moment. As if something were preventing you from thinking clearly."

But his companion was no longer listening. Once more addressing Wayfinder, Tigris demanded: "And where are we to go? How far? But no, never mind, of course you cannot tell me that. I have been given a direction. The real question is, should we walk, or run, or will we need a griffin?"

Again Valdemar shrugged. Of course the Sword was not going to tell them how far away the goal, whatever it was, might be.

The young man saw little future in trying to do anything but cooperate with this woman for the time being. She was evidently a practitioner of evil magic, but she had also rescued him from death and perhaps worse.

Once shown a clear course of action, Tigris was decisive. Already she was giving a magical command, together with a shrill whistle, calling her own griffin from the camp a hundred meters distant.

In another moment it was Valdemar's turn to be distracted. He was awed, and frightened, watching the griffin approach and land beside them.

Getting aboard the hideous winged beast required some courage of Valdemar. It was not, of course, that he really had any choice. His huge frame was cramped in the small space available in the left side pannier, but the extra weight seemed to make little difference to the griffin. The young man had heard that these creatures' powers of flight depended far more on magic than on any physical strength of wing.

His captor was already aboard, straddling the central saddle, glaring down at Valdemar in his lower seat with imperious impatience. In a moment they were breathtakingly airborne. Tigris steered the beast, sometimes by kicks, sometimes by silken reins, or murmured words, or all of these means in combination—steered so that the Sword always pointed straight past the creature's leonine and frightful head.

They were heading approximately west.

Tigris soon resumed her conversation with Valdemar, demanding help from him, impatiently listening to his replies, revealing more than she intended about her desperate situation. She was trying every approach she could think of, in an attempt to fathom this youth's mysterious importance, perhaps absolute necessity, to the success of her effort to escape Wood's dominance.

Suddenly she demanded: "What do you know about me, grape-grower?"

"Not much, lady. Only the very little you have just told me. And . . . one thing more."

"What?"

"It's plain enough, isn't it? When I had the chance to hold Wayfinder in my own hands, and demand guidance from it—that very Sword that you are now depending on—it guided me to you."

"What?"

Patiently Valdemar explained what his question had been, and concluded, "The Sword must have directed me to you. I asked my question of Wayfinder, and followed its directions consistently—and here you are."

The enchantress almost laughed—but not quite. Though inexperienced with Wayfinder, her theoretical knowledge of the Swords was substantial. She realized that this one's devious indications, like the powers of any Sword, had to be taken very seriously indeed.

She said: "You mean you think I am somehow going to help you find your bride-to-be?"

"I hardly think that you are meant to be my bride, so I suppose it must be that." Valdemar added after a pause: "First I was led to another woman, who was not the one I wanted to marry, but I suppose somehow brought me closer to her. And now I have been brought to you."

Tigris allowed a sneering comment to die unsaid. She supposed that in a way the Swords were all quite democratic; to Wayfinder, the status of its wielder, or the gravity of the quest, would not matter in the least. Vinegrower or duke, king or swineherd, princess of magic or homeless beggar, all would be on an equal footing to the gods' weapons. And so would the goals they sought.

Wayfinder still pointed straight ahead; the griffin still bore on untiringly. A good thing, Tigris congratulated herself, that she had not decided to try walking.

"It could be worse, grape-grower. Had this mount not been available, we might be riding Dactylartha's back." Even as Tigris spoke, she looked round warily once more.

"Is that the name of another griffin?"

"No creature so mild and friendly as that."

The youth looked back too, seeing nothing but the clouded sky. Was this mysterious Dactylartha the being that she feared? He inquired: "This creature, as you call it, follows us?"

"It does, right closely—but at my own orders."

Then your fear, the young man thought, must be for someone or something else.

Valdemar gritted his teeth and continued to endure the journey. At moments when, because of weather or an unexplained lurching of the beast beneath him, things got particularly bad, he tried closing his eyes. But being deprived of sight only made things worse.

Once or twice he asked: "Where do you expect the Sword to guide us?"

"To a place where I can find what I need."

From time to time Tigris spoke again to Wayfinder, questioned it, in a language Valdemar did not know. He inquired: "Is it too much to ask—I couldn't hear you clearly—exactly what query you have just put to our guide?"

Tigris ignored the question. Her face was grim.

The great wings beat on, marking out slices of time and space. With every fleeting moment Tigris felt an incremental growth of fear. An increase of the driving, nagging, growing terror that she would not be able to reach her goal before her Ancient Master caught wind of her treacherous intention. The goal to which the Sword was guiding her, for all she knew, might still be halfway around the world.

She had not asked the Sword of Wisdom for safety.

And Wayfinder, upon which her life now depended, was forcing her to bring this peasant clod along. And still she had no inkling why.

11

On having Wayfinder fall so unexpectedly into her hands, Tigris had needed only a moment to make her great decision. She would strike for freedom, gambling impulsively on the Sword of Wisdom's tremendous power. After all, there was no telling when, if ever, an equal opportunity would arise. She had expected quick meaningful answers from this weapon of the gods, affording her a fighting chance of success in her revolt against her Swordless Master.

But so far, to her growing terror and rage, things were not working out as she had hoped.

In her anger, she lashed out at the grape-growing peasant Valdemar. He was the handiest target; and besides, there was something intrinsically irritating in the very nature of this young man with whose presence the Sword had saddled her for some indeterminate time to come.

Bridling her impatience and fury, concentrating her attention, straining to be logical, she resumed her questioning as they flew. She dared not harm this oaf seriously until she could determine just what his purpose in her life might be.

The peasant answered her questions with an irritating lack of fear—as if he were confident in being indispensible to her.

But she had practically no success in extracting useful information from him.

In something like despair she demanded: "So, what am I to do with you when I reach the end of this flight?"

"You will let me go my way, I hope. Perhaps my bride will be there."

Tigris told him what he could do with his bride. Then, as the griffin bore them over a lifeless wilderness of splintered rock, an idea struck her, with the force of inspiration.

"I wonder if I have now carried you far enough," she mused aloud. "Perhaps the Sword will be satisfied if I leave you in safekeeping here, while I go on, unencumbered, to solve the next step of the puzzle, whatever it may be."

Safekeeping? Valdemar, not knowing what she had in mind, or

whether to be pleased or worried, clung to his seat in silence. Decisively the young enchantress reined her griffin around in a horizontal loop, and caused the beast to land on a rocky pinnacle perhaps twenty or thirty meters high. The small flat space that formed this spire's top was totally inaccessible from the ground.

"Now get off," she commanded.

"Ma'am?"

"You heard me, insolent fool! Get out, get off. If this mode of transportation bothers you, you may be free of it for a time at least. I will be back for you, I suppose, when I have performed the next step required by the Sword."

Silently, somewhat awkwardly, Valdemar climbed out of his basket, planting one foot after the other carefully on the one square meter or so of flat rock not occupied by the crouching body of the griffin itself. He stood there carefully, not saying anything. He was thinking that the Sword had brought him to this pass, and there must be some benefit in it for him. At least in potential.

Tigris settled herself in the central saddle and flicked the reins. Her mount sprang back into the air.

But then, when she would have urged on her steed again, she found the damned Sword in her right hand pointing inexorably straight back to the abandoned man.

Muttering abuse and imprecations, she steered the animal back to land on the spire again, a process that made Valdemar crouch and cling in fear, ducking under one of the great wings to keep from being knocked into a deadly fall.

"Get on!" his persecutor commanded.

The youth needed no second invitation. In a moment they were airborne again, the satisfied Sword once more pointing almost due west. Valdemar, settling himself more comfortably in his basket, remarked against the rush of air: "So, it seems that Wayfinder insists that our fates are somehow bound together."

Tigris did not answer.

"Do you know where we are going?" he asked patiently.

Eyes of blue fire burned at him. "Plague me with one more question and I'll slice out your tongue!"

"No, you won't."

The griffin, urged on by its mistress, was swiftly gaining speed, far beyond anything attained in the first leg of their flight; the terrible wind of their accelerating passage whipped Valdemar's words away and tore them to shreds. Now Tigris made a magical adjustment to screen the wind somewhat, and managed to hear what her captive had said when he bravely repeated it. But she said nothing in reply.

Valdemar, fighting to keep calm, continued: "As I see it, you can't afford to do me any serious harm. Because the Sword insists that you need me for something, but you don't know what it is. I'd like to know the answer too, and it might help me figure it out if I knew exactly what you are trying to get the Sword to do for you."

Tigris, resisting the urge to commit magical violence upon this fool, stubbornly remained silent.

Still she had no more idea than did her reluctant passenger of where they were going, and under her controlled calm the terror of her own ignorance, her fear of Wood, was threatening to overwhelm her. Her imagination could readily supply a hundred destinations, objectives to which Wayfinder could be sending her. But she had no real reason to credit any of them.

Hours passed, tempting Tigris to despair, while their great steed still hurtled toward the west, now angling somewhat to the south, at mind-numbing velocity. Valdemar was stunned to see how the sun's normal westward passage slowed, then stopped for them, then began to reverse itself. The griffin's wings had long ago become an almost invisible blur. Great masses of cloud, above, below, and near them churned past.

Tigris, almost lost in her own thoughts, became chillingly certain that Wood had by now had more than enough opportunity in which to suspect, if not actually prove, her treachery. And it was not the Ancient One's habit to delay punishment until he was presented with airtight proof.

And then, just when the enchantress had begun to wonder if her Master's magic had already found her and begun to destroy her life, and the terrible flight was going to endure forever, the Sword of Wisdom suddenly swung its sharp point downwards.

Tigris hastily moved to instruct her magic steed, directing it carefully toward the indicated goal.

Obediently the griffin descended, through layers of cloud and slanting sunlight to the waiting earth.

They emerged from the clouds at no more than mountain-top altitude. Valdemar, reviving from a kind of trance brought on by cold and monotony, observed in a dull voice that the object of their journey appeared to be nothing but an extensive desert. He had no idea how far they were from the wasteland where their flight had started.

Tigris, moved by some impulse toward human feeling to engage in conversation, agreed. Thinking aloud, she speculated that Wayfinder might have brought them here in search of the Sword of Vengeance.

"Farslayer? How would that help you?"

"A dullwitted question. A bright young man like you must know the virtue of that Sword."

Within a minute or two the griffin brought its riders safely to a gentle landing on the earth.

Muttering words of control into the nearest ear of the huge leonine head before her, Tigris climbed lithely from her saddle with drawn Sword, to stand confronting a harsh, lifeless-looking landscape under a midday sun. Valdemar promptly joined her, without waiting to be commanded. All was quiet, except for a faint whine of wind moving a drizzle of sand around their feet.

The Sword in the young woman's hand was pointing now in the direction of a barren hillock nearby.

Together Valdemar and Tigris began to walk that way.

As they drew near the hillock, he raised a hand to point toward its top. Up there, the cruciform outline of a black hilt showed against the distant sky, as if the point of a Sword were embedded in the ground, or in something that lay on the earth.

Silently, keeping their discovery in view, the pair trudged toward the modest summit. What at a distance had appeared to be a Sword was one indeed. At close range the weapon was identifiable as Farslayer. The Sword of Vengeance was stuck through the ribcage of a half-armored skeleton, nearly buried in the sand.

"So," Tigris breathed, "I was right. It is to be his death. That is my only chance to escape from him. So be it, then."

Valdemar noted that the garments adorning the anonymous skeleton had once been rich, and gold rings still adorned some of the bony fingers.

Tigris, murmuring some words of her art in an exultant tone, stretched out her hand to take hold of the black hilt. But scarcely had she possessed Farslayer, when there sounded a deep, dry whispering out of the low clouds above. Valdemar, looking up sharply, could see them stirring in turmoil.

"What is it?" the young man asked in a hushed voice. At the same time he unconsciously took a step nearer his companion, as if some instinct told him that he needed her protection.

Before Tigris could reply, there emerged from the lowering cover of clouds a churning gray vortex, a looming threat the size of a griffin, but barely visible to Valdemar. He found the silent onrush of this phenomenon all the more frightening because his eyes were almost willing to believe that nothing at all was there.

"It is Dactylartha," Tigris said in a low, calm voice. "Just stand where you are."

Valdemar nodded. Meanwhile, though his eyes had little to report, wind shrieked and roared about his ears, and those of the woman standing beside him on the hill.

That was only the beginning. The wind soon quieted, but Valdemar's stomach was literally sickened by the presence of the creature that now appeared; now he realized that this entity in the air above him, or something like it, must be what had sickened him before.

But Tigris was speaking to the thing, then boldly challenging it, with the businesslike air of a woman long inured to facing things this bad, and even worse.

Valdemar stood swaying slightly, averting his eyes from what was almost impossible to see anyway. He did not need his companion to tell him that, for the first time in his life, he was having a direct encounter with a demon.

Tigris, facing the thing boldly, appeared to be perfectly comfortable and in control. She spoke to the demon sharply, calling it by the name of Dactylartha.

Valdemar, retching helplessly despite his empty stomach, his knees shaky, had all he could do to keep from collapsing to the ground. Instead he forced himself to stand almost upright.

To his relief the great demon was paying him no heed. Dimly Valdemar could hear the voice of Dactylartha, a sound that reminded him of dry bones breaking. The demon was speaking only to Tigris, saying something to the effect that it would join her in rebellion, or at least refrain from reporting her to the Master, provided she immediately loaned it the Sword of Wisdom.

"Never."

"Then will the gracious lady consent to ask the oracle of the gods one question on my behalf?"

Tigris sounded as if she might have the wit and nerve to be able to win an argument with the creature. "Why do you want that?"

"I wish to locate my own life, great lady," muttered the ghastly voice of Dactylartha. "Where it has been hidden I do not know. But only by finding it again shall I be able to free myself of the power that the Ancient One now has over me."

Valdemar, trying to remain sane, and to understand, remembered with a shudder what little he had ever heard of the man who was sometimes called the Ancient One. Valdemar could also recall hearing somewhere that the only way to truly punish or control a demon—or to kill one—was to get at its life, which was almost invariably hidden, sometimes a long way from where the creature appeared and acted.

Whether Dactylartha was telling her the truth or not, Tigris did not, would not, believe him. She was thinking that she dared not trust any of his kind—this one, perhaps, least of all.

Valdemar watched her as she balanced the Sword of Vengeance in her hands. Such was Farslayer's power, he knew, that Tigris—or anyone else —armed with it would be able to cut down Wood himself, or any other foe, at any distance. Only one other Sword, only Shieldbreaker itself, could provide a defense. What, then, was holding her back? Only the ominous presence of Dactylartha, it would seem.

"Will you ask the question I want asked of the Sword of Wisdom?" the dry bones snapped.

"After I have won my own struggle. Support me in my fight first!"

They were shrieking at each other now, the woman and her demonic antagonist. Valdemar reeled and shuddered.

He put his hands over his eyes, then brought them down and stared. To his horror the demon had now assumed the form of a giant manlike shape in black armor, standing frighteningly close.

"Will you fight for *him*, then?" Tigris, her voice become unrecognizable, demanded of the thing. "You had better revolt, with me!"

"It may not be, great sorceress, it may not be! When *his* life ends, so does mine." The aerial blur of Dactylartha's presence seemed to intensify. A crushing weight seemed to be descending upon the stomach, and the soul, of Valdemar.

The woman was ready for combat. She had sheathed Farslayer, and her hands, one holding Wayfinder, rose in the subtle gesture of a great magician. "If I must slay you first, I will!"

The struggle was closed between Tigris and Dactylartha.

To Valdemar's limited perception, the outcome appeared horribly uncertain.

Made more desperately ill than ever by the increased activity of the monstrous demon, the young man thought he might be dying. But suddenly he found himself completely free of illness, for the moment, as the magical powers of the two contestants strained and nullified each other.

Terror of the demon overrode all other fears. Valdemar lunged desperately for the Sword still sheathed at the slender waist of Tigris. In a moment he had seized the black hilt of Farslayer, pulled it from its scabbard, and was hurling it with all his strength at Dactylartha's overwhelming presence—it was a crude effort, such as any unskilled fighter might make in desperation, throwing any sharp object at a foe.

The Sword of Vengeance, relentlessly indifferent to its user's skill or lack thereof, shot straight through the demon's flickering, half-substantial image, and in a moment had vanished over the distant horizon.

Valdemar had forgotten for the moment that the demon's life must be hidden elsewhere.

Dactylartha, frozen in position, stared for a long moment at his two human foes, glaring with eyes that were no longer eyes, out of a face no longer even a passable imitation of humanity. And in the next moment the demon died, shrieking a great shriek, his image exploding in spectacular fashion, and yet so quickly that he was able to do no harm to Tigris or Valdemar—nor carry any reports back to the Ancient One.

His guts hollow with fear, but his eyes and mind once more clear, Valdemar discovered Tigris down on one knee, struggling with the aftereffects of the contest.

Stumbling closer, he seized her by the arm. "It's gone. I think it must be dead."

"Dead and gone," Tigris confirmed, in a dull voice. Moving slowly, also stumbling at first, she regained her feet. Then some energy returned. Shaking herself free of Valdemar's grip, she cursed him for a peasant coward: "I could have managed that demon without wasting Farslayer on it! But nothing else will give me a chance to kill my Master, or to break free! I will be helpless without it . . . Damn you! Damn you, grower of poisoned grapes! I might have coped with the fiend by my own strength! You have cost me my chance for freedom, and damned me to hell!"

The youth recoiled, shaken. "We might get it back—"

"There will be no time."

Valdemar asked humbly: "What do we do now?"

For a moment Tigris brandished Wayfinder, as if she meant to cut him down with it. Then, in a voice bleak with depression, close to despair, she admitted: "Still I dare not hurt you."

Valdemar could find nothing helpful to say.

The woman cried out: "Sword, what am I to do? How am I to survive?"

Wayfinder, displaying the infinite patience of the gods, silently indicated Valdemar.

Tigris glared speculatively at her silent counselor. Then a gleam of hope appeared in her eyes. "Is it possible that the Sword of Wisdom has allowed for your idiocy in wasting Farslayer? In that case, peasant, it appears there may still be hope."

"I suppose we are to travel again?"

"Is that it, Sword? Yes, I'll drag him with me again, wherever you command. But which way?"

Promptly Wayfinder directed her to the griffin, which had been cowering like a beaten puppy in the demon's presence. Now, with Dactylartha gone, Tigris was quickly able to reinstill in the lesser creature something like a sense of duty.

As soon as she and Valdemar were airborne, Wayfinder aimed them back eastward, in approximately the same direction from which they had come. Tigris accepted the command without comment.

Once more they went hurtling above the clouds. Their speed soon filled Valdemar with awe by bringing on a premature sunset behind them. Both of the griffin's passengers drew the obvious conclusion from their direction: that Wayfinder was guiding them back to somewhere near— perhaps very near—their original point of departure, at the overrun Blue Temple camp.

Tigris said little as they flew. Her thoughts were dominated by the notion that the pair were getting closer to Wood with every passing moment.

Once her companion was able to hear her questioning herself, or fate: "Am I to go to him, try to lie to him, defend my actions? That cannot be! As well plead with him for mercy."

The young man, despite his own desperate situation, felt a stirring of something like sympathy.

The enchantress muttered several somewhat amended forms of her wish for survival and for freedom, asking the Sword for some means of protection against the Ancient One, rather than the ability to destroy him.

"Sword, save me from him! Save me, somehow!"

From the very beginning of her contemplated escape, Tigris had been aware of the extreme danger involved in defying a wizard as powerful as the Ancient One. And Tigris knew, far better than most people, how powerful he was.

Even so, she now feared that she had almost certainly underestimated the truth.

"What am I to do?" she breathed. She was looking at Valdemar as she spoke, though perhaps not really seeing him.

He glared at her sourly. "Do you now want my willing cooperation?"

The sorceress snarled back, "From the first moment I saw you, I have suspected that you could not be as innocent as you appeared. Very well, if you have any revelations that you have been holding in reserve, let's have them now.

"Or else," she continued a moment later, speaking now as if Valdemar were not there, as if she were talking to her griffin, "some other power may be cleverly using this peasant as a catspaw." Suddenly she faced her prisoner again. "What say you to that, grape-grower?"

He shook his head, as calmly as he could. "Why is it necessary for me to be something other than what I am?"

The eyes of Tigris, filled with pain and fear, seemed to be boring into him. "When one has lived with Master Wood for any length of time, as I have, nothing can any longer be considered simply what it is. It is necessary to approach every question in those terms."

"Why did you choose to serve him, then?"

This, it appeared, was an unanswerable question. Tigris faced forward again, and the griffin flew on, magically tireless. Valdemar wondered if it would ever have to stop and rest, or feed.

When Tigris's attack had fallen on the Blue Temple encampment, Sergeant Brod had been close enough to observe the results, and to be shaken by the experience. But by good fortune he had also been distant enough to survive, unnoticed by the attackers.

In Brod's estimation, the new conqueror, even if she did appear to be hardly more than a girl, was obviously powerful enough to be a worthy patron. He wanted to attach himself to her somehow, if that were possible without taking too much risk.

Torn between fear and ambition, the Sarge considered approaching the camp, and representing himself to its new masters as a victim of the Blue Temple. But soon caution prevailed; there were events in progress here that he could not begin to understand. Later, perhaps, when he had learned more. For the time being he decided to sneak away instead.

Ben, hiking industriously toward home, warily scanning the skies ahead, was just saying that, in his opinion, they might be going to get away with Woundhealer after all. At that instant he heard Zoltan scream behind him.

Spinning round, Ben was almost knocked off his feet by a swooping griffin. The thing must have come down at them from behind, and was now rapidly gaining altitude again with both Zoltan and the Sword of Mercy in its claws. While Ben stared, open-mouthed and helpless, the great beast swung round in the air, and rapidly departed in the direction of the Blue Temple camp.

On the ground Ben ran hopelessly, shouting curses, after the rapidly receding griffin. "Drop the Sword!" he screamed at his hapless comrade. "Drop—"

But Zoltan either could not hear him, or was powerless to obey.

Meanwhile, the Ancient One's most malignant suspicions of Tigris were in the process of being inflamed by a whispered report from a certain lesser, junior demon. This creature had just arrived at Wood's headquarters with the report that Dactylartha had been slain.

And even that was not the worst news: To the surprise of the attackers, the Sword of Wisdom had been in the Blue Temple camp—and Tigris had seized that mighty weapon for herself, and taken it away with her.

Wood, seated now on a plain chair in a small room near his laboratory, did not move a muscle. He said quietly: "She sent me no report of any such discovery."

The bearer of bad news offered no comment on that fact.

"Her official report," the great magician continued, "was very vague. Something about 'great success'—and that was all. I suppose there is no doubt of any of these disquieting things you tell me?"

The creature made no attempt to conceal its unholy glee. "Absolutely none, my Master! And—no doubt of this fact either, great lord!—Dactylartha was slain by Tigris herself!"

"So."

"With the Sword of Vengeance!"

Wood sat listening carefully to the few additional details that he was told. His eyes were closed, his face a mask. He tended to believe the allegations against Tigris. Yet he could not be *absolutely* sure that his most favored aide has in fact turned traitor—this report might be a mistake or a lie, the result of some in-house intrigue.

But with at least one, and perhaps more, of the ten surviving Swords at stake, he was certainly not about to take any chances.

One thing that the Ancient One did secretly fear intensely, without trying to deceive himself about the fact, was Farslayer. Though he betrayed no sign of this externally, in his imagination he could feel the great cold of that steel as it slid between his ribs, or split his breastbone.

But the Sword of Vengeance had evidently gone to finish Dactylartha.

Wood actually did not know where that demon's life had been hidden, except that he thought it had been at a reassuringly great distance. Well, there was nothing to be done about that problem just now.

But Tigris. . . . If she was indeed now armed with the Sword of Wisdom, she would be very dangerous. He could not afford to put off action for a moment.

As night fell, and the stars came out above her speeding griffin, Tigris, still mounted in the saddle with her prisoner Valdemar huddled beside her in his basket, felt increasingly certain that her treachery must now be known to Wood. She knew a foretaste of the terrible punishment that it would no longer be possible to avoid.

Her worst fears were coming true. In an abyss of terror, feeling her mental defenses crumbling, Tigris realized that nothing could keep her Master from trying to wreak terrible vengeance upon her.

Valdemar stared at his companion helplessly. He could see by Tigris's behavior that she thought something terrible was happening or about to happen to her, and he was afraid of what this would mean to him.

At this point Tigris in her panic redoubled the urgency of her demands on Wayfinder. She stormed and pleaded with the Sword, that it must show her a way to escape.

"Help me! Save me!"

The Sword still pointed straight ahead, along the griffin's rippling neck.

Then, staring hollow-eyed at the Sword, the blond sorceress almost despaired. "Or is it," she whispered, "that even the gods' weapons cannot help me? That you can only guide me straight back to him—that *he* is too strong—even for you?"

A moment later, with her passenger watching and listening in frozen horror, the terrified young woman was retracting that statement, fearful that she had offended the mighty powers ruling Wayfinder.

Valdemar, hesitant to speak, gaped at his companion. In this raging, cursing, pleading woman there remained no visible trace of a figure he thought he had once glimpsed, a wistful girl who had once paused to listen to a robin sing.

Suddenly some part of her terrible rage was directed at Valdemar. She glared at him and snarled.

Turning in the central saddle, she raised the Sword of Wisdom in both hands, to strike.

This madwoman was on the brink of killing him! There was no way to dodge the stroke. He was trying to straighten his cramped legs in the basket for a hopeless effort to seize the deadly Sword—when a sudden and violent change transformed the finely modeled face above him.

Suddenly and unexpectedly, the last curse died in the throat of Tigris. Her body lurched in the saddle. Her eyelids closed. Wayfinder, which she had been brandishing for a death-stroke at Valdemar, slipped from her hands and fell.

12

ZOLTAN was gone, and Woundhealer with him, and there was nothing Ben could do about either loss. Doggedly the huge man had resumed his trudge into the north. From that direction, as the bird-messengers had told him, the Prince of Tasavalta and his force were now advancing; and if all went well he ought to meet Mark soon.

But Ben was unable to make much headway. Time and again flying reptiles appeared in the sky, forcing him to lie low, waiting in such shelter as he could find until the searchers were out of sight again.

At night, great owls, dispatched by Mark as forerunners of the advancing Tasavaltan power, came to bring Ben words of counsel and encouragement. They kept him moving in the right direction, and helped him to remain hidden successfully through the hours of darkness. Freighted with tokens of Karel's shielding power, the owls drifted and perched protectively near Ben while some of Wood's lesser demons prowled through the clouded skies above.

Yambu lay in another self-imposed trance, placed by her captors in a newly erected tent in what had once been the Blue Temple camp. The Silver Queen's condition was the subject of cautious probing by minor wizards who had been part of Tigris's attacking force. These folk were prudently waiting for orders, from their vanished mistress or from Wood himself, before they took any more direct action regarding this important prisoner.

Only partially, intermittently aware of the world around her, Yambu lay drifting mentally. Her dreams were often pleasant, rarely horrible, on occasion only puzzling. Most of the dreams in the latter category concerned the Emperor.

As often as not, Yambu's recent near-rejuvenation now seemed to her only part of the same continuing dream.

* * *

At the moment when Wood's vengeance fell upon Tigris, a thunderbolt no less startling for having been expected, her last coherent thought
was that the Sword of Wisdom had somehow failed her.

The crushing spell aimed at her mind permitted her a final moment of
mental clarity in which she gasped out some curse against the Sword.
After that she was aware of crying out in desperation for her mother.
And then a great darkness briefly overcame her.

Tigris—or she who had been Tigris—was still in the griffin's saddle
when an altered awareness returned, and her eyes cleared; but when her
lids opened they gazed upon a world that she no longer knew.

When Valdemar saw the hands of stricken Tigris relax their grip upon
Wayfinder's hilt, he lunged upward and forward from his basket. He was
making a desperate, almost unthinking effort to catch the Sword of Wisdom as it fell.

The hilt eluded his frantic grab; the blade did not. Cold metal struck
and stung his hands. His try at capturing the Sword succeeded, but the
keen edges gashed two of his fingers before he could control its weight.

For a long moment he was in danger of falling out of the swaying
basket. At last he recovered his balance, now gripping the Sword's hilt
firmly, in hands slippery with his own blood. Valdemar glared at the
dazed woman whose face hovered a little above his own. In a tone somewhere near the top of his voice he demanded: "What happened? What's
wrong with you?"

The young woman was slumped down in the saddle, the reins sagging
in her grip. She swayed so that he grabbed her arm in fear that she might
fall; but still she appeared to be fully conscious. Her only reply to Valdemar's question was a wide-eyed smile and a girlish giggle.

Meanwhile the griffin, evidently sensing that something well out of the
ordinary had occurred, was twisting round its leonine head on its gro-
tesque long neck, trying to see what was happening on its own back.

Tigris giggled again.

"Fly!" Valdemar yelled at the curious beast. "Fly on, straight ahead for
now!"

The hybrid monster, presented with these commands by an unaccustomed voice, kept its head turned back for a long disturbing moment,
fixing the youth with a calculating and evil gaze, as if to estimate this new
master's strengths and weaknesses. After that long moment, to Valdemar's considerable relief, it faced forward again and went on flying. The
reins lay along the creature's neck, where Tigris had let them drop.

The evening sky was rapidly darkening around them. Demon-like masses of shadow and cloud went swirling by with the great speed of their flight.

The young woman raised her head and spoke in a tiny, childish voice. "What did you say?" he asked.

She blinked at Valdemar. "I just wondered—where are we going?"

Her smile as she asked the question was sweet and tentative. She looked somewhat dazed, but not particularly frightened. She seemed really, innocently, uncertain of where she was.

The dropped Sword, the cut fingers, the sudden change, were briefly all too much for Valdemar. He felt and gave voice to an outburst of anger. He threw down the Sword—making sure it landed safely in his basket—and raved, giving voice to anger at his situation and at the people, all of them by his standards crazy, most of them bloodthirsty, among whom the precious Sword had plunged him.

Meanwhile, the strange young woman who was mounted just above him recoiled slightly, leaning away from Valdemar, her blue eyes rounded and blinking, red mouth open.

What was wrong with this crazy woman now? But even that question had to wait. The first imperative was to establish some real control over the griffin. Now the beast's unfriendly eyes looked back again. The course of their flight was turning into a great slow spiral.

The first step in dealing with this difficulty, obviously, was to use the Sword. Valdemar did so. While Tigris looked on wide-eyed but without comment, the young man asked to be guided to a safe place to land. Wayfinder promptly obliged.

The indication was toward an area not directly below. Therefore Valdemar was required to head the griffin there. Strong language and loud tones accomplished the job, though only with some difficulty. When he thought the creature slow to turn, he even cuffed it on the back of the neck. As a farmer's son, he had had some practice in driving stubborn loadbeasts, and saw no reason why the same techniques might not work in this situation—at least for a little while.

Presently they were over a good-sized lake, with a single island of substantial size visible near the middle, a dark blob in a great reflection of the last of the sunset. Soon Valdemar managed to guide the creature to a successful landing on the island.

Tigris, her face, arms, and lower legs pale blurs in the deep dusk, remained in her saddle until her companion told her to dismount.

At the same moment Valdemar began to climb out of his own basket, then hesitated, worried lest the griffin fly away once they both got off. But he could not very well remain permanently on board. Tigris had already leapt from her saddle to the ground, and in a moment he followed.

The griffin turned its head and snarled; the young man spoke harshly and gripped his Sword, wondering if the great beast might be going to attack them.

Well, that was simply another danger they would have to accept for the time being. Still carrying Wayfinder, and keeping an eye on the griffin, the youth went over to where Tigris was standing uncertainly. Angrily he began to question the woman who, an incredibly short time ago, had taken him prisoner.

Truly, the change had been drastic, whatever its cause. Valdemar was now confronted by a stricken girl who looked back at him anxiously.

Feeling angry all over again, he demanded: "What is this, some kind of joke? Some kind of pretense?"

Recoiling from him, the young woman abruptly burst into sobs. There was a convincingness about this sudden relapse into childishness that caused Valdemar to feel the hair rise on the back of his neck, an unpleasant sensation that even the demon had not managed to produce. This was no game or trick, but something completely out of her control.

She mumbled something through her tears.

"What's that you said?"

"I'm—afraid," she choked out. Tears were making some kind of cosmetic run on her eyelids, blotching her cheeks. Another moment, and she was clinging innocently to Valdemar as if for protection.

Automatically he put his arms around her, comforting. Paradoxically, Valdemar found himself even angrier than before at Tigris. Angry at her and at his general situation.

Not only angry at her, but still afraid of her in a way. What if she were to recover from this fit, or whatever it was, as abruptly as she had fallen into it? He didn't know whether he wanted her to recover or not.

Whatever magic might still have been binding Valdemar at the moment the sorceress had been stricken—obviously there had not been enough to keep him from lunging for the Sword—was now undone. He had felt the last remnants of that enchantment passing, falling from him, like spiders' webs dissolving in morning sunlight.

"Where are we?" she was asking him again, now in what sounded like tearful trust. She wiped at her eyes. "Who are you?" she added, with more curiosity than fright.

"Who am I. A good question. I ask that of myself, sometimes. Here, sit down, rest, and let me think." Seating his oddly transformed companion upon a mossy lump of earth—she obeyed directions like a willing child—

Valdemar paced about, wondering what question he ought now to ask the Sword.

His cut fingers, still slowly dripping blood, kept him from concentrating, and he used the peerless edge of Wayfinder to cut a strip from the edge of his own shirt, thinking to make a bandage. The crouching griffin kept turning its head watchfully from time to time, as if estimating its chances of successful escape or rebellion. Valdemar thought that the beast's eyes glowed faintly with their own fire in the deepening night.

Tigris, sitting obediently where he had put her, had ceased to weep and was slowly recovering something like equanimity. Now, when he got close enough in the gloom to see her face, he could tell that she was smiling at him. It was a vastly transformed smile, displaying simple joy and anxious friendliness. A child, waiting to be told what was going to happen next.

As Valdemar stared at the metamorphosed Tigris, a new suspicion really hit him for the first time: the suspicion that this impossible, dangerous young woman could be, in fact, his Sword-intended bride to be.

Going to her, he unbuckled the empty swordbelt from her slender waist, and, while she watched trustingly, fastened it around his own. Then he sheathed Wayfinder. Waving the little bloodstained rag of cloth which he had been trying to tie up his hand, he asked: "I don't suppose you could help me with this?"

"What?"

"It's just that trying to bandage my own fingers, working with one hand, is rather awkward."

And when he held out the cloth to Tigris, she made a tentative effort to help him. But the sight, or touch, of blood at close range evidently upset her, and the bandaging was only marginally successful.

Gripping the black hilt of the Sword of Wisdom in his now precariously bandaged hand, Valdemar drew it and asked: "Safety for myself—and for my intended bride—*whoever* she may be!"

The Sword promptly gave him a direction. Generally south again. He decided that, since this island had been certified safe for the time being, further travel would have to wait till morning.

The next question, of course, was whether the griffin was going to get restless and fly away before sunrise. Or grow hungry, perhaps, and decide to eat its erstwhile passengers.

Valdemar sighed, and decided they would take their chances here for the night.

* * *

The remaining hours of darkness were spent uncomfortably, with each passenger sleeping, or trying to sleep, in one of the side-baskets, which were still fastened to the griffin's flanks. Some cargo in the right basket—the most interesting items were food and blankets—was unloaded to make room for Tigris. Valdemar thought it would be hard for the magical beast to attack them while they were on its back; and if the thing felt moved to fly during the night, it could hardly leave its passengers behind. As matters worked out, the griffin remained so still during most of the night that Valdemar wondered from time to time whether the beast had died. But he definitely felt more secure staying in the basket.

As if his current crop of problems were not quite enough, Valdemar continued to be nagged by worries about his untended vines back home, and about his lack of a wife. The images rose before him of several of the women with whom he had had temporary arrangements; all of them, for various reasons, had proven unsatisfactory.

At last he slept, but fitfully.

In the morning, when it seemed that no more sleep was going to be possible, Valdemar stretched and took stock of the situation. Tigris, as he could see by peering across the empty saddle, was still sleeping like a babe. She actually had one finger in her mouth.

The griffin, on feeling its heavier passenger stir, looked round lazily; but at least it had done nothing—yet—in the way of a serious rebellion.

Valdemar had the Sword of Wisdom still gripped in his right hand. Raising it again, he bluntly demanded: "Where is the woman I should marry?"

His wrist was twisted by an overwhelming force. Remorselessly the weapon continued to point out Tigris.

Dismounting with a grunt, straightening stiffened limbs, Valdemar walked around to the animal's right flank and awakened his companion, who rewarded him with a cheerful, vacant smile.

Then, chewing on some of the food they had removed from that cargo basket, he attempted to nail down the Sword's meaning beyond any doubt. Addressing Wayfinder, he demanded: "Are you trying to tell me that this, this one with me now, is the very woman? That this creature is not simply meant to be a help of some kind to finding my rightful bride?"

The Sword, without a tremor, still indicated Tigris.

"Oh, by all the gods!" the young man roared. Such was his disgust that he felt a serious impulse to throw this Sword away.

He did in fact make an abortive gesture toward that end, but such was his practical nature that the Sword went no farther than necessary to stick the sharp point in a nearby tree. A moment later and Valdemar had hastened to retrieve the weapon of the gods. Wayfinder might produce some unpleasant surprises, but still it seemed to be the only hope he had.

A few minutes later they were preparing to fly again. This time Valdemar occupied the saddle, and Tigris went indifferently into the left basket, where he had ridden as her prisoner.

Time for the orders of the day. Valdemar put some thought into his request. "Sword . . . I want to go home, to my own hut and my own vineyard. I want to reach the place safely, and I want the world to leave me in peace once I am there. Also I want to have there with me— someday, somehow—the woman who should be my wife. Whoever she may be."

Pausing, Valdemar eyed Tigris. Sitting obediently in the basket where he had put her, she returned his gaze with an eager, trustful look that he at the moment found absolutely sickening.

He returned his concentration to the sharp Blade in his hands. "With all those goals in mind, great Sword, give me a direction." The response was quick and firm. "Very well! Thank you! Griffin, fly!"

He gave the last command with as much confidence as possible. If the griffin only turned its head and looked at him, he was going to be forced into some act of desperation.

Fortunately, things had not yet come to that. Gathering its mighty limbs beneath it, the creature sprang into the air.

This morning's flight lasted for about an hour, and during its entire course, controlling the griffin continued to be something of a problem. Tigris, giggling and babbling what Valdemar considered irrelevancies, distracted him and made his job no easier.

Wayfinder at least was predictably reliable. In response to Val's continuing requests for safety for both passengers, the Sword guided them through several aerial zigzags that had no purpose Valdemar could see. And then, point tugging sharply downward, it indicated a place to land.

At that same hour, a great many kilometers away, the Ancient One found himself able to spare a little time and thought to contemplate the treachery of Tigris, and to decide upon the most satisfactory method of revenge.

Another of Wood's inhuman secret agents had just brought confirmation that he, Wood, had been able, from a distance, to inflict a severe loss of memory upon his most faithless subordinate.

"And not only that, Master, but a complete regression to near-childhood. The foul bitch is deliciously, perfectly, helpless!"

"It is a rather powerful spell." Wood nodded, somewhat complacently. "I am not surprised at its success. If the Director of Security for the Blue Temple could not resist it, our dear Tigris had no chance . . . of course in her case, this treatment is meant as no more than a preliminary penalty. One might say it is not really a punishment at all, only a form of restraint. I want to neutralize the little wretch until I can spare the time and thought to deal with her—as she truly deserves." He frowned at his informant. "Now who is this companion you say she has? No one, I trust, who is likely to kill her outright?"

"Only a man, Master. Don't know why she brought him along. Not much magic to his credit. Youthful, physically large. A lusty fellow, by the look of him, so I don't think he'll want to kill her very soon. He has of course taken over the Sword Wayfinder now."

"And I suppose he has been making use of it—but to what end, I wonder?"

"No doubt I can find out, great lord. Indeed, you have only to give the word, and I will step in and take the Sword away from him. I, of course, unlike the faithless Tigris, would bring the prize directly to you, without—"

"You will not touch that Sword, or any other!" Wood commanded firmly. "From now on that privilege is mine alone!"

"Of course, Master." The demon bowed, a swirling movement of a half-material image.

"I," the Ancient One continued, "am presently going to take the field myself."

There yet remained in the old magician's mind some nagging doubt that his lovely young assistant had really turned against him—his ego really found it difficult to accept that.

Perhaps it would be possible to learn the truth from her before she died.

At first she had been somewhat frightened, coming awake out of that awful dream—or sleep, or whatever it had been—to find herself straddling the back of a flying griffin. A griffin was an unfamiliar creature—certainly there had been nothing like it on the farm, home of her childhood, scene of most of her remaining clear memories—but it was not completely strange. She remembered—from somewhere—certain things about the species. Thus it proved to be with many other components of this strange new world.

By now, the young woman who had been Tigris had just about decided that this world in which she found herself—the world that had in it such an interesting young man as her companion—was, taken all in all, a sweet, wonderful place.

She who had been Tigris, her sophistication obliterated and her knowledge very drastically reduced by the magical removal of most of the memories of the later half of her life, continued to be very confused about her situation. But in her restored innocence the young woman was mainly unafraid.

From her place in the passenger's basket she gazed thoughtfully at Valdemar, looked at him for the thousandth time since—since the world had changed. Since—whatever it was, exactly, that had happened.

Since, perhaps, she had awakened from a long sleep of troubled dreams—and oh, it was good to be awake again!

She found herself still gazing at the strong young man. And she found him pleasant indeed to look upon.

It was something of a shock—it was almost frightening—to realize abruptly that she did not know his name.

In a loud clear voice she asked him: "Who are you?"

Turning a startled face, the youth in the saddle stared at her. "It is now something like a full day, my lady, since we met. I have told you almost as much as I can tell about myself. Have you no memory?"

She who had been Tigris did her best to consider. "No. Or, I have *some* memory, I suppose, but—I don't remember who *you* are. Tell me again."

The young man continued to stare at her. For the moment he said nothing, only shaking his head slightly.

Gently she persisted. "But who *are* you? Where are we?"

When Valdemar did not answer, she began to be a little afraid of him. She saw him as a very formidable person—even apart from his obviously gigantic physical strength. He had an air of confidence and reliability.

After a while she told him as much, in simple words.

He gazed at her with returning suspicion. "So, I am to believe that you are only a child now, and easily impressed? Is that it?"

She laughed girlishly. She could not really remain afraid of this young man for long. He was too . . . too . . .

"Ah, Lady Tigris, if only I could be sure . . . but how can I determine what you are really—but you have let me have the Sword, haven't you? Oh, truly you are changed!"

The lady was frowning. "What did you call me?"

"Tigris. Lady Tigris."

"But why do you call me that? Are you playing some game?"

"No game, no game at all. Not for me, certainly. By what name should I call you, then?"

"Why, by my own."

"And that is—?"

"How can a friend of mine not know my name?" She paused, thinking, her red lips parted. "But then I didn't know yours, did I? . . . my name is Delia. And now I remember that you did tell me your name before—Valdemar. That has a strange sound, but I like it."

He looked at her for what felt like a long time. "What else do you remember about me?"

"Why, that you are my friend. You have been helping me to—do something." Gradually, with an effort, Delia was able to remember a few other things that he had told her about himself, before—before the world had changed.

Valdemar asked: "And what do you remember about the Sword of Wisdom?"

She blinked at him. "What is that?"

He stared at her, the wind of flight whipping his long dark hair. "We'll talk about it later," he said at last.

The longer the flight went on, the longer she looked at him, the more definitely she who had been Tigris began to flirt with Valdemar, innocently and sensuously at the same time.

Valdemar at first took no real notice of her smiles and subtle eyelid-flutters, and occasional voluptuous stretches. He was watching the griffin grimly, and from time to time he repeated his latest question to Wayfinder: "Point me—point both of us—the way to safety."

Under his inexpert piloting, the great winged creature, continuing to change course on demand at frequent, irregular intervals, carried the couple back to some place that was half familiar-looking; Val, who as a rule had a fairly good sense of direction, had the feeling they were not far from the armed camp from which Tigris had marched him—it seemed like a terribly long time ago.

Obviously Wayfinder was not guiding them directly toward his vineyard. Well, having once decided to trust his life to the Sword's guidance, he supposed he had better trust it all the way. And anyway, he wouldn't want to arrive home with a griffin.

They landed in the middle of a small patch of forest.

Wood, once having made his decision to take the field in person, had not delayed. Within a few minutes he was airborne, flying on his own griffin.

On his arrival at the camp which had been taken by Tigris, he took charge at once, and ruthlessly. By dint of seriously terrorizing her former subordinates, he was soon able to confirm—if any confirmation was still needed—that Tigris had indeed captured the Sword Wayfinder, and had deliberately failed to notify him.

All of Tigris's people who remained in or about the camp automatically fell under grave suspicion in the eyes of the Ancient One. Those who Wood thought should have prevented her defection were placed in the hands of interrogation experts.

Wood had been in personal command of the camp for less than an hour when an alarm was sounded. But this time the news was good: another griffin, bringing in the Sword Woundhealer, along with a prisoner.

After gloating briefly over the Sword—no hands but his own took it from the semi-intelligent beast—Wood turned his attention to the prisoner. At the moment the wretch looked more dead than alive.

Thinking he recognized the fellow as Prince Mark's nephew, the Ancient One employed the Sword of Mercy to heal his injuries—quite likely he would be worth something in the way of ransom.

In a moment, as soon as Zoltan's eyes were clearly open, Wood asked him gently: "Where is she now? Tigris?"

On recognizing where he was, and who was speaking to him, the youth looked gratifyingly sick with terror. "I don't know," he whispered hopelessly.

"No? Well, I suppose there's really no reason why you should. But I'm sure there are interesting things you *do* know, young man. Things that I shall be pleased to hear—you and I must have a long chat."

That was postponed. More news arrived: yet another new prisoner had just been picked up in the vicinity of the camp, upon which he appeared to have been spying.

Wood turned his attention to this man.

Brod, dragged in and supported by several guards, tremblingly assured the wizard he had only been watching the camp because he had long wanted to devote himself to the service of the mighty magician Wood as a patron. He had been trying to find the best means of approach when he was taken.

The Ancient One stared at him. Nothing pleased him so much as a proper attitude of respect in those he spoke to. Brod, who thought he could feel that gaze probing his bone marrow, clutched at the only hopeful thought which he could find: at least he had not been trying to tell a lie.

"Tell me, Brod . . ."

"Yes, sire?"

"What would you ask, if you were given the chance, from the Sword called Wayfinder? I take it you know what I am talking about."

"Oh yes sir, yes sir. I know that Sword." The Sarge swallowed with a great gulp. "Well sir. I'd ask a way, a direction, that would let me fill my ambition of getting into your service, Lord Wood sir, and continuing in your service, successfully, for a long, long time . . ."

The Sarge stopped there, because the great wizard called Wood was laughing; it was a silent and horrible display.

13

PRINCE Mark was heading south. He rode astride a great black cantering riding-beast, with the bulky form of the old wizard Karel similarly mounted at his side. They were long out of sight of home. Days ago the Prince had ridden forth from the great gate of Sarykam at the head of a hundred cavalry, supported by magicians, beastkeepers, a couple of supply wagons, and semi-intelligent winged scouts and messengers. Ever since their departure the Prince and his expeditionary force had been riding hard to reach the region where his friends and enemies were still contending for a pair of priceless Swords.

The Prince was wearing two swordbelts, each supporting one sheathed Sword, so that a black hilt showed on each side of his waist. During most of the day Mark had little to say. His gaze was usually fixed straight ahead, and his countenance grim. He was ready for a fight, armed to the teeth, coming to the struggle with both Sightblinder and Shieldbreaker in his possession. The Swords Stonecutter and Dragonslicer, considered unlikely to be of much use in the current situation, had been left in the armory in Sarykam.

The swift-moving Tasavaltan column kept moving generally south, in the direction of the region from which Ben had last reported his position. Scouts, both winged and human, ranged ahead continually.

Mark as he rode was nagged by the feeling that he ought to have brought Stephen with him. But he knew it was better that he had not; he felt comforted by the idea that the boy would be with his mother and perhaps afford her some relief from her endless gloom.

At sunset, the Prince and his troops reached the fringe of the barren country lying to the southwest of the Tasavaltan border. Mark ordered a halt. This would be a dry camp; tomorrow would be time enough to look for water.

Several times during the past few hours, winged scouts had returned from the southwest to meet the column on the march. Now yet another of these great birds, speeding from the same direction across the twilight sky, arrived at the encampment.

This scout reported the ominous presence of griffins in the area.

The Prince cursed at the indications that the enemy was now in the field too, in force. Mark ordered the beastmaster to dispatch more birds to investigate.

"Day-flyers, sir, or night?"

Mark ordered some of each sent into the air.

In the light of a lowering sun, Mark glanced at the three or four specially trained loadbeasts accompanying the column, which appeared to be bearing hooded human riders. Actually the figures on the loadbeasts' backs were the swathed forms of giant owls, whose heads and shoulders became visible as the hoods were removed. These birds would presently be launched to scout and harass the enemy under cover of darkness.

When Mark chose the campsite, Karel and his magical assistants busied themselves weaving protective spells around the area. The Prince personally oversaw the posting of sentries, ate lightly, then entered his small tent. Grimly impatient for morning, he wrapped himself in a blanket, stretched out on the ground, two swordbelts beneath him, his body in contact with both of his sheathed Swords, and tried to get some sleep.

The Prince sometimes tried to calculate whether he had spent more of his life in the field, in one way or another, than he had under a roof. Certainly he sometimes felt that way. The familiar sounds of a military camp—low voices, a fire crackling, someone sharpening a blade—were soothing rather than disturbing. Yet sleep eluded Mark. His mind could not cease struggling with plans and calculations.

The ominous signs of Blue Temple presence, and worse, in the land ahead suggested that one of his chief enemies might well now be in possession not only of Woundhealer, but of Wayfinder as well. But the Prince could take comfort in the fact that against the Sword of Force, even the Sword of Wisdom would be no more useful than a broken dagger. Wayfinder, Mark felt confident, could never tell its owner how to locate Shieldbreaker or Shieldbreaker's holder, or how to avoid any danger posed by him.

The Prince shifted position on his blanket, feeling as wide awake as ever. What would he do if he were Wood?

Of course, Wayfinder would be able to tell its owner the whereabouts of the magician Karel, say—or the location of the Sword Sightblinder—

and from that information an enemy might well be able to deduce that
Mark was somewhere near. No Sword or combination of Swords could
solve all problems.

Sleep eventually came to Mark, in the form of a troubled doze. And
with sleep came disturbing dreams that shattered into unrecognizable
fragments as soon as he awoke, leaving a feeling of anxiety.

And one thing more. He had awakened with a new plan.

The Prince conferred with the wizard Karel just before dawn, and
Karel agreed that Mark should ride on, alone but carrying both his
Swords, ahead of the main body of his troops.

The old wizard had some forebodings about what seemed a chancy
scheme, and at first had argued against it. But Mark was impatient, and
stubborn enough to adopt the idea even against Karel's opposition.

At sunrise, as the Prince swallowed hot tea and chewed on a hard
biscuit, preparatory to riding out alone, Karel warned him that carrying
Shieldbreaker and Sightblinder at the same time, even with both Swords
sheathed, could cause him problems.

"I must warn you, Prince, that holding both of these Swords drawn at
the same time may well produce some powerful psychic effect even on
you, who in some ways seemed to possess a curious partial immunity to
the Swords' power."

"I have done as much before."

"Perhaps. But I warn you that your immunity is far from complete."

"I understand that, Uncle."

"Have you, since leaving home, tried either of the Swords you carry?"

"Not yet."

"Then do so."

Now, in the relative privacy of his uncle's tent, Prince Mark drew from
its sheath the god-forged blade that rode on his right hip.

Sightblinder, as always, produced some spectacular effects when it was
drawn. Mark was aware of no change in himself. But he knew that in the
eyes of his uncle he was somehow transformed into a figure evoking
either terror or adoration. Even the great magician Karel, here in his
own tent, surrounded and supported by all his powers, and knowing
intellectually that the figure he saw was only a phantasm of magic, was
powerless to see the truth behind the image.

"What do you see, Uncle?"

The old man passed a hand across his eyes. "The details of the deception do not matter. I no longer see you in your true nature, of course, but

an alien image which frightens me, even though I know . . ." The old man, averting his eyes from Mark, made a gesture of dismissal.

Prince Mark sheathed Sightblinder, which he had held in his left hand, and saw Karel relax somewhat. Next the Prince drew Shieldbreaker. The Sword of Force was silent, and inert, because no immediate danger threatened. Mark gripping the black hilt was aware of the vast power waiting there, but he felt no more than that.

Then, still gripping Shieldbreaker, the Prince pulled the Sword of Stealth from its sheath once more, and stood holding both Swords at the same time.

He saw by the change in his uncle's face that his own appearance had once more altered, perhaps even more terribly than before. The nerves in Mark's arms and shoulders tingled; the effect was strange, but well within his range of tolerance.

Carefully Mark sheathed both Swords again, Sightblinder first.

He tried to reassure Karel, but the old man remained cautious, and perturbed. He warned the Prince, unnecessarily, not to be caught in combat with an unarmed foe whilst holding Shieldbreaker.

"I know that," Mark patiently reminded his counselor.

Karel still looked worried.

The Prince, putting a hand on the old wizard's shoulder, reminded him that he, Mark, was no stranger to the Swords. And he assured the old man—though not without a certain mental reservation—that the effect of holding the two Swords at once had not been strong enough to cause him any real concern.

At the same dawn hour when Mark set out alone from his camp, Ben was urged out of a light sleep, into instant alertness, by the tug of a rapier-pointed claw upon his garment.

Crouching over him where he sat with his back against a tree was a winged messenger from Mark. This helpful, friendly bird, having been instructed by Karel, brought Ben the welcome news that Tasavaltan troops were not very many kilometers away, and the Prince himself was even closer.

The birds' sense of horizontal distance was notoriously inaccurate, so Ben did not derive as much comfort from this news as he otherwise might have.

As the hours passed, Valdemar continued to observe the destruction of the personality, even the physical identity, of the sorceress who such a short time ago had come riding at the head of a force of demons and human thugs to slaughter her enemies and kidnap him.

Not that Delia appeared to care in the least—she kept humming little snatches of simple, cheerful songs—but her clothing was now sodden with rain and getting dirty. Evidently it was now deprived of what Valdemar supposed must have been the magical protection afforded the garments worn by Tigris. Even the woman's face was notably changed from that of the conqueror who had devastated the Blue Temple camp. Valdemar wondered if he could have recognized this as the same individual, had he not seen with his own eyes the several stages of the change. Rain and circumstances seemed to have washed and scoured away an aura of bad magic, and perhaps some subtle though mundane makeup as well, from her countenance.

Only the physical parts of the transformation had taken any time at all. Never, since the thunderbolt fell, had Valdemar caught any hint that any part of her older, wasted and vicious personality might have survived.

Valdemar had no doubt that the metamorphosis had resulted from a blow struck at Tigris by the great and mysterious magician she had feared so terribly, and from whom she had been so desperately trying to escape. One of the oddest things about the whole situation, as Valdemar saw it, was that the blow, the sudden transformation, had not really done her any harm. As far as he could tell, quite the opposite.

And here was another turnaround to consider: He, who had been the prisoner of Tigris, was now Delia's captor. Or more properly her keeper. Now he, the simple farmer, had become the worldly, experienced mentor. It was not a role he relished, but there was no one else to take responsibility for her, and the idea of simply abandoning her was unacceptable. Though in her previous persona she had treated him unjustly, still her new helplessness was disarming. And her new childlike personality was charming in its innocence.

Delia was more talkative than Tigris had been. Almost every time Valdemar looked at her, he found her gazing back at him as if she sought his guidance. And she kept asking naive questions.

Earlier, under relentless questioning from this young woman, Valdemar had tried to explain how he had been guided to her by the Sword of Wisdom. He thought that Tigris had never quite believed that story; she had been chronically suspicious, and perhaps incapable of understanding a simple truth. Now, when he told Delia the same tale, she somehow had no trouble at all believing if not comprehending what he had done.

"This Sword has brought us together, you and I," Valdemar, patting the black hilt, assured his new companion.

"That's good." Her tone suggested complacent acceptance, if nothing like full understanding.

"It is a magic Sword."

"Magic. Ah." And Delia nodded solemnly, with an appearance of wisdom.

"Are you acquainted with magic, then?"

"No," she said vaguely. "No, I don't think so. Except—"

"Yes?"

"Except sometimes, when I still lived on the farm, I think . . . there were things that I could do."

"What kind of things?"

"When plants were sick, sometimes I could make them well."

"Really? Then I will have to tell you about my vines."

A shadow, as swift as it was insubstantial, abruptly fell over the two young people.

Simultaneously Valdemar was once more stricken with the helpless sickness in his guts; this time he recognized the cause, and now his fear was greater than before.

The presence this time was smaller and more nearly bearable than Dactylartha's had been. But the young man had no doubt that this sudden intruder was a demon too.

He clutched for dear life at the Sword of Wisdom, and cried to it for help. He did his best to lift it, as if to strike a blow.

The demon only chuckled, a truly hideous sound. The ghastly wraith-shape of it drifted in the air in front of Valdemar.

"What do you mean to do, young man? Strike me with your Sword?"

"I . . ." At the moment, brave words seemed impossible to come by.

"Wayfinder will not protect you . . . nothing will . . . if I simply reach out to you . . . like this . . ."

Fear and nausea gripped him, then dragged their slimy presences away. Val wondered why the demon did not simply seize Wayfinder out of his almost paralyzed hands. But the shadow drifted on, and the Sword of Wisdom was still his.

It was, it had to be, only playing with them, like a cat with a pair of mice.

Delia, utterly miserable, pathetically ignorant, clung to him, wanting to be comforted.

Val's fears were confirmed. The vile creature had only pretended to depart, for now it came drifting back. Its vague shape gathered over Delia, and it whispered something frightful into the young woman's ear.

Shocked, uncomprehending, Delia screamed and wept.

Valdemar tried to summon up his nerve, his will, to rise to her defense, but physical and mental cramps assailed him, and he fell back groaning.

Delia shrieked again. Horrible memories had stirred in her when she heard the demon speak Wood's name.

Then, as unexpectedly as it had come, the demon was gone.

Delia expressed her fear that the Ancient One was coming to get her. "Val, that's what it meant. That—*thing* which spoke to me just now— whatever it was. It told me things that made me start to remember—Val, hold me!"

And Valdemar, still sick and trembling from the recent presence of a demon, found himself doing his best to comfort Delia.

He held her while she wept, and promised to protect her—and in his ignorance he could even believe for a time that he might be able to afford her such protection.

As for the Ancient One himself, with every passing hour, each incoming report, he was becoming more firmly convinced of his former assistant's treachery. Though by this time, as Wood assured himself grimly, the objective truth concerning her guilt or innocence really no longer mattered. He had decided to consider her guilty, and that was that.

Whatever she had really done or not done, after this he would never again be able to trust her even minimally. Too bad; at one time she had shown great promise . . .

Wood now welcomed back—as warmly as he ever welcomed any being —the demonic scout who had just tormented Tigris.

Listening attentively, the Ancient One received from this creature a new report. The news, related with much demonic merriment, was that Tigris had certainly been reduced to childish helplessness. And now— this was the crowning effect—seemed to be on her way to a new existence as a farmer's wife.

The Ancient One reacted to this announcement with a great deal of amusement and satisfaction.

He went so far as to reward the messenger—at least, he promised a substantial, though unspecified, reward, to be delivered in the future.

The demon praised its master's generosity—its gratitude sounded as sincere as the virtue that it praised. And it slavishly rejoiced at having brought good news.

"Yes. Well, well." The human nodded. "All things considered, such a fate will do quite well as the first phase of our settlement of accounts with her."

"And the next phase of her punishment, Master?" The servile creature almost gibbered with delight. "When may we expect to enjoy that?"

Tersely, in a voice tinged with regret, the Ancient One explained that for the next few hours or perhaps days he was going to be too busy dealing with his chief opponents to pay this traitress much attention.

He concluded: "But do keep me informed."

"Most gladly, Master!"

Valdemar still asked the Sword for safety, and the Sword still required him and Delia to fly. The flights thus commanded were random jaunts, as far as Val could see, getting them nowhere in particular, but rather keeping them in the same area of almost uninhabited country, uncomfortably close to the camp from which Tigris had kidnapped him—how very long ago that seemed!

And Val was growing increasingly worried about the griffin. He supposed that the creature had grown tired, lacking its proper magical nourishment, or reinforcement. Or perhaps, thought Valdemar, the beast was simply becoming increasingly restive in the control and company of these two milksops.

When he asked Delia if she remembered anything about the animal's diet, she only shuddered and insisted that she knew nothing whatever on the subject. Valdemar couldn't decide whether she was telling the truth or not.

When he asked the Sword for help in feeding their chief means of transportation, Wayfinder obliged. Evidently there was some kind of food the griffin favored, and when Valdemar turned to the Sword for help, Wayfinder directed them to a landing place where the creature browsed contentedly for a time, burrowing its head into the dense foliage of a grove of peculiar trees. Valdemar was unable to tell at first glance whether the beast was eating leaves, fruit, or perhaps something more meaty that dwelled in the high branches; he made no effort to find out.

"Is it a very big magic, then?" The young blond woman was staring gravely, wide-eyed, alternately at Valdemar, and at the Sword he was consulting with regard to their next move.

He was disconcerted by the way she put a thumb or knuckle in her mouth, her pink lips sucking at it.

Also he wanted to tell her that her garments needed some adjustment. He was more certain than ever that in her previous persona her clothing must have been protected by some magical means. Now this enhancement was no more, and seams and fabric, not made to withstand rough usage without help, were here and there starting to give way. Her blouse, or tunic, or whatever the right name was for the upper garment she was wearing, was tending to come open in front. Matters were tending toward the immodest. How could he think of her as a potential bride?

Valdemar told himself that he was not really accustomed to dealing with children.

He said: "Of course this Sword is magic, magic of tremendous power. Haven't I just been telling you?"

The griffin was showing signs of reasonable contentment as it continued feeding. Valdemar assumed that he and Delia would soon be riding on the monster's back again. He wondered if some curse was on him too, that circumstances kept arising to delay his return home.

Of course, once he had reached that goal, another problem would arise: What ought he to do then with the Sword? Any such treasure would inevitably draw trouble, as Valdemar saw the situation. He would have to hide it, get rid of it, trade it off somehow as soon as an opportunity arose.

But that could wait until he was safely home. Once Wayfinder had seen him that far, Valdemar was sure he wanted nothing more to do with any magic of the gods.

As for his wife . . . whoever she might be . . .

He sat looking long and soberly at Delia.

"What am I to do with you, girl, when we've got that far? I don't know. Will you at least be safe from demons when we've reached that point?"

She could no more answer that question than an infant. She looked back at her caretaker with mild concern, waiting for him to find some reassuring answer.

"At least," Valdemar growled, "I'll know where *I* am then, and I'll be able to do something . . ."

He picked up the Sword and once more asked it to show him the way home.

14

THE Sword of Wisdom failed to respond at all to this important question, or to the others Valdemar asked. Valdemar took this to mean that he too should adopt a course of inactivity. That would be all right if it didn't last too long; he could use the rest. Anyway, the griffin had not yet finished its protracted feeding.

Also Val was still being bothered by his cut fingers. The skin around the little wounds was red and sore and even felt warmer than the adjacent flesh, as if he were getting a local fever. Healing was slow, not helped by the fact that he had to keep using his hand.

Delia, despite her claim to have spent her childhood on a farm, protested that it bothered her to have to deal with blood and injury. But when Valdemar coaxed her, she agreed to do what she could to help him.

First, wearing an absentminded look, she searched among the nearby bushes and eventually came up with what she said were useful herbs, varieties to help the small wounds heal.

While engaged in this search, she took time out to complain, she had not been able to find the kind of berries she would really like to eat. "There should be little red berries, in the spring . . ."

"I suppose your farm was a long way off from here."

"I suppose it was," the young woman answered vaguely. Then she lifted her head sharply. "Listen!"

"What?" Valdemar turned uneasily, hand groping for his Sword.

"The birds. Hear them? Except they're not the same kind that used to sing on the farm."

Eventually, with Delia's assistance, Val succeeded in getting an effective bandage on his hand. The poultice of leaves that she bound on stung a little at first, but then felt vaguely comforting.

As Delia finished tying the last knot in the little bandage, he continued to stare at her thoughtfully. Long ago Valdemar had abandoned the last suspicion that this shocking innocence was some kind of a trick, a pose on her part. And she showed no signs of snapping out of it. No, it seemed that she was his responsibility now.

So far the pair of them had had enough to eat; fortunately the griffin had been carrying some field rations, mostly hard bread and cheese, in one of its panniers. But those supplies were quickly running out, and Valdemar realized that to keep himself and his supposed bride going he was going to have to somehow scrounge more nourishment from other sources.

He would have to think seriously about that problem soon. At the moment he was very tired.

The Sword of Wisdom would of course lead them to good things to eat, as soon as he wanted to make that his priority. But Valdemar had the feeling that they were under pursuit, if not direct attack, and he had learned that the Sword could only handle one question—or one main goal—at a time. He would not risk his life and Delia's for food until actual starvation threatened.

Sitting against a tree, he was pulled back from the brink of sleep by his companion leaning over him.

"Is it a very big magic?" Delia now repeated, innocently. She was gazing thoughtfully at the Sword, which lay in Valdemar's lap, his hand on the black hilt.

Earlier, Valdemar remembered with a sense of irony, this woman—or rather this woman's other self—had been the one to accuse him of feigning an innocence too great for the real world.

"It is indeed," Valdemar replied at last, with the slow patience of near exhaustion. "It is a gigantic, tremendous magic. And also very sharp—be careful!" He had thought for a moment, from the eager way his charge was leaning forward, that she had been about to run a testing finger right along the edge of Wayfinder's Blade.

She who had once been Tigris had never objected to Valdemar's having complete charge of the Sword of Wisdom. But from the way she was gazing at the weapon now, it was obvious that something—whether it was the bright beauty, the supernal keenness, or the intricate under-the-surface pattern of the steel—held a strong fascination.

He slid Wayfinder back into the sheath still fastened at his waist.

And then he leaned back against the tree. His eyelids were getting very heavy, and he would rest for just a moment.

Delia, feeling a mixture of mischief and curiosity, reached for the Sword again as soon as Val, losing his battle to exhaustion, dozed off.

And at that moment the griffin, as if sensing that something of importance was about to happen, silently turned its head, watching Delia keenly as she reached for Wayfinder.

She could not test the sharpness of the edge while the Sword remained sheathed. Softly she put her hand on the black hilt and drew the weapon forth, so quietly that Valdemar slept on.

Holding the Sword with a double grip on the sturdy hilt, made Delia feel strange. Her arms and hands were going tingly in a way that she knew—somehow—had something to do with magic. The sensation made her forget about testing the physical edge. She held up the Sword to smile at it in innocent admiration.

Val had told her that the Sword answered questions, and helped people. "What should I ask?" she whispered aloud. The question seemed addressed more to herself than to the instrument of the gods.

The griffin, at the moment chewing its mysterious nourishment, chewing with the jaw-motions of a cow, and the fangs of a gigantic lion, had no answer for her.

Warily Delia turned her head, looking carefully at Valdemar to make sure that he was still asleep.

Then inspiration came. Small hands white-knuckled with the strain of gripping the black hilt, she raised the heavy Sword of Wisdom and whispered to it again.

"Show me the way to make him want to keep me with him," she whispered devoutly. And smiled a moment later—because sure enough, Wayfinder had just twisted slightly in her hands—pointing at what?

At nothing in particular, that she could see. Just at some bushes.

Moving eagerly and quietly, holding the heavy Blade extended carefully in front of her, Delia investigated. The Sword led her through a screen of brush, and on a few meters more, to a point where she heard the sounds of murmuring water just ahead.

Still following the Sword's guidance, she soon arrived at a small stream, partially dammed by a fallen tree and lodged debris. Above the dam a pleasant little pond had formed, partially shaded by standing trees. The day was warm and sunny for a change, and the pool invited her to test it with her fingers. Not prohibitively cold. Certainly it looked deep and clear enough to provide a bath. Sniffing fastidiously at her armpits, she grimaced, and could not remember ever before being this dirty.

What had awakened Valdemar he did not know, but full consciousness suddenly returned. Sitting up straight, with a reflexive wrench of all his muscles, he felt a cold hand at his heart when he saw that the Sword of Wisdom was no longer in its sheath, which was still belted securely at his waist.

Delia was missing too. Maybe she had only stepped into the bushes to relieve herself. Jumping to his feet, Val called her name, first softly and then at considerable volume. To his vast relief, an answer came drifting from somewhere in the middle distance. A moment later, he thought he could hear prolonged splashing.

Quickly the young man pushed his way through the bushes to investigate.

He stopped abruptly as soon as the pond came into view. The Sword at least was safe, stuck casually into the moist earth at the water's edge.

Delia's clothing, including an undergarment or two which Valdemar had never seen before, lay beside the upright Blade. The young woman herself, completely unclothed above the waist, covered by water below that, waved at Valdemar from midstream, no more than an easy leap away. She called cheerfully for him to join her in her bath.

"Val, come in, come in!"

"I'm coming!" he heard himself reply. His voice was a mere croak. Already he was striding forward, as if hypnotized. Somehow it was as if he were watching his own behavior from outside. He was aware of stripping off his own garments, and stepping down into the current . . .

Half an hour later, Delia, still unclothed, lying at ease amid the spring grass and early flowers a little inland from the water's edge, was frowning prettily. She had hold of the huge hand of Valdemar, who, as naked as she was, lay almost inert beside her, and was turning it this way and that, as if interested in the articulation of the wrist.

"And now your bandage has come off again," she was complaining. "What are we to do for your poor fingers?"

"Never mind my fingers." Valdemar's voice had a newly calm and thoughtful quality.

Something crackled in the brush nearby, galvanizing him into action, first lunging, then crawling awkwardly, to reach the Sword. With his bandaged hand on the black hilt he turned—to find himself facing nothing worse than the griffin, driven by curiosity to see what its two masters were about.

Delia, who had crawled after him, started tickling him playfully.

Another half hour had passed before Delia asked Valdemar whether the magic Sword could heal his fingers.

"No, there is another Sword, called Woundhealer, that would be needed to do that."

"Woundhealer? Where is it?"

"I don't know. It was with me for a while, before I met you—or rather

I was with some people who were carrying that Sword. But where it is now . . . just help me put on a bandage again. My fingers will be all right, and we face bigger problems than a couple of little wounds."

The bandaging went more easily this time, perhaps because Delia was less afraid of hurting him.

As she tied the last knot, Val said regretfully: "Better get dressed. We must be moving on."

The griffin appeared to be through feeding, for the time being anyway. But Val's renewed questioning of the Sword, with safety as his goal, this time elicited no clear indication from Wayfinder.

Valdemar, strolling about with his arm around Delia, bending now and then to kiss her, kept trying to picture her as his wife, working beside him in the vineyard. Yesterday such a vision would have seemed impossible. Now it was much clearer.

He began to talk to her about his vines and grapes, and about the good wine that could be made from them in a year or two when the plants were fully matured.

Delia, listening to Val's description of his work, and his plans for the future, saw nothing frightening or unpleasant in the prospect. In fact she found herself quite pleased.

His description of the vineyard stumbled to a halt. "Does this suit you, then?" he asked.

"Yes," she told him simply. "All I want now, Val, is to stay with you."

"Oh. Oh, my dear. Delia."

When the pair of them were busy gathering what food they could, foraging to augment the supplies still remaining from the griffin's fast-diminishing store, she demonstrated a definite magical affinity for growing things—making thorny vines bend to and fro, to yield her their juicy berries without pricking her reaching hands and arms.

"I foresee a great future for you in the country, little woman."

"I keep telling you, I have always lived on a farm."

"And do your parents live there still?"

"I'm not sure." A shadow crossed the young woman's face. "I don't want to think about them."

"Then don't."

Once more Delia, at a moment when her companion was inattentive, got her small hands—hands no longer as pale and soft as they had been —on the weapon of the gods. In simple words she whispered a new question to the Sword of Wisdom, asking it to guide them to the Sword called Woundhealer, so that her lover's cut fingers could be healed.

Yet again they mounted the griffin. Valdemar, thinking that his own most recent query was the one to which the Sword was now actively responding, gave the beast commands. Quickly they were airborne.

They had not flown far before the young man noticed that a flying reptile was following them. He could not be sure whether it was actually trying to catch up with them or not, but the griffin was flying so slowly that that seemed a possibility.

Grimly Valdemar urged their mount to greater speed. The nightmare head turned on the long neck. The eyes, seeming to glow with their own fire, looked straight at him. But the griffin ignored the command.

"Faster, I said!" Val waved the Sword, as if threatening the beast with it.

The threat was a bluff, and it proved a serious mistake.

With a move that appeared deliberate for all its speed, the beast reached up, with an impossible-looking extension of one of its almost leonine hind legs. The blow from the great claws caught Wayfinder cunningly, knocking the Sword of Wisdom neatly out of Valdemar's hand.

Val uttered a hoarse cry of surprise and dismay. There was no use trying to grab for the Sword, it was already gone. In the next moment he saw the pursuing reptile catch the falling treasure in mid-flight, and with the gleaming blade between serrated teeth, go wheeling away on swift wings, carrying the prize.

At the moment of the Sword's fall, as if a successful and unpunished act of rebellion had given it courage, the griffin became totally unmanageable.

Skimming low over forest and wasteland, it launched into a series of aerobatic moves, as if determined to dislodge at once its two uncongenial masters from its back. Val and Delia hung on all but helpless, shouting at the creature and at each other. Sky, wasteland, and patches of forest spun round them as the griffin looped. The couple clung desperately to saddle and basket.

Suddenly a blue-white wall of water loomed, a pond or miniature lake. Hardly had the body of water come into sight, when the crazed animal plunged straight into it, diving and swimming like a loon.

The water's liquid resistance finally dislodged the humans. Valdemar, choking, almost drowning, felt a piece of basket rim break off in his hand. Swimming in water over his head, he fought his way to the surface, just in time to see his escaped means of transportation floundering ashore. From the wooded shoreline the griffin leapt into the air again, displaying magical celerity.

Where was Delia?

Treading water, turning this way and that, Val hoarsely called her name.

A long moment passed before he saw her—floating face down.

Desperately he stroked to reach her, got the muddy bottom of the pond under his boots, and carried her ashore. By that time, to his great relief, she was coughing and moaning feebly. She spat out a mouthful of muddy water.

When he would have helped Delia to sit up on the bank, she cried out in pain. Her back had been somehow injured in the watery rough landing. She protested that she could not walk, could hardly move.

Standing now on the shoreline, with a chance to look around, Valdemar thought that this territory looked vaguely familiar. As far as he could tell, they had returned to a point at no very great distance from the place where a young woman named Tigris had kidnapped him, and their adventures with the griffin had begun.

The scouting reptiles informed the Ancient One that Tigris was not very many kilometers away.

A beastmaster relayed the information. "She is in worse shape than ever, Lord! The peasant who is traveling as her companion strips off her clothing, and uses her at will."

Wood chuckled. For the moment he continued to be satisfied with the progress of his punishment.

"And we have taken their Sword from them!" the reporting human gloated.

The Ancient One's demeanor changed. "I hope that none among you has dared to touch it?"

Hastily the subordinate explained. No one had disobeyed orders. One of the more simple-minded flying reptiles had caught the falling Sword Wayfinder in midair, and was bringing it in, flying slowly under the unaccustomed load.

Wood was not really surprised by the news regarding the Sword. He had been working for some time, and on several levels, to get Wayfinder away from Tigris and Valdemar, and into his own hands.

It had been part of his plan to obtain the Sword without letting any of his associates possessed of human intelligence, or greater, get it into their own hands even for an instant.

The task had been further complicated by the fact that Wayfinder itself had doubtless been employed to protect its possessors from him. But as matters had turned out, his plan succeeded anyway. Perhaps, he was tempted to believe, the Sword's magic was not invariably supreme.

Soon the Sword itself was brought in. But, almost immediately after getting Wayfinder into his hands, Wood was distracted again from thoughts of pleasant vengeance by reports from both demons and reptiles, confirming that a force of about a hundred Tasavaltan riders was on its way south, heading almost directly toward his camp.

On hearing this, one of the Ancient One's currently most favored human subordinates immediately suggested evoking a large force of demons, and dispatching them all against the hundred cavalry and their support people and creatures.

The proposed tactic would undoubtedly serve well to determine whether Mark was accompanying this main Tasavaltan force or not. But if Mark was indeed there, the discovery might cost the discoverer, Wood, a whole force of demons.

He decided prudently to begin by sending only one or two of the vile creatures.

As for attacking Mark personally, he had other ideas about that.

Having been aware for some years of the presence of Shieldbreaker in the Tasavaltan arsenal, Wood assumed that the Prince would be coming against him armed with the Sword of Force. Shieldbreaker was undoubtedly the mightiest piece of armament in the world, capable of nullifying the power of any other weapon, even another Sword, that might be deployed against it.

With these facts in mind the Ancient One, pleased as he was to be finally holding Wayfinder, took it for granted from the start that any attempt to locate Mark directly by using the Sword of Wisdom was bound to fail.

So Wood, on first obtaining the Sword of Wisdom, made only a perfunctory attempt to locate Mark. When that was unsuccessful, he acted rather to locate the wizard Karel, or the Sword Sightblinder, on the assumption that Mark would be found very near that person or object.

When the Ancient One's small squad of demonic skirmishers attempted to strike at the force from Tasavalta, they would encounter, in fat old Karel, a magician of sufficient stature to beat the attackers off—though not as quickly and effectively as Mark would have been able to repel them.

In Karel's archives, as he was soon explaining to an anxious pair of military officers in his tent, were listed the locations of many demons' lives. And the old magician gave assurance that he knew how to find out more such locations very quickly, if and when the need arose.

Besides, Karel had the power to make things unpleasant for a lot of demons whose lives he lacked the knowledge to terminate—so unpleasant that they would even prefer to incur Wood's displeasure, rather than persist in this attack.

Wood, observing the fate of his demon skirmishers as closely as he could while still remaining at what he considered the best distance to exercise command, felt reasonably confident that Mark was no longer accompanying his cavalry and his chief magician.

Then where was the Prince of Tasavalta? Mark's archenemy chewed a fingernail, heretofore well-kept, and pondered.

Wherever the Prince might be, Wood felt sure that he would be armed not only with the Sword of Force, but also with the Sword of Stealth. Such a combination would make a formidable antagonist out of the veriest weakling; in the hands of a warrior like Mark, the effect was bound to be overwhelming, against all but the strongest and most crafty defense.

Well, Wood considered that he was ready.

In less than a minute, before Wood's demons could begin their serious attack, even before most of the Tasavaltan force had been made aware of the impending threat, Karel's magic had slain or dispersed the handful of magical skirmishers.

But the confrontation, once begun, continued between Mark's uncle and the Ancient One. The two commenced sparring at long range.

Wood had long wanted to test directly the occult strength of Kristin's overweight uncle. Now, having at last made immediate contact, the Ancient One had grudgingly to admit that, although he felt confident of being able to wear this veteran adversary down in time, the struggle was bound to be a long and draining one. Wood did not choose to spare the time and effort to fight it to a conclusion now. He was going to need all his powers to deal with Mark, armed as the Prince must now be.

Not that Wood thought Mark was going to represent the ultimate test. The Ancient One had received certain magical indications that his own final success or failure, in his bid to dominate the world, was going to depend upon another confrontation, now still relatively remote.

Against the Dark King, and the horde of demons that one could call up? Wood considered it unlikely that his rival Vilkata had really been permanently removed from the scene. But no, not even the Dark King would represent the ultimate challenge.

Sooner or later, the Ancient One was thinking now, it would be necessary to concentrate his efforts with the Sword of Wisdom on locating the Emperor, in anticipation of a final combat with that man.

The Lady Yambu, lying on an ebon couch, covered with a white sheet, her head now pillowed on rich fabrics, was being more or less forcibly maintained by her newest captor in a state of responsive consciousness. Finding it necessary to converse with him whether she wanted to or not, she expressed to Wood her surprise that his first questions to the Sword of Wisdom did not seem to have been concerned with establishing his own safety.

She asked him the reasons for this lack of caution.

He assured the Silver Queen that he scorned to be so timid.

"You will understand that, I am sure, my lady. You yourself have never been accused of excessive caution."

"No doubt that is intended as a compliment."

"Of course. I have always regarded you with the greatest respect." Wood paused, before adding in a low, convincing voice: "I would never have deserted you in your time of need."

"Meaning that the Emperor, who was my husband, did?"

"You are the best judge of his behavior in that instance." Without hesitating, the Ancient One continued: "Support me now, and I will give you real youth. Eternal youth and beauty, a far more lasting change than even Woundhealer will ever be able to provide."

Her head turned on the brocaded pillow. "And Tigris? Did she have the same promise from you?"

"What has happened, is happening, to that woman is no secret. But dear lady, I made her no promises. I never found that woman half as interesting as I find you."

"I have no interest in what is happening to her. Now will you let me rest?"

"Of course, dear lady. For a time."

Walking alone, a few moments later, Wood developed a shrewd suspicion: this lady was really trying to find, to rejoin, her former husband. Though he thought it doubtful that the Silver Queen herself was fully aware of her own motivation.

Perhaps he, Wood, ought to announce his readiness to help her in this quest.

Because he really wanted to find the Emperor too.

On an impulse drawing Wayfinder, Wood took time out from his immediate struggle to command that Sword to guide him to the Great Clown.

The Sword's reaction was simply to point straight down to the spot of earth on which Wood was standing. He could readily find one interpretation of this answer: If he remained where he was, the Emperor would come to him.

Of course there were other possibilities.

"Am I to dig into the earth? I hope not. Or do you simply mean that I must wait? Faugh! The secrets of the gods are welded into this bar of metal, and all I can do is ask questions like any other supplicant, and hope, and wait!"

Faced with this behavior by the Sword of Wisdom, the Ancient One began to wonder if his calculations regarding Mark's behavior could have been wrong.

He wondered also whether it might be the Emperor, instead of Mark, who was now armed with Shieldbreaker.

When Wood tried to locate Mark directly, Wayfinder became as inert as any farmer's knife.

Wood, who had also taken possession of Woundhealer on entering the camp, was considering that he might eventually want to trade that treasure for a Sword he wanted more—though he would dislike having to give up the Sword of Healing, having certain uses for it in mind.

He thought that the next time he talked with Yambu, he would elicit some comment from her on the subject of trading Woundhealer.

15

MARK in a grim mood kept riding forward. The country through which he traveled was largely desert, and for a time remained almost flat. The land got rougher as he drew closer to a river's rocky gorge.

He had now been traveling alone, ahead of the advancing column of Tasavaltan cavalry, for more than a full day.

The Prince had had no conscious contact with anyone, friend or foe, since he had separated from his hundred picked troopers, from Karel, the assistant magicians, and the rest of the fast-moving force.

On parting from his friends, Mark had ridden for a short time without drawing either Sightblinder or Shieldbreaker. But rather soon the Prince decided that he had better not advance any farther without having in hand one of his two Swords—or, better, both of them.

Mark wanted to have the Sword of Stealth in hand before he was seen by the enemy's reptile scouts.

And he wanted to draw Shieldbreaker before coming within range of any enemy weapons.

Since leaving Karel behind, the Prince had several times sensed the power of contending magical forces, and he realized that something might be happening to delay his uncle and the cavalry. But even with Sightblinder in hand to enhance his powers of observation, he had been unable to perceive the details of the magical combat between Karel and Wood, or of Karel and Wood's demons.

Mark supposed that, barring such magical hindrance, his Tasavaltan escort ought to be not much more than a couple of hours behind him.

Carrying Sightblinder drawn for protection deprived Mark of information he might otherwise have received from scouting birds and made him unable to send winged couriers to his friends. Confronted by magic powerful enough to deceive humans, the birds, with their limited intelligence, could hardly be expected to disregard the visual image—they would either perceive Mark as some fearful presence, and refuse to approach him, or they would see him as some beloved object—another bird, he supposed, or a favorite handler—not the two-legged master for whom they had been trained to carry messages and fight.

Thus on occasion, when he saw a friendly messenger in the air, Mark risked sheathing Sightblinder again.

Under these conditions, the Prince had received indications that Wood himself was now somewhere in this general area. The most recent of these communications was a note from Ben, explaining that the Blue Temple force had been destroyed, and its camp taken over by an expedition under the command of Tigris.

Mark observed several flying reptiles at irregular intervals of time. Their paths in the sky converged at a place no very great distance ahead of him. This fact warned the Prince that he was almost certainly closely approaching some enemy; from this point on he rode with the two Swords continually drawn.

And now the subtle blending of their two powerful magics, Shieldbreaker in his right hand, Sightblinder in his left, both Swords more fully activated than when he had tried them in Karel's presence, gave Mark strange, exotic feelings of power and glory. Wave after wave of giddiness threatened to unbalance him in his saddle. His uncle's warnings clamored in his memory, but Mark forcibly put them from his mind—just now, both of his Swords were necessary.

Old Karel had more than once cautioned him that these, like other forms of power, could be addictive. Not that Mark had needed the warning; he had long been old enough to understand that for himself.

The Prince retained a firm faith that Shieldbreaker's protection would hold absolutely against any spells or other attacks that Wood might launch personally, or might order to be made by others.

As Mark grew closer to the enemy, the powers slumbering in the Sword of Force awoke and made a tapping sound. He knew that this noise signalled a hostile presence, somewhere close enough to represent an immediate danger.

Now and again, as Mark moved forward, the dull sound arose, only to sink back almost to inaudibility. In the circumstances, knowing the power of this Sword, the Prince found the faint noise more comforting than alarming.

As when the duel commenced between Karel and Wood, Mark's experienced senses provided him with a vague but disturbing warning of evil magic, strange presences, nearby. He could feel these groping in the air around him, and then withdrawing thwarted.

* * *

Wood, on taking over the camp established by Tigris, had quickly reorganized its layout and defenses.

The Ancient One now occupied a blue and silver pavilion in the center of an elaborate and heavily safeguarded bivouac.

The powers, human and inhuman, who had come here with the treacherous young enchantress had all by now been formally charged with incompetence or worse. Every one of them had now been taken away in chains, or the magical equivalent thereof.

Having, as he thought, magical capabilities to spare, and no real concern for problems of logistics, the Ancient One had also set out to make this facility luxurious.

In the few moments he thought he could spare from more immediate concerns, he studied the condition of his prisoner Yambu, and talked with her on several subjects.

The Ancient One, with the help of several subordinates, was also conducting, or preparing to conduct, experiments with some new magical techniques. He nursed at least feeble hopes that these would enable him to get around the defense posed by the Sword of Force.

But it did not take long to confirm his most gloomy auguries regarding the new methods. These were doomed to fail as absolutely as any other inferior magic ever set in opposition to a Sword.

He was angry, but he had really expected no other result.

"It is no use," he admitted, his voice descending to a quiet rasp of rage. "Shieldbreaker's protection remains absolute."

These new techniques had required some human sacrifice, and the Director had been chosen. The Lady Yambu had asked whether she was being considered as a candidate, and Wood had looked pained at the suggestion.

The Ancient One did truly regret that Tigris was not currently available in his camp, so that she could do him a final service as the sacrifice.

It would be hard, he thought, to imagine anything more satisfactory than watching her be fed slowly to a demon—unless of course he should manage to lay his hands on Woundhealer and Tigris together. Then new possibilities would open. He would be able to treat her, after all, to that little vacation in one of his remote strongholds for which she had once so eagerly expressed a wish . . .

Yes, Wood already missed his little comrade, and he was going to miss her more. Oh, if only she had remained loyal to him a little longer! It was unsatisfying to have the decision on when to end a relationship taken out of one's hands, so to speak.

*   *   *

Wood talked with Brod, and in the course of this discussion he formally enlisted the Sarge as one of his followers.

Brod groveled in gratitude.

"You may demonstrate your thankfulness by performing a certain mission for me. Do this job well, and I will give you something more important."

"Anything my Master commands!"

"I want you to seek out a certain woman—you will be given her approximate location, and magical means by which you will be able to certainly identify her—and bring her back here, to me, for my personal attention. You need not be too concerned about her sensibilities while she is in your charge."

"I take your meaning, Master."

"I think I made it plain enough."

Ben, forced to seek shelter almost continually, had been able to make little or no progress to the north. But he kept trying.

On rounding a bend in a path that wound its way through scrubby forest, he suddenly came upon a vision that stopped him in his tracks— he was confronting a young woman, tall and strong, with clear blue eyes and bright red hair, who stood regarding him steadily.

It was Ariane, his long-lost love.

Intellectually, Ben knew better. He realized almost at once that he had really encountered Mark, carrying the Sword Sightblinder, so that the Prince must appear to his old friend, as to anyone else he met, as some object of overwhelming love or fear.

Knowing well the powers of Sightblinder, and also that Mark would almost certainly have armed himself with the Sword of Stealth, Ben had braced himself mentally for such a moment. Still the shock was almost overwhelming.

Mark, on seeing his friend turn pale, and sit down as if his knees had betrayed him, sheathed Sightblinder, and advanced to offer words of greeting and reassurance.

In a minute Ben had pulled himself together, had given Mark the bad news about the loss of Zoltan and the Sword of Healing, and was ready for whatever had to be done next.

The Prince took a turn at walking, loaning weary Ben his riding-beast for an hour or two. In this manner the pair headed south again. Mark told Ben that he had been for some time reasonably certain that an enemy camp was not far, because he had observed the converging reptile flight-paths.

Ben confirmed that the lost Sword of Healing had been carried that way too.

At dusk, advancing cautiously, the two men observed sparks of firelight ahead, suggesting the presence of a camp.

Taking counsel together, the two experienced warriors decided that, armed as they were with Swords, they stood an excellent chance of being able to launch a successful raid without waiting for the arrival of the Tasavaltan troop and Karel.

Mark emphasized: "If Wood is indeed in this camp, I want to get my hands on him before he has a chance to fly off with the Sword I need."

Ben raised a hand to silence him.

Someone was approaching.

Valdemar had been forced to leave the injured Delia in an abandoned hut, which at least offered shelter against the intermittent cold rain, while he sought help.

Even in the gathering dusk, he quickly recognized Ben's hulking figure. But standing beside Ben . . . in that first moment . . . was an almost-forgotten horror out of Valdemar's own childhood, a faceless figure of which he could be certain only that it was frightful.

And in the next moment, even as he recoiled in horror, the young giant beheld the image of horror replaced by one of his beautiful wife to be . . . and then that form faded too. Beside Ben there was only a tall man, sheathing what appeared to be a Sword.

In a few moments introductions had been made, and explanations begun. From Valdemar Mark soon heard, in a drastically condensed version, the story of how the woman who had been Tigris was now lying in an abandoned hut, reformed and injured, in dire need of help.

Valdemar in the course of this relation reported how Tigris had abducted him from this site, and mentioned the loss of Wayfinder.

Ben expressed his doubts. "You think she's reformed, young one? Maybe her magic's been taken away, but I'll shed no tears for that. It's some kind of trickery she's worked upon you."

"It's not!"

Quickly and firmly the Prince squelched this argument. There was no time for quarreling now. Even if the situation was in fact just as Valdemar described it, he, Mark, could not, would not, go off on a tangent now to help some woman in distress, however deserving she might be.

And then the Prince made a plea of his own. "Help me now, Valdemar. Help Ben to guard me against attackers when we invade this camp, and I swear that I in turn will help you as soon as I can. With all the power of Tasavalta, and of the Swords, that I can bring to bear."

The towering youth let out a sound of frustration, something between a sigh and a snort. "I must accept your offer, Prince. It seems I have no choice."

Mark decided that they would not attack the camp till dawn, giving them all a chance to eat and rest. He shared out the food from his saddlebags. Before bedding down for the night, Mark and Ben discussed tactics with the inexperienced Valdemar. The two veterans made the point that the only enemy tactic they really had to worry about, whatever forces might oppose them here, was that of people deliberately disarming themselves and then hurling themselves on the Prince who carried Shieldbreaker.

Valdemar nodded; the theory of the situation was easy enough to comprehend. As for putting it into practice: "I will do the best I can."

"Can't ask for any more than that."

In the first gray light of dawn, the three men soon came close enough to Wood's encampment to hear the sounds of people stirring, and smell the smoke of campfires.

Evidently the Ancient One, confident in his strength, had made no particular effort to conceal his position.

Mark, made wary by this lack of concealment, wondered whether Wood was more or less expecting him, perhaps even trying to lure him into making a solo attack.

It turned out that Wood's camp was magically protected against casual discovery, but with Shieldbreaker in one hand and Sightblinder in the other the Prince crossed the invisible boundary unharmed and unimpeded. Had it not been for a softly augmented thudding from the Sword of Force, he would not even have realized that he had encountered any defenses.

Matters were different for the two men who formed his escort. Ben, despite his experience and alertness, was unaware of the magical protection until unnatural light flared around him and Valdemar, and immaterial weapons slashed at their minds and bodies.

Shields and snares of magic closed on the three intruders, only to recoil an instant later like snapped bowstrings, broken by the unyielding central presence of the Sword of Force. Shieldbreaker's voice beat loudly, light flared across the early morning dimness, and the claws of magic lashing out at it were instantly blunted and beaten back. Valdemar and Ben were staggered momentarily, but the power that might otherwise have destroyed them was quenched before it could have serious effect.

Hoarse cries in human voices went up from near the center of the camp. Ben thought that perhaps the backlash of the broken spells had taken toll among the minor wizards there. Certainly by now the entire enemy camp was aware of an intrusion. Soldiers in blue and silver, magicians, and others came pouring out of their tents. The trio of invaders stood in plain sight of most of them, and Sightblinder immediately provoked primary confusion among the defenders, human and inhuman.

The first human sentry to get a clear look at Mark, near the edge of camp, ran forward hesitantly, sword half-raised by an arm that jerked uncertainly, as if the man himself did not know whether he meant to salute or strike. Evidently this man perceived the invading Prince as Wood himself, or as some hideous demonic power.

An instant later, a real demon came hurtling down out of the lowering morning sky. Even had Mark been lacking Shieldbreaker, he would have confronted the foul thing with a wary respect, but not with terror. As the Emperor's son, he had always possessed the power, without understanding why or how he had it, to drive away even the most powerful of those evil creatures, simply by commanding them to depart. In the past the Prince had been forced to demonstrate this ability several times, often enough to give him confidence in it now.

And the Sword of Force, he felt sure, added another impenetrable layer of protection against demons. Such beings, as old Karel had once explained to Mark, were creatures of magic and pure malevolence, born of great explosions at the time of the Old World's dying. They could will nothing but evil, and Karel thought that they could take no action of any kind except by means of magic.

Magic employed to inflict injury was by definition a weapon, and Shieldbreaker was proof against all weapons, material or otherwise. A human being abandoning all weapons could win barehanded against the Sword of Force—but a demon could hardly disarm itself without ceasing to exist.

Perhaps, Sightblinder notwithstanding, this morning's demon understood at once just what antagonist it must be facing. Because the thing vanished out of the air again, as quickly as it had appeared, and of its own volition.

And now—inevitably but foolishly—a few material weapons were deployed directly against the holder of the Sword of Force. Mark's body, no longer under full control of his own will, stretched back and forth with magical celerity, darted to right and left, executing parry, cut, and thrust with ruinous violence and precision—but all under cover of Sightblinder's cloak of deception. The visible counterfeit of Mark—some image of terror or love—beheld by each friend or enemy, more often than not appeared weaponless and unmoving, a single enigmatic figure standing immobile in the midst of causeless carnage.

Enemy swords, spears, missiles and shields were hacked and harvested in a spray of fragments. Shieldbreaker chopped up human flesh and body armor with ruthlessly complete indifference. The Sword in Mark's right hand—in those moments when that weapon could be glimpsed—became a silver blur. The hammer-sound blurred also with its speed, and swelled up to a steady thunder-roll.

Valdemar had never seen or dreamed of anything like this before. Few people had. There was, there could be, in the whole world nothing else like this to see. The young man was momentarily stunned into immobility.

One man, Mark, advancing with his weapons, sent the first wave of blue and silver opposition reeling back in confusion.

So far the Prince's double bodyguard had not been required to do anything but stay close to him. If they stayed close enough, they remained within the aegis of protection of the Sword of Force. Shieldbreaker flashed invisibly between their bodies and around them, smashing slung stones and arrows out of the air.

But now, sooner than either Val or Ben had expected, some of the enemy began to come against Mark unarmed.

Val saw the first one, a squat, strong soldier in silver and blue, come charging barehanded between two of his fellows armed with short spears. The Sword of Force put out its flickering tongue of power, and both spearshafts were severed in a blink. The unarmed enemy who would have charged between the spears to grapple with the Prince instead encountered the battle-hatchet swung accurately at the end of Val's long right arm. The vineyardist had never killed before; but he was left with no time now to meditate upon the fact. Another unarmed foe was coming.

Ben and Val, stepping forward one on the Prince's right hand and one on his left, acquitted themselves well in the first fight with the initially disorganized foe.

There came a brief lull. Panting, Mark gave his orders: "We go forward again. I must find Wood! Whatever Swords are here will be with him."

Advancing boldly, pressing their initial advantage, he and his escort penetrated to one of the central tents. Ripping open fabric with a Blade, the Prince cursed on realizing that his chief antagonist was not here either.

But a moment later, to their joy, the three attackers discovered in this tent a pair of important prisoners. Zoltan and Yambu were both stretched out on narrow beds, eyes staring and bodies rigid, obviously under some magical constraint. Any humans who might have been stationed to guard them had already taken to their heels. In only moments the Prince and his flankers were able to set the pair free.

Into the right hand of each prisoner, briefly and in turn, Mark pressed the hilt of the Sword Shieldbreaker. This instantly and permanently broke the grip of the magic Wood had bound them with.

Zoltan, on being released from imprisonment, sat up with a strangled gasp of relief, to see Valdemar and Ben before him, standing one on each side of a black-eyed mermaid. Zoltan understood that he was facing the Sword of Stealth, when a moment later the mermaid's image turned into that of Wood himself, and then into a nameless, shrouded figure of horror, a memory from nightmares of his childhood.

Whatever horror the Lady Yambu might have experienced in her captivity, or on waking to see Mark wielding Sightblinder, she bore the burden well.

Less than a kilometer away, the young woman who had once been Tigris was still lying injured, half delirious, inside some peasant's half-roofless and long abandoned hut.

Fearing equally for her own survival and for her lover's safety, Delia drifted in and out of feverish sleep. In her lucid moments the young woman hoped and prayed to all the gods that the two of them would be able to get away from this seemingly endless conflict, to the peaceful vineyard Val had so proudly described to her.

Almost Delia felt that she already knew that place, that she and Valdemar had already lived there together. In dreams she saw the little house, the garden, a green and summery vision of delight, a paradise once possessed, now gone again and unattainable.

In her pain and distress she had lost track of how much time had passed since Val had left her here alone. Many hours, certainly. She was afraid it had been days. She feared, in her state of suffering, that the man she loved had suffered some horrible fate. Or, worse, that he had cruelly deserted her.

Zoltan, still suffering somewhat from Wood's maltreatment, could provide little relevant information about Wood, nor could he guess what

Swords the Ancient One might hold. But Yambu was able to confirm that Wayfinder had been here, in this camp, and in Wood's hands.

Where the Ancient One was now, or whether he had with him that Sword, or any other, she did not know.

Mark assumed that Wood had carried the Sword of Wisdom away.

Now, in the center of the camp, Mark and his augmented bodyguard faced a development the Prince had not really expected—a carefully prepared series of enemy counterattacks by a surrounding composite force of armed and unarmed men, specially trained to fight against Shieldbreaker.

At the next pause in the action, Mark suspected, and his panting friends agreed, that the Ancient One must be somewhere near at hand, directing these attacks.

The beleagured handful craned their necks, trying to spot their enemy in the clouded sky. The Prince grunted: "He'll be riding on a griffin, or I'm surprised. He'll be too shrewd to mount a demon, when he expects me to be present."

Before anyone could answer him, there sounded from somewhere in the distance what Mark and his compatriots could recognize as a Tasavaltan horn.

"That's Karel, thank all the gods."

"Let us hope some cavalry is with him."

Karel himself, riding forward with a courage matched only by his physical clumsiness, doing his best to keep up with the cavalry, had been able to determine with fair accuracy, despite Wood's attempts at concealment, just where the enemy camp had been established. Some of the Tasavaltan scouting birds had been deceived by enemy magic, and others temporarily outfought by reptiles. But the uncle of the Prince and Princess could also determine, even without much help from feathered friends, that Mark was now in the vicinity.

He signalled to the cavalry commander to sound the charge.

In moments the Tasavaltan mounted troopers, supporting and supported by a truly formidable magician, were heavily engaged with the forces surrounding Prince Mark and his small bodyguard.

Drawing a deep breath, Mark commanded an advance, toward their allies.

There were plenty of fallen weapons about with which the former prisoners could arm themselves.

They advanced.

Meanwhile Wood, still carrying Wayfinder, was airborne. Mounted on his own especially large and vicious griffin, he circled above the fighting, dispatching relays of reptiles with urgent messages to his officers below. He sent other winged couriers with orders to speed the advance of his additional ground forces already marching to the scene.

What had once been an orderly camp was now a ruined, trampled field of mud, fallen bodies and ruined and discarded weapons, and collapsed tents. Time and again, the Prince's personal bodyguard saved his life by beating off unarmed attack. He, and the unmatchable power in his right hand, rescued them in turn. The onslaught of the Tasavaltan cavalry had relieved some of the pressure from surrounding forces, but still Mark and his handful in the center had all that they could handle. So far, thanks to skill and luck and the weapons of the gods, none of them were more than slightly wounded.

Wood, hovering on his chosen griffin, darting away and coming back, now and then swooping low enough to get a good look at the figure he knew must really be Mark, sometimes perceived instead a man he recognized as the Emperor. Again the Ancient One beheld a shadowy figure, insubstantial yet angular, somehow almost mechanical, something out of the Old World. He knew that the Sword of Stealth was tricking him into seeing Ardneh.

Though Shieldbreaker had prevented Wood from using Wayfinder effectively to plan his counterattack on Mark, the Sword of Wisdom continued to be effective against Mark's allies, Karel and the Tasavaltan cavalry. The trouble was, as long as Mark himself was on the scene, Wood could not spare the time to accomplish their destruction.

The next time he dove his mount low enough to get a close look at the fighting around Mark, the Ancient One beheld, to his own freezing horror, the hulking, foul image of the king-demon Orcus—a being now ages dead, along with Ardneh his great antagonist.

Putting aside the initial shock of this perception, Wood summoned up his intelligence and will, gritted his teeth, and stubbornly denied what both his eyes and his best magical perception were assuring him to be true.

That was Mark. And with the two Swords, Mark was winning.

A number of Wood's people, who as a rule were more afraid of their master than of any other conceivable enemy—or at least of Mark—fought like fanatics.

But on encountering the armed Prince of Tasavalta, a majority of these unfortunates perceived Mark as Wood, and they saw confronting them a figure even more terrible in its wrath than the original. And the very terror with which the Ancient One had sought to bind his fighters to him, resulted in their defection.

Yambu had been struck down, and was out of action for the time being.

Those of the Prince's friends who were still fighting beside him could only hope, if they should lose sight of Mark for a moment, that when they again saw a figure they took to be him, it was not really that of Wood or another enemy instead.

For Wood, snarling rage was giving way to a kind of calm. He prepared to risk everything on a single move.

"My plan is failing, because my fools down there lack wit and nerve to execute it properly. Very well, then. I see I must grapple with him myself."

Wood reined his griffin round to circle in a wide loop, gaining momentum for a final charge. Meaning to hurl himself unarmed on Mark, he began divesting himself of weapons right and left—but stopped when he came to Woundhealer and Wayfinder, sheathed at his side.

"Not yet. Both Swords may have to go, but only at the last moment, when I'll know that he still has Shieldbreaker in hand."

Mark's tiring riding-beast tripped and fell, hurling him violently to the ground. Though protected against all enemy weapons, Mark had been knocked out of the saddle by accident.

The Prince lay temporarily stunned.

Zoltan, being closest to him on his right side, grabbed up Shieldbreaker.

Val, who was in the best position on the other side, took up Sightblinder, which had fallen from Mark's left hand.

Moments later, having seen from a distance how their Prince went down, Karel and some of the Tasavaltan cavalry attacked fiercely, and broke through to surround and defend him.

In the double confusion of a melee and a joyful reunion, Valdemar was easily able, even had he lacked Sightblinder, to step away without being noticed.

The Ancient One, circling away momentarily, failed to see Mark go down.

Coming back, swooping very low to the ground for a final attack, Wood observed only a confused struggle in the place where he expected Mark to be. The Ancient One's hopes rose—perhaps his plan of attack had succeeded after all.

The griffin, great wings blurring with its speed, roared low above the struggling throng, sustaining what to it were minor wounds from Tasavaltan stones and arrows.

Closing swiftly on the knot of central activity where Mark must be, Wood saw Zoltan standing in the Tasavaltan ranks.

Shieldbreaker would be down on the ground there, somewhere underneath that scramble. The direct attack on Mark would have to wait for his next pass—or if the Prince was already slain, such a desperate tactic would be, after all, unnecessary. But here was another choice target, and this run would not be wasted. Swerving his mount slightly at full speed to meet the altered target, the Ancient One swung Wayfinder with all his strength against Zoltan—and the world seemed to explode with tremendous violence in Wood's face.

The shocked griffin literally somersaulted in midair, and the body of its rider went hurtling from the saddle. Some of the onlookers were quick-witted enough to realize almost immediately that Wood must have swung Wayfinder against Shieldbreaker, and that the Sword of Wisdom had been dazzlingly destroyed.

In every quarter of the field, increasing numbers of enemy soldiers were panicking into flight. No matter how thoroughly their secret training had prepared them for a fight against two overwhelming Swords, the reality was overwhelming, and they found themselves unable to stand against it.

The surviving Tasavaltan troopers, taking heart from the fall of their archenemy, fought all the harder.

The physical combat flared and receded and flared again. The fighting was fierce, the slaughter great, the number of fallen in blue and silver much larger than those in blue and green. Wood had been determined to wear down his foe by numbers, if he could win in no other way.

Mark, still sprawled on the ground, but now fiercely protected by his friends and his surrounding troops, was starting to regain consciousness.

Part of his trouble was due to the strain of carrying two such Swords into battle at the same time. Karel now was at the Prince's side, mumbling a reminder of his own warnings on the subject; but at the same time the elderly wizard protected Mark and all the Tasavaltan forces against anything that Wood's lesser magicians were able to try against them.

Valdemar, his perceptions enhanced by having Sightblinder in his grip, went running toward the place where he had seen Wood's plummeting body strike the earth. The crashing weight had half-collapsed a large tent in an area of the battlefield now otherwise deserted.

Inside the standing portion of the tent, Valdemar discovered that the falling body, half-armored in bright metal, had torn its way right through the fabric as it came down. The corpse lay on its back, rain falling on the face, the whole head looking hideously altered from the human. The terrible wound of Shieldbreaker's latest riposte showed plainly in the center of the chest, where armor of steel and high magic had been shredded as effortlessly as skin.

The Sword of Mercy still reposed in its sheath at the waist of the dead wizard.

The proof of the identity of this deformed and otherwise nearly unrecognizable corpse was in its right hand: dead fingers still gripping the black hilt of what had been the Sword of Wisdom, the hilt itself still bearing a stump of broken blade, once-magnificent metal dulled and lifeless now.

After the briefest of hesitations, the young man identified the sheathed and intact Sword beyond any doubt: he did this by drawing it forth and using it to treat his own small injuries recently received in battle.

Then Valdemar, working quietly and quickly and unobserved inside this half-collapsed pavilion, wrapped up Woundhealer in tent fabric, having used the blade itself to cut a piece to size. And then he promptly made off with it, trusting to Sightblinder in his right hand to afford him an unimpeded exit from the battlefield.

Valdemar had no trouble justifying this action to himself. The fight seemed to have been won, or at least was in a lull, with every prospect for an eventual Tasavaltan victory.

He told himself that he had done his share, and more than his share, of the necessary fight against the evil folk who would have hounded Delia to her death or worse—their glorious enemy, the Prince of Tasavalta, was still alive, now protectively surrounded by his own fiercely defensive troops, all of them, unlike Valdemar, trained fighters.

Overshadowing all other considerations, of course, was the fact that Delia desperately needed help, the help that he could bring her now—

and that he feared might never reach her, if he were to trust the Sword of Mercy to someone else.

With both leaders now fallen, a lull had fallen over the field of combat. The enemy had retreated to regroup, or were perhaps recovering from a rout, or else they were following the Tasavaltans who in turn were trying to retreat with their injured Prince. Val could not immediately see just what was happening, and in fact he did not greatly care. He moved out boldly, armed with the Sword of Stealth.

Making steady progress, not looking back, he separated himself from whatever was left of the battle. He was going to bring help and healing to the woman he loved.

He told himself as he trudged away that after he and Delia were safely out of trouble, the Prince of Tasavalta would be welcome to the Sword—to all the Swords.

The Prince had not seemed a bad man, but Valdemar really put little faith in Mark's promises of help—obviously the Prince was going to be fully engaged in his own problems for some indefinite time to come.

Val could not blame him. In Mark's place, he would have done the same.

Presently the fighting flared up again around the Prince and his close companions, so that their search for the now-missing Valdemar, just tentatively begun, had to be abandoned for a time.

Zoltan and Ben exchanged guesses as to whether Valdemar had been killed. Of course there was nothing to be done about it if he had been.

Men had been dispatched to look for Wood's body, for he might have been carrying a Sword or two. The corpse of the fallen wizard was discovered, and, with the help of Karel, recognized. But no unbroken Swords were with it.

Sightblinder was gone from the field, but Shieldbreaker in Zoltan's hand fought on, with devastating effect. Any minions of Wood whose morale had survived the loss of their leader, and who were still misguided enough to strike directly, with material weapons, at the holder of the Sword of Force, saw their spears and swords and missiles shattered and broken, and they themselves were slaughtered when they came within range of Shieldbreaker's matchless force.

Similarly, any who tried to attack that person with magic saw their spells, too, broken by the Sword of Force. Some minor wizards in Wood's camp expired with startling visual effects.

And again and yet again, cleverly trained and fanatically led, one frantic would-be wrestler after another cast down his weapons and tried to close with the figure assumed to be Mark.

Again and again that man's new bodyguard beat back these attempts with ordinary blades, cudgels, skill and strength.

16

VALDEMAR, struggling against exhaustion after the prolonged fighting, kept moving as fast as he could, trudging on through rain and muck. He snatched brief periods of rest, when quivering knees and faintness told him that he must.

In the first stage of his journey, carrying two Swords, he passed many wounded, numbers of them crying out pitiably. Setting his jaw, he closed his ears to the sounds of pain and carried Woundhealer wrapped and hidden past the victims of the fighting, telling himself that he had already done more than his share for the Tasavaltan cause. At moments when he closed his eyes, every groan of pain seemed to be sounding in Delia's voice. He kept on moving as quickly and steadily as he could, back toward his beloved.

When Valdemar was half a kilometer from the camp, he thought he heard the sounds of battle started up behind him yet again. He did not look back, but kept going, and the noises slowly faded once more.

Resting only when his weariness compelled, Valdemar traveled for about an hour before coming in sight of the abandoned hut where he had left Delia. Running the last few meters, calling her name, he heard a welcome answer, and found her inside waiting for him.

He remembered to put Sightblinder away before he entered.

Delia, lying almost exactly where Val had left her, cried out to him in weak but joyous welcome.

Woundhealer drawn, he rushed forward to his woman's side.

Minutes later, the couple were resting and eating, preparatory to starting their long journey to Valdemar's vineyard, when a dull shadow fell across the doorway, blocking the dim light of the rainy day. Val looked up to glimpse a massive figure clad in Wood's blue and silver livery.

The young man had taken off his belt, and left both Swords imprudently just out of easy reach. In the next instant Val lunged for them, only to be felled by a stunning blow on head and shoulder.

"Good day to you both, young folks," said Sergeant Brod.

Delia hurled herself on the intruder, but Brod, laughing, easily caught her and clamped her wrists behind her back in one of his huge hands.

He said: "Things have gone a little wrong with the Master's magic—but I see the spell he gave me to find you here is still working just fine."

But on taking a good look at the woman he had just caught, who continued to squirm and hiss and scratch, Brod had some difficulty in believing this ordinary-looking female had once been Tigris—even though he had never had a good look at the enchantress. It seemed to the Sarge that Wood's long-range punishment had been devastatingly effective. In fact, if Wood had not thoughtfully provided him with a certain magical means of identification, he would probably have failed to recognize her at all.

Val lay on the floor of the hut groaning, by all indications unable to move.

The Sarge, making sure he had Delia in a safe grip, bent over to get his first good look at the weapons on the earthen floor, the tools Val had just been trying to reach. He was astonished and momentarily distracted by what he saw.

"Swords!—by all the gods!"

Shifting his grip on Delia's arms, he muttered: "Let's jus' see which ones we got . . ." And bent over, meaning to look closely at the black hilts projecting from the swordbelt.

It was now or never. Val, seeing double, his head and neck aflame with pain, a deadly weakness dragging all his limbs, summoned up what strength he could and hurled himself forward, grappling Brod around the knees.

Brod struck viciously at his assailant, stretching the already injured man out helpless on the floor. But he had to let go of Delia in the process.

In the moment when Brod was busy defending himself from Val, Delia managed to pull one of her hands free. Diving to reach the Swords, she was able to pull Sightblinder from its sheath.

With the same movement of her arm, she threw the weapon as far as she could, so it went flying into a far corner of the hut.

When Brod instinctively released her and went plunging after the Sword, she stuck out a leg and tripped him, so that he came down with a slam that drove the breath out of his body. A moment later she had seized Woundhealer and without hesitation thrust its bright blade straight into her lover's chest.

The Sarge, regaining his feet and lunging forward once more after the tantalizingly available Sword of Stealth, had almost got his fingers on its hilt when the great weight of Valdemar's body, once more fully functional, landed on him from behind. Skidding forward with Val's momentum, both men went crashing out through the old hut's flimsy wall.

Wrestling hand to hand, the two went rolling over and over. Brod's effort to knee his opponent failed. Valdemar's huge arms quivered, straining against muscles every bit as powerful as his own.

Suddenly the Sarge stiffened, looking over Valdemar's shoulder at a terrible male figure that towered above them both. The figure's blue eyes glared, its empty hands were extended in the gesture of a wizard about to loose a blasting curse.

Valdemar saw nothing of this apparition. He only felt Brod's body convulse, and heard him scream out: "Master Wood!" before he retched up blood and died.

Turning, Valdemar beheld only Delia. He saw her in her true form, for she had let go the hilt of Sightblinder, whose blade remained embedded deeply in Brod's heart.

Val, struggling to his feet, recalled once urging Ben to use Wound-healer to save this very man. And Val muttered now: "No. No more. You've had enough chances."

Tethered at a little distance from the hut they found Brod's riding-beast, along with a spare mount saddled and ready. The saddle-bags of both animals contained food and other useful items.

"He said something, didn't he, about having been sent to bring me back?" Delia shuddered.

"It wasn't you they really wanted, love. It was that other woman, Tigris."

"I don't want to hear about her, or think about her."

In less than half an hour the pair, wishing with all their souls to put the horrors of their last few days behind them, were hastening away from the scene of their most recent struggle.

Delia, her spirits risen again with the return and triumph of her lover, began to play with Woundhealer, giggling and marveling at the inability of this sharp Blade to cut her fingers off, or even scratch them.

How different this Sword from the one that had so treacherously hurt Val's fingers earlier!

Watching her perform such tricks gave Val the shivers, and he ordered her to stop. For once in a meek mood, she obeyed without a murmur.

Valdemar noted also, with belated apprehension, that the Sword of

Mercy had only partially, if at all, restored Delia's memory. He supposed that Wood's expunging of her evil experiences, both as perpetrator and victim, would not be construed as an injury.

Somehow, out of renewed spirits and talk of a future that suddenly seemed clear, the topic of marriage came under discussion.

The urge for wedlock came with the greatest intensity upon Valdemar. His sense of propriety, an innate conservatism in matters of society and morals, was really stronger than Delia's.

Delia wondered aloud if she was too young for matrimony, and whether she ought to take such a step without consulting her mother.

"Would that be possible?" her companion asked, vaguely surprised.

"No. No, I don't see how. I don't know if she's still alive."

Valdemar was in a mood to insist on a ceremony. "Otherwise it would be shameful to continue to take advantage of you in this way."

"Is that what you call it? 'Take advantage'? Come, take advantage of me again!"

On the next morning the couple awakened to idyllic sunshine. From the state of the morning sky it seemed likely that, for a change, a whole day might be going to pass without rain.

"Delia?"

"Yes?"

"I think perhaps the most proper thing for us to do is to perform some kind of wedding ceremony ourselves."

Chewing on a grass blade, the young woman thought over this idea. "Yes, we can do that if you like."

Having won his point, the youth still felt it necessary to explain his thoughts and feelings. "Otherwise the difficulty, as I see it, is going to be in finding someone qualified to marry us.

"Even when we get back to my vineyard, there'll really be no one. The nearest village is about a day's walk distant. And I don't know if there's anyone in that village I'd want to perform my wedding ceremony."

"That's too bad." But in fact Delia did not seem very much upset.

Val continued: "A White Temple priest or priestess would be the best, I think. Maybe someday we can get to a White Temple somewhere. I pray to Ardneh sometimes. Actually I pray to Ardneh a great deal. He's not dead like the other gods."

Delia was now listening carefully, wide-eyed and nodding. As far as her companion could tell, she was accepting everything he said as truth. That made him feel the importance of weighing his words carefully.

He added moodily: "I could almost wish that we still had the other

Sword. Wayfinder would show us where to find the right priest or official."

"Is it that important to you, finding someone to say words over us? We
could pretend we still have the Finding-Sword."

Half in jest, half seriously, Valdemar closed his eyes, held out his hands
gripping an invisible hilt, imagining or pretending that he still had the
Sword of Wisdom.

He said: "Sword, if you can do so without keeping me longer from my
vineyard, or putting us in danger—show me the way to someone who
could marry us."

Of course there was really no weight tugging at his hands, no bright
metal to point and give him a direction.

But Delia's fingers were pulling at his sleeve. Opening his eyes, Valdemar discovered that they were no longer alone.

Standing on the other side of the little clearing, regarding them in a
friendly way, was a middle-sized, dark-haired, thirtyish man wearing
boots and practical trousers of pilgrim gray, his upper body covered by a
short white robe which made him look like a White Temple priest on
pilgrimage. He appeared to be unarmed.

Valdemar scrambled to his feet. "Greetings to you, sir. I am Valdemar,
and this is Delia."

The man nodded his head briskly. His eyes were faintly merry. "And
greetings to you, in Ardneh's name. I am . . . the man you see before
you."

"Sir?"

"The truth is that I have taken a certain vow. For a time I may not
speak my real name."

Delia appeared to find this interesting. "A vow to a god? Which one?"

The other shrugged slightly, a deprecating gesture. "A vow to myself,
that's all. You might call me Brother White, if it is easier for you to call
me something."

"Brother White—" Valdemar was suddenly anxious. "Are you a priest
of the White Temple, as your robe suggests?"

The newcomer nodded in acknowledgement. "I am. Among other
things."

"Then . . . Reverend Brother? Would you be willing to perform a
certain ceremony for us, sir?"

"That is what you both want?"

Delia and Val looked at each other, then said together: "It is."

"Then it would please me to be your witness, if you will perform the
ceremony for yourselves."

Valdemar looked again at Delia, then agreed. He was beginning to have the distinct impression that he had known this man somewhere before, but he could not recall where or when.

And then, abruptly, a hint of insight came to Valdemar. He asked: "Sir, do you know the Lady Yambu?"

"I do."

"Then—sir, are you, possibly, he who is called the Emperor? She spoke to me once of such a man, who was once her husband."

"Indeed I am." The answer was very matter-of-fact, neither a boast nor an apology.

Val didn't know exactly what to say next. At last he announced: "Sir— the Blue Temple covets your treasure."

"I'm sure they do." The Emperor smiled, then looked almost wistful for a moment. "But I doubt they know how to get at it."

Delia's thoughts were elsewhere. "If we are to be married," she murmured thoughtfully, "I wish I had a new dress to wear." There had been nothing of the kind in Brod's saddlebags.

"Let me see," said the Emperor. And he bowed to Delia slightly, as if asking her permission for what he was about to do. Then he took her by one hand and turned her, spun her gently, considerately, as if he were the skilled partner of the world's most graceful dancer. "White? Perhaps white would be best. Why, I see nothing in the least wrong with what you are wearing now." And with the spinning, in the time it took young legs to dance a step, her stained, frayed garments changed, became a dress, a gown, of purest ivory.

Val would have expected a White Temple priest presiding at a wedding to read from some kind of a book, but instead the Emperor—or Brother White—simply took each of the young people by the hand, held their hands clasped together in his own, and asked them questions about their commitment to each other.

The girl became very solemn for a time when this rather ordinary-looking man looked at her, and spoke to her and to Valdemar.

The setting was a pleasant place, and, true to the morning's promise, for once it was not raining.

When the ceremony had been concluded, and Valdemar had kissed his bride, he turned to Brother White and said: "Sir, we are young and healthy. We intend to avoid war in the future—so we have no need of either of these Swords that we are carrying. Or, rather, others have greater need of them than we do. And we have had proof, more proof than we needed, that the possession of such treasure can bring disaster as well as healing. So—I want to give them to you."

Brother White listened carefully, and nodded. "A noble gift, and I thank you. And I am proud to accept. Still, others have greater need than I. So my acceptance must have one condition."

"Yes sir?"

"That you carry these Swords, which are now mine, with you a little longer. Hand them over to the next person you meet who appears to be in need of their powers."

Valdemar and Delia nodded.

The Emperor waved them on their way.

Very well pleased to be formally united as man and wife, Delia and Valdemar continued their progress homeward on Brod's pair of riding-beasts—not hurrying now, but not wasting any time. She had noticed, with no great surprise, that as soon as she and her husband were alone again her wedding dress had turned into clothes very much resembling her own garments, but not worn or grimy.

They pressed on. At times when the way ahead still seemed long and difficult, Valdemar reminded his new bride and himself that he had come on foot, in no very great number of days, from his home to this region; and that they therefore ought to have no great trouble walking home again. Especially not with the Sword of Stealth to guard them on their way.

The land around them had become more hospitable, and there were increasing signs of human habitation, and Valdemar had begun to ride with Sightblinder sheathed instead of drawn. Perhaps he had also begun to lose a little of his alertness. He was halfway across a narrow bridge, spanning a small stream, when he raised his eyes to see Ben of Purkinje, armed and mounted, waiting for him on the west bank.

Val slowed his riding-beast, and put a hand to the black hilt at his side.

He hoped devoutly that Delia would know what to do—to stay in concealment where she was, back on the east bank. They had not yet entirely forsaken caution as they traveled.

The bridge was a single great log, carved flat on its upper surface. The brisk stream splashed and gurgled underneath. Speaking a little more loudly than was strictly necessary, Valdemar called out: "Ben. Surprised to meet you here."

The ugly face smiled faintly. "Can't say I'm that surprised to meet you. Matter of fact, a lot of us have been out looking for you—and for a couple of Swords—and for a certain woman—ever since we won the battle."

"I was sure our side had it won. Else I would not have left." Even as Valdemar spoke the words, he wondered if they were strictly true. Urging his mount slowly forward, he halted again when he came close to Ben, who with his riding-beast was almost blocking the west end of the span. Then Val looked around. "Are you alone?"

"I wanted to talk to you about that," Ben said mildly, and reined his mount back slightly from the narrow path, giving Val plenty of room to pass. Val urged his own steed forward. A moment later, just as Val was passing, Ben seized him round the waist, and dragged him from the saddle, gripping him fiercely to keep him from drawing any weapon.

Delia came cantering briskly across the narrow bridge with Sightblinder raised to defend her husband.

At the sound of hoofbeats, Ben looked up; and what he saw momentarily paralyzed him.

Before he could recover, Val had knocked him out.

When Ben came to himself—with the feeling of just having made a magically quick and complete recovery—he found himself sitting beside the little path. Valdemar, a Sword in his huge right hand, was standing looking down at him.

Obviously the couple were packed up and in the act of moving on; the sound of a woman's voice came from somewhere just out of Ben's sight around the next bend of the path, as if she were gently fussing with a couple of riding-beasts.

Ben's own mount was waiting patiently, just beside him.

"Where is she?" Ben leaped to his feet, looking around.

"Who?"

"Ariane. I saw her here . . ." His voice trailed off, as some version of the truth dawned on him.

Valdemar shook his huge head. He threw his weapon to the ground, where metal clashed on metal. "One of the two Swords that we are leaving you is Sightblinder."

"That you are leaving me?" Ben inquired stupidly. Following Val's gesture, he looked down uncomprehendingly. Two magnificent black-hilted blades lay crossed on the ground in front of him, waiting to be picked up.

"Yes," said Valdemar. "We are leaving them with you. Chiefly because of a promise we have made. And one of these Swords, I repeat, is Sightblinder."

"I ought to have expected that."

"Yes . . . do you understand now? Whatever woman you thought you saw before I knocked you out was never actually here."

"Ah."

"Yes. The woman with me is my wife. And we're leaving both Swords with you . . . does the Lady Yambu still live?"

"She does," said Ben slowly. "And the Prince too."

"Good. I hoped Mark was going to survive. Heal them, and heal Mark's Princess."

"I will," said Ben, and let himself sit down again, heavily, in the grass. His legs, so recently touched by the Sword of Healing, were as strong and healthy as they were ever going to be, and yet his sitting down was a collapse. He was going to be all right. He was all right. But some losses even Woundhealer could not restore.

Ariane was still gone. Gone forever.

At a little distance he could hear Valdemar mounting, and then the two animals moving away, accompanied by the voices of their riders. But for some considerable time Ben of Purkinje only sat where the givers of gifts had left him, staring at his magnificent paired Swords.

THE LAST BOOK OF SWORDS:
SHIELDBREAKER'S STORY

1

Hunched in his saddle on the flying demon's back, buffeted by winds of air and magic, Vilkata the Dark King confronted catastrophe with a snarl of defiance. In his left hand Vilkata gripped the magical reins of his monstrous steed, and in his wounded right fist he clutched the black hilt of the naked, god-forged Mindsword, its flashing steel blade stained lightly with his own blood.

The cuts on his right wrist and hand had been inflicted perhaps three minutes ago. After that the Mindsword had been sheathed again, its powers muffled; but when the Dark King had finally succeeded in getting control of the Sword, only a few moments ago, his first act had been to fling the scabbard clear, unleashing all Skulltwister's magic.

Too late.

Even armed and mounted as he was now, the ancient wizard, survivor of a thousand dreadful perils, could not doubt that this time, at last, the doom of utter destruction had overtaken him.

With facial muscles clenched hard around the long-empty sockets of his eyes, the Dark King uttered a tremendous scream, venting all the agony of his soul in a bellowing curse, a malediction as profound as it was impotent, directed at all his enemies, known and unknown, and at the universe itself for spawning them.

The Dark King's enemies were many, and what was happening now gave proof, if any proof were needed, that some of them were very strong.

Around Vilkata, from the quasi-material throats of the two dozen or so flying, shape-changing demons who formed his hideous escort, there rose despairing howls of such pitch and volume as to suggest that the end of the world had come.

He, Vilkata, together with his mount and his entire escort—these now including in their number the mighty demon Akbar, at one time the Dark King's mortal foe—the whole swarm of them, despite the Mindsword's presence, regardless of anything that any and all of them could do, were being swept away, helpless as leaves in a tornado.

* * *

Only moments ago, a mere few heartbeats in the past, the wizard Vilkata had been, as he thought, on the brink of triumph. He had been locked in airborne combat above the torchlit palace of his archfoe, Prince Mark of Tasavalta. And then, in the twinkling of an eye, not only had the Tasavaltan palace passed quite out of the Dark King's sight and reach, but so had the whole night-shrouded city of Sarykam, as well as all of the human enemies and temporary allies by whom Vilkata had been surrounded. It seemed that he had been cut off from the whole world.

And the Dark King knew the cause. It was impossible to avoid the bitter truth, even if he could not understand it. He had heard the incantation of his doom, foolish-sounding but irresistible, shouted by Prince Mark.

An instant after those words had fallen upon the air, the shouts, the clash of metal, the glare of torches, all were gone. Vilkata and his demons had been wrapped up, bundled together as if by hands of divine power, and thrown away. Now blackness and near-emptiness surrounded him and the two dozen hideous, half-material creatures whose loyalty the Mindsword had compelled. They were now encapsulated within an almost featureless void that was pervaded by a sense of movement, caught in helpless hurtling flight at some indeterminable but awesome speed.

They were in rapid motion, certainly. But toward what destination? Speed and destination were both completely out of their control. Gravity, as modified by the flying demons' magic, seemed to come and go in yawning leaps. All sense of direction had been lost; even "up" and "down" no longer seemed to have consistent meaning.

Vilkata understood that his own greatest weakness, as was so often the case among humans, was the mirror image of his strength. The fact was that the Dark King's own skills in magic had long ago led him to depend almost absolutely upon demons. The man was physically blind, by his own hand and choice, and had been so for most of his long life. Only by magically borrowing the vision of a demon was he able to see at all, but ordinarily the vision thus provided was keener than that of any merely human eyes. Not now. Currently his perception of his surroundings was only sufficient to suggest that the tornado of material and non-material energies evoked by Mark was carrying him and his inhuman escort into a strange realm indeed.

The exact nature of this realm, or condition, was obscured by the same forces that enveloped Vilkata and bore him through it. But at least his immediate fate was not to be annihilation, as he had feared at the outset.

Perhaps, he told himself, there even remained a glimmer of hope for ultimate recovery.

Meanwhile, defeat, even if it should prove only temporary, was made all the more bitter by the fact that only moments earlier he, the Dark King, had been, as he thought, so close to final victory. So close to winning, to gathering in the gods' great Swords all for himself! But that chance had now been obliterated. He, who had long played the great game for ultimate authority, was in the grip of forces that held him helpless as an infant. Now, despite the awesome power of the one Sword he still possessed, despite the strength of the demonic mount between his knees and the other terrible monsters flying near at his command—despite all this, disaster.

Still, moment after moment flew by, and he remained alive. The ultimate blow had not yet fallen.

At least he had no fear that the demons droning and murmuring around him now were going to turn against him. No, Vilkata's sense of magic assured him that, even here in this peculiar domain of darkness and of hurtling movement, the Mindsword still retained its power to compel obedience, loyalty, and worship.

Only moments before Mark's curse of banishment took effect, Akbar and Vilkata had been opposed to each other in deadly combat. But then, suddenly, the demon had been deprived of Shieldbreaker, the Sword which had for some time protected him, and almost at the same time the Mindsword had come into Vilkata's hands. Akbar, along with every other thinking being within its radius of operation, had fallen immediately under the domination of the Sword.

Now silence held. And duration, in this strange and shadowy and almost timeless realm, had become difficult to quantify. Now, more than ever, the man could tell that he was dependent upon his demonic escort for his continued survival, his very existence. Compelled by the power of the Mindsword to an uncharacteristic loyalty, they were magically supplying him with air to breathe, as well as eyes to see with. It was as if the sealed-off space which enclosed Vilkata and his creatures during their helpless flight had quickly come to lack any atmosphere of its own.

Yes, the calculation of time was certainly a problem in this state. . . . More and more the wizard became convinced that time here—wherever "here" might be—was evolving very strangely. Had this enforced passage endured for a day, an hour, a month, a year? Vilkata had lost all confidence in his ability to tell.

* * *

Whatever might have been the correct objective reckoning of time, an epoch at length arrived when one of the demons, murmuring deferentially as it hovered near its worshipped master, informed him that it had fabricated for his priceless Sword a new sheath (the original was irretrievably lost), of some leathery material obtained from the gods knew where. In this sheath he could put his priceless Sword to rest while he tried to heal his injured hand. That was all right; the Dark King knew from experience that the Mindsword need not be held unsheathed continuously to maintain its compulsion, once that influence had been established.

Sword sheathed, he was able at last, with a sigh of relief, to let go the reins of the huge magical creature he was still riding. Let go, for the time being, and try to get some rest. In truth he was very weary. At a murmured command from him the saddle he had been sitting in reshaped itself to suit his comfort, becoming something like a bed or hammock. The demon-beast he had been riding reshaped itself as well, a trick they could do practically at will; then it vanished for the time being from his ken. Still it continued to re-orient itself as necessary, providing for its worshipped master some semblance of consistency regarding "up" and "down."

For many, many years the Dark King had had no eyes to close; but now he did the trick of magic that allowed him to disconnect his borrowed vision. With sight now gone, he could still hear and feel his faithful demons around him.

Ever since disaster struck he had drawn some measure of comfort from the fact that he certainly was not going unaccompanied into the peculiar night which had so totally engulfed him. His erstwhile enemy, the mighty Akbar, was drifting near him now, and the Dark King with only a minimum of effort, performing an act magically analogous to slitting his eyelids open, was able to see, through Akbar's inhuman perception, his own physical body: albino white of skin and hair, tall and strong and ageless. And currently somewhat damaged.

The demon Akbar, doubtless taking note of this activity, commented sadly and unnecessarily that its master had been wounded. Vilkata's right arm and hand had by now ceased to bleed, but were still somewhat painful, gashed from an earlier accidental contact with the Mindsword, the Blade of Glory. This particular weapon was known, among other things, for the ugliness, the resistance to treatment, of the physical wounds it could inflict.

"See what you can do in the way of healing me," the magician ordered brusquely. He held up his right hand, on which all of the blood was not yet dry.

"Yes, Master."

The damned monsters could probably do some good if they tried, Vilkata thought. Though in the ordinary course of events the healing of any living thing, especially a human, would certainly be among the least likely actions to be expected of any demon.

Once before, years ago, the Dark King had enjoyed an extended possession of the Mindsword. When in that epoch he had carried the weapon into battle, his demonic vision had shown it to him as a pillar of billowing flame long as a spear, with his own face glowing amid the perfect whiteness of the flame. And so the weapon appeared to him now.

Hand resting uneasily on the hilt of his newly resheathed Sword, he totally blanked out his vision once again and endeavored to rest. But anger and resentment prevented anything like complete relaxation.

And exactly what was it that had mobilized this impersonal and overwhelming force against Vilkata? Almost nothing, or so, in his present state of brooding helpless rage, it seemed to him.

No more than a few words of incantation cried out by his archenemy, Prince Mark.

Such was the mysterious power against demons, and against those who depended upon demons, enjoyed by Mark, the Emperor's son.

When the Dark King decided that he had rested enough, and reclaimed his demonic vision, there was really almost nothing to be seen. This bizarre state of darkness and movement which had been imposed upon Vilkata and his escort by some enigmatic, overwhelming power, this rushing passage into an incomprehensible distance, protracted itself for what he began to find, subjectively, to be a very long time indeed. It seemed to him that he endured an immeasurable epoch, divorced from any objective standard of duration.

Little more in the way of deliberate, articulate communication passed between the man and the members of his demonic escort while the journey lasted. Vilkata had begun to fear that this condition might prove to be eternal, when at last hints of change broke the monotony. A murmuring developed among the demons. Something like a normal flow of time seemed to resume, and presently demons and man alike were able to sense that the darkness and the sense of rushing movement were also coming to an end.

And now, Vilkata realized with mingled relief and apprehension, the compelled journey had at last concluded. The sense of encapsulation persisted for the moment; but seeming weightlessness had been supplanted by gentle gravity. Once more "up" and "down" had become perfectly consistent—though the magician retained the odd impression that his body was now considerably lighter than it had been.

Now finally the sense of encapsulation was fading. Man and demons were free to move about. For the first time since the Prince had cursed him, Vilkata could feel a solid surface under his booted feet, a surface that felt like sandy soil.

Issuing crisp orders, making sure his compulsively loyal escort were deployed as a bodyguard ranked closely about his own person, Vilkata magically grafted the vision of first one of his enslaved creatures and then another to his own mind, in hopes that at least one of their viewpoints would be able to provide him with useful information.

Having thus done his best to transcend the handicap of his own empty eye sockets, the Dark King looked about him warily.

He was standing on a dusty, heavily cratered, windless, airless plain—he could breathe, he sensed, only because his demons were loyally providing him with air. The Sun glared, with abnormal brilliance, out of a black sky. The temperature of his surroundings was extremely high, well past the point of human endurance, had he not been magically protected.

Vilkata's first impression of this environment was that it was a hellish place indeed to which the Emperor's son had exiled him. This land, this airless space, were virtually as dead as the encapsulation he had endured on the long journey. This place was breathless and silent, in fact altogether lifeless, to a degree that the Dark King had never before encountered or even imagined.

Now, beyond the foreground of dusty, almost level plain, he could perceive hills of assorted sizes, rounded and smoothly eroded but harshly cratered. The farthest of these elevations marked out a sharp horizon under the clear but dark sky, which was strewn with unlikely numbers of hard, unwinking stars. Already, as the last traces of encapsulation disappeared, there were many stars to be seen, and more were steadily becoming visible.

In the middle distance of Vilkata's field of view were clustered a dozen or so strange buildings. These were unmistakably relics of the Old World, structures fabricated of unknown crystalline and metallic materials, the basic dome shape elaborated in incomprehensible variations. Certainly no human skills available in Vilkata's world could have created anything like them. Some were no bigger than peasants' huts, others the size of manor houses.

The inventions of the Old World were not completely foreign to the Dark King, whose education had not been restricted to matters of state-craft and magic. Like every serious scholar, he had read how the arrogant humans of that long-gone era, armed with their mysterious *technology,* had admitted no limits to their ambition—and yet had been overtaken by destruction all the same.

Issuing orders to his demons in a steady voice, Vilkata sent a couple of them ahead to scout among the buildings. In less than a minute the pair were back, saying they could detect no danger. Irritated by what he considered their casual attitude, he told them to go and look again, to make absolutely sure.

But despite his irritation the Dark King had been reassured, and in his impatience he did not wait for his scouts' second report. Hand ready on the Sword hilt at his side, he started to walk toward the apparently deserted settlement. As soon as he began to walk, new strangeness almost overcame him; his strides on this ground were awkward and bouncing, almost a slow bounding, as if his body had indeed somehow been deprived of most of its weight.

Before he had covered half the distance to the nearest of the strange, domed, half-crystalline structures, his pair of scouts, who could move with the speed of quasi-material beings, were at his side again. Still the two demons had discovered no clear and present danger. But they were obviously excited and worried by things they had just observed, babbling to their Master about Old World *technology* beyond anything that they had ever seen before. Below the visible settlement there stretched extensive underground passages and rooms, many of them still in a good state of preservation; and in some of these there appeared to be wonders indeed.

The Dark King brushed aside talk of Old World things; he simply was not interested. "And people? Is this place inhabited?"

"Not as far as we can tell, Master. There has been no one, I think, for a very long time indeed."

Vilkata grumbled some more at the excited creatures and kept on walking. It was not that he had any wish to explore this alien land, where so much strangeness, so much—*technology*—was going to make it difficult to concentrate on the familiar and important things of magic. But the Dark King wanted to learn where he was as quickly as possible because he was eager to reassure himself regarding his chances of returning to more familiar regions without inordinate delay. Only when he had done that would it be possible to get on with his own business. And he had plenty of vital business demanding his attention: first, of course, glorious revenge, and, when the lust for revenge was stated, a return to the methodical accumulation of power.

Walking toward the Old World buildings with steps which were still mystically light and springy (even though not magically assisted), over a crunchy soil, the Dark King put the question of location to another of his demonic servants. Instinctively he chose for this purpose the demon who might be expected to be most knowledgeable and capable, the Mind-sword's most eminent recent convert, Akbar himself.

"Where in the world are we, Akbar? Tell me, you cloud of slime, are we still on the same continent as Tasavalta and Sarykam?"

Akbar now assumed in Vilkata's perception the shape of a sturdy, reliable manservant who walked beside him, crude boots crunching in the soil. In apologetic tones the manservant informed the Master that the journey they had just concluded had evidently been indirect as well as protracted. They had been helplessly following for approximately two earthly years a long, wandering course through airless space. Akbar, in his usual smooth, oily fashion, did his best to take credit for making the experience as relatively comfortable as it had been for the human wizard.

But Vilkata, staring incredulously at his informant, was shocked. Outraged! Two years, wasted in confinement, as surely as if he had been clapped into a dungeon!

The Dark King snarled at his faithful demon, sending the manservant image cowering back in fear and disappointment. A demon could ordinarily take any shape it chose, within broad limits, and Akbar's likeness was now abruptly transformed into that of a young woman. Her body, voluptuous and nearly nude, minced along on delicate bare feet beside Vilkata, moving hesitantly and awkwardly, as if she were on the verge of darting away to take shelter behind one of the boulders occasionally dotting the landscape. The look on the young woman's nearly perfect face confirmed the impression of her utter helplessness and fear. In fact, her countenance reminded Vilkata strongly of a young servant girl whose name he had forgotten—it was years since he had amused himself for an evening by torturing her to death, but he still retained fond memories of the experience.

At the moment, the adoption of this particular image by the demon struck the Dark King as disgustingly stupid. Akbar could be that way at times—as though he thought his Master wanted or needed distraction, when his true need was to concentrate intensely on his problems!

Akbar, as Vilkata thought to himself, had always been one of the most cowardly and self-effacing of demons, though by no means one of the least powerful. The race were hardly noted for their bravery; but always this one had preferred to avoid even the slightest risk of death or punishment, whenever possible using other creatures—human, animal, or demonic—to attain his ends.

But right now the wizard had more important problems demanding his attention than trying to fathom the depths of a demon's character—if one could attribute such a quality as character to any member of the race. His physical environment was the first thing he had to understand. Where exactly was he, and in what kind of place? Here the pervasive ascendancy of forces other than magic made him uneasy.

He paused in his springy walk toward the enigmatic buildings. His demonic escort stopped as well, and waited, droning and half visible, in the space around his head. He was close enough now to the Old World structures to see that many of them were ruined. Whatever information might be discoverable among them could wait. Just now, with the utter alienness of his surroundings impressing itself upon him with ever-increasing force, he wanted a simple answer to a simple question: Which way was home, and how far?

Distractedly, Vilkata ran trembling fingers through his white beard, which—as he just noticed for the first time—had indeed grown long during the involuntary voyage just completed. Staring around him at the strange hills, he once more demanded the clear answer he had not yet been given.

"And where have our coerced wanderings brought us? What is this place?"

The cringing image of the young woman, becoming suddenly even more attractive, looked up brightly and edged closer. Her eyes turned bright and hopeful as she replied: "Sire, we are now standing on the Moon, upon that portion of her surface perpetually most distant from the Earth."

2

THE demon who had pronounced the shattering words, together with all his colleagues, peered in anxious silence at his Master, concerned to see what effect this news might have upon him.

Vilkata, stunned by the announcement, said nothing for a few moments. It was impossible to hear such an unprecedented claim without doubting it. Yet the unearthly strangeness of the environment, impressing itself upon him more intensely with every moment, immediately undermined his doubts. And the Dark King reminded himself again that the Mindsword compelled perfect loyalty; whatever his demons' natural inclination, they would not, could not, lie to him. Not unless they deemed that their Master's best interests would be served by such deception— and that condition hardly seemed likely to apply in the present situation.

Was it conceivable that a demon could be mistaken in such a matter? No, not likely either.

Seeking to establish beyond all doubt the truth of his situation, and wanting the best advice he could obtain on what to do about it, the Dark King summoned the whole number of his faithful demonic horde close about him. There were about two dozen of them in all, at the moment assuming a variety of human and almost-human shapes. Though Vilkata recognized them all individually, he had never taken a count of their exact number.

One reason for this summoning was that he did not want any of the demons straying for any dangerous length of time beyond the physical distance at which the Mindsword's influence would, in time, begin to fade.

When he was sure he had the full attention of each member of his escort, he demanded proof of the incredible statement one of their number had just made. Characteristically, he phrased the request in the form of an accusation.

"We are on the *Moon?* Do you really expect me to believe *that?*"

Judging by the expressions on the faces of his slaves and guardians, such belief was indeed what they, in their current state of enforced loyalty, had expected. The angry tone of their Master's question disturbed them.

"What proof can you offer?" the Dark King demanded.

If he had expected Akbar and the others to be perplexed by this demand, he was mistaken. To prove to their choleric Master as clearly as possible that they spoke the truth, they lifted him gently and carried him at arrow-speed over the rolling hills of the peculiar landscape, directly away from the clustered Old World domes. When his bearers put him down a minute later, the Dark King found himself gazing by means of his borrowed vision at an almost recognizable Earth, just risen straight ahead of him above the sharply defined and not-too-distant horizon.

The great orb, vastly larger than the Moon as seen from Earth, and nearly full, was now hanging motionless among the crowded stars, for all the world like some blue-white Moon, monstrously swollen.

There was half a minute of silence before the Dark King, in a changed voice, murmured: "That is . . . what I think it is?"

"Indeed, Master."

As he stared at his native planet, Vilkata's magically augmented vision was able to descry, beneath the white film of distant clouds, the shape of continents and oceans. The sight was finally convincing.

Suddenly his homeworld, so eminently recognizable, also looked so *close,* almost within reach. Vilkata wanted to reach up and pluck blue Earth from black sky, crush all the juices from the planet in his grip.

Impulsively he demanded: "How long will it take us to get back there? Surely not a matter of years again? Such delay would be unendurable!"

Akbar, speaking with a fanatic's vehemence, and quickly supported by a chorus of his lesser colleagues, assured his Master that they would find a way to make the homeward leg of their journey infinitely faster.

"Never years, Master!"

"Never!"

Vilkata glared at them all. "Months, then? That would be almost as bad. Assure me that the return trip to our own world will not be prolonged over months."

Akbar now turned supremely smooth and reassuring. "Days only, Master, I am sure. Never more than days."

"How are we to travel? I have the feeling that this place is still connected to the Old World, that it does not support magic as well as it might. *Technology* . . ."

"Yet magic here works well enough for your purposes, Master, for here *we* are. As for getting home, I can see already that there are several ways. We will soon determine the swiftest and most secure," the demon promised.

"How?" Vilkata's voice, demanding particulars, grew louder, threatening. He waved the glowing torch-vision of his Sword. Even before the lengthy voyage just concluded, he had flown uncounted times on demons' backs, and was very familiar with the process. The idea of deliberately setting out to travel from the Moon to the Earth by such means was unsettling, whatever magical protection might be provided.

"We will discover the best way," Akbar assured him vaguely. The demon, evidently sensing that his Master considered the maidenly form inappropriate just now, had taken that of a stout male warrior. "I suggest we begin, great Master, with a thorough investigation of those buildings we had sighted."

"Be it so."

Again Vilkata was lifted gently by his guardians, and in moments they were all back at the abandoned Old World settlement—if that was the right word for this collection of enigmatic and apparently deserted structures. As they flew above the pockmarked surface, the Earth once more slipped back below the strangely foreshortened lunar horizon.

With the complete dissipation of the encapsulating force, whatever it had been, which had confined the man and demons together through their outward voyage, the demons' vision had dramatically improved, as had that of the wizard who shared their perceptions. Now a truly unreasonable number of stars were crowding the dark sky. Standing out in the display were a pair of the brighter planets, the latter familiar to Vilkata from his long-ago studies in astrology. And always there was the mercilessly glaring Sun, which so far had shown little inclination to move from the place low in the sky where the Dark King had first seen it.

Flying, he was able to observe more clusters of human construction in the distance. Whatever the true nature of this place, whatever its true location (he still clung fiercely to an atom of doubt about being on the Moon—he did not *want* to be there!), it was certainly marked, in scattered locations, with other clustered, abandoned settlements, the ruins of strange buildings and devices.

Vilkata had learned the fact in his studies long ago—had learned but until now had never totally believed—that the arrogant humans of the Old World had indeed, even without the benefit of any magic at all, colonized the Moon.

One of the first things he had observed upon his arrival here was that the landscape was heavily cratered, pocked and blasted with marks as of violent impacts or explosions. These concavities came in all sizes, from kilometers in diameter—all distances here were hard for a stranger to estimate by sight, and Vilkata thought that ordinary human vision would have done no better than his—down to only centimeters. Some of these scars, whatever their provenance, overlay older craters and were as fresh looking as if they had been formed only yesterday. In depth and width and conformation these craters seemed to testify to titanic explosions, waves of heat which had slagged and melted native rock and buildings alike.

Directing his demonic guardians to put him down again in the middle of the first cluster of Old World constructions they had observed, the Dark King could see that many or most of the house-sized domes were more than half destroyed, looking empty and airless as the surrounding landscape.

Hand on his Sword hilt, moving again with enforced slow springy strides, Vilkata at last stepped warily in through one of the fractured walls, entering one of the broken, glassy shells. The tiled floor, looking quite ordinary, was by far the most familiar thing in sight. Now at last he was able to see enough details to convince himself completely that these buildings were the work of the legendary folk of the Old World, constructed with the aid of all their mysterious technology. Indoors and outdoors the place was littered thickly with the leavings of that antique race of humanity, the piled debris of their colossal failure. Even as the tracks of their booted human feet remained here and there visible in the crunchy soil around the buildings, evidently preserved neither by technology nor magic, but only by the unearthly nature of this environment.

The Old World culture of technology, Vilkata knew, had died some fifty thousand Earthly years ago.

In response to mumbled orders from the increasingly tired and bewildered wizard, his escort soon located for him, in one of the better-preserved ruins, a real bed, solid furniture upon a solid floor. They filled his vision with bright, cheerful light, supplied his new quarters with air, and found for him, miraculously preserved by more Old World technology, wine to drink and real food to eat. A volume of comfortable living space the size of a small house was magically sealed off.

Once a secure and comfortable physical environment had been provided for their Master, half a dozen demons, borrowing the shapes of young and beautiful humans of both sexes, came crowding together on his bed to tempt him with their bodies. He considered this display thoughtfully for a few moments, then snarled at its creators. Waving the naked, flaring Mindsword at them, he bade them get out of his sight, ordered them on pain of destruction to concentrate their efforts upon vigilantly standing guard.

When, about eight hours later, Vilkata awakened from the first real sleep he had enjoyed since his banishment—his first in two years, if Akbar was right about the time—with the hilt of the sheathed Mindsword still gripped in his long-since healed right hand, he felt considerably better. The Dark King was once more in command of himself, and ready to resume control over his own destiny.

A good thing, too, that he felt rested. Because within a few minutes of his awakening his demons came to inform him of certain unsettling discoveries they had made while he slept—there were ominous hints from beneath the lunar surface of a whole domain of ongoing mysterious activity seemingly not native to the Moon. The centerpiece of this phenomenon seemed to be a certain very ancient but still active individual presence, no more than a hundred kilometers away.

At the moment when his demons brought this news, the Dark King was standing before a mirror of magic which presented him with a demonic vision of his own eyeless countenance. He paused in the act of magically depilating his two-year beard.

"What sort of activity and presence?" he demanded. "What are you talking about?"

The demon-image of a voluptuous woman—this time one of Akbar's lesser colleagues was acting as spokesman—observed him warily. "Great Lord, it is certainly connected with the Old World, and yet it is not entirely of that."

" 'It'? What? What kind of information is that? Either tell me something definite and meaningful, or— or—"

Again it was Akbar's turn to speak. He loomed in insubstantial form, a talking cloud. "Great Lord, it is very hard to say exactly *what* it is that we have discovered. There is much *technology,* as one might expect in any Old World settlement, and besides that there is much that is alive."

"Alive? Where? What is alive?"

"As to where, Sire, some kind of life exists here under the surface, in places not readily accessible to our examination. We cannot be more specific at the moment because there are barriers, magical and otherwise, to our close approach. We might assault those barriers successfully. Whether we might gain or discover anything that would be worth the cost . . ."

The Dark King thought. "Human life? You told me earlier that there was none."

Akbar's cloud shape contracted, suggesting a humble bow. "To our infinite shame, Tremendous Master, we may have been mistaken. What kind of life it is is hard to say without obtaining a closer look."

"Dangerous to us? To me?"

"I think not, Sire. Rather such life as exists here seems—quiescent. Of course, what might happen if we probe harder in our investigations . . ." Akbar gave the image of a shrug.

"You are babbling," Vilkata accused his faithful slave. Then he took thought before he added: "I do not intend much exploring here. I suppose you have already carried out some local investigation, or you would not have detected this supposed life."

"A rather thorough probing of our surroundings within a kilometer or two seemed only prudent, Master."

The Dark King had to admit as much. "What else have you found? But never mind, it's plain I must look the situation over for myself. You can tell me of your discoveries while I walk."

An hour after he had awakened, the man, holding the Mindsword drawn, was standing in a tunnel several meters below the lunar surface, at the very rim of the territory his demons had already thoroughly explored.

Within a few hundred meters of the room where he had rested ran at least half a dozen underground tunnels, all lighted at convenient intervals with undying globes or panels of Old World radiance. One of these passages, bending deeper underground than others, seemed to lead on to the heart of the domain of mystery, the locus of the individual presence which, according to his demons, might or might not be alive.

Vilkata, now probing alertly with his own magical sensibilities, soon perceived certain attributes of the thing his advisers had been struggling to describe. Great but ambiguous power in repose. *Some* kind of life. And, as seemed inevitable in Old World matters, *technology*.

The Dark King had to agree with his servants. The evidence so far, he thought, the fine emanations picked up by his demons and himself, indicated that somewhere in the deeper passages there dwelt an intellect, an awareness of some kind, neither human nor demonic—and certainly not bestial.

"We think it is asleep, great Master," a minor demon offered timidly.

" 'It'? What do you mean?" But the Dark King did not really expect an answer to the question.

In his own estimation he was being patient. He yearned—for no partic-ular reason—to beat and punish his slaves, but sensed that in this case such treatment would only interfere with their genuine efforts to be help-ful.

Acting on impulse, he advanced again.

Within a hundred paces he came to a halt, standing before a sign carved high on a wall.

This was an array of large, clearly marked symbols in a type of Old World script that neither he nor his inhuman companions, all of whom possessed several languages, could begin to read. The notice—he esti-mated no more than a score of words—was cut into the wall with Old World precision, just above the place where the passage Vilkata was following changed direction and turned sharply downward.

"What do the symbols mean?" To Vilkata's thinking they had an ur-gent, imperious look about them.

"Master, we regret that none of us, in our abysmal ignorance, possess the capability of reading them. Certainly they are an Old World script."

"I can see that, fool!"

Considering his situation, the Dark King, somewhat to his own sur-prise, now felt a certain perverse temptation to continue along the de-scending passage, to explore this world much more thoroughly. But it was only a faint craving and easy to resist. Instead of yielding he ordered a retreat.

On the way back to his comfortable quarters, trudging with springy steps through one branch of tunnel after another, he forbade his slaves to go digging any further after such potentially dangerous mysteries; what he really wanted was to get back to Earth, and his servants should all concentrate their efforts to that end.

As for the presence slumbering beneath the lunar surface, Vilkata approved the arrangement Akbar had already made—three demons posted as sentries round the suspicious area, lest the nature or attitude of what was there should undergo a sudden change.

Whatever the true nature of the mysterious underground lunar entity, the Dark King thought it well to be wary of it. It could not be *greater* than Sword-power, he supposed—he believed that no force could be—but if it was inanimate he could not expect it to be subject to the Mind-sword's control.

Meanwhile his demons had turned their energies to the problem of getting their Master safely home. Since the Old World folk had obviously come here in substantial numbers without benefit of magic—the lack of

any serious power of enchantment was really what defined the Old World
—it followed that they must have used *technology* for the purpose, and
some of their machines of transportation, like those of other types, might
still exist.

The researches of Akbar and his colleagues in the field of transportation had not made much headway before they were interrupted by yet
another discovery. This, too, was of something underground, but at a
distance of a hundred kilometers or more from the first. Here again was
life, of a kind much more familiar to Vilkata and his demons, and which
seemed to have nothing directly to do with that earlier mystery.

Cautiously responding to loud inhuman cries, demands for rescue audible on both psychic and physical wavelengths, the Dark King's demons
notified their Master before taking any other action. Vilkata had himself
transported to the site, and ordered further exploration. His demons
cracked rock and cleared it away, and he himself dissolved binding spells
of enormous power.

The passage through solid lunar rock, along which the Dark King and
his faithful slaves so tenaciously fought and forced their way, ended in a
great hollow shell of a chamber, like the interior of a glassy ball ten
meters in diameter, physically and magically sealed away from the outside world. Filling this chamber and reverberating through the nearby
rock, almost deafening the human explorer, was the nerve-shattering
droning, tormented screaming of the nearly immortal beings who were
confined within.

Demons, of course. A swarm, a score of them at least, a horde whose
existence the Dark King had never suspected until now, had been here
mercilessly imprisoned.

Nearing the place by means of a freshly blasted tunnel, Vilkata approached with the Mindsword drawn this fearsome chamber inside a
convoluted, crystallized and enchanted mass of lunar rock. Breaking his
way into the howling kennel, then entering it boldly, the Dark King
shouted to silence the evil creatures who were bound within, and with the
same shout proclaimed to them that they were now his slaves.

Unfamiliar though these captive demons were to him as individuals,
Vilkata immediately found communication with them easy enough. They
spoke, in addition to several archaic human tongues, the basic, common
demonic language in which he was well versed. In moments he had
learned their names, which, like their identities, were utterly unfamiliar
to him.

The largest of these newly-discovered beings, named Arridu, at once assumed the role of spokesman. Arridu, who gave the impression of being much stronger than even Akbar, went so far as to describe himself as equal in power to Orcus of ancient legend, and Vilkata, awed despite himself, was not sure that the fiend before him was exaggerating.

Then the human wizard, assisted by Akbar, set about finding the proper modes of magic with which to free Arridu and his colleagues from their present bondage. The mere forcing of a tunnel into their prison was not going to suffice.

To say the locks and keys and barriers of enchantment were stubborn was to understate the case. But the Dark King was able to work on them without being himself confined, and he was one of the premier magicians of the world. Some hours of concentrated labor were required, but in the end his success was assured.

Vilkata was greatly impressed by this imprisoning, and not at all sure that he could have managed anything of the kind himself. Who, he demanded to know, had entrapped them thus?

The Dark King was at first amazed when Arridu and the demons with him insisted that they did not know their conqueror. But then Vilkata realized that the partial destruction of these demons' memories must have been part of their punishment, perhaps necessary to keep them so long confined.

Arridu, when pressed, related some disconnected scenes, about all he could remember, from the early years of his existence—or at least his version of events, which, under the Mindsword's compulsion, might be assumed to be close to what he actually believed, if not really the truth. But the fragmented memories were of little help. All that could be said with certainty was that some thousands of years ago, how many thousands the speaker could no longer tell, he and a handful of his most evil colleagues had been sealed by overwhelming magic—or by some other energy having the effect of magic—into this sublunarian vault, or crypt.

Questioned by Vilkata regarding the strange underground domain of non-demonic life and technology which lay approximately a hundred kilometers from the site of their confinement, the newly-freed demons were unable to give him much, if any, information.

Next Vilkata demanded of them: "Tell me, all of you, where are your lives?" Almost without exception among demons, it was the rule for the life, the vulnerability, to be concealed in some ordinary physical object, generally innocuous in itself, often at a considerable distance from the creature's manifest presence.

Akbar and his colleagues would have eagerly surrendered to the Dark

King their life-objects as well as their names—but, in fact, the formerly imprisoned demons did not know where their own lives were.

The Dark King at length had to admit the truth of this surprising development—he supposed it only natural that if the creatures' gaolers had known where their lives were hidden, they would have killed them.

But even without the extra advantage which would have been offered by possession of the life-objects, these demons were now the Dark King's slaves. Vilkata's eyes gleamed with ambition, with dreams of revenge and conquest, when he assessed the strength of the force over which the Mindsword had now given him absolute authority.

Arridu and his colleagues would have been disappointed that their deliverer should be a mere human, and that this mere human seemed quite capable of managing them—they would have been so disappointed, even dismayed, had not the Mindsword shown them their deliverer as the incomparable being that he was. From the moment the Dark King, with Skulltwister drawn, approached their place of confinement, their age-long despair had given way to elation, to transcendent joy. It was the one perfect being in the Universe who had come to make them his servants and worshippers!

Akbar chose a moment when all of the Dark King's new servants were elsewhere to approach his Master with a warning. Compelled by the Sword into genuine concern for Vilkata's welfare, Akbar warned the man that loosing a demon of Arridu's power and malignancy upon the world, no matter under what conditions of magical compulsion, could not but be fraught with peril.

"Tut. My Sword controls him, does it not? Even as it compels you, and the others."

"But I like it not, Master. I like it not."

And Akbar, who until now had rightfully considered himself the pre-eminent demon in the Dark King's service, sulked a little in jealousy. But under the Mindsword's influence even Akbar was compelled to rejoice at any development that really augmented Vilkata's power.

Within minutes after the lunar demons had been released, the imperfect memory of one of the long-term residents contributed to an important find:

Here was a large underground chamber filled with Old World devices intended to be used for interplanetary transportation.

Leading Vilkata along an underground passage the man had not

walked before, Arridu and his contemporaries soon revealed to their
Master the collection of spacecraft they had discovered.

A vast underground chamber contained a great number and variety of
units, obviously Old World machines, the smallest as large as a small
house. Investigation disclosed more than one underground hangar, occupied by ranks of bubble-type devices, with all the appropriate launching
and support and control equipment.

Vilkata at first resisted the idea that these devices could have been
meant to fly—there were not even rudimentary wings, such as birds,
reptiles, and griffins sported, and even demons wore, at least in his demonic vision, when they soared into the air. These works of technology
appeared almost magical in their outward simplicity: rounded, almost
spherical things of glass and metal, interiors furnished with seats and
couches of various styles, showing that the things were indeed intended
for human occupation. The richness and variety of interior furnishings
indicated strongly that they were definitely not meant as mere cells for
confinement.

Over the course of the next few hours or days—the man tended to lose
track of days because, compounding the unearthly nature of this world,
there was only a very gradual shifting of the position of the Sun against
the pattern of stars in the black sky—some demons cautiously experimented with these spacecraft.

Others ransacked certain Old World stores surviving in the deep caves.
There the faithful, jealous creatures discovered supplies of air, and of
preserved food and drink, more than sufficient to last their master comfortably through the return journey. This time, he warned them, he
meant to retain his full awareness and alertness.

In moments when Vilkata allowed himself to be distracted from his
mission of getting home, he again curiously questioned the old lunar
demons, seeking to learn what they could tell him of the events leading
to their imprisonment.

But all their most important memories were permanently gone. At
certain moments some of the creatures spoke with chilling familiarity of
the Old World, as though perhaps it was something they had seen for
themselves, and of Ardneh and Orcus, of whom they must have heard
much; but as for the mysterious regions, the other life possibly existing
on the Moon, they could only warn their beloved new Master to stay
clear. These warnings only reinforced his own inclinations.

Having learned what little his new recruits could tell him that seemed of any practical value, Vilkata, giving his most savage imitation of politeness, invited new demonic recruits and old servants alike to join him in his conquest of the Earth, which had been delayed, but not, he was now sure, prevented.

His formal invitation was, of course, accepted enthusiastically. Not that his hearers had any choice, being as tightly bound as ever to loyalty under the Mindsword's influence.

Knowing as much about demons as he did, the Dark King felt certain that, even apart from their enforced loyalty, his escorts were as spontaneously glad as he was to be returning to the Earth, to a place where they would once more be creatures of great size and importance.

Within an hour after the command had been given, his protectors—mighty Arridu now claiming priority among them—announced that they were ready to bear him, and his protective bubble of atmosphere, on the flight. Either magically or depending almost totally upon the powers of the Old World craft.

The Dark King's return flight was already under way—the hurtling glass-and-metal sphere escorted by quasi-material demons, some inside the craft and some outside, the huge blue roundness of the Earth dominating the black sky ahead—before one of the escorting creatures inquired: "And whereabouts on Earth, Master, are we to land?"

"What better place than the very spot from which we left? Conduct me back to the palace at Sarykam! I have unfinished business with that proud Prince who hateth demons. And business with his people too."

The Old World spacecraft was satisfactorily comfortable, much more so than the limbo-like conditions of the outward voyage. Shortly after leaving the Moon, Vilkata began to consider seriously at what hour he wanted to arrive at Mark's palace. In the middle of the night? Or just before dawn? That was always a favorite hour for a surprise attack. But it was more important, he soon decided, to time his arrival at Sarykam for a day and an hour when he could be sure that Mark himself was elsewhere—he was not pleased by the prospect of being immediately whirled away into another two years' exile.

Therefore, all his brave speech and muttered vows to the contrary notwithstanding, the Dark King did not really want to fly directly to the palace. No, it would be vastly preferable to land somewhere nearby—in the ocean, possibly, or along the rocky Tasavaltan shore—somewhere where he could hide his Old World flying device until he could discover how things might have changed in Sarykam in two years, and just where Prince Mark was now.

"We will discover a good place, sire."

Ought he to send a demon ahead to scout? That was a decision requiring careful consideration. If he did so, he would have to take the chance that the thing might well be tempted to turn against him when it had been away from his Sword for some hours at a distance of hundreds or thousands of kilometers.

Still, he had controlled demons before he had the Sword, and expected he could do so even if deprived of Skulltwister's advantages.

Vilkata decided to send at least one scout ahead, and perhaps several more after the first; to begin with, he wanted to select one of the demons whose lives he already carried with him. He had in mind a creature who on occasion had served him as his eyes, whose life-object, a small mirror, rode securely in the Dark King's pocket, and whose loyalty the man felt confident he could compel even without depending on the Mindsword's power.

What better choice than Akbar himself?

3

NEAR the middle of one of the shortest nights of early summer, a single bright light, an Old World lamp of cool and eerie brilliance, burned in one of the deepest and most heavily guarded rooms of the central armory below the palace at Sarykam. A brace of fascinated moths were circling the round lamp of strange, smooth glass and metal in its mounting on an oak beam over a workbench. The lamp showed no flame and required no external source of power, but cast superb illumination, balm for tired eyes, upon the bench, the surrounding walls of white-washed stone, and the faces of the two people present.

One of these was Prince Mark's fourteen-year-old son, Stephen, who had been hard at work for half a day and half a night upon a certain private project; the other was an elderly man called Bazas, one of the senior armorers, who had volunteered to stand by and give advice. The young Prince was making it a point of honor to do all the actual labor on this particular job with his own hands.

The task Stephen had set for himself was that of crafting some piece of armor (whether a breastplate or a shield was still to be determined) from dragons' scales. And the project was private, more accurately semi-secret, because the product was intended as a gift for Stephen's father, on the occasion of Prince Mark's fortieth birthday.

Prince Mark was currently absent from the palace, not expected back for two or three days, when he would return in time for the semi-official birthday celebration. At the moment Mark was some sixty kilometers from Sarykam, having spent the last several days in a lightly populated region of his compact realm. Mark and Princess Kristin had gone there, with a small military escort, to help some citizens who had recently suffered from a local plague of dragons. The scales Stephen was working with were a byproduct of the relief expedition.

From the five Swords available in the Tasavaltan armory at the time of his departure, Stephen's father had chosen to carry with him only two—the harmless Woundhealer and the ruthlessly efficient Dragonslicer. The latter Sword had been returned to the armory, under guard, as soon as the need for it in the countryside had passed.

For more than a year now the land of Tasavalta had been at peace, save for the occasional natural violence of dragon-incursion, or of earth-quake—thank Ardneh, there had been only minor temblors lately.

Inside the palace, peace reigned with special felicity. These days the royal couple, Stephen's parents, were doting on each other, spending by choice a great deal of time in each other's company; although they were temporarily separated now and then by the need to accomplish important business in two places at the same time, they were firmly reconciled, following an earlier period of near estrangement.

For more than a year Kristin, thanks to Woundhealer, had been completely recovered from the physical injuries she had incurred at the time of the Dark King's assault upon their palace.

Approximately two years had now passed since the vicious attack by Vilkata. That onslaught, the cause of so much pain and suffering for everyone in Tasavalta, was only a bitter memory.

But tonight, Prince Stephen's thoughts were concentrated on the matter of a birthday gift. To make a shield of practical size, two dozen or more of the hand-sized scales would have to be fastened to a wooden frame, arranged in overlapping rows. Putting together a suitable frame ought to pose no problem; but working a dragon's scales was something else. Try to cut or simply bore a hole in one, at least in any scale which was big enough to use for armor, and you were likely to wear out your tool or weapon of mere mundane steel, no matter how well forged and honed, before you had made much of an impression on the material.

Stephen had argued, and the expert armorer had grudgingly admitted, that dragonscale shield or armor, provided it proved feasible to make at all, ought to offer some real, practical advantages over any metal breastplate or shield—gram for gram of weight, such a defense would probably be a lot tougher and more protective than any human smiths could make of steel.

The special material for this project, the actual scales of a genuine landwalker, had of course been harvested in the field in the course of the recent emergency, by a skilled fighter who had been loaned the Sword of Heroes for the task. The detached scales had been brought back to the armory with the Sword, and were now being shaped with the same god-forged implement which had slain the monster and had cut the scales loose from its otherwise almost impervious hide—the only feasible way to do the job.

The setup on the bench in the armory workshop, with a Sword, one of the world's enduring wonders, clamped in place like some mere ordinary tool, was remarkable to say the least, and in the earlier, daylight hours of the job other workers had occasionally stopped to stare at the work in progress. Stephen had sworn each new witness to secrecy until Prince Mark's birthday came and the gift could be presented.

Stephen's hands, well coordinated though not yet extremely skillful, were already big, and hardened from frequent work with tools and practice weapons; his arms and shoulders were still on a smaller scale, not nearly as thick and strong as they would be in a few years.

At the moment the boy's hands were gripping a single dark scale, approximately the shape of a giant freshwater clamshell, slightly convex on its upper, darker surface, and with something of a clamshell's rugose texture.

Clamped immovably into place (earlier attempts to use it as a drill bit had been abandoned), the magical weapon began making its customary shrilling sound as soon as Stephen began to work the scale against the more-than-razor keenness of the Sword's bright tip. Using point and edge in alternation, the youth was with comparative ease shaving, carving, and boring holes in the material which would have quickly dulled or broken any ordinary tools.

Stephen, impatient to get the job finished before his royal father could be expected home, pushed harder, and suddenly the scale, tormented by the shrilling Sword which carved at it, broke neatly down the middle. The youth narrowly avoided cutting his own fingers.

It was not the first time during the past few hours that such a problem had arisen. The tough, hard scales seemed soft and malleable as cork when Stephen put them to the test with Dragonslicer; but the material was stubbornly reluctant to yield in the precise way the young craftsman wanted. The floor near the bench was littered with the debris of these mishaps.

The Sword's noise ceased abruptly when it lost contact with the scale. Into the sudden silence Stephen swore, using soldiers' oaths with a veteran's casual instinct, his adolescent voice breaking awkwardly in the middle of the utterance. He had heard a great deal of soldiers' talk during the last year or so, when the armory had suddenly become one of his favorite places. The armorer meanwhile looked on dourly, this time restricting himself to a single laconic comment; in truth old Bazas had never thought much of the plan of making a shield, or anything else, from dragonscale. In his view, if the idea had any real merit, some expert would have done it long ago.

As far as the old armorer had ever heard, only one being had ever used dragonscale armor: the god Vulcan, the limping smith who'd forged all of the Swords. Mere humans—so Bazas was ready to tell the world, royalty or not—mere humans ought to be content with the kinds of armor humans had always worn.

Now Stephen bit his lip. In his cooler moments he was well aware that he needed to demonstrate patience and control his chronically difficult temper if he was going to make a real success of this job.

For one thing, his stock of available scales—his original intention had been to use only those in a narrow range of size and color—was far from unlimited.

Wiping his hands on his simple workman's shirt, he went to work again, longish hair falling over a face that was swiftly losing its childish looks; his hair was growing dark, soon to be even darker than his father's had been until a year or so ago, when Mark's hair and beard had started to show some gray.

Long hours ago, during the sunbright afternoon, the youth had been sweating from his work, but now the deep armory was almost chill. Tasavalta was a coastal land, whose climate, though subject to abrupt and sometimes unpleasant variations, lingered for the most part in a state approximating perpetual spring.

Now for a time the work went more smoothly. But the young prince soon paused again, with a technical question for his old adviser, one for which old Bazas, as usual, had a ready answer. Other voices, those of bored sentries exchanging passwords outside the thick walls, drifted in faintly through a high grilled window. It had been necessary for Stephen to inform Karel, the realm's chief wizard, and also General Rostov, the military commander, that he was opening the heavily guarded Sword-vault to get out Dragonslicer. But he had not needed any special permission to work with the dragonscales. At least he had not asked specifically, though he had told his mother what he was going to do, before she left Sarykam with her husband.

Now, having shaped one more dragonscale to his own satisfaction, the boy added it to the small pile of finished work and picked out a fresh scale from a small box nearby. Then once more he set to work under the critical eye of the grizzled armorer.

* * *

Mulling over the subject of gifts in his own mind as he worked, wondering whether he ought to try to discuss it reasonably with Bazas, Stephen's thought turned briefly to his two-years-older brother, Adrian, who was now absent from home while performing—or undergoing—the last stages of a years-long tutelage in advanced magic. This was a subject for which Adrian, unlike Stephen, had a tremendous natural aptitude. It now occurred to the younger brother, trying to carve scales, to wonder what, if anything, Adrian might be getting their father for his birthday. Mark himself, though a child of the Emperor, was no magician, apart from one great and apparently inherited talent—his amazing ability to hurl demons into distant exile.

Now for a time Stephen forgot about his brother and the subject of gifts in general. On the workbench things for a change were going well. Presently another of the exotic scales had now been cut and bored into the desired shape. Stephen held it up, inspecting the small, neat holes in the hand-sized slab, openings through which tough thongs could be laced, binding it to a light wooden frame. The surface of the shield (or, alternatively, the breastplate) when it was completed would be comprised of rows of overlapping scales, like shingles on a roof, each protecting the otherwise vulnerable lashings of the scale below.

With satisfaction the young Prince laid the latest scale on his small pile of finished work. Five or six more of the same size, he told himself, ought to be enough.

Soon Stephen paused again, briefly, to ask Bazas another question having to do with certain details of the shield-maker's craft. Months ago when he began to frequent the armory the young Prince had discovered that it was necessary to speak loudly to the old man, who had been left somewhat deaf by his years of labor at the anvil. Except for Stephen's loud voice the vaulted room beneath the palace was very quiet at this hour, now that the Sword on the bench had once more ceased the shrilling sound it made in action.

In the near silence, the lad noted in the back of his mind that there did seem to be, after all, at least one other worker present there at midnight. The faint thudding sound of someone industriously, almost continuously, hammering came drifting in from one of the armory's relatively remote chambers.

The young Prince made some passing comment on this sound, mentioning the evident presence of another worker to his companion. Old Bazas, who had not yet been able to hear the noise, only grunted noncommittally. He was a proud man, who at any time during the past several years could have had his hearing restored by Woundhealer for the asking—but had not wanted to admit he needed help.

Stephen went back to work—he had become grimly determined to finish cutting, in this session, all the scales he was going to need. And the old armorer, gnarled hands behind his back, resumed the pose of an alert overseer.

But before another minute had passed, another difficulty arose with the scale currently being carved. Maybe, thought Stephen to himself, the shape of this one just wasn't quite right to begin with. . . .

Thud thud thud thud . . .

The sounds from the other room were growing louder, becoming a real distraction. Not just because they were loud; during the afternoon just past, the armory had been a much noisier place than it was now. No, the young Prince thought, the disturbing thing was that something fundamental must be going wrong with whatever project was under way in the other room. He hearkened to another random, senseless-sounding barrage of impact-sounds from that direction.

Abruptly Stephen looked up, frowning, and turned his head, listening intently; that didn't sound like rational constructive hammering at all, but rather like some angry workman taking out his spite upon his bench. No, not like that either, but more like some deranged drummer, who had been locked inside a big chest and was trying to get out.

No, not even that.

Really what it sounded like was—was—

Stephen's eyes, widening, met the suddenly frightened gaze of the old man who stood across the bench from him. Even Bazas could hear the racket now, and in this he had been quicker-witted than his young Prince.

Realization had come to man and boy at the same time, and they both uttered almost the same words, almost in unison: "It is the Sword of Force!"

Shieldbreaker only gave such warning when actually in use, or when combat impended. So Prince Mark had taught his sons; and Mark had impressed upon the two young Princes also that in his experience the Sword was never wrong when it sounded the alert. This current uproar from the chamber where the Sword of Force was kept must mean that a serious assault was about to fall upon the palace at any moment.

Stephen, having been taught the lore of Swords almost from his cradle, realized that whatever kind of armed attack might be impending, they had only a few minutes, or perhaps only a few seconds, in which to act before it struck.

The troublesome dragonscale fell unheeded from the hand of the young Prince. Everything but the alarm forgotten, Stephen turned away from the workbench, his first impulse being to run up the nearest stair into the palace, shouting out a warning . . . but before he had taken more than two steps, he realized that there was no figure of real authority near at hand, none close enough to relieve him of the burden of decision and action which had been so suddenly thrust upon him.

He had no time to seek out Great-Uncle Karel, or General Rostov, or even the officer of the day; besides, the latter was not privy to the secret code of magic necessary to get the Swords out of their vault and bring them into action. Neither were any of the regular armorers, not even trusty old Bazas. The only person able to act immediately and effectively was the young Prince himself.

With swift agility Stephen turned in the opposite direction. Two driving strides and he was running at full speed toward the chamber in which the Swords were kept.

Just in the last few moments Shieldbreaker's noise had swelled to a hammering bedlam of terrible urgency. The young Prince experienced a choking sensation as he thought that there might be just time for someone as near to the repository as he was, someone able and willing to act boldly, to get the Sword of Force out of its case and into action before the threat, whatever it was, arrived.

The constriction in his throat proceeded from a fear of failure. He, a Prince of Tasavalta, should have know better, he should have known the sound of the Sword at once for what it was, he should have been alerted to the danger long minutes ago! Possibly the unthinkable had already happened, he had ignored the warning for too long, it was already too late for him to act. . . .

In the few heartbeats of time which had elapsed while those thoughts ran through his mind, Stephen's running feet had brought him to the Sword-chamber. He jolted to a stop just outside that room's single doorway, darkened now. The opening lacked any material door but was gauzed with almost invisible but effective barriers: his Great-Uncle Karel's powerful magic, spells keeping everyone out with an action like that of unseen hands.

Muttering the necessary secret password under his breath, the boy felt the hands immediately cease their opposition, the barrier of enchantment divide like a curtain to let him in.

He sprang through into the vaulted space where all of the Swords in the possession of the realm of Tasavalta, along with a few other very precious things, were ordinarily kept safe.

The low-ceilinged Sword-chamber was octagonal, and comparatively small, extending no more than about five paces between opposite walls. Two of the walls supported racks of ceremonial crowns and weapons, kept here for the sake of their jewels and gold. There were a few sword-belts and empty scabbards, there as works of art; other shelves held jewels and comparatively minor treasures. A few lamps and candles, none of them lighted at the moment, stood about on stands and ledges. The place was cool and very dim, particularly to eyes so recently accustomed to the brightness around the workbench. In fact the chief source of illumination in the Sword-chamber at the moment was the indirect glow of the Old World lamp still burning two rooms away.

Only a small handful of individuals had ever been empowered to enter this room. An even smaller number had been granted the immaterial keys required to open the inner vault and remove a Sword. The necessary secret magic, simple enough for even a non-magician to use, had not been entrusted to Stephen until very recently, on the occasion of his fourteenth birthday.

This expression of his parents' confidence had made him very proud. He had used the spell (with his mentor, Karel, looking on) for the first and only time only yesterday—actually a mere matter of hours ago, in the morning just past—to get Dragonslicer out of its case for his secret project.

Thud-thud, thud-thud, thud-thud—

Here under the low vaulting, the sound of hammering seemed notably amplified. There could now be no possible doubt about the source. The white stone walls, and Stephen's bones alike, reverberated with Shieldbreaker's pounding tocsin.

The actual place of storage for the Swords was a waist-high coffer or strongbox built into the center of the room. In this Shieldbreaker and its peers were locked away, behind a pair of carven, slanted doors of wood and metal. This coffer had been constructed of mixed materials, mostly rounded masonry, but incorporating the wood of certain exotic trees as well as several kinds of metal, ivory, and horn, all woven fast within tight nets of Karel's magic. Precious metal had been incorporated as well, gold and silver used more for their magical qualities than as mere decoration. Even rings of unidentifiable material from mysterious Old World devices had been built into the structure.

* * *

THUD, THUD-THUD, THUD—

As Stephen stretched out his hands toward the slanted doors of the inner vault, he was vaguely aware of someone behind him. Glancing back momentarily over his shoulder, he saw that the old armorer had come hurrying after him from the workroom, come as far as he could, to just outside the guarded doorway. Bazas must have acted quickly and purposefully, delayed only by the need to free Dragonslicer from the clamps which had held the Sword upon the bench. Now the elderly man, his progress stopped by the invisible hands of Karel's magic, had come to a halt. He was holding up the keen Blade in his right hand, and had his free hand raised as well, as if to test the magic sealing of the doorway, or pronounce a benediction.

The armorer called out urgently: "My prince! The Sword of Heroes must be put in a place of safety."

The words of Bazas were partially muffled by the intervening magic, but Stephen nodded his understanding. Dragonslicer was not the weapon of choice with which to repel a raid or an invasion—except in the highly unlikely event that one's foe came riding on a dragon. It was the expression on the old man's face that made the young Prince experience a sense of awe. A seasoned soldier was actually looking to him for leadership, and this realization gave Stephen the night's first moment of genuine fright.

It was not to be the last.

Nodding, the boy wordlessly turned his back on Bazas. Facing the sloping plane formed by the closed doors of the inner vault, he quickly let his right hand rest on the hard surface. There was no physical handle or knob on either door, no bolt or latch, but the guardian powers required identification of the petitioner for entrance. He started to recite the brief spell of opening—

—but before Stephen had managed to utter more than three of the seven necessary words, he choked and stumbled in his recitation. At the same time the world turned sick and strange around him, the stone floor seeming to tilt alarmingly sideways underneath his feet.

This was far more, far worse, than the choking of anxiety. Involuntarily he cried out, and heard what seemed a responding cry from just outside the room. Looking again in that direction, Stephen saw old Bazas, Dragonslicer still in his right hand, slumping to the floor. Now another figure, strange and startlingly gigantic, completely filled the doorway, its image wavering so that it looked to the young Prince both more and less than human. There was nothing about it that Stephen's mind wanted to acknowledge as a face. With a transparent appendage that was like and yet unlike a human hand it appeared to be working to put aside the defenses put up by the master-magician Karel. So far those defenses were holding back the thing, the presence, whatever it might be—

Yet already the invader could project some form of power past the barrier. Stephen was aware that he was losing consciousness, and with what shreds of sense remained he knew the cause: he was being confronted by a demon at close range. Though the young Prince had been brushed by demons' wings before—he had been in the palace during Vilkata's attack two years ago—he had never experienced anything like the force of this evil manifestation, and he found it all but completely overwhelming.

Again the world seemed to tilt crazily, wrongly around Stephen, and he clung helplessly to the rounded stonework side of the inner vault, swaying with physical illness.

In his terror Stephen involuntarily closed his eyes. But this was no help, for the monster immediately started to force its image under his eyelids.

And now a voice, a sound of dead leaves crushed that had to be the demon's voice, was calling to him. It was commanding, demanding that he do something for it.

He answered with a nearly helpless, incoherent mumbling: What was it that he had to do?

The dried leaves swirled and rustled. "You must recite for me the spell I need. Undo for me the barring of this chamber door, and let me in . . . ."

Stephen tried to think. But he couldn't think. Not beyond the knowledge that he was going to be killed—yet there remained something he *must* do.

Of course. The Swords.

For the moment his body would not move. But remembering a purpose gave him strength, and he tried to talk to the thing that was about to kill him. "Who are you? What—?"

The tones of the demon's utterance, taking form more in the mind than in the ears, were an inhuman rattling among dead bones. "You must know, child of the Prince of Scum, that I am called Akbar. . . . I say that you must open this door."

Akbar. Indeed Stephen knew the name from his father's stories, and from a hundred other tales, and that it meant overwhelming malignancy, sheer terror. He must not give way, he must not open the gate for it—no, he had to open the inner vault, recite the spell that would let him reach the Swords.

And now the demon had succeeded in forcing another part of itself— an arm that was not really an arm—partway in through Karel's barrier. One giant finger—something half-material that was not quite a finger— flicked at the young Prince.

The impact knocked Stephen off his feet, sent him rolling across the stone floor, out of reach of the doors which he must open. Scarcely aware of the bruising of his knees and elbows on the stone, he tried to scramble out of the way as the quasi-material thing came probing, reaching, after him again.

Again it struck at the young Prince, and this time a veil of darkness started to descend across his mind.

4

DAZED and battered as he was, the young Prince retained enough awareness to hear Bazas screaming weakly and hoarsely, the old man lying on the floor just outside the doorway of the Sword-chamber.

Stephen himself was also sprawled on the stone pavement, but well inside the doorway where the demon's groping power had flung him. Where he ought to be protected by Karel's magic, but yet seemed to be not quite out of Akbar's reach. His knees and elbows hurt from the fall on the stone floor. The whole world felt sick and strange around him.

Drawing a deep breath, clenching his fists and his jaw as tightly as his eyelids, Stephen denied sickness. A hundred times his father had told him of the several confrontations he, Mark, had had with demons, occasions when he had been able to banish the foul creatures with a command. These were not matters of which the elder Prince ever spoke boastfully. Rather Mark described those encounters in the manner of a man still trying to understand how he had served as a conduit for powers greater than himself. And many times, Mark's younger son, when listening to the stories, had wondered whether he himself might have inherited his father's ability.

Now the boy's voice cracked again as he desperately shouted the mysterious formula which had never failed his father: "In the Emperor's name, forsake this game! Get out!"

In Stephen's own ears the slurred words sounded more like a scream of panic than a firm command. But at once the multiple foul images of the demon vanished from under the young Prince's eyelids. Some force had obviously intervened against his attacker, and the hideous thing, which a moment earlier had seemed on the point of crushing Stephen like an insect, was being forcibly separated from him. Akbar reacted with a bellow of outrage.

Raising himself on his elbows, Stephen dared to open his eyes.

His monstrous antagonist, its form still only half visible, was thrashing about as if some unseen power larger than itself had seized it and was

pulling it by main force out of the doorway of the Sword-chamber, farther and farther from its intended human victims—

A moment later the demon was entirely gone.

As the young Prince scrambled back to his feet, he was dimly aware of
distant screams and yells, in voices far more human than the demon's. At
the moment he could not tell whether these outcries proceeded from
upstairs within the palace, or from outside. But he thought it did not
matter. The whole palace, the whole city, must be under attack.

Now that the demon had been ejected from the armory, Bazas, just
outside the doorway of the Sword-chamber, was slowly regaining his feet.
The old armorer, shaking his head and quivering in all his limbs, was still
holding Dragonslicer in one hand and propping himself with the other
against the wall.

Stephen turned immediately back to the task he must perform, that of
opening the inner vault which held the Swords—but the moment he
again began the incantation to unlock the doors, he became aware, more
with his mind than with any of his physical senses, that the demon he had
caused to be hurled away had not gone very far.

*Howling and screaming its rage at him, its insane hatred of all humanity
but the adored Master, Akbar was racing, flying back—*

Again the incantation must be interrupted. Again the young Prince
had only a moment in which to bark out a command. This time, heartened by the partial success of his first attempt, he managed to put more
authority into his voice. Gritting his teeth, he willed and yelled his swelling anger at the beast.

Again a scream from an affronted demon—again the banishing was
successful. Because the mental contact which had been established between himself and Akbar still persisted, Stephen could feel that this time
his foe had been hurled to a somewhat greater distance. But the youth
had no doubt that Akbar would be doggedly, relentlessly, returning yet
once more to the attack. And Stephen was vaguely aware of the presence, somewhere in the background, of another demon—more likely
several of them—approaching.

Meanwhile, Stephen's latest repulsion of the enemy had earned him
the moment of time, the breathing space he needed.

Half leaning against one side of the inner vault, the young Prince once
again reached a physical position from which he could lay his right hand
on the slanted doors. Breathlessly he hurried through the few and simple
words, dreading lest he stumble in his pronunciation of one of the essential syllables, and so be forced to begin yet again.

But this time Stephen managed to do the incantation properly. The vault doors of their own accord jerked open with a double slam. At once the wordless voice of the Sword of Force, no longer muffled, boomed out through the armory.

Three god-forged Swords, as well as two empty, Sword-shaped spaces, were revealed within the vault. Each meter-long blade and white-marked hilt lay nested in a velvet lining of the blue-green color of the sunlit sea. The faint wash of Old World light coming into the chamber from two rooms away touched the bright magical lines of steel, and the flat sides of the three perfect blades gave back a mottled triple reflection—Shieldbreaker, Sightblinder, and Stonecutter.

In appearance the Swords were indistinguishable from each other, save for the white symbols on their black hilts.

Three Sword-belts of fine leather, each with an empty scabbard attached, were racked separately at one side within the inner vault. The receptacle for belts, like that for the Swords, displayed two empty spaces and three filled.

Despite the immediate threat posed by the returning demon, Stephen knew a sense of awe that compelled him to a heartbeat's hesitation. These were the weapons of the gods, forged more than forty years ago by the deity Vulcan himself, with the human aid of Jord, a human smith—Jord who was also Prince Mark's foster father, and thus the grandfather of Stephen. The young Prince and his brother Adrian had grown up hearing the marvelous old stories, as often as not from their foster-grandfather's own mouth.

One of the pair of empty Sword-shaped niches within the vault was of course the usual resting place of Dragonslicer. The other space sometimes accommodated Woundhealer, which was also very often, as now, absent from this repository upon some mission of mercy. Part of Stephen's mind took note of the fact that a tiny spider was even now spinning a web in the space reserved for the Sword of Mercy.

But Stephen just now had no eyes or thought for any of the Swords but one. That one, snug in its nest, positioned a little above its fellows, was now emitting a frenzied war-drum sound. The warning boomed out louder than ever, and a verse of the Song of Swords raced through his mind.

> *I shatter Swords and splinter spears;*
> *None stands to Shieldbreaker.*
> *My point's the fount of orphans' tears*
> *My edge the widowmaker.*

The young Prince's right hand darted into the vault, ready to seize the black hilt marked with the small white image of a hammer.

—and meanwhile the demon Akbar had once more returned and now was rushing again upon him, sweeping from the doorway the last shreds of protective magic—

The Sword of Force came literally leaping up out of its velvet casing to meet Stephen's grasping fingers. He needed no particular skill in magic to feel the god-power surge along his arm. Such was the effect that in that instant he gasped with relief, as if the battle were already won.

Nor was the young Prince now required to display any skill or strength at arms. Darting out of its case as if by its own volition, Shieldbreaker continued its upward movement, pulling the young Prince's right arm violently with it.

Shieldbreaker, hammering thunderstrokes, lashed out violently against the demonic intruder. Stephen's right arm was pulled helplessly forward even as his body staggered back. Pain stabbed at his shoulder, where the movement of the Sword twisted it.

The demon, an image of horror seeming to loom larger than the walls of the Sword-chamber, emitted no bellow of outrage this time, but rather a choked cry, a grating and unbreathing sound that was to haunt the young Prince in nightmares. In the next instant Akbar's image burst like a pricked bubble. The sickness provoked by the demonic presence immediately disappeared, as if it had been flushed into oblivion by cleansing waves of air and light. And then Stephen was vaguely aware that the creature which had called itself Akbar was no longer anywhere, anywhere at all.

Relief lasted for only a moment; another ghastly scream warned Stephen that he had no time at all for triumph. Turning with alarm, gazing toward the now-unguarded doorway, he beheld Bazas standing in that opening with Dragonslicer in hand. In the last few moments the old armorer's face had undergone a ghastly transformation, had become a mask of exalted rage and hatred.

Glaring at the young Prince, screaming Stephen's death and the exalted name of the Dark King, Bazas leapt forward with his Sword raised to kill—and struck, with a trained warrior's skill.

The young Prince, still reeling from the demon's onslaught, had no time to try to understand, to think, or even to react consciously. Fortunately he needed to do none of those things. As the blade of Dragonslicer swung toward Stephen's head, slicing almost horizontally under the low ceiling, Shieldbreaker of its own accord pulled his arm along at invisible speed to parry the blow.

Steel clashed with steel, both products of Vulcan's forge. With a single *thud,* monstrously loud, and a flash of light, the Sword of Heroes passed out of existence, dissolved in a burst of flying fragments that rang from stone or embedded themselves in flesh.

Stephen, his injured shoulder wrenched again, body sent staggering back against the central vault, caught one clear glimpse of the fact that Dragonslicer was gone, while the Sword in his own hand remained perfectly intact. Stephen himself was uninjured by the explosion—armed as he was now, no weapon had the power to hurt him—but he could see at once how fragments of the Sword of Heroes had torn the body of Bazas into bloody rags, dropped the old man in his tracks.

For a moment or two the consciousness of the young Prince dimmed toward faintness, then full awareness of the world came back. Breathing heavily, Stephen found himself once more slumped against the open Sword-vault, left hand clinging to the decorated stonework, right arm pulled down by the weight of the Sword of Force. His right shoulder burned with a sharp pain as if something inside it had been torn, and his palm and fingers were magically glued to Shieldbreaker's black hilt.

The weapon was almost quiet at the moment, the magical hammer-sound muted, having subsided until it seemed that the Sword might be only talking to itself.

Clutching at one of the open vault doors with his free hand, gazing with shock and horror at what was left of Bazas, Stephen fought down an impulse to vomit. He wondered what could have driven the old armorer so violently, abruptly mad. The old man had shouted something just before he swung his Sword at his young prince and died—something crazy having to do with the Dark King. . . .

At that moment the frightening truth began to dawn on Stephen: Only the Mindsword could produce such instantaneous and frightful alterations in the thoughts of good and worthy people. Skulltwister must have been once more brought into play by his father's enemies.

While struggling to cope with that idea's horrendous implications, the youth became dazedly aware that his right hand was no longer magically welded to Shieldbreaker's hilt. A lull in combat now obtained, for the moment at least, and he could if he wished put down the Sword of Force.

He actually started to do so, but then instead, despite his injured shoulder, gripped the black hilt with convulsive strength, at the same time whimpering with the thought of how near he had come to letting go —that would have meant death, or worse than death. Only Shieldbreaker could have saved him, must be saving him even now, from the same awful madness which had afflicted Bazas, almost within arm's length.

The cheering, roaring noises which now came drifting down from the upper palace confirmed Stephen's horrible suspicion that the Mindsword must be in action. This insight, along with the undoubted presence of demons in the palace, and the fact that Bazas in his madness had shouted the Dark King's name, strongly indicated that this latest attack, like that two years ago, must be led by the terrible Vilkata.

But so long as he, Stephen, had the Sword of Force in hand, so long was he protected against any other weapon, including Skulltwister. In fact he alone ought to be able to defend the palace against any kind of attack—any kind save one.

As Prince Mark had impressed over and over again upon his sons, the only way known to defeat Shieldbreaker was to disarm oneself completely and then grapple as a wrestler with whoever held the Sword. But, as Stephen had known in theoretical terms for years, there was no way a demon could ever disarm itself; the foul creatures *were* nothing but weapons, at least as far as this Sword was concerned. Whenever they attacked its wielder directly, Shieldbreaker was capable of slashing them out of existence, as surely as if its edge could be laid against whatever material objects concealed their unclean lives.

Yesterday Stephen might have had a difficult time believing that, no matter what his teachers taught; but now that he had seen and felt the Sword of Force in action, had witnessed the virtual annihilation of another Sword and a powerful demon, he no longer felt any doubt.

And now the Dark King had come again to Sarykam, attacking, no doubt seeking frightful vengeance for his past defeats.

Stephen twisted his feet, as if he would dig the heels of his boots into the stone floor. Straightening his back, he set it firmly against the open Sword-vault. Then, ignoring the continuing pain in his right shoulder, he raised his Sword to guard position, unconsciously adopting the tactics in which he had been drilled with ordinary weapons.

Then, confident in his armament though still feeling stupid with surprise and weariness, he waited for the next attack.

Moments passed, and the suspense stretched out unbearably. Not for a moment did the young Prince believe that the danger of combat was over. Shieldbreaker, quivering with the muscles of the young Prince's right arm, muttered and stuttered to itself. Now, gradually, he could not doubt the fact, the sound was growing louder once again.

Think! he commanded himself, shaking his head in an effort to clear it of shock and pain and horror. At the moment, as far as he could tell, the fate of the whole realm was indeed resting on him, and he had to think. Shieldbreaker could be, was, an overpowering weapon. But—

But the Dark King, or any other human ally of these attacking demons, would be able to disarm himself of other weapons, and to wrestle Stephen for possession of the Sword of Force—in such a contest the unarmed human inevitably won. And with the Mindsword in action, Vilkata and his demons would have a host of fanatically eager human allies, doubtless including everyone else who had been in the palace when the enemy struck. Bazas as a newly converted madman could have attacked successfully unarmed, had he only waited until Stephen actually had the Sword of Force in hand.

Even as the young Prince did his best to think, to prepare, to nerve himself to meet whatever form the attack was going to take next, Vilkata the Dark King was dismounting from a demonic steed which had just landed on the highest level of the palace.

The Dark King's planning for this attack had prudently included the caching in a secret place, the deepest recesses of a coastal cave not inconveniently far from Sarykam, of several of the glassy Old World spacecraft, one of which had only hours ago completed its task of carrying the wizard back to Earth from the distant Moon. Akbar's promise had been made good, and the return voyage had taken no more than two Earthly days. Much as Vilkata still distrusted *technology*, it was plain that such devices could in many ways be useful.

Now, even as Vilkata set foot on the palace roof, he cast a sharp glance toward a pair of bodies lying nearby. Two sentries, their useless weapons scattered at their feet, had been silently murdered by demons within the past few minutes. The pair of corpses, still clad in livery of Tasavaltan blue and green, now drained of blood and psychic energies, resembled dried-out, somewhat less-than-lifesize dolls.

Vilkata looked up higher. The narrow, towering eyries of the fighting birds and winged messengers, stone spires rising even above the roof where the Dark King had alighted, had been savagely raided already. Eggs had been smashed, grown birds and nestlings slaughtered, and some of the interiors of wood and straw were burning.

Vilkata nodded with satisfaction. Surprise had certainly been achieved, and at the moment no opposition to the invaders was in evidence. The Dark King had not only made sure that Prince Mark was elsewhere, but had warily planned his attack on the palace and armory so that his own personal entry should be slightly delayed. Let his demons confront the heavy counterattack, if there was to be any; he would see what happened to them before entering the fight himself.

Naturally cautious in the matter of personal risk, Vilkata had considered the possibility that he might have to face Shieldbreaker in combat today. Of course he was well acquainted with the proper way to fight against the Sword of Force; but he had two very strong objections to personally disarming himself, if and when he should be confronted with that weapon.

First, since a demon counted as a weapon, disarming would almost certainly mean giving up his demonic vision for some unknown period of time.

That would make things difficult; but the second objection, in the Dark King's estimation, was even deadlier. He clearly could not disarm himself without giving up the Mindsword, the very foundation of all his current power. He dared not hand over that weapon to any of his followers, human or demonic; nor did he doubt for a moment that, within a few heartbeats' time after he should put Skulltwister down, someone, friend or foe, would pick it up. Even if one of his loyal slaves should pick it up, having in mind some purpose tending to Vilkata's advantage, still at that moment the fierce devotion engendered in everyone else by the Sword would swing to a new object.

Most definitely unacceptable!

The Dark King could easily picture a hundred disastrous scenarios sprouting, diverging, from that point. In the worst of them his own demons, instantly converted to some fresh loyalty, pounced on him and tore him into psychic shreds—a fate infinitely more painful even than the analogous physical destruction would have been.

No, if, against his best hopes and expectations, he were confronted today by the Sword of Force, he planned to retreat, with Skulltwister still securely his. There would be time and opportunity to plot and strike again.

Having surveyed the palace rooftop and dismissed his demon-mount with orders to stay vigilantly nearby, Vilkata observed an open doorway not far ahead of him. Mindsword held before him like a torch, he approached the entrance cautiously.

For the time being he was alone, save for Pitmedden, his demonic provider of vision. This creature, hovering invisibly at the Dark King's side, was currently his sole companion and bodyguard. None of the demons who had made up the first wave of the attack had yet come back to report, and this disturbed Vilkata vaguely. In particular, he had hoped to have an almost immediate report from Akbar, who had been charged with seizing control of the room or place in which the Swords were kept, and guarding it fiercely until his Master should come to take over his new property.

Having reached the open door leading down from the rooftop, Vilkata stood gazing down the first flight of descending stairs, which were dimly, indirectly lighted by some lamp or cresset somewhere on the next lower level. Surely, he thought, the mighty Akbar could not be very far ahead of him. The creature, like its colleagues, was bound by the Mindsword to Vilkata in perfect loyalty. They were all compelled to gain for its master all the treasures of magic buried here, in particular the Sword Shield-breaker—but under strict orders not to pick that weapon up, not even touch it. Only to keep anyone else from picking it up until Vilkata himself could reach the site and do so.

With a few brisk words to Pitmedden, the Dark King entered the palace, passing down the first stairs with confident strides. He knew that as the human beings in the rooms and passageways surrounding him were engulfed by the Mindsword's sphere of influence, every one of them without exception—each person, waking or sleeping, within an arrow-shot or so—would automatically become his fanatical ally and worshipper.

More, he felt confident that his demons would be largely unopposed—because Prince Mark was absent.

5

For a long time, for years even before his first attack on the palace at Sarykam, Vilkata had been grimly aware of the fact that strong magical powers (quite apart from Prince Mark's special talent) were continuously on sentinel duty there. These protective forces, ordinarily quite adequate to keep demons and other malign entities at a distance, were primarily under the control of old Karel, who was Princess Kristin's uncle, and also one of the most formidable magicians on Earth. The Dark King was not sure but that that old man might not be his equal—assuming, of course, that the Mindsword was left out of the calculation.

But even without counting the Mindsword, the powers now at Vilkata's command were far greater than ordinary. When the new attack fell on the palace and the surrounding city, Karel's sentinels, human and otherwise, were able to give the inhabitants only a belated warning, and could delay the giant attacking demons only briefly.

This first line of Tasavaltan opposition was swept out of the way in a matter of moments.

Within moments after the first of his demons went bursting into the palace, Vilkata also personally entered the royal residence, determined to descend as quickly as possible into the lower regions, where he knew the armory was located, and where Prince Mark's collection of Swords was ordinarily stored. Within moments he was moving quickly downstairs, the Sword of Glory drawn cheering and roaring in his hand.

Around the invader and in advance of him there spread a murmur of mingled joy and sorrow, voiced by first one, then a dozen, then a hundred human throats. These were the voices of servants, guards, palace inhabitants of every station, all of them taken unawares, in their beds or awake, each converted in an instant into a fanatical servant and worshipper of the Dark King. Most of those falling under the Mindsword's influence were in other rooms or corridors than those through which Vilkata passed, and they failed to witness their new Master's arrival or his first passage.

Even those who had not yet seen the invader or his Sword knew ex-

actly the name and titles of the man they were suddenly constrained to
worship, and could have marshalled arguments to demonstrate that their
sudden change of heart in favor of Vilkata was perfectly rational and
honorable. Their joy was at his glory, their poignant sorrow at their own
blind failure to acknowledge him for so long, until their lives were transformed by this moment of transcendent revelation.

The sharpest outcries came, naturally enough, from those few people
who happened actually to encounter their new Master, Mindsword held
before him like a bright slice of light, in his first swift passage through the
palace. Trusted servants and old family retainers, who moments earlier
would rather have died than betray their Prince and Princess, were be-
witched into wretches stumbling and stammering in their eagerness to
repent of these feelings. Their yells of joyous shock brought out from
their rooms of sleep or work a steadily growing throng of new converts,
men and women nightshirted or wrapped in blankets, all eager to adore
Vilkata.

The invading wizard pushed his way through these where they were in
a position to impede his progress. He proceeded rapidly on foot through
torchlit or darkened hallways—Old World lamps were far too rare for
common use.

The Dark King had now been rejoined in his progress by a close bodyguard of demons, these latter worked up and raging with fear and hatred
of their enemy the Prince.

After having made doubly sure that Mark himself was absent from the
palace, they lashed out at surrogate victims, even at doubly helpless converts, with murderous fury and tremendous violence.

Gleefully they reported that their colleagues outside the palace were
devastating the dwellings of known enemies throughout the city.

For sport the demons now escorting Vilkata butchered in passing some
of Mark's formerly faithful servants and loyal followers, an amusement
for which their indulgent master granted them permission by default; but
any humans who Vilkata thought might be privy to the secrets of the
Tasavaltan government were forbidden as prey.

Chief among these last was Karel himself, the uncle of Princess Kristin, a stout, apple-cheeked old man who was by far the realm's most
powerful wizard. Against the Mindsword, of course, the old man was as
defenseless as the lowest kitchen servant. He came stumbling out of his
modest palace apartment in his nightshirt, tears already streaming down
his round red cheeks at the thought of how he had so long and wickedly
opposed the very Master of the World.

Vilkata, remembering past defeats, would have found it very satisfying to kill Karel and certain other of his old foes, now that the opportunity had come. But he did not indulge this craving. In fact he issued strict orders to his demons to see to his old enemies' survival. Of course utilizing as many of these important people as possible in the service of his own cause was undoubtedly the more intelligent course, and that was the plan Vilkata chose to follow.

Eager as the Dark King was to reach the armory, he stopped to question and to listen to some of these freshly converted important folk. All of them were anxious to tell the Dark King (who, as any right-thinking person must understand at once, was the only being in the universe truly worthy of loyalty and worship) under what kind of protection, and approximately where in the deep central vaults of the Tasavaltan armory, Mark's trove of Swords was kept. One after another these teary-eyed defectors also hastened to inform their incomparable new Master that, to the best of their knowledge, at least a couple of Swords were still there.

The Dark King delayed his descent into the depths of the palace an instant longer to demand: "And are any of the royal family at home?"

The converts looked at one another uncertainly. All of them were desperately eager to be helpful, but at the same time in dread of inadvertently giving the Master wrong or incomplete information. It was Karel himself who finally answered: "Only the young Prince Stephen is here, great lord!"

Bad luck! But better one small fish than none. "And where is he?"

Not in his usual sleeping quarters, that was quickly reported by a scouting demon. Nor did the modest bed in Prince Stephen's room appear to have been slept in during the past few hours. The youth was old enough to have been visiting the bedroom of some maid or mistress, Vilkata supposed; or perhaps he had been taking advantage of his parents' absence to enjoy some other form of carousal.

No one had any useful suggestions to offer. Vilkata ordered an immediate and thorough search of the palace for Prince Mark's brat, and demons and converted Tasavaltans went rushing and whooping away to carry out his order. But the invading wizard was not going to spend any time on that effort himself; certainly not just now, when down in the armory there might be Swords to be had for the picking. At all stages of his planning for this attack, the Dark King had made the armory his primary target, his first concern being to seize at once whatever Swords might be available—particularly Shieldbreaker.

On to the armory!

The descent of the Eyeless One continued through the many levels of the palace, becoming something of a triumphal procession. Ceaselessly the Sword of Glory worked its magic, emitting its customary roaring cheer as the Dark King bore it forward and downward like a torch.

As he advanced, descending, he wondered again what had become of Akbar, whom he had sent on ahead. At least the demon would not be up to any treachery, the holder of the Mindsword told himself—he could feel perfectly confident of that.

Down in the Sword-chamber, the young Prince at that moment was still leaning with his back against the open vault in which the Blades were customarily kept. Stephen was just emerging from a brief and successful struggle with his own fears—fear of death, and, worse just now, fear of making the wrong decision.

With the exception of his long work session with Dragonslicer, just interrupted, Stephen had never been allowed to handle any of the Swords unsupervised. But at one time or another, as part of his education, he had been given every Sword available to hold at least briefly, and had been taught the theory and something of the practice of their use. The result was that now he felt reasonably well acquainted with these weapons, whose history was so intimately intertwined with that of his own family.

It had come as no great surprise to the young Prince that Shieldbreaker had leaped up obediently to meet his touch, and then with matchless violence had disposed of a giant demon, as well as Dragonslicer and the unfortunate man who had been holding it.

But Stephen's education regarding the Swords also assured him that now, with the palace in the hands of a strong enemy force, Shieldbreaker was not going to be enough. He was well aware that if he were armed with that Sword only, it would be only too easy for a knowledgeable human attacker to overcome him.

He turned his head to look back and down into the Sword-vault, studying the two weapons still remaining in their velvet nests. Stonecutter would not help him in his present circumstances, and could be disregarded. But there was one other Sword still in the vault, and that one was quite another matter. The boy realized that his duty, and his very hope of survival, required him now to pick up Sightblinder as well as Shieldbreaker.

The Sword of Stealth is given to
One lowly and despised.
Sightblinder's gifts: his eyes are keen
His nature is disguised.

Yet Stephen hesitated. He also understood full well that the decision to hold two Swords drawn at once was not one to be taken lightly. On his recent birthday he had been allowed, very briefly and under Karel's supervision, to make the attempt with these very two. His father, Mark, had demonstrated the ability to do that effectively. (For the first time, as a boy, and then holding them only briefly, Mark had had the feeling that a great wind had arisen and was about to blow him off his feet. That the world was altering around him, or that he was being extracted from it. Then Mark had fainted; this, too, the grown Prince had told his sons.) But the effect on Stephen had been the same as it would have been on most people: confusion, mental anguish, disorientation.

Shieldbreaker and Sightblinder together, the young Prince knew, would provide anyone who held them with an almost absolutely unbeatable offense and defense. He knew of only one real flaw in this armament, but it was a daunting one—the inevitable psychic burden of carrying both Swords drawn at the same time. That would impose a disabling handicap on all but a few very capable men or women.

But he knew he was going to have to take the risk.

Shieldbreaker continued its muttering, the black hilt thumping soft magical impacts against Stephen's palm. His right arm, still hurting at the shoulder, was tiring from the weight of the heavy Sword, and he let the arm sag again until the unbreakable point of the Sword of Force trailed on the stone floor; with this weapon there was no need, after all, to hold a ready position.

And then, frightened of what he must do next, but unwilling to put off the attempt any longer, Stephen thrust his left hand boldly into the vault and closed his fingers around the black hilt with the white outline of a human eye—Sightblinder.

This Sword did not come leaping up to meet his reaching grasp. But immediately on Stephen's making contact with the Sword of Stealth, its magic surged along his arm and through his mind and body. A power similar to Shieldbreaker's, yet different. This, on top of the lingering effect of the young Prince's first brush with the demon, made him once more dizzy, and afflicted him with deep anxiety, the fear that reality might be about to crumble. The savage noises still drifting down from the upper palace seemed to be swallowed up in the sound of a great wind; it was distracting, even though the young Prince understood that the wind really existed only within his own mind and perception.

But Sightblinder's heavy magic worked its benefits as well. The power of the Sword of Stealth enhanced and focused Stephen's own perception sufficiently to let him feel assured that the human voices he heard above were truly those of deadly enemies—no matter that most of those who spoke and sang had once been loyal friends—and that more demons were indeed swarming in the near vicinity.

Feeling mentally menaced and disconnected, undergoing sensations so peculiar he would have been unable to describe them, threatened by impalpable winds of change, almost on the point of fainting, Stephen was suddenly sure that he could not, dared not, remain here in the presence of the enemy. Armed as he now was, though, he could and would get away, and would carry to his parents the two greatest treasures of the armory.

The great problem with this plan, as the young Prince realized even before he tried to move, was that in this state of fierce giddiness induced by double magic he would have all he could do simply to stand erect. He feared he would not be able to walk across a room, let alone travel to a distant village, holding both Swords drawn. He would have to put one of the two weapons at least into a scabbard even before he tried to climb the stairs and leave the palace.

Knowing that the Mindsword must be perilously near, Stephen did not dare to release his grip on Shieldbreaker's hilt even for a moment. Propping up Sightblinder in a position where he could grab it again instantly, he worked left-handed to extract two sword-belts from the Sword-chamber's inner rack. Working with his left hand and his right elbow, he managed, after a long struggle that at times seemed hopeless, to get the two belts fastened around his waist, so that one long leather scabbard hung at his right, the other at his left. Then he took up Sightblinder again, enduring the weight of double magic long enough to sheath the Sword at his right side, from which position he should be able to draw it handily left-handed.

Looking at the doors of the inner vault, which still stood open, Stephen made a great effort to think coherently. Stonecutter of course was still inside the vault, but it would simply have to stay there. Yes, no doubt he ought to close those doors before he left—that would set at least a small additional obstacle in the path of whoever was about to overrun the palace wholly. He grabbed one door and slammed it; the other one came with it automatically. No special closing incantation was required.

As the young Prince prepared to leave the armory, Shieldbreaker in his right hand kept muttering to itself as if in eager expectation of the joys of combat. Cautiously, being very careful never to let go for an instant, he changed his grip on the black hilt from his right hand to his left, to better balance the physical weight of the sheathed Sword of Stealth. He thought that any difficulty he could eliminate, even the most minor, might make the difference for him between success and failure.

On his way to the door he had to detour slightly to avoid stepping right over the old man's body. But before setting foot out of the Sword-chamber the young Prince paused, fascinated against his will, to take one more horrified look at Bazas.

Almost straddling the corpse, which lay sprawled upon its back, Stephen for the first time took note of the ruined hilt of Dragonslicer, black wood splintered and still smoldering, still clutched in the old man's hand.

At that sight, another thought went fluttering through the youth's shocked, half-disconnected mind: *But how now was he ever going to be able to complete his father's gift—?*

Shaking his head in an attempt to clear it, the young Prince shuffled past the dead man and stepped through the doorway. He turned his back on the Sword-vault chamber, and started automatically for the nearest stair. He had done very little conscious planning, but was holding to the fixed idea that his parents several days ago had gone to the village of Voronina, some sixty kilometers away, and that he must reach them there with the two important Swords.

If only, Stephen prayed, circumstances did not compel him to travel any distance with both Swords drawn. And if only he could decide correctly which one he had to have drawn at any moment. . . .

Walking with a persistent slight unsteadiness, he was halfway across the room in which the abandoned workbench stood holding its neat and meaningless pile of dragonscales, and where the Old World lamp now burned unheeded, when what seemed a better plan of action struck him with the force of inspiration.

The house of Stephen's grandparents, of Mark's mother, Mala, and foster-father, Jord, was right here in Sarykam, at no enormous distance from the palace. Surely he, Stephen, would be able to carry his two Swords on foot successfully at least that far. In the house of Jord and Mala he would be able to get help.

But now more demons were coming toward him. The vile creatures were moving somewhere near. . . .

Hastily Stephen snatched Sightblinder lefthanded from its sheath. Once more his head went spinning with the force of double magic, but now he could see, feel, exactly where the foul things were. Still more than a hundred meters distant, they were no immediate threat, but at any moment that might change.

Restricted by his burden to a staggering and seriously uneven progress, the young Prince went forward carrying both Swords drawn. He would continue to do so, he told himself, at least until he could get out of the palace.

Experiencing recurring waves of a feeling that the world was twisting itself into knots around him, a sensation unpleasantly reminiscent of the night last winter when he'd secretly experimented with drinking too much wine, Stephen kept going.

He had gained no more than a couple of rooms' distance from the Sword-vault, traversing with difficulty the darkened armory on a course for the nearest ascending stairs, when through a concentric pair of doorways on his left he observed movement, that of one person walking.

The enhanced perception granted the young Prince by Sightblinder showed him the single figure clearly: that of a man bearing in front of him a Sword raised like a torch, who had just now descended to the level of the armory by another stair, several rooms away.

For a moment Stephen could not react. The mental strain of carrying the two Swords was growing worse, not lessening. Invisible surges of power seemed to blend inside his nervous system, with unpredictable effect. Nevertheless Sightblinder still augmented the boy's sight sufficiently to allow him to become aware of the invader before the invader saw him; and it also enabled Stephen to identify the Dark King with certainty, even from several rooms away. That man had just come hurrying—alone, except for the one demon which clung to him like an incubus, and functioned as his eyes—down, down into the dimly lighted armory.

Not that this towering, eyeless albino, in the ordinary course of events, would have been very difficult to identify.

Stephen tensed, and in his sudden concentration even came close to forgetting for the moment that he was carrying two drawn Swords.

Vilkata. The Dark King.

This was the man—say, rather, the monster—who, two years ago, had almost killed Stephen's mother, inflicting upon her months of physical and mental agony. The evil magician who was the deadly enemy of Stephen's father. The fiend who preferred the society of demons to that of people, and who had wrought great havoc upon the whole world—the realm of Tasavalta in particular.

The boy's naturally combative nature, and his princely training in the theory and practice of war, asserted themselves, and he was ready to attack.

6

A T once, without the need to pause or think, the young Prince turned away from the stairs he had been about to climb and began to retrace his steps toward the Sword-chamber. He was moving to intercept the invader. Scarcely conscious of the continuing pain in his shoulder or the bruises on his knees and elbows, Stephen stalked his hated enemy. Shieldbreaker was once more in his right hand, drumming softly as he held it ready for a thrust. In the left hand of the young Prince, Sight-blinder continued to exert its silent power; with the help of the Sword of Stealth the youth was able vaguely to perceive the demon accompanying his foe, a half-transparent cloud of something in the air beside the wizard's head.

Meanwhile the eyeless magician had satisfied himself that he was now on the deepest level of the palace. The bright image of the Tyrant's Blade, gripped fiercely in the Dark King's right fist, emitted a muted roaring, to itself and to the world, the sound of a fire started by some enthusiastic mob.

Unaware of Stephen watching him from three rooms away, Vilkata paused briefly at the foot of the stairs to gaze about him with his unnatural vision. In the next moment the Dark King, without looking back, beckoned to someone or something above and behind him, at the top of the stone stairs; then the man turned his back on the stairs, and turning away from Stephen also, strode forward purposefully.

In response to the Master's commanding gesture, a small squad of demons, fanatical and protective, came pouring after Vilkata down the stairs, to take up their positions swirling behind him like an evil mist. None of these creatures darted ahead to scout, because the Eyeless One had already warned them that he must be first to enter the room where the Tasavaltan Swords were kept. The Dark King walked at the head of his powers alone—except, of course, for Pitmedden, who continued to provide his sight.

Yes, Vilkata was thinking, the weapons and tools arrayed here in profusion left no doubt that he had reached the armory. Now, to locate the room of Swords . . .

Holding the murmuring, faintly roaring steel of Skulltwister—in his own demonic vision a towering spear of pale fire—raised before him as he advanced toward the Sword-vault through the lowest level of the palace, Vilkata sighted from the corner of his eye a movement on his left which was not demonic. To his surprise he became aware that someone else, a single human figure, was walking there in the dim light, indeed was steadily approaching him.

A moment later, scowling doubtfully, the Dark King felt an inward chill as he identified the newcomer as the newly-converted Karel. Yes, Princess Kristin's wizard-uncle, the same almost-tearful convert who just a minute ago, up on one of the higher levels of the palace, had informed Vilkata of the words of the incantation necessary to open both inner and outer sealings of the Sword-vault.

As Pitmedden's vision presented the image of the Tasavaltan magician, the old man's hands, slightly upraised, were empty. Karel's mien was humble, his smile gentle and apologetic, as befitted a convert in the full flush of his enthusiasm.

Vilkata was vaguely puzzled. Only moments ago he had left Karel behind him, at the head of the last flight of descending stairs. Had the Tasavaltan wizard so quickly disobeyed orders and followed him downstairs out of some irrational concern for Vilkata's welfare? Or did Karel perhaps come bearing urgent information? Some fresh news of Prince Mark? Or—?

"What is it now?" the Dark King snapped at the approaching one. Meanwhile his swarm of demons hung over his head, snarling and droning among themselves, like poison bees around his ears. However Vilkata's bodyguard perceived this human walking toward them, the figure caused them no alarm.

Stephen, having closed now within a few paces of his enemy, seeing the tall man's pale face with its scarred and empty sockets turn toward him, felt a chill of fear, despite his intellectual confidence in Sightblinder's protection. When the villain snapped a question at him, the young Prince, suffering another wave of confusion, hardly understood what the man was saying.

Under the continuing burden of the two Swords' double magic, Stephen wondered who the Dark King took him for . . . a moment passed before the lad realized that it hardly mattered. Vilkata was not alarmed or alerted. There was no need for him, Stephen, to pretend anything. The Sword of Stealth would do all the necessary pretending for him.

But duration and reality were crumbling. His next step toward the Dark King seemed to take forever. The young Prince tried to steel his nerves by reminding himself that his father, even as a boy, had held two Swords simultaneously and had survived the experience.

Stephen advanced another pace toward his foe, and yet another. In fact he was walking almost at normal speed, yet each stride seemed to be protracted through endless time. It seemed to be taking him minutes, hours, just to get from one room of the armory to the next.

The tall, hideous figure of his enemy shrugged, and turned away from him again . . . but the double magic of the Swords was roaring in Stephen's ears, and now, whatever else happened, he was going to have to stop, for just a moment, to try to organize his thoughts. . . .

Brutal, physical noise cleared the cobwebs of magic from his mind, and momentarily shocked the young Prince back to full awareness. Ever louder and more savage had grown the sounds of disturbance drifting in through the high, barred windows of the lower levels of the palace. The cheering, roaring tumult issuing from the Mindsword itself was being drowned out, swallowed up in the rush of similar sounds from human throats. It sounded as if a joyous crowd was pouring out into the streets around the palace to welcome the arrival of their glorious new Master. The conversion had overtaken hundreds, perhaps thousands of the citizens of Sarykam in their sleep, had engulfed everyone within the palace and the houses on the nearby streets, all who had been within an arrow's flight of the Sword of Madness along whatever route its bearer had used to enter the city.

Now the roaring had become more raucous. Individual screams and challenges testified that something like all-out war had erupted in the precincts of the city surrounding the palace. Of course, besides the possible thousands of new converts, there would still be an even greater number who had remained outside the Mindsword's sharply defined range. The fanatical converts could not but see the latter now as deadly enemies, no matter that they might have been close relatives or friends an hour ago—and the converts were ready to strike for their Master in deadly earnest, and with the full advantage of surprise.

Stephen blinked and looked around, to find himself alone. Now where had Vilkata got to? He must be up ahead, he must by now have reached the repository of the Swords. Now the young Prince, still doubly armed, clinging to his sanity and alertness as best he could, forced himself to follow.

* * *

The Dark King had already forgotten for the moment the perfect image of a nodding, smiling, speechless Karel, approaching him obsequiously, because Vilkata was sure that he had now reached the Sword-chamber itself. Still holding the Mindsword raised before him like a torch, he had arrived at the doorway of a vaulted room which, if the directions he'd been given were correct, must be the very one he wanted.

The wizard placed a sensitive hand high on the stone wall, fingers delicately stroking. Shreds of old Karel's protective magic clinging to the doorway, ineffective now but still perceptible, assured the invader that he had come to the right place—and supporting evidence, tending to confirm that this was no ordinary room, was visible in the form of a dead body, physically mangled, on the floor inside.

Vilkata paused, scowling. Just here and now, he could not interpret the presence of a corpse as a sign that things were going well.

His escort of demons, droning almost mindlessly, still filled the air around him.

Using the glowing point of Skulltwister, the tool readiest to hand, the Dark King quite easily, almost absent-mindedly, put aside whatever bits of Karel's handiwork still survived about the doorway. Taking note of the nature of these remnants of enchantment as he did so, and of how completely their fabric had been torn apart, he thought: *Akbar has certainly been here.* That senior demon, and few other beings, human or demonic, could have shredded Karel's defensive handiwork in such a way. But then the question persisted: Where was Akbar now?

After stepping across the threshold of the Sword-chamber, Vilkata paused again before approaching the inner vault, whose doors he saw were closed. He delayed a moment to study more closely the body on the floor. With faint disappointment the Dark King saw that the dead man was no one he could recognize as an enemy.

Particularly the intruder now took note of the blasted Sword-hilt in the corpse's hand.

Vilkata bent to investigate further; even without touching this relic he thought he could identify it, even drained of magic as it was. There was no doubt that these scorched wooden splinters, no gram of metal left, had once been part of the Sword Dragonslicer.

No doubt at all?

"Pitmedden."

"Master?"

"Do you pry his fingers open. I want to get a better look at that black wood, to make absolutely sure."

Some part of the vision-demon's nature took on the form of a dwarfish, malignant-looking human child, unnaturally hairy, crouched by the dead man's outflung right arm. In a moment the dead fingers loosed their grip.

The white dragon-symbol, offering a final confirmation of the smashed weapon's identity, was still visible upon the hilt.

A shattered Sword just now was even a worse sign than a dead body, because it was a sure indication that Shieldbreaker had already been brought into action.

Vilkata, scowling at this discovery, was suddenly no longer sanguine about his chances of finding the Sword of Force available when the inner Sword-vault—obviously this construction standing in the center of the chamber—should be opened.

In another moment he had employed the secret incantation given him by Karel, and the two doors thudded back.

Vilkata frowned to find the vault already emptied of its best treasure.

Only one Sword, obviously Stonecutter, was still in its rack. For the time being, Vilkata let it stay there. Above and below the single occupant, four empty velvet spaces yawned.

A moment later Karel appeared—for the second time in a few moments, as Vilkata thought. Princess Kristin's mighty uncle, as helpless in the Mindsword's grip as the humblest of servants, having now in great concern for his Master's welfare followed him downstairs, caught up with the Dark King in the Sword-chamber, discovered in his turn the body of Bazas, recognized the man, and expressed grief over the loss.

"What loss is that?" demanded the Eyeless One.

Karel murmured something to the effect that it was to be hoped that Bazas before dying had also seen the light, the glorious truth about Vilkata.

Vilkata mumbled viciously. "Old idiot, are you going to prove as useless as you look? What does it matter what a dead man thought or felt? The real loss is here; the most important Swords are gone. I want to know who has them."

Karel obediently turned his attention to the inner vault. He was clearly surprised, and every bit as chagrined as Vilkata, by the absence of Sightblinder and Shieldbreaker. "I do not know who has them, Master," he admitted sadly.

Vilkata shook his head impatiently at this evidence of ineptitude. "Well, where was Shieldbreaker when you saw it last? And Sightblinder? Surely they *are* customarily kept here?"

"Yes, sire. I had thought they would be here now." The old wizard continued to look stricken at the loss.

"Well, find them! You know the people here, the lay of the land. Use your vaunted powers!"

The elder wizard looked gently pained. "Master, if whoever now possesses those two Swords does not wish to be found, neither my powers nor any others will search effectively." And the graybeard made a helpless gesture.

Of course he was right. The Dark King gestured too, and muttered, summoning into the armory more demons, who rolled down the stairs like so many billows of smoke. A moment later, fearing Shieldbreaker in the hands of some unknown enemy, he shouted to bring more human converts to his side as well, potential unarmed champions and defenders if he should need them.

To the young Prince, who had been brought to a virtual halt two rooms away, these additional demons, which would ordinarily have sickened him to the point of disability, now seemed no more than storm-wraiths passing at a distance. Armed as the boy was, they could neither harm him nor even really see him; each demon, Stephen supposed, must be perceiving him as one of their own kind, or as the wizard whom they worshipped, no matter that the real wizard was visible only a few paces distant. Such was the power of the Sword of Stealth. . . .

Stephen's mind was for the moment clear again, though he had to struggle to keep his perceptions and his balance steady. Once more his feet were carrying him relentlessly, almost silently, toward the Swordroom, and in each hand he still held a heavy weapon poised.

Whatever conscious fear he had experienced a few moments ago was now completely gone, and even his dizziness and disorientation were now abated, swallowed up in a burst of murderous rage directed at this intruder. Shieldbreaker's steady, muffled hammering sounded no louder than the beating of his own heart.

When he saw who stood beside the Dark King in the pose of an adviser, Stephen's rage, unreasonably enough, extended to Karel. But Karel at the moment was in no danger; he was not the one who had to be struck down.

The young Prince's quarry, a powerful man, an almost matchless wizard, seemed unable to hear or see the doom which was coming upon him. This tall creature before Stephen, pale and eyeless as a cave-worm, repulsively malignant and at the same time helpless, was the evil man who two years ago had almost killed Stephen's mother and had come near bringing disaster upon the whole realm.

Yet again the moment of final confrontation was postponed. One of the flock of circling demons, evidently caught up in an ecstatic urge to worship the figure it perceived as its true Master, came flitting toward Stephen—then, at the last moment, turned in terror, on the point of flight from whatever sudden alteration it now saw in the shape before it.

In a spasm of hatred and revulsion the youth armed with the two Swords killed the demon. An effortless flick of the young Prince's right wrist, a single drumbeat from the Sword of Force, and the hideous thing was gone—he wondered why the man who was going to be his next victim should not at least have heard that much warning? Because, the demon-killer quickly understood, Sightblinder muffled and transformed everything. . . .

Yet perhaps the Dark King had heard something after all. His demeanor changed; he was almost alert. Warned by his powers that some new violence had occurred, but unable to pinpoint precisely what had taken place or where, he looked about him nervously. . . .

The magical and physical searches of the armory and lower palace, which moments ago Vilkata had commanded certain demons to perform, had already been carried out. Helpless against the Sword of Stealth, the searching demons had discovered no human presence unaccounted for—none save their Master's own, and that of his loyal converts.

The searchers were once more swirling round him even now, reporting. "There is no one here who means you harm, great Master, no enemy at all. . . ."

But of course, the Dark King thought, cursing suspiciously, such a negative result was all one would expect in the case of an enemy working under Sightblinder's protection—the searchers however diligent and clever, would be unable to perceive—

In the next moment, just as Stephen with weapons raised approached the door to the Sword-chamber, Karel, the real Karel standing just inside, turned an astonished countenance to confront him briefly.

"Master?" the old man asked, in wild bewilderment. Then, turning from Stephen to the genuine Vilkata standing just beside him, he uttered the same word once more.

"Master?" And with that the helpless old magician, befuddled like all Sightblinder's victims, fell down in a near-trance of terror or worship, and was for the moment forgotten by the dueling powers that were about to come crashing into conflict.

Vilkata's thought on the subject had no chance to develop further. Stark terror gripped the Dark King's guts and seemed to stop his heart.

Because a figure of utter and abysmal terror had just stepped from somewhere into the very room where he was standing. This entity came seemingly from nowhere, and immediately the Dark King knew in his bones that this confrontation meant his doom.

Facing him now was Prince Mark, in full battle gear, smiling a terrible smile of triumph, and lifting Shieldbreaker for the killing blow—*or was the truth yet worse than that?*

The fact that the approaching figure was being transformed even as Vilkata watched it made the apparition more terrible rather than less— the truly powerful were often capable of appearing in any guise they chose. The Eyeless One now perceived with merciless clarity, he was for a moment utterly convinced, that he was confronted by Orcus, the king demon, archfoe of Ardneh.

Not Mark. Still worse even than a triumphant Mark.

Orcus of old legend, the equal at least of Arridu in strength, peerless even among demons in sheer malignity, and somehow now rendered immune to Sightblinder's control . . .

But in the next moment the figure was transformed again, and the Dark King beheld Ardneh himself, a body looking squarish and half-mechanical, ancient and utterly terrible to demons; the implacable enemy as well of wizards who preferred demons to humanity.

And yet again, repeatedly, Vilkata's perception of the figure changed. Flickering in rapid succession, there came an image, more an intimation, of Vilkata's own archrival in evil magic, Wood—then he was certain he was seeing Wood, pretending to be Orcus. Then vice-versa.

And now once more he beheld Prince Mark, fully armed with the Sword of Force, immune to any influence Skulltwister could exert. . . .

Whipsawed by these various possibilities, the Dark King was left in a state of terror beyond thought, worse than what could have been evoked by any single, simple presence. His instinctive reaction was to pull a trigger of enchantment, to activate a long-prepared reflex of flight.

He knew that his Enemy, whatever mask It wore, whatever powers It wielded, was One. Certainly someone, a single being, had slipped inside Vilkata's ring of ferocious demonic bodyguards, had confused and blinded them, neutralized them, with such ease and strength that they might as well not have been there at all.

* * *

And in these moments of Vilkata's freezing terror, the young Prince approaching, his deliberate strides now bringing him almost within Sword's-length of his foe, his own perception now feverishly enhanced by holding Sightblinder, was able to do more than recognize with absolute certainty his father's great and almost lifelong enemy the Dark King.

Now Stephen found himself empowered, even compelled, to study the man, in the most chilling and disgusting detail.

The face strongly featured, except for the ghastly empty eyesockets—a face looking neither young nor old—the clothing, rather nondescript for a great king and wizard—the pallid, powerful body.

With a feeling of unutterable loathing, the young Prince stepped forward and willed to strike with the Sword in his right hand.

And, at the same time, the thought existing simultaneously, Stephen consciously reminded himself that he must be ready to try to rid himself of Shieldbreaker on short notice, should his enemy at the last instant be unarmed. Then he, Stephen, would have to use the weapon in his other hand instead; use Sightblinder as a simple piece of sharpened, weighty steel, a physical killing device like any other sword. The Swords were all of them, save Woundhealer, effective in that simple deadly way.

And Vilkata in that same instant, overwhelmed by a mind-bending agony of fear, instinctively raised his own weapon, and at the same time willed with all his soul his magical escape. . . .

The man's body was almost completely dematerialized in flight before metal clashed on metal and one phase of the gods' great magic broke against another.

In the almost instantaneous surge of combat, the Sword of Force responded at once to the movement of Vilkata's Sword, and simultaneously to Stephen's will to kill. There was a jar of opposition, an instant of overwhelming violence—the Mindsword was blasted into splinters.

A stunning explosion accompanied the clash, an echo in the ears of Stephen of the recent blast in which Dragonslicer had perished. This latest detonation stung at Karel's helpless, fallen body, and wounded more than one of the converted people who happened to be standing near. The demons nearby too felt pain from the passage of those smoking fragments.

* * *

Stephen, as in his earlier encounter with Bazas, felt his arm pulled violently through a hacking motion. Fresh pain shot through his shoulder.

The young Prince assumed for a moment that his enemy must be dead. Then, when he could see clearly again, he realized that none of the bodies he could now see on the stone floor was that of the Dark King.

Vilkata had been slightly injured by the Sword-blast, but not enough to interfere with his escape. He continued instinctively to concentrate all his remaining energies upon the magical retreat he had already willed.

The Dark King's vanishing, to somewhere outside the palace walls, was magically swift, quick enough to save him from most but not all of the Sword-fragments.

Had Vilkata's flight been an eyeblink slower Stephen could have and would have killed him on the spot, thrusting Sightblinder awkwardly, left-handed, into the guts of the suddenly unarmed man.

That thrust was ready, but it was never made.

7

With a crash that resounded in his own ears like a minor thunder-clap, Vilkata's body arrived—somewhere.

So rapid had been his magical escape from the underground armory that he had even been separated from Pitmedden, the demon who provided him with vision, thus rendering himself at least temporarily sightless. Still, the flight-spell had succeeded admirably, and the Dark King felt reasonably sure that for the moment at least he was physically safe.

The utter, weak-kneed terror induced by his confrontation with the ultimate horror in the armory was gone. He had escaped, and for the moment he was alone. . . .

But where was he now?

All he could be certain of was that he was lying awkwardly facedown upon a curved surface that felt like wet stone, his body caressed by a whispery breeze that suggested outdoor air, amid invisible surroundings which smelled like a mudpuddle. This place, wherever it was, was quiet, shockingly so after the abrupt termination of the Mindsword's cheering noise. But somewhere nearby water was trickling audibly.

Against the power of the spell Vilkata had just uttered, mere stone walls, regardless of their thickness, could have had little or no constraining effect, and he had no doubt that he was now outside the palace walls.

But where?

A quick groping about him with both hands provided no very helpful information. His body was draped, in what occurred to him must be a most undignified manner, over a hard, wet surface curved, now that he thought about it, like the rim of one of the fountains in the central plaza of Sarykam—certainly the shape felt more like a fountain than a watering trough. He remembered a number of each located in the plaza before the palace, and along the adjoining streets.

And the Dark King could still feel, clutched in his right hand but emptied of all magic, the Mindsword's hilt. Reflexively he passed the fingers of his left hand over the raw, splintered end, making absolutely sure that all the Blade with all its power was really gone.

Long moments passed in which the Dark King continued probing his immediate environment by groping around him with both hands and listening intently. He learned very little by these means, but did get his body into a less awkward position. He was sitting now on the fountain's rim, his booted feet on some kind of pavement. Wherever he was, his sight-demon still had not caught up with him.

Another thing to worry about. Suppose the creature had not survived the encounter with Shieldbreaker? That was a distinct possibility. And could Pitmedden's fellows, the Dark King's entire force of demons, have been scattered or destroyed as well?

He, Vilkata, continued to be utterly alone and Swordless. Gradually his body reassumed the crouched defensive posture he had instinctively adopted as his magic shot him like a spirit out of the armory.

Muttering spells, he loaded and surrounded his own sightless body with further protective magic. Afraid to move, he crouched where he was, and continued to concentrate upon his hearing.

Below a variety of other sounds, he could detect those of nearby crickets, cheerful elementary creatures remarkably unperturbed by human and demonic travail and violence. Farther off were a couple of barking dogs, and a distant outcry of human voices. And, at the moment, very little else.

Vilkata grunted as he came to realize—somewhat belatedly because of the general wetness of his surroundings—that he was bleeding from several small wounds, tears and punctures in his arms and legs. The wounds called themselves to his attention by starting to grow painful—inordinately so, it seemed, for their size. Gingerly he probed them, one after another, with a finger. They were throbbing as if they might have been made by some poisoned weapon. After a moment's thought the Dark King realized that these injuries had very likely been made by tiny fragments of the shattered Mindsword.

He muttered curses to himself, and waited. Another seemingly endless interval—it was really only the space of a breath or two—passed before the demon Pitmedden managed to catch up with his angry Master and, apologizing abjectly for the delay, magically reattached itself to his very brain.

The Dark King's sight immediately came back, his anger weakened with his relief, and he could see that his first thought about a fountain in the plaza had been correct. His trousers and boots and half of his upper garment were dripping wet. Now he disentangled himself completely from the low stone structure and stood erect, glaring about him into the night.

Looming almost over him, less than a hundred meters distant, was the bulk of the Tasavaltan palace; his swift escape had carried him a lesser distance than he had thought. Behind many of the huge building's windows lights were coming alive and moving about uncertainly. From those same apertures there issued the sounds of exotic human ecstasies and sufferings, results of Skulltwister's recent passage, making the Dark King smile.

Only now, having regained his sight and determined his location, did the Dark King slowly unclench his fingers from the dead hilt of what had been the Mindsword. He stared, with borrowed vision and gradually growing understanding of the implications, at the lifeless fragment on his broad white palm.

Meanwhile his servant-demon Pitmedden had not only restored the Dark King's sight, but in quick response to his urgent commands had started trying to heal his freshly bleeding wounds and relieve their pain.

Soon this unlikely physician reported that the injuries resisted the usual methods of magical treatment. The patient only snarled in response; the wounds were not vital, his tolerance for physical pain was high, and he had greater matters to worry about just now.

Along some of the main streets converging on the plaza, there burned gaslights, famed for their decorative effect; other main thoroughfares in Sarykam, like the plaza itself, were lit by magically-enhanced torches set on metal poles at regular intervals. Even as the demon finished its attempt at healing, Vilkata was distracted from his various problems by the sight of human movement nearby. A single passing stranger, a man of nondescript appearance simply garbed in gray, definitely a commoner by the look of him, had just turned onto the plaza from one of the adjoining streets and was now crossing the paved and planted area as if on his way to some early morning job. The fellow was carrying in a bag what might have been a set of gardener's tools, as well as a spade or shovel over his shoulder.

Whether the briskly moving gardener—or perhaps a gravedigger, out on some early job—walked through darkness or through light, in the shadows from the plaza's lamps or under their direct illumination, Vilkata could see part of him—not much more than an outline—equally well. The details of his person, perceived only through demonic vision, came out poorly—attempts to see certain things by that means were doomed to failure.

Beholding the man through the demon's often selectively distorted perception, Vilkata thought at first that he appeared to be wearing a simple mask—and a minute later that the fellow had no face at all. The Dark King growled at Pitmedden, and the demon squealed in anguish, but the seeing got no better.

Meanwhile the man in gray was behaving as if he could see just as well as the Dark King could, or better, though Vilkata thought the place where he himself was standing must appear to normal human eyesight to be in heavy shadow.

This passing gardener, sexton, or whoever he was, favored the now-Swordless conqueror with a little saluting gesture. His voice was brisk and cheerful. "Good evening, sir. Or should I say good morning?"

Vilkata only stared back at this workman who sounded courteous, though not at all like one freshly enslaved by the Mindsword. No doubt the fellow had been just beyond Skulltwister's reach before the Sword was destroyed, and had no idea of his narrow escape. Even now the increasing uproar of the converts in and around the palace was spilling out into the streets; but the workman, as if deaf, was totally ignoring it.

Before going on his way, the other paused to add: "The choice, I think, is up to you."

No more than a few breaths after the arrival of his vision-demon Pitmedden, within the short interval of time after the workman had walked on but before any other human had yet discovered him, the now-Swordless Dark King with an effort of will managed to recover a large measure of his self-possession.

Suddenly his spirits rose. Here came Arridu, whistling down out of the night, a giant subdued and harnessed, compelled by the even greater power of the Mindsword to feel anxiety for the welfare of his human Master.

And here at last came a small handful and then a score of converted humans, including Karel himself, running across the plaza, as joyful as so many demons to see Vilkata alive and not seriously injured. Raising his voice to speak to all of them at once, Vilkata related to his followers a condensed and unemotional version of the confrontation in the Sword-vault, and his own hair's-breadth escape. He mentioned nothing of his own abysmal terror.

On hearing of the Dark King's close call, Arridu, inflamed with the need to protect his Master and avenge his injuries, screamed demonic outrage and flew back into the palace to scout. Arridu returned a few moments later to say that the enemy, whoever it had been, was no longer in the armory.

Vilkata only grunted. The demons freshly come from the Moon perhaps did not fully grasp the power of the Mindsword yet.

Arridu stood before him in the shape of a titanic warrior, armored all in black. "But who was it who attacked you, Master?"

"I—could not be sure." He paused, looking about him at the rest of his retinue. "Understand, all of you, that this enemy is probably equipped with the Sword of Stealth. Perhaps I will have to explain more fully just what that means." Vilkata himself had needed long moments after his escape to come belatedly to understand that the being he thought he had seen down there must have been only a phantom generated by Sightblinder, the deceptive image of some real person who not only enjoyed the powers of the Sword of Stealth, but worse, who struck with Shieldbreaker. . . .

And only now, when he began to try to put the event into words, did full comprehension dawn. Vilkata's first sensation on realizing the deception was one of shuddering relief; he had faced only some well-armed human; *that being* was not coming after him. But then . . .

"Shieldbreaker," the Dark King breathed aloud.

Pitmedden and Arridu were concerned, as was Karel and other converted humans; the number gathered around Vilkata was steadily increasing. "My great lord?"

"Nothing."

Whoever his real opponent in the armory had been, he, the Dark King, had survived an armed encounter with the Sword of Force, a feat few men or gods or demons ever had accomplished . . . and those only when they had been able to break the skirmish off.

But even Shieldbreaker was not the whole story. He had actually, Vilkata now realized, survived a simultaneous confrontation with Shieldbreaker *and* Sightblinder. The figure which had terrified him so had not in fact been Orcus or Wood, but someone, some human enemy, not only armed with two Swords but able to use them both virtually simultaneously.

Vilkata realized that his arms were trembling. He was *very* lucky indeed to be alive.

Again he briefly studied the Mindsword's dead hilt, and having done so started to hide the piece of useless wreckage in a pocket of his clothing—then he abruptly changed his mind and cast it violently away from him.

At least, he thought suddenly, he now had a good explanation for what had happened to Akbar.

For years Vilkata had been carrying that demon's life around with him. Now he reached into a pocket with trembling fingers, brought out and unwrapped the object—like many chosen abodes of demons' lives, it was in itself a simple, homely thing, in this case a small mirror of quite ordinary appearance.

Inside its untouched wrappings, the mirror had been diced, not broken, into a hundred fragments, as if by some steel edge keen enough to deal with glass like paper.

The time elapsed since the Dark King's arrival at the palace did not yet amount to half an hour.

He threw away the glittering bits of what had been the demon's life-object; no magical virtue of any kind remained to it.

Over the next minute or so Vilkata was distracted from the contemplation of his various problems, and somewhat heartened, by the continued arrival from the direction of the palace of still more of his demons, howling their joy to find him safe; and, within moments, more dozens, scores, hundreds of people, all rejoicing loudly in his living presence and outraged by his wounds. These starry-eyed folk came running up to gather round him at a respectful distance in the predawn darkness.

The numbers of these human worshippers seeking him out continued to increase. The thought occurred to the Dark King, bringing with it a wave of bitterness, that these folk were certainly the last converts the Sword of Glory would ever make.

Karel was far from being the only high-ranking defector from the palace. A number of others could claim with justification to have been quite high in Tasavaltan councils. These important people in particular kept trying to get closer to Vilkata, though with violent gestures he did his best to keep them all at a little distance. With touching remorse they tried to plead with him for his forgiveness for their own evil deeds, their years of support of that vile renegade Prince Mark, for their protracted and stubborn and incomprehensible opposition to the Dark King's beneficent rule.

Now that their eyes had been opened by the glorious Sword of Glory— so some of them now loudly assured their new Master—they could see the light of truth, appreciate the proper and natural order that ought to hold in human affairs.

Karel himself was among the first converts to locate his new Master outside the palace. The fat old man ran up gasping and wheezing, then knelt down trembling, to give thanks for the Dark King's survival; the fact that he prayed to Ardneh evidently did not strike his convert's mind as inconsistent; Vilkata himself was faintly amused.

And then Karel began to do his best magically to heal the sting of the wounds made by the Sword-fragments. In this he was soon more successful than any of the demons had been.

But dominating Vilkata's thoughts amid the prayerful babble of this swelling human mob was the realization of how soon these turncoats were going to turn on him again. With his empty sockets the Dark King glared balefully at them all, Karel included. Nothing was more certain than that, with the Mindsword gone, most of these contemptible scum would be his mortal enemies again in a matter of only a few days—in some cases only hours would pass before there was reversion.

That posed a grim prospect for him and his plans; but there was one aspect of it which he could enjoy in anticipation: When the time of their recovery came, these sycophants would regard their present behavior with a loathing as great as that they now expressed for their own supposed sins in helping Mark.

Vilkata questioned Karel about General Rostov, Prince Mark's chief military commander, and learned that Rostov could not be immediately accounted for. The General had been on an inspection tour of the northern provinces, and, like the Prince and Princess, would have to be dealt with somehow later.

The Dark King's next question was about Ben of Purkinje.

With the exception of Mark himself, Ben was undoubtedly the individual whose appearance in an enslaved state would have most gladdened the conqueror's heart—but Vilkata had already been told, and had received independent confirmation of the fact from several sources, that Ben also had been out of town when the attack struck. Karel gave assurances, and Vilkata's other informants agreed, that Ben had gone with the Prince and Princess, and was most likely with them still. His home in town had already been visited, and he was not there.

By this time Vilkata, now surrounded by a thick swarm of anxiously protective demons and a cheering mob of human converts, had almost completely recovered his wits and his nerve. His usually savage temper was returning too.

What to do with these eagerly worshipful humans? In his sullen anger the elder wizard considered ordering them, while their fanaticism was still at its height, to kill each other off—but, on the verge of issuing that command, he had what struck him as a much better idea.

Presently, with the idea of deriving as much benefit as possible from their enthusiasm before it faded, Vilkata ordered the creation, from the ranks of the palace's converted soldiers, of several assassination squads. These were to sally out into the countryside, targeting whatever unconverted Tasavaltan leaders they might find there, especially Prince Mark. There was at least a fair chance, the Dark King supposed, that before the Sword-based conversion of these troops wore off one of them might actually manage to destroy Mark. At worst, they would be scattered, and at a considerable distance from himself, when their current adoration began to turn to hatred.

Vilkata found he was still unable to free himself totally of the lingering notion that, despite his logical deductions regarding Sightblinder, despite the reassurances of Karel and of Arridu and others, his opponent in the armory might after all, somehow, have been Wood—or one of the other possibilities, which bore thinking about even less. Shuddering with the recent memory of that awesome presence, the Dark King could not connect it with any mere sniveling Tasavaltan princeling.

But when Vilkata questioned his retinue on the subject of Wood, he soon learned from one of his demon aides, or from some converted soldier or magician, that about a year ago that master wizard had fallen to his doom and death before the power of Shieldbreaker in the hands of Prince Mark's nephew Zoltan.

Had Vilkata still retained the state of mind in which he had begun the attack, had he not been obsessed by the fresh loss of the Mindsword, the news of Wood's death would have been reason for celebration—one important competitor eliminated. Vilkata also heard, with some satisfaction, that the Sword Wayfinder had been destroyed by the Sword of Force at the same time that Wood fell.

An hour ago the news of that destruction, too, would have afforded the Dark King satisfaction, because that recently it had still been his ambitious plan eventually to acquire and somehow eliminate all of the Swords except the Mindsword.

If the report concerning Wayfinder were true, then he now had good evidence that five of the original Twelve Blades had already been destroyed—Townsaver and Doomgiver some years ago, and now Wayfinder, Dragonslicer, and the Mindsword. Yet seven more—Shieldbreaker, Sightblinder, Coinspinner, Farslayer, Woundhealer, Stonecutter, and Soulcutter—were still in existence somewhere.

Of course it was Shieldbreaker which Vilkata most dreaded, and most craved to possess—as would any prudent man in his current position. He could still feel the shock of that Sword-smashing impact running up his arm. His minor wounds still stung despite the demon's, and even Karel's, ministrations.

But there was hope. Now a human convert physician, the latest to have served the royal family in the palace, was in attendance on the Master. The woman was putting on salves and urging patience.

. . . Yes, when one was setting out to subdue the world, Shieldbreaker had to be one's Sword of choice, even beyond such fearful tools as Sightblinder and Soulcutter. As had just been so violently demonstrated, the Sword of Force was quite capable of nullifying any other weapon, magical or physical, that might be used against its owner. Even the Sword of Vengeance, which otherwise, launched from the hands of a determined enemy anywhere in the world, could end his own much-hated life at any moment. Meanwhile, the ugliest weapon of all, the Tyrant's Blade, was a wild card with the potential of overthrowing all the calculations of Vilkata or any other human.

Ultimately the Sword of Force was going to present a special problem, even after Vilkata came into control of it, as he thought he eventually must do if he was ever going to rule the world—a special case, because so far he had been able to conceive of no way in which Shieldbreaker itself could ever be destroyed. Even had he eventually been able, by means of the Mindsword, to perfect his mastery over the thoughts and bodies of every thinking being on the Earth, yet the Sword of Force, however he might attempt to hide or bury it, would present a perpetual danger to his rule.

There might be discoverable some method, though, by which it would be possible to eliminate Shieldbreaker. He did not consider the matter hopeless—but at the moment, of course, he was a totally Swordless man, and had to make his plans under all the disadvantages being in that state entailed.

For a minute or two he had been thinking about Swords, concentrating on the problems they posed to distract himself from the pain whilst his small wounds were cauterized by the palace physician, with Karel's help.

Presently Vilkata, now thoroughly and protectively surrounded by a clamorous escort of outraged demons and human converts—those of his human worshippers who could best tolerate being near the demons—decided that, Swords or not, he should delay no longer his re-entry of the palace. Certainly he was not going to conquer Tasavalta, or prevail against his superbly armed assailant of the armory, by huddling indecisively out here in the street.

But before he passed into the building again, the Dark King dis-

patched a small army of human converts ahead of him—he was determined to get as much use as possible out of these people while he could
—to scout and act as a temporary occupying force.

Of course, since Sightblinder was missing from the Sword-vault and
presumably had already been taken up and used by an enemy, no one
could be sure that the same enemy was not still lurking nearby somewhere.

The demon Arridu and the great converted wizard commiserated with
their lord and Master.

It was Karel who came up with the suggestion that any one person
armed with two Swords, especially Shieldbreaker and Sightblinder, must
almost certainly be undergoing psychic difficulties from the strain; the
problem would be worse if the simultaneous use of the Blades continued
for any length of time.

This was faint comfort to the Dark King. "But who was it, really, old
man? Can you tell me that?"

The old wizard discounted the idea that Mark himself could actually
be near, in the palace or even in the city; the royal couple were known to
be at some little distance.

Then Karel suggested that Vilkata's sole opponent in the armory had
very likely been young Prince Stephen. Who else known to have been
present would have been able to gain access to the Swords? Rostov had
been away.

The fact of Stephen seemed inevitable.

Karel went on: "The Mindsword having been so unfortunately denied
us, as you say, great and dear Master, we must try to find some other way
to make plain to the lad the truth of your superior nature. Failing that, of
course, we must find some way to get those Swords away from him. He is
badly misguided, but there must be some way."

"I eagerly await your discovery of an effective method." Vilkata looked
round him in all directions. "Meanwhile, I am not going to be kept out
here on the street because of the mere possibility of trouble."

Even as Vilkata re-entered the palace, this time going in through the
main entrance from the street, he was met by a minor demon bearing
electrifying news: the confirmation that at least one intact Sword, Stonecutter, was still available in the deep armory. This information was whispered in the Dark King's ear by a messenger sent out by Arridu, who
himself was mounting jealous guard upon the find.

This was no news to the Dark King, but now he decided that he had
better pick up at once the Sword which was available.

That the enemy had not taken Stonecutter was shrewdly regarded as evidence that the enemy might already be having trouble carrying Swords. This in turn argued for the young Prince rather than some more experienced and capable wizard or warrior.

Despite his eagerness to return to the underground storeroom of the Swords, the Dark King thoughtfully took care to disarm himself completely before doing so. He would rely upon his escort to deal with any problem that needed weaponry to solve. Now, let any enemy armed with Shieldbreaker dare to threaten him!

No enemy could be detected when the Dark King again descended to the level of the armory. No Sword-phantom appeared—at least he thought not. Of course, with Sightblinder one could never be sure.

Vilkata, on being welcomed and escorted back into the conquered palace of his enemies by a horde of joyous converts, was soon able to bring Stonecutter peacefully under his control.

Bitterly, Vilkata again cursed his failure to seize Shieldbreaker, or at least Sightblinder, in the first rush of his surprise attack.

Having opened the vault in the Sword-chamber unmolested, the Dark King stood staring earnestly at the sole intact Blade before him—yes, this was undoubtedly Stonecutter. He pulled the Sword of Siege unceremoniously out of its rack, looked at the small white wedge-sign on the hilt, and hacked a notch or two in floor and wall, just by way of final demonstration. Stone slid and crumbled away like butter before the Blade, which in action made its own hammering noise, heavier and slower than that of Shieldbreaker.

Vilkata tried to think whether there was any way in which this remaining Sword could be of notable benefit to him. Karel and Arridu, when consulted, could suggest nothing. Rather regretfully, the Dark King had to concede that Stonecutter had no immediate use. For the time being the Sword of Siege could stay here, under close guard and protection.

Meanwhile, other problems demanded the Dark King's immediate attention. Chief among these were the implications of the loss of the Mindsword. He understood that he had to put on a bold front in the presence of his subordinates, many of whom probably did not yet realize that Skulltwister was gone. Those who did were themselves still under the dazzling influence of its power, and so Vilkata thought they might not be able to grasp the importance of the loss. And, by the time they did, they would be tempted to rebellion.

Still staring into Prince Mark's Sword-vault, which was now empty but for the Sword of Siege, it occurred to Vilkata to wonder whether he ought to try to deceive his adversaries, and the world at large, into thinking he still wore the Mindsword at his side. Certainly it would be beyond his art to replicate the powers of Skulltwister, but he was quite a good enough magician to be able to create a visual simulacrum good enough to deceive the world, or almost all the world, for some time.

Then the Dark King was struck by a simpler idea. If deception was truly desirable, he could carry Stonecutter sheathed at his side in lieu of the Mindsword, letting others glimpse only the black hilt with its white symbol concealed.

8

MOMENTS after the explosion, Stephen came stumbling his way out of the Sword-chamber, leaving it for the second time in a few minutes. He felt half dead with exhaustion. The overwhelming challenge of the surprise attack had fallen upon him at the end of a long and wearying day of physical work, and in the first moments of that onslaught his body had been injured and his mind twisted. He had been allowed no time to recover from his skirmish with the demon before being subjected to the psychic burden of carrying the two Swords.

Now the young Prince had undergone the shock of combat with a mighty wizard, a clash in which the Mindsword had almost certainly been destroyed—the young Prince wanted desperately to believe that, but in his dazed state at the moment felt he could take nothing for granted. And his chief enemy, a man he considered worse than any demon, had been repulsed, if not killed. Vilkata had certainly disappeared, perhaps was dead.

The burdens of ongoing responsibility, and of the two Swords' magic, would not allow Stephen the luxury of triumph. At the moment he could think of little else but the sanctuary and help awaiting him in the house of his grandparents.

With regard to Jord and Mala, a horrifying possibility had already crossed their grandson's mind—suppose they had become the Mindsword's converts too? The youth would not, could not, allow himself to consider that possibility seriously. He told himself that most of the city must have escaped. The Dark King's attack must have been aimed first and primarily at the palace, with the objective of seizing the Tasavaltan Swords before an alarm could be sounded. But if, as seemed probable, the Mindsword had been destroyed before the area of its evil influence could be expanded, then the great majority of the city's population, all those more than a long bowshot from the palace, should have retained the mastery of their own minds and souls—and this majority should have included Stephen's grandparents. Fiercely the young Prince assured himself that it must be so.

A few of the Mindsword's final converts, servants and soldiers and palace functionaries so recently loyal to Tasavalta, now shrieking and crying their concern for their new Master's welfare, had come belatedly following Vilkata down to the lower level of the palace. Now these people had been thrown into panic by the Dark King's sudden disappearance, and were raising an alarm.

Stephen, his right shoulder and his bruises aching, all the muscles of his body weary, heard these folk, many of whom had been his friends, babbling their concerns for the fiend's welfare. The young Prince ignored them as he had ignored Karel after the most recent Sword-blast. Stephen went on dragging Shieldbreaker and Sightblinder, the bare blades trailing, up a broad flight of stairs to the ground floor of the palace. The two Swords seemed too heavy now for him to carry in any normal way.

On the stairs and above them, turmoil continued. Demons and shrieking human converts seemed to be everywhere, on the ground level of the huge building as well as in the basement. Most of the faces of Skulltwister's victims were familiar to Stephen. Others he would have known, but did not, because their ecstasies of hate, rage, and devotion transformed them into strangers.

Since leaving the Sword-chamber, the young Prince had not dared to sheathe either of his deadly Blades. He could only assume that Sightblinder was working effectively as always, because so far none of the enemies surrounding him on every side had challenged him, but rather were promptly giving way. Most went hurrying past him on the stair with averted faces. On the rare occasion when one came near, Stephen drove the man or woman away with a sharp gesture, a wave of one of his Swords. What Sightblinder made the other see when he did this, he did not know, but the method was effective.

So far Stephen had been able to overhear only disconnected odds and ends of speech from the strange beings, converts and demons, among whom he was suddenly an isolated stranger. And still he had no way of determining whether his family's archenemy Vilkata had survived the Mindsword's negation or not. Those around Stephen who were chanting Vilkata's name in ecstasy said nothing to indicate that he might be dead.

Well, supposing that the Dark King still lived, the young Prince just now had neither the means nor the intention to seek him out. Not while Stephen's own soul felt as bleak and exhausted as it did just now, his battered body aching, and his head spinning with Sword-magic until he feared that he would faint.

* * *

The young Prince came to a pause, body swaying slightly. He had, without quite realizing it, reached the top of the long flight of stairs. He now stood on the ground floor, in one of the many rooms of the old palace whose original purpose had never been quite clear to him. But this room and its furnishings were perfectly familiar, and from here it was an easy task to choose a passage through the building which brought him quickly to one of the small side doors. A moment later Stephen was outside, and a minute after that he was opening an iron gate, leaving the palace grounds.

At every step, the young Prince kept hoping to catch some hint of a place nearby, a sanctuary where he might find a moment's safety, a chance to rest. But so far he had seen no hint that anything of the kind existed. He had only the Swords, and his own will, to depend on.

The city, or at least this portion of it, was as hectic as the palace itself had been. Screaming converts, some waving weapons and torches, some divesting themselves of their Tasavaltan livery of green and blue, seemed to be everywhere, indoors and out. Out in the street, just as in the palace, the dark night air seemed filled with demons. Shieldbreaker effectively warded off any sickening or other untoward effect caused by the presence of the foul creatures, but still Stephen was aware of the vast forms moving above him and around him, like ominous shadows behind thick glass.

Even after the youth had distanced himself by a full block from the palace grounds, he did not dare to sheathe either of his Swords. As a result, the psychic strain upon him continued to mount.

Only after he had dragged his double burden two full blocks from the palace did the number of visible enemies around him begin to diminish noticeably. But it seemed he had been wrong, the city away from the palace had not been spared by the attack. Horror, in several forms of human death and ruin, continued to dominate the streets around him.

Here Stephen walked among the blood and havoc those sounds of distant fighting had produced. His mind, already reeling with shock, took in the dead and wounded people, the smashed windows—a number of the shops and houses close to the palace boasted real glass—the wantonly slaughtered work-animals and pets, and general destruction. Here was a building totally destroyed, crushed like a toy by some wanton child, the ruins sprouting greedy flames. No one was paying any attention to the wreckage or the fire.

Several times during these first minutes of Stephen's struggle through the city he considered sheathing Shieldbreaker—but he could not be completely sure that Skulltwister was really gone. The Sword of Force intermittently muttered drumbeats of warning, and he dared not take the chance. Even had he been willing to put the Sword of Force away, it sporadically adhered by magic to his palm and fingers.

Neither could the young Prince nerve himself to muffle the power of Sightblinder. The Sword of Stealth, gripped tightly in his left hand, continued its silent and effective service. People and demons alike, whether individuals or roving bands, took one look at the image shown them by Sightblinder and silently, unanimously, gave Stephen a wide berth. To judge by the expressions on the human converts' faces, many or all of them must have been convinced that they were face-to-face with one of Vilkata's nastier demons. As long as Sightblinder continued to do its job, he might hope to avoid more shoulder-wrenching exercise with Shield-breaker.

The young Prince struggled on, squeezing the hilts of both his god-forged weapons, as if by that means he might moderate the dizzying currents of their power. But when he had progressed a little more than two blocks from the palace, he had to pause, gasping, and sit down on the curb. He was forced to concede that he could not long sustain the unremitting struggle with this double burden of magic.

Still, for the moment at least, there could be no thought of abandoning the struggle. Sternly Stephen put from him all thoughts of failure. Briskly he got to his feet and tried again. But his steps wavered, and before he had gone twenty paces more, dizziness and a feeling of mental fragmentation compelled him to stop again, to try to rest, and try to think. The trouble was that the Swords gave him no rest, no, not a moment's.

This time the young Prince had seated himself—almost he had collapsed—on a carriage block in front of the wrought-iron fence of one of the tall, elegant houses which here lined the avenue. Gritting his teeth, he continued to clutch the two black hilts. In the absence of any direct threat, his right hand at the moment had the power to sheathe and release the Sword of Force; but now Stephen was afraid that if he sheathed either Sword, or even put one of the pair down in search of a moment's relief, he would find it impossible to resume the double burden.

The strain was being intensified by the physical injuries the boy had suffered before coming under the protection of the Sword of Force, as well as by the shoulder damage inflicted by that very weapon. In his dazed and terrorized state immediately following his first encounter with a demonic foe, these hurts had passed almost unnoticed; but now they were making themselves felt.

Stephen, trying very awkwardly to rub his sore shoulder with the back of the hand still holding Sightblinder, realized with sudden insight that one weapon against which the Sword of Force could never protect him was itself. In his dazed condition, trying to rub his bruised left elbow with the back of his right hand, he cut his shirt, and came near wounding himself, with Shieldbreaker.

After trying without much success to rest and think, the young Prince again got to his feet—this time it cost him even more of a struggle than before—and resumed his effort to do what he knew that he must do. Every instinct shrieked that only disaster lay ahead unless he could find help, and soon.

Only a few more blocks, he told himself. Only a few hundred meters. He told himself that he ought to be able to run that far, and back again, in the time he'd already spent on this slow struggle.

Then he thought that trying to deceive himself, to make the matter sound easy, was a childish trick, and it wasn't going to work. He might as well tell himself it was kilometers instead of meters; the one was going to be as impossible as the other.

But no, it wasn't impossible. He was a Prince of Tasavalta, and his father's son, and he could do it, because there was no other choice. He'd just rest here another minute, or try to rest, and then . . .

The direction and location of his goal both remained clear in the mind of the young Prince. Jord, Stephen's grandfather, knew how to deal with Swords as well as any man alive could be said to do so—perhaps Jord, though he was no magician, really understood better than anyone else, because he had been the only human actually present and directly involved in the Twelve Blades' forging, more than forty years ago.

No longer, Stephen decided, were most of the people converts who came hurrying past him in the street. In this neighborhood the faces and the voices were different, terrorized but not fanatical. The great majority, like Stephen himself, were heading away from the palace, and a considerable number were actually fleeing in a panic. There were women with small children, a man trundling his household belongings in a cart. Even in their haste and fright they continued to give Stephen plenty of room, as did every demon swirling past him overhead. Demons were much scarcer here, and, as far as the young Prince could tell, those which appeared were not attacking the population now, but seemed rather to be continually patrolling, searching . . . more than likely, he realized, he himself was the object of their search.

On top of all Stephen's other difficulties a sense of guilt began to nag at him. Even armed as he was, almost invincibly, he was retreating and leaving the enemy in possession of the palace. Now and again he looked back over his shoulder. Sturdily he clung to the thought that his first instinct, to save the great treasure of the two Swords, had been correct: It would be impossible for him to vanquish or even seek for his hereditary enemy now, while he himself was so nearly incapacitated.

In fact the young Prince was being forced to a bleak decision: If the stress of magic continued as it was much longer, he might be compelled to abandon one of the Swords before he could get as far as his grandparents' house.

Jord and Mala's modest cottage had been built some years ago in a neighborhood of roughly similar homes, each with a small plot of grass and garden and a few shady trees. Through the darkest time of the late night the young Prince struggled on, holding in his mind a vision of that grassy shade where he had so often played as a small child.

Here was the street at last, and Stephen eagerly increased his pace. But as he turned the last corner his heart sank at the fresh signals of disaster. Straight ahead in the pre-dawn darkness he saw the glow of fire, and smelled fresh smoke.

Did he have the right street after all? Yes, there were landmarks—a shop where Mala had bought him candy, a tree girdled by a circular bench—to give grim confirmation.

The young Prince rubbed his weary eyes with the back of one Sword-bearing hand. But no, his eyes were not at fault. There was smoldering fire ahead where there ought to have been no fire; low flames flickering up, trying to gain strength to consume an entire building, provided illumination enough for him to confirm that there was only a collapsed and smoldering ruin where the familiar house had stood.

9

IMLY Stephen was conscious of the fact that the houses on either side of his grandparents' had also suffered heavy damage, though neither was as badly off as the cottage he had so often visited. One of the adjoining buildings was also smoking, as if it might soon start to burn; and two or three additional fires were visible at some distance in the neighborhood.

But just now the young Prince had no time or thought to spare for neighbors. He ran forward, still convulsively gripping a black hilt in each hand, though for the moment he had almost forgotten why it was essential to retain the Swords. Stephen's weary arms were allowing the two unbreakable points to drag, god-forged steel striking sparks from the cobblestones of the street.

Three or four neighbors, in nightshirts and hastily thrown-on clothing, had been standing within a few meters of the smoldering ruins. However these folk perceived the bearer of the Sword of Stealth, they at once drew back to give him plenty of room. One of the onlookers, getting a close look at Sightblinder's version of Stephen's approaching figure, screamed and ran away.

The other bystanders had not taken to their heels, at least not yet. For the moment the young Prince ignored them all, keeping his attention riveted on the jumbled ruins before him. Maybe, he thought wildly, Jord and Mala hadn't been home in their bed when disaster struck. Maybe . . .

Gasping, his whole body burning and aching with strain and weariness, Stephen halted under a fruit tree in what had once been his grandparents' grassy yard. It was all sickeningly unfamiliar now. A few meters ahead of him, small flames snapped avidly at freshly splintered wood, illuminating ruin. The fire seemed eager to establish a solid foothold in the timbers and siding which lay tumbled and broken among the shattered masonry and tiles.

"Grandfather! Grandmother!"

There was no reply.

Once more Stephen called upon his tired arms to lift his Swords so that the long blades ceased to drag. So armed, he edged closer to the ruin. The flames were not big enough—not yet—to force him back, nor were they growing swiftly. Intermingled in the wreckage with the broken and burned pieces of the building's structure were household items: pots, pans, furniture—there was a padded chair he thought he recognized—bundles of old clothes . . .

The gaze of the young Prince moved on, came back. In a moment he realized with horror that what he had thought for a moment were two bundles of old clothes, three-quarters buried in the rubble, were really the bodies of his grandparents, clad in nightshirt and nightgown. Gray hair was visible, exposed pale arms and legs.

Suddenly all of the night's horror, which had been starting to seem dreamlike, regained immediate reality. The grandson of Mala and Jord noted that the couple lay almost side by side, as if they had been together when the walls of their home crashed in around them—or possibly one had come to try to help the other. . . .

"Prince? Prince Mark?" Someone was pulling tentatively on Stephen's arm, speaking to him in a voice he dimly recognized. Turning, Stephen came face to face with a nextdoor neighbor, a man whose name he could not remember at the moment, but whom the boy had sometimes seen and spoken with on visits. The neighbor's face was altered, and he, like Stephen himself, seemed almost paralyzed by horror.

"Prince Mark?" the man repeated.

That name administered a shock of hope. The young Prince looked around dazedly, to see if his father might indeed be present. He needed a moment to realize that Sightblinder must be presenting him to the neighbor in his father's image.

"What is it?" Stephen at last responded to the man who stood beside him.

"May all the gods defend us, Prince Mark, the demons have done it. Killed the old people, knocked down their house and ours, too. The rest of the neighborhood is damaged, as you see. But now that you're here, you can shout the demons away again—you can do that, can't you? You must!"

For the moment, Stephen could only stare helplessly at the man.

The neighbor gazed back, pleadingly, his eyes now focused just over the top of Stephen's head—no doubt where Sightblinder was showing him the face of the taller Mark.

"Prince? We're going to win now, aren't we?" The man's voice cracked. "The army's coming?"

The moaning sound was slight at first, and Stephen almost failed to hear it over the background of nibbling flames and distant uproar in the streets. But it brought his eyes back to the crushed bundles under the rubble, and a moment later he saw movement in one of them. The moaning grew.

Though he could not be sure of the exact source of the sound, it testified that at least one of Stephen's grandparents—he could not tell who—still breathed.

"They're alive—!"

Upon making this discovery the young Prince cried out incoherently and gestured awkwardly, with Sword-filled hands. Realizing that he would need his hands free to save his grandparents from the slowly growing fire, he sheathed both Swords, an operation that seemed nightmarishly slow and awkward—he had to thrust several times with each steel tip to find the narrow opening in its respective sheath.

When Stephen released Sightblinder's hilt, the neighbor standing beside him recoiled, startled.

"Prince Stephen—but where's your father? He was just here." The man was blinking and stammering in confusion.

Stephen mumbled some kind of answer, even as he turned his back on the man to go climbing awkwardly into what was left of the ruined building, scratching his legs and ankles in the process. Reaching for Grandfather and Grandmother, whose bodies, partially buried, both lay just below reach, he started to dig into the rubble with his bare hands.

The long scabbards hanging on each side of Stephen's waist got in his way with every movement when he crouched to attack the wreckage. With feverish haste he slipped both Sword-belts off, setting them down within reach.

Grabbing a long, thick beam in an attempt to lift and move it, the young Prince succeeded only in burning his fingers, and discovering that his strength was not equal to the task.

The neighbor who had been talking to Stephen now climbed energetically into the rubble beside him and did his best to help. With that example before them, two more people, who had evidently been watching from a little distance, now came to give assistance.

With four pairs of hands to dig and lift, there appeared to be some chance of getting the two old people out of the wreckage—but one long beam was still wedged in place, preventing the rescue.

Even the united strength of everyone on hand was not going to be enough. The beam was held down at both ends.

The lad promptly turned to his Swords again, and slid the long blade of

Sightblinder from its sheath. With the other rescuers standing back to give him room, he dug other pieces of wreckage out of the way, then braced his feet and swung the Sword like a long axe, chopping at the beam.

As soon as he took up the Sword of Stealth again, his image once more changed in the eyes of everyone watching.

As Stephen had expected, a Sword's indestructible blade proved a good digging tool, an excellent chopper, an unbreakable pry bar. You had to be careful, of course, about stabbing or slicing the victims you were trying to rescue. In this case, fortunately, there was adequate clearance, and the bodies plainly visible.

It occurred to Stephen that, if the rules of Sword-magic worked as he had reason to believe they did, Shieldbreaker used as a digging or cutting implement ought not to hurt the flesh of an unarmed victim buried in the wreckage. But it crossed his mind also that either Jord or Mala could be armed, having grabbed up some weapon when an alarm was sounded.

Letting the Sword of Force rest in its scabbard, he continued chopping with the Sword of Stealth.

Stephen labored on, using the keen, indestructible edge to sever the fallen roof beam which at first had frustrated the rescue efforts. The seasoned wood was as thick as his leg; but the weighty sharpness of the steel made the Sword at least as good as an axe for this mundane purpose.

One of the neighbors, seeing what good success Stephen was having, grabbed up Shieldbreaker and used it to chop with too—the young Prince noted distinctly how the Sword of Force remained silent at this mundane task, like some proud warrior forced into routine, supposedly less heroic, labor.

As soon as the beam had been chopped through in two places, the helpful neighbor put Shieldbreaker awkwardly, but almost reverently, back in its sheath.

Now that the beam was cut, Stephen used Sightblinder as a lever, leaning his weight on the Sword to force up the remaining length of timber while others pulled the bodies free. Moments later, the bodies of Jord and Mala had been dragged and lifted as carefully as possible out of the smoldering rubble and laid gently on the grass.

This latest effort left the young Prince swaying on his feet with weariness. Tears of grief, anger, and fatigue were running down his cheeks, even as he looked down on the bodies of his grandparents. Mala and Jord were quiet now, and motionless. Stephen could not be certain for the moment that either of the old folk still breathed; but neither was he absolutely sure as yet that either one was dead. Both were marked with blood.

Sightblinder was still in the right hand of the young Prince when he bent anxiously over the old people to try to talk with them. Now he could be sure that his grandmother was dead; but Jord was muttering, trying to say something clearly.

Some helpful neighbor had gone to get water. Coming back, he tried to give the old man a drink.

Jord's eyes focused slowly on Stephen crouching beside him. In a moment the old man muttered: "Don't leave me, Mark."

Stephen hesitated, then retained his grip on the black hilt. He would let his grandfather see Mark, if that was what Jord wanted.

"I ought not to have kept a Sword on the wall, son. . . ."

Stephen had heard the story, from his father, often enough. It came from Mark's childhood. "It's all right, gr—. It's all right."

The old man let out a feeble breath. He had almost no voice left. "I shouldn't have forged Swords. Not that Vulcan gave me much choice."

And presently Stephen realized that those were the last words Jord was ever going to speak.

Stephen, preoccupied with grief, was still holding Sightblinder, unsheathed, when the great demon Arridu came swooping down upon the scene. The distraught young Prince did not even notice the wave of sickness brought by the demon until the foul thing was very near, until the neighbors had either scattered in blind terror, or fallen down in fear and demon-sickness. . . .

When Stephen turned his head at last, to his horror he beheld the figure, larger than humanity, of a man in black armor, bending to grab up the sheathed Sword of Force from the place where the Sword's last user had set it down.

A demon, an ungodly great demon by the look of it, had Shieldbreaker; though the Sword of Force was still undrawn, inactive in the enemy's hand—

The monster turned an almost paralyzing gaze on Stephen, and spoke. Nearly frozen in terror, the boy could scarcely hear or understand the words of its soft, rumbling voice; nor did he realize that they were uttered in humility: "The great Sword lay unattended here, dear Master. Any of these human beasts might have grabbed it up. I hold it for you—"

On the verge of fainting, Stephen lashed out at Arridu as best he could.

"In the Emperor's name, forsake this game—!" The young Prince

thought he could feel the veins standing out upon his forehead as he yelled.

And the Sword of Force and its hideous bearer were both gone, whirled aloft and out of sight in an instant.

Not until the demon had been banished, and a measure of sanity and stability had returned to the locality, did the young Prince realize the extent of his own blunder—*Shieldbreaker must have gone with the demon!*

Now that it was too late, the horrible memory came clear: his glimpsing the undrawn Sword of Force in Arridu's grip . . .

Stephen knew tremendous horror and guilt at the great loss . . . and fear that at any moment the demon, invincibly armed, would be coming back to eat him alive.

Meanwhile the last terrorized neighbor had crawled away somewhere. Stephen was alone in the night, with the crackling fire and the howls of riot and murder coming from the distant reaches of the city.

There was no disputing the fact that now both his grandparents were dead. There was no disputing either that the loss of Shieldbreaker was, for the moment at least, irretrievable. The doom of its return was hanging over him, and over all the Earth.

Staring numbly at the dead bodies of his grandparents, listening to the disorder and the horror of Sarykam around him—Arridu's brief presence had stirred up new tumult over an area of several square blocks—Stephen swayed on his feet with weariness.

Where now? What now? From somewhere in the back of his mind a simple, natural suggestion presented itself: He might try going to the house of Ben of Purkinje. Conscious planning might well have rejected that idea: If the enemy had sought out people as far removed from power as Jord and Mala, surely the home of Ben and his family would have received much more intense attention; if that house survived at all it would be watched.

Stephen started walking, seeking sanctuary, without being aware that he had made any decision about where he ought to go. Already the thought of Ben's house had slipped from his conscious awareness.

At least Sightblinder was still his—his hand still gripped, unconsciously, the hilt of the sheathed Blade—and he was vaguely aware that, unless an enemy armed with Shieldbreaker came against him first, the Sword of Stealth would get him safely out of the city and to his parents.

But first he must find a place where he could rest.

Walking slowly, still moving without a conscious plan, the young Prince felt himself in the grip of bitter guilt over the fact that he'd lost Shield-breaker. Stumbling, he felt himself abruptly overwhelmed by tiredness. There were moments when the world turned gray, and he came near fainting on his feet.

Before traveling very far away from the ruins of his grandparents' house, without even getting anywhere near the city gates—even before deciding what his next move had to be—he left the street, seeking some shelter where he could rest.

Turning from the noise of the street to pass through the open gate, he found himself behind high stone walls, in the garden of Ben's half-wrecked and freshly deserted house. This was definitely a more elegant neighborhood than Jord's and Mala's. . . .

Only after he had entered the grounds surrounding the big house did he consciously recognize this as the home of Ben of Purkinje and his family. It was not a place that Stephen had often visited. The roof had been smashed in, but here, too, the enemy had come and gone. Perhaps that meant it would be a safe place, for a little while, in which to rest. He'd rest for only a moment, relying on the Sword of Stealth, and then he'd move on. . . .

The young Prince stretched out in a grassy place under some bushes . . . but for the time being, sleep refused to come. The horned Moon, lately risen, and the stars provided all the light he needed. He lay directly on top of the naked Blade of Sightblinder, the fingers of both his hands interlaced around the hilt . . . he would rest for just a moment . . . he supposed there was nothing for it now but to make his way to Voronina, the village where his parents were—or where they had been. As soon as they got the news of the attack, they'd be on the move . . . somewhere.

But he'd find them. He could still bring them Sightblinder, and while he had that Sword and no other to carry, the journey ought to be quite feasible.

One Sword he still had—and that one he was not going to let go of. His life, and likely much more than his own life, depended on his ability to retain the Sword of Stealth.

Now, if he could only rest, close his eyes for a few moments, he would be able to push on again.

Vilkata, tightening his grip on the palace in the last hour before dawn, had secreted himself in one of the upper chambers, from which he kept issuing a stream of orders to demons and converts, patiently establishing his new base of operations in rooms which only hours ago had belonged to his great enemy.

Meanwhile the Dark King was steadily recalculating, reconsidering his situation. Like other people on both sides of the conflict, dwellers within the city as well as outside its walls, he was profoundly interested in what interference, if any, could be expected from the Swords still remaining in the world, or what advantage gained from them.

He assumed that Shieldbreaker and Sightblinder were still in the hands of his lone enemy of the recent confrontation. The locations of Soulcutter, Farslayer, and Coinspinner remained unknown as far as the Dark King was concerned; and each of these weapons in its own way was capable of completely turning the balance of the great game.

Grimly, Vilkata had determined that the loss of the Mindsword was not going to plunge him into a panic. His enemies were reeling too, and badly hurt; he had struck a hard blow at their leadership by converting Karel and others, he had slaughtered a number of their proud and stiff-necked populace, and occupied their capital.

Mark, he supposed, and the surviving Tasavaltan military, would need a day or two at least to make preparation for some attempt at striking back. In about that time, also, the converts' zeal would be starting to turn to ashes. So it was plain to the Dark King that in one or two days he might well have to retreat—unless in the meantime he somehow managed to acquire substantial human help, of some kind not dependent upon the Mindsword.

He considered the option of retreating now. He could summon his loyal demons, declare that he had intended nothing more than a raid on Sarykam, and withdraw from the city, perhaps to the seacoast caves where he had secreted the Old World spacecraft. But the idea of retreating at the first setback, sharp though it had been, rankled; and the Dark King quickly decided that to withdraw, now, at least, would be premature.

Also Vilkata tried to formulate some way to pursue or entrap Mark, who, on leaving the city a few days ago, had evidently taken with him from his special armory no other weapon besides the Sword of Healing. Karel and other converts had amply confirmed that fact.

The idea of a massive hostage-taking was beginning to grow in Vilkata's thoughts. Whatever problems might be about to confront him, having a few thousand hostages on hand would be a good idea.

He snapped out decisive orders to get the process started. Let a thousand or more of the city's people, without any particular selection, be rounded up, disarmed, and herded into the palace complex. Converts good for nothing else would do perfectly well as hostages, and would be as fanatically eager to assume that role as any other.

* * *

The elder magician Karel, with all a convert's eagerness to be of help, had volunteered to be Vilkata's counselor, and appeared with an offer to send a treacherous message to Prince Mark.

Vilkata, raising an eyebrow in approval, listened judiciously.

Kristin's uncle was eager to do all he could for his new lord. "The best tactic, Master, might be to persuade the Prince that I, Karel, have not been converted after all."

"You think you could convince him?"

"I think the tactic worth considering. If we can thus get Mark, and my dear niece—ultimately for their own good, of course—"

"Of course."

"To give up this foolish and unequal struggle."

Vilkata had grave doubts that any such plan to work. But he asked the old wizard to work out the details.

When informed of the plan to take hostages, Karel was not so enthusiastic. But, in his converted opinion, if people refused to see the light, they really deserved no better than a miserable death. Of course it was too bad about the children; but their fate could hardly be blamed upon the glorious Dark King, who never did anything wrong.

The Dark King, having now ordered repeated searches of the palace and its grounds, believed that his recent opponent in the armory had been no one but the young Princeling, Stephen. That puppy had gotten away with two of the most dangerous Swords.

Karel offered firm assurances that the stripling would never be able to carry such a double burden of magic very far.

Then, quite unexpectedly, the wizards' conversation was interrupted. One of the Dark King's new human slaves, still strongly under the Mindsword's lingering influence, came running in with word that Arridu was clamoring to be admitted to Vilkata's presence. The great demon was announcing his intention to give the Dark King a great gift.

Vilkata, having had no report from the monster demon for several hours, had begun to fear that Arridu had gone the way of Akbar, had become a victim of Shieldbreaker in the Tasavaltan Princeling's hands.

In a moment the gigantic fiend, in the guise of a black-clad warrior, was entering his Master's presence, one hand outstretched and far from empty. Arridu was making a present to his beloved Master of a sheathed and belted Sword, its power for the moment safely muffled.

One glance at the black hilt showed Vilkata that the weapon being put into his hands was no less than Shieldbreaker itself.

The Dark King cried out with joy, with near-disbelief at his own good fortune.

The loyal one, the great demon Arridu, stood back in silence. Quickly recovering from the Mindsword's influence, he might already be starting to have second thoughts about the wisdom of turning over this Sword— but those thoughts came at least a minute too late.

Vilkata waved the Sword of Force, and roared with triumphant laughter.

10

THE news of the attack on Sarykam reached Princess Kristin and Prince Mark in the sleeping village of Voronina just before sunrise. These first disjointed signals of the horror arrived in confused and fragmentary form, borne in the small brains and uncertain speech of two half-intelligent bird-messengers, the only creatures of their kind who had succeeded in escaping the demons' onslaught on the palace.

Actually it was Ben of Purkinje, sleeping in his blanket-roll under the stars, who was first awakened by the beastmaster; and it was Ben, huge and ugly Ben, who then, grumbling and blaspheming all the gods that he could think of, came bringing the unwelcome tidings on to Mark and Kristin, in the yeoman's cottage where the royal couple were being housed during their visit.

Prince Mark was jarred out of some dream that was very strange, skirting a strange borderland between beauty and ugliness, by a knocking on the yeoman's door. Mark was in general a lighter sleeper than his wife, or any member of the farmer's family.

Working himself out from under the light cover, and then from under the outflung right arm of his sleeping wife, Mark, a tall, strong man now forty years of age, stood beside the bed and reached for some clothing. He had made his way downstairs and was listening to the news before anyone else in the house was properly awake.

He had had time to hear Ben's message before blond Kristin, four years younger than her husband but looking younger still, followed Mark downstairs with a blanket wrapped around her, to join her husband where he was standing with Ben and the beastmaster in the morning twilight at the front door of the little house.

Kristin stood beside the three men listening carefully, grasping swiftly many of the implications of what was being said, herself having little to say at first. Shortly after she arrived, the farmer himself, next to be awakened, came to stand with his extraordinary visitors, listening too, holding a flaring brand from the hearth that gave at least uncertain light.

None of those who listened had much to say at first. The news of the attack came as a ghastly shock to all who heard it. Could there be any possibility of a mistake?

"Where are the birds now?" the Princess presently asked. "I want to hear directly from them whatever they can tell me."

"Yes, let's see them," Mark agreed.

Ben bowed lightly, a graceful gesture in so huge a man, and turned and led the way across the darkness of the farmyard. Mark and Kristin followed him to where a lantern was burning in the barn. Here the beastmaster had established himself with his little squadron of messengers. Bird-eyes glowed down in pairs from the high loft.

The two feathered creatures who had just arrived with the black news from Sarykam were of the species of giant nightflying owls. One of these messengers had arrived wounded and with its feathers scorched—ominous confirmation of the ghastly news. The uninjured owl had been flying half a kilometer from the city when the attack came; the other had somehow managed against all odds to make its escape from the ravaged aeries and blunder its way through the cloudy night to Voronina.

This bird, the smaller of the pair, speaking in its halting, half-intelligent small voice, could give few actual details of the attack. But it reported the presence in Sarykam of many demons, which strongly tended to confirm Mark's and Kristin's immediate suspicion that the Dark King was involved.

The Princess, listening, sighed and said: "Well, let us rouse our squad of soldiers."

But there was no need, most of the men had been sleeping outdoors near the barn and were already stirring. A small military guard, some fifteen or twenty mounted troops under the command of a captain, had accompanied the Prince and Princess on what had been expected to be a relatively uneventful trip.

In fact, at least half of the small village now seemed to be awake. Perhaps, the Princess suggested to her farmer-host, everyone should be awakened, since all had a right to know the situation.

The commanding officer of the small military squad, Captain Miyagi, came up to find Prince and Princess scanning the lightening skies, concerned about a possible attack on the village by demons or flying reptiles.

The Master of Beasts was also part of the military detachment who had come out from the capital. Fortunately, as a routine measure, he had brought along a complement of messenger-birds, intended to keep the royal couple in touch with all the relatively far-flung portions of their realm.

Now the Prince and Princess gave the beastmaster explicit orders. He saluted and moved briskly away.

Kristin looked at Mark. "Stephen," she said. All her concern and hope were audible in the one word.

Ben was standing by, muttering words of counsel when requested. At the same time he was privately and intensely worried about his family left back in the city, though he acknowledged that by his own choice he'd seen neither wife nor daughter for some months.

Following a night of violence and terror unprecedented in Sarykam, the early stages of a summer's dawn, heralded by the traditional signs of cockcrow, fresh dew, and a changing sky, were now overtaking the normally bustling outskirts of the city.

This morn was unusually quiet for an area so populous and ordinarily so filled with activity. At the moment the main road approaching the capital from the west carried almost no traffic. Conspicuous was a single rider, mounted on a large, magnificent riding-beast. This animal was bearing the rider's considerable weight toward the city at a brisk pace, even after laboring under the same burden through most of the night.

This close to the city the road was broad and smoothly paved, and a recent shower had left the pavement wet. The rider sniffed the heavy, smoky air and seemed to grant the morning his approval. He was a bulky, gray-haired man in his early sixties. His powerfully built body, scarred by a hundred fights, was wrapped in a gray cape, which in the eyes of naive observers would have identified him as a pilgrim. A more accurate reading would have been that he preferred just now to be anonymous.

The Moon, a waning crescent with horns aimed approximately toward the zenith, hung in the eastern sky, where it had just emerged from behind a tatter of cloud. A morning star was visible as well, Venus, to the east beyond the city and above the sea, a planet so round and lustrous that many people seeing it on that morning took it as an omen. The weary rider had little faith in omens, as a rule. But something in which he did have faith rode at his side in a long sheath, under his gray cape. Half-consciously he touched the black hilt with a large hand, as if to make sure it was still there.

When he had come within half a kilometer of the city walls, the traveler reined in his mount slightly, slowing his progress the better to observe a certain gray-clad man on foot who was carrying what looked like garden tools, notably a shovel, over his shoulder. This fellow was plodding along, coming from the direction of the main gate, and evidently bound for the loop of road that would take him to the coastal highway heading south. On becoming aware of the mounted man's inspection, the man on foot returned his glance and waved, without breaking stride, as if to some fellow pilgrim.

The mounted traveler waved back, without really giving the gesture any thought. Then he faced east and urged his riding-beast forward once more.

As the bulky man on his strong mount entered the area of practically continuous settlement just outside the city walls, he took note of half a dozen columns of smoke, each of a steady thickness, all together far in excess of what might have been expected from morning kitchens or other common activities. These smoke-plumes, ascending from unseen sources within the walls, blended at high altitude into a sooty cloud smeared by the morning breeze all across the lightening eastern sky. The sight suggested to the traveler that in the city several buildings, perhaps a great many, must be burning. Indeed, the volume of smoke suggested that no one in Sarykam was making much of an effort to put the fires out.

The traveler was not particularly worried that the whole city ahead of him was going to go up in flames. For one thing, there had been the recent rain to wet things down. For another, he was familiar with Sarykam, and recalled that most of the buildings inside the walls were constructed of stone and tile. A third and more fundamental reason for the traveler's equanimity was that he personally did not really care whether or not the city and everyone in it might be burned to cinders.

Steadily he pushed on, approaching the main inland gate of the Tasavaltan capital.

Just before he reached that tall portal the visitor turned once more, frowning, to look after that other supposed pilgrim—there had been something odd about that man and his tools—but the road behind was empty now.

With a shrug the mounted man proceeded about his business.

When the mounted traveler's methodical pace had brought him right up to the main gate where the high road went through the walls, he paused again to look the situation over. The gate, as a rule alertly guarded, now stood wide open, and there were no lookouts visible on the high city walls. These were ominous signs, even on such a superficially peaceful morning as this.

Even as the traveler sat in his saddle watching, there emerged from the gate a very young man wearing only a nightshirt, tall and thin to the point of fragility, looking both distressed and dazed. Blood that seemed to have run down from a recent untended scalp injury was drying on his forehead. This youth came wandering out of the open gate and along the high road for a couple of dozen paces, then off the road into an adjoining ditch. There he stood, staring at nothing, pulling thoughtfully at his lower lip like a scholar trying to remember the answers to a test. When the mounted traveler hailed him, the tall youth did not respond.

Well, thought the man in the saddle to himself, *I certainly cannot say that I have not been warned.*

But he had business here. He was not about to be turned back by warnings so indirect and impersonal as these.

Again the mounted traveler moved on slowly. By listening carefully he could hear, coming from somewhere inside the gate, a distant roaring, as of a crowd or mob, acting at least roughly in unison. The traveler's riding-beast, which seemed to be listening too, pawed the stones of the road and snorted.

Taking into account the several indications he had now been given, the observer decided that something in Sarykam was seriously amiss. He felt no great surprise at the discovery.

And now, even as the visitor watched from his saddle, he observed a new banner, of gold and black, being hoisted on the watchtower beside the gate, replacing the accustomed blue and green of Tasavalta. The latter banner was now hurled rudely to the ground by soldiers—if they were soldiers—of ragtag appearance, at least half out of uniform.

The observer thought the new emblem's stripes were somewhat uneven, as if the flag had been hastily sewn together. And looking in through the open gate he was able to catch a glimpse of another such flag going up on the tallest mast of the towering palace, well in beyond the walls.

The rider nodded; it was a brisk and private gesture of satisfaction, that of a man having a prediction confirmed. In the hues of the new banner he recognized the livery colors of the Dark King.

Whenever the traveler's gray cape moved aside a little on the left, the sword at his waist once more became visible. Harder to make out was the fact that this was no ordinary weapon, but a Sword, the Sword of Chance.

Before definitely deciding on his next move he partially drew Coinspinner and consulted the Sword, making the pommel point one way and then another, observing a vibration in the blade and feeling it through the black hilt.

Then briskly he dug heels into the ribs of his tired mount, and once more confidently rode forward, straight in through the main gate.

As the journeying rider entered the city the indications became even more obvious that here remarkable and violent events had very recently taken place.

At frequent intervals Coinspinner's wearer guardedly drew, or half-drew, the weapon. Each time the Sword cleared enough of the sheath to allow the owner to feel the surge of magical power, indicating to him which turning he should take next. The course thus mapped by Coinspinner was about as straight as the streets would allow, and took him in the direction of the palace.

From time to time during the intervals when he was not actually consulting the Sword, its owner repeatedly looked down at the black hilt, or felt for it to make sure that it was still there. Each time he was reassured; but with the Sword of Chance, one could never be really certain from one moment to the next where in the world it was going to be.

Coinspinner, uniquely among the Twelve, had always been fundamentally its own master. Following its usual pattern of moving itself about mysteriously, magically, the Sword of Chance had some months ago come into the hands of the adventurer Baron Amintor.

Having ample experience with the Swords, enough to trust their powers implicitly when Fate granted him the privilege of doing so, Amintor had been overjoyed at his good fortune. He had wasted no mental effort or energy trying to account for such a blessing, but had followed Coinspinner enthusiastically.

Firm in his expectation that Coinspinner would continue to provide good luck, Amintor now continued to follow the Sword's guidance through the maze of streets. It was leading him in the general direction of the palace.

The sky over Sarykam had changed again, getting past the stage of dawn, assuming now the colorless glow of very early daylight. The sun was still obscured in fog, somewhere above the eastern sea. The streets of the capital were quiet at the moment, but the visitor decided that this hush must have been a very recent development. A brace of dead bodies lying unattended in the middle of the thoroughfare testified with silent eloquence to an exciting night just past.

The traveler was not one to be dismayed by a few dead bodies; no stranger, he, to either war or civil tumult. And at present he felt comfortably well armed. Alertly he allowed his Sword to guide him forward. His riding-beast, also a veteran campaigner, pricked up its ears as it stepped past the bodies, but the animal betrayed no great excitement either.

As the bulky man in pilgrim gray continued along one of the main streets, still being guided by his Sword in the general direction of the palace, the signs of recent disturbance and violence were multiplied. In the distance many voices were chanting something. They were human voices, he felt quite sure, not the utterance of beasts or demons, but he could not make out the words. The Baron saw no reason to assume that all the violence was over—quite the opposite—but he had always been ready to accept a reasonable amount of risk when he thought there was also a good chance that a profit of some kind could be made.

He rode past several more dead bodies lying in the street, and another hanging halfway out of a second-story window. Here was a building upon whose sides someone had scrawled, in red paint that was still fresh, gigantic words. These might have been in some way helpful to the seeker after knowledge, but unfortunately the building had collapsed soon after being thus decorated—in fact it appeared to have been flattened by some superhuman power, which was perhaps the fact—reducing the messages to gibberish. No way for anyone to read those fractured, crumbled slogans now.

Amintor's methodical, Sword-guided advance was now bringing him very near to the main plaza and the palace. He detoured, without stopping, closely around a building that was burning fiercely, while a handful of people with buckets made an effort, only desultory, to wet down the neighboring structures.

But the fire had not drawn a crowd. It was attracting no more attention than did the bodies of the victims of violence. Plainly, on this strange morning the majority of the good citizens of Sarykam—presumably a majority still survived—had little thought or emotion to spare for the death and destruction which had been wrought among them overnight. Looking into the glittering eyes of some of the survivors, the visitor thought that another and transcendent excitement consumed their minds and spirits.

At least half of the people he had seen so far, living and dead, were still in night-dress, and one or two stark naked, with no one paying much attention. A number of other folk, the traveler noted, had hastily improvised a livery of black and gold for themselves to wear. Many had been marked by the night's festivities with soot and ashes, and some with blood. Not just your city riff-raff either. To judge by their generally well-fed appearance and neat barbering, they might have been until very recently among the city's most prosperous and reasonable inhabitants. Now the good burghers marched and chanted, even while some of their houses stood freshly ruined and others were burning down before their eyes. Folk of the Blue Temple (although the Blue Temple had only a very modest foothold in this city), the Red Temple, and the White, were all behaving uncharacteristically.

On one streetcorner stood a group of a dozen people singing, or trying to sing. The syllables they were chanting so hoarsely rang plainly in the visitor's ears. They made up a man's name and title, and they, like the livery of gold and black, belonged to an individual he recognized. Nay, one he thought he knew quite well.

Hand on his Sword-hilt, his own eyes now glittering with hopeful ambition, Amintor advanced. Now the palace was only two blocks ahead.

He had been less than half an hour in the city, but that was more time than the Baron needed to realize that in his long and far from sheltered life he had several times before seen conduct very similar to that now being displayed by the citizens of Sarykam. These people around him, engaging in such uncommon behavior, reminded him less of drug-overdosed devotees of the Red Temple than they did of folk fresh-caught by the Mindsword's spell.

A loud shout made the new arrival turn his head. He reined in his mount when he discovered that the cry had been directed at him. A group of six or eight young people, mounted upon a motley collection of loadbeasts and riding-beasts, was trotting toward him down a side street. All were wearing armbands of gold and black. The stocky youth who rode at the head of this small armed band now shouted another challenge at Amintor.

As they came up to him, the leader declared in a loud, raucous voice that they were seizing Amintor's riding-beast.

"Our glorious new King, Vilkata, will have need of many servants and many soldiers, of cavalry and messengers!" As he reached out to take the reins from Amintor, the stout youth glared at the visitor as if daring him to dispute the fact.

For just a moment as the Baron considered this demand, his broad, lined face was utterly blank of any expression. But an instant later he was smiling broadly as he swung himself down from the saddle. With a gesture at once proud and commanding he handed over the reins to his challenger, making the donation into a personal accomplishment.

In the circumstances Amintor was perfectly ready to abandon his tired riding-beast—let someone else feed the animal and care for it. He was confident that Coinspinner would find another mount for him whenever one was needed.

The Baron walked with a moderate limp, noticeable as soon as he alighted from his mount.

The little band of youths, a couple of them girls, all their faces slack, sat blinking down at him from their saddles or bareback mounts. Obviously they had been put somewhat off balance by the apparent enthusiasm of Amintor's compliance. It was equally obvious that they remained suspicious of this stranger, and that they wanted to be sure of his complete devotion to their great and glorious leader, the rightful ruler of the entire world, Vilkata the Dark King.

Certainly no doubt remained in the Baron's mind about the identity of the man who must have descended on this city during the night, bearing the drawn Mindsword and thus creating his own apotheosis.

Vilkata. Yes, indeed.

Amintor, rubbing his chin thoughtfully, remembered a great deal of that potentate's long history. The most recent highlight in that saga had been Vilkata's magical banishment, along with a flock of his demons, about two years ago, from this very metropolis. Since that time, as far as the Baron was aware, the world had heard nothing from the Dark King.

But now . . . yes indeed, the Dark King's demons. Amintor thought that he could smell them in the air. Vilkata always had demons with him.

While the fanatical youths were muttering among themselves, trying to decide what they ought to demand of him next, the Baron looked around the sky apprehensively.

He was recalled from this concentration on what he considered more serious matters by a fresh challenge from the stocky youth, who now sat holding the reins of Amintor's riding-beast as if uncertain what to do with them.

The Baron glowered at him. "What did you say?"

"We insist upon an oath of loyalty," the youth repeated grimly.

It was Amintor's turn to blink. But then he laughed. "An oath? Why not? Have you a formula devised, or would you like me to create one for the purpose?"

This provoked open disagreement among the self-appointed committee of conformity.

The Baron let them argue for a time among themselves. Then, interrupting further fervent, quasi-religious babble, he inquired of them firmly: "And just where, at this moment, is that flawless divinity, the Dark King we all adore?"

None of the young enthusiasts seemed to detect the mockery in their elder's tone. They looked at one other with helpless expressions; it seemed that no one in the small group had any real idea of where their divine leader could be found, or what he might be doing.

One of the band finally suggested, humbly, that their great Master might be in the palace.

Amintor, casting a wary glance in the direction of that tall building, made a face of disgust upon noting that Vilkata's bodyguard of demons were at least intermittently in evidence. Half a dozen or so of their half-material shapes could be seen flitting in and out of the upper windows. He decided that he would rather not go there just now—unless the Sword of Chance advised him to do so.

Yet again he drew and tried his Sword, half expecting the magic of the gods to warn him to move in the opposite direction from the palace; but Coinspinner was quiet in his grip. Doubtless, Amintor thought, the demons were relatively harmless just now. After a few buildings had been flattened in sheer demonic exuberance, and some key prisoners taken if that proved possible, the Mindsword's holder had doubtless given orders that his new and soon-to-be-useful human subjects and other property were not to be molested.

A new clamor jarred him from his private thoughts. Now several of the little band of youths, their faces alight with sudden inspiration, were daring to demand of him his Sword—now that he had called their attention to it.

Again, the Baron's mind had been elsewhere, and he had to ask for the demand to be repeated. "What?"

"I said, that looks like a good sword you have there. Hand it over, in the name of the Most High King."

The Baron favored with a mirthless smile the one who made this demand. "No, my Sword you will have to take from me by force." Doubting that any of this slack-jawed crew had yet recognized the true nature of his weapon, he added: "But in fairness I warn you, making any such attempt would be a serious mistake."

Only one persisted in demanding that he give up the Sword. And Coinspinner, working more silently than dice, saw to it that the offender was punished for his temerity without any effort on Amintor's part. A loose stone bigger than a fist came tumbling from the parapet of a half-ruined building to strike the fellow's head a glancing blow, and bang his shoulder. When he lurched in his saddle and cried out, his riding-beast reared up and threw him to the street.

Disregarding this warning—or perhaps unaware of cause and effect—the stout youth, utterly intent and sincere in his fanaticism, persisted in his attempt to challenge Amintor. At this the old man boldly claimed acquaintance, even hinted at strong friendship, with these people's new god.

"I enjoy already the privilege of acquaintance with the magnificent, the, the indescribable—how shall I put it?—the ineffable Vilkata."

A claim so bold caused the last challenger's companions to withdraw a little from him, looking worried.

Amintor in a firm voice dared them, if they really doubted he knew Vilkata, to put the matter to the test.

That overawed, even if it did not entirely satisfy, the last fanatic. The Baron knew that if they were really convinced he was a danger, a menace to their new god, they would have fought him and his magic Sword to the death, to the last man or woman; and in that event Amintor had no doubt that, despite the odds and his advancing age, Coinspinner would see to it that he was still unscratched when none of the others were still on their feet.

But in the end matters did not come to that. The Baron's arguments, as usual, proved convincing. Presently the little band moved on and allowed Amintor to do the same.

As soon as he was free to move about again without harassment, the Baron's own demeanor changed, with a facility worthy of a skilled diplomat.

For the next half hour or a little more—while the sun finally cleared its high eastern horizon of oceanic fogbanks, to glare down pitilessly upon the wounded capital and its dead bodies—Amintor wandered the city. When he thought himself about to be once more challenged as a stranger, he went into an act, contorting his face and waving his arms like one in ecstasy, pretending to be enthralled like the most ardent of those he beheld around him.

Slowly, traversing a zigzag course through several nearby streets, he completed an entire circuit of the palace and its grounds. The uneven new flag of black and gold hung limply from the highest tower. The great stone edifice itself, now plainly visible from every angle, appeared to have suffered more from the attack than most of the rest of the city. Baron Amintor could see where some of the bars protecting the lower windows had been torn aside. Structural damage was apparent, a forcible entry had been made upon one of the higher levels, as by something that could fly and was heroically destructive.

He smiled thinly, wondering if any of the royal folk inside had survived the night to become the Dark King's prisoners. Whatever else was happening, there would be real satisfaction in seeing the proud rulers of this land brought low.

At this point Amintor observed some of the first gatherings of Vilkata's hostages, a ragged formation of a few score folk, largely women and children, being rounded up by a demon and herded, shuffling and limping, toward the palace.

It was obvious that a sizable minority of the group were converts, for they were going willingly, in fact were earnestly singing some improvised hymn in praise of their transcendent Master, even as they flinched, averting their faces from the stalking figure of the demon who had them in his charge. The majority were helpless captives, herded by demons and by stern convert guards.

The Baron stood motionless, watching the ragged little procession out of sight. He wondered for precisely what purpose these Tasavaltans had been conscripted. Not for labor, for there were many poor specimens among them, and a number of powerful demons available if Vilkata wanted heavy work accomplished. It would seem that he wanted hostages.

And now there was no doubt that demon-smell, far more psychic than physical, hung in the air. Amintor sniffed, and shivered.

Demons aplenty, but no great number of human soldiers. In fact the visitor could see none at all but Sword-converts of passionate but precarious loyalty.

Opportunity waited in this city, Amintor was more than ever convinced of that—Coinspinner would not have led him here for nothing. He would have a lot to offer in a partnership with the Dark King. And Vilkata, if his power here was to have any permanence, would soon have to base it upon something more than magic and demons.

11

As the sun burned its way through the last of the morning's high fog, Amintor wandered rather aimlessly about the city, getting no clear direction from Coinspinner, remaining in sight of the palace but not approaching it closely. He told himself that his Sword's seeming indifference, the fact that it was giving him no advice and arranging no meaningful chance encounters, simply meant that he was in the right place. All he needed to do for the time being was wait.

His saddlebags had gone with his riding-beast, but at the moment he had no need for any of their meager contents. When a need for anything arose, Coinspinner would provide.

Presently, feeling somewhat tired and hungry after his long ride, Amintor seated himself on a bench, hailed a street vendor whose enterprise had not been totally discouraged by recent events, and ordered some breakfast: hot tea, fried bread, and broiled fish, the latter fresh-caught here in this seaport.

The vendor's pushcart shop-on-wheels was not the only business establishment now open. There were increasing signs that at least an imitation of normal economic activity was getting under way. Also the Baron observed that an improvised body-wagon was beginning to make the rounds, staffed by white-robed acolytes of Ardneh—it would be interesting to see what the Dark King tried to do with the White Temple—picking up the casualties of the hours just past. A Red Temple, a tall, narrow brick building with hedonistic statues writhing and posturing across its façade, was also among the first businesses to open, the click and whir of gaming wheels starting to sound from inside the main room on the ground floor.

All in all, the city was now giving an impression of starting to come awake from its nightmare, of pulling itself together—to some extent. Not that conditions were back to normal, or anywhere close to that. Still, the Baron saw many people putting aside weapons, beginning what must be their daily routines, despite the glazed and wary look in their eyes. Probably, thought Amintor, observing carefully, some who were not really

Mindsword-converts were pretending that they were, thinking thus to protect themselves against attack. And perhaps real converts were playing the game the other way, as *agents provocateurs.*

Hundreds, it seemed, were discarding and burning garments and flags of blue and green, making up new ones out of black cloth and any yellow fabric that might pass for gold.

Still other folk, as if exhausted by noisy demonstration or activities still more energetic, sat quietly now, their hands and garments sometimes smeared with blood, their faces numb and blank, as if they might be considering the inner meaning of their lives.

The Baron, while munching on his bread and broiled fish, made use of his time to do some thoughtful considering of his own. Looming large was the fact that he himself had been in the city for a couple of hours now but was still unbewitched. The most likely explanation of that, of course, was that the Mindsword's influence had only passed over these people and moved on elsewhere; Skulltwister was no longer on the scene, or at least no longer drawn and active.

Another possible explanation, one Amintor considered much more unlikely, was that he was being individually protected by some magic of a potency equal to that of Shieldbreaker—if any such equality could be imagined.

Had Coinspinner somehow, without his knowledge, obtained for him immunity to Skulltwister? The Baron shook his head. He thought the chance of that extremely remote, though he could not rule it out absolutely. In general the Sword of Chance provided protection by keeping its possessor away from danger. Coinspinner had brought him here to Sarykam, and so here he ought to stand in no great peril.

The thought of Shieldbreaker reminded Amintor that the Sword of Force was, or had been, generally thought to be in Sarykam, under the control of Prince Mark. Well, if so, the Prince had obviously not been able to get his hands on it in time to save his city. If several Swords had really been kept here in the palace armory, as was popularly believed, a successful surprise attack might have captured one or more of them.

The Baron's thoughts drifted. What he had always wanted, really wanted in his heart of hearts, was the chance to be a general—better yet, a field marshal; to command a victorious human army, to win or at least have a fighting chance of winning the great game of power, the struggle in which for forty years all the Swords had played such a central part.

And over the past several months the Sword of Chance, coming suddenly into his possession like an answer to his prayers—not that he had really offered any prayers—had allowed him to realize his dream, at least as far as forming the army he had wanted.

As for being able to lead his army into battle, well, he supposed that wish would be granted him, in the Sword's good time.

It occurred to the watching Baron that other travelers must be approaching the city this morning, as on any other morning, and that a few of these, at least those with the strongest reasons for doing so, must be actually entering, despite all the obvious signs of disaster.

In fact he was soon able to observe some of these, who with evident trepidation were making their way to a place near the central square. The Baron watched with measured interest as at that point they came to grief through not being quick enough to emulate the fanaticism by which they now found themselves surrounded.

Amintor's natural disinclination to interfere with whatever was happening to the victims was not disturbed by any counsel of his Sword. Coinspinner lay inert at his side.

Sipping tea from the vendor's cracked mug and trying to better understand the situation, the Baron made an effort to mentally reconstruct last night's events here in the capital. It seemed to him that Vilkata, armed with the Mindsword and doubtless accompanied by his usual swarm of demons, must have launched his sneak attack upon Sarykam no more than a few hours ago. Then the Dark King, having quickly secured the palace and achieved his own apotheosis in the hearts of a key segment of the population, must have given orders to take hostages. Having taken that precaution he had himself moved on, no doubt in pursuit of Mark or other enemies. And, of course, Vilkata would have taken Skulltwister with him.

It seemed likely that the conqueror would be returning to his conquered city fairly soon. Certainly the Dark King knew as well as anyone how impermanent were the Mindsword's spells; unless they were renewed every couple of days, Vilkata would stand in serious danger of losing his grip upon the capital.

With these facts in mind, Amintor looked up at the skies, frowning, alert for the sight of demon or griffin with the Dark King on its back, the rider with a gleaming, cheering Sword in hand. Skulltwister bothered him. The Baron was ready to accept risks, even high risks sometimes, but he had a chronic terror of falling under the Mindsword's spell. Often enough he had seen what that weapon did to others.

He turned his head sharply to study a new disturbance at ground level. Here came another little mob of chanting fanatics, marching down the street right past his bench. The Baron stared back at them coldly as they went by. He shivered slightly, and felt for the reassuring black hilt at his side.

Well, he supposed he could continue to rely on his own Sword for indirect protection—and for more than that. Coinspinner had guided him to Sarykam, and he thought it must have done so to help him achieve more than mere survival.

Everything the Baron knew about the Sword of Chance suggested to him that opportunity for great gain or advancement, perhaps of several kinds, abounded here in this conquered city. Now, if only he could determine how best to take advantage of the occasion. . . .

But naturally Coinspinner would show him how, if he only gave it the chance.

Amintor started to sip his tea again, then impulsively threw half a cup of the vile stuff away. Getting to his feet, he limped about again. He felt it was time to be moving.

Several times in the space of the next half hour he consulted his Sword, trying to attract as little attention as possible in the process. Each time he frowned at the negative result and strolled on. In his own perception he was doing little more than killing time; but as far as he could tell, the Sword of Fortune, giving him only slight indications or none at all, was advising him to continue.

An hour or so after breakfasting, the Baron was sitting in a sidewalk shop, imbibing still more hot tea—this of slightly better quality—and waiting for opportunity to present itself. The state of keyed-up alertness in which he had entered the city had long since faded; nature was asserting herself, and he was beginning to get sleepy, having been in the saddle most of the night. The tea at least was helping him to keep his eyelids open.

Then abruptly Amintor was jarred to full wakefulness. The voices around him had suddenly taken on a new tone. He became aware of an accelerated swarming and gathering in the streets, a concerted movement finally involving thousands of people, all converging upon the central square before the palace. The normal business of the day, tentatively begun, was once more being put aside.

Amintor reacted decisively, getting swiftly to his feet and moving with the crowd. Proceeding at a fast limp, sometimes almost running, he wondered whether he should draw his Sword again. But he decided that was unnecessary for the moment, as Coinspinner had certainly brought him here. He allowed himself to be carried along.

The stream of people in which he moved joined other streams, from other streets, all eddying in a great pool across the central plaza. The Baron drew in his breath sharply upon recognizing, despite the distance, the virtually unmistakable figure of the Dark King. The tall, blind albino had come out on one of the second- or third-level balconies on the high palace of gray stone. There was the usual half-visible blurring of demonic presence in a small cloud above the wizard's head, and Amintor thought —though it was difficult to be sure at that distance—that he could see small bandages in several places on Vilkata's body.

Rapidly the enthusiastic crowd—if Amintor's private calculations regarding the number of converts were correct, the throng must be heavily augmented by folk only pretending to be converts—pressed forward, gathering as closely as possible underneath the balcony. There were thousands or tens of thousands of people now, looking up with evident awe and worship. When Vilkata's distant figure gestured that they should be still, they fell for the most part into reverent silence.

Amintor, cheering and falling silent in tune with those around him, felt somewhat uneasy, despite his own firm grip on the hilt of the Sword of Chance. He considered prudently working his way back through the crowd to the far side of the square; but surely the Mindsword's power, if it should be drawn, would extend that far.

He took some comfort from the fact that at the moment neither of Vilkata's pale hands were holding any Sword, though there might well be one sheathed at the man's side.

Vilkata soon began an oration, of which Amintor could hear no more than a few isolated words because of the fresh outbreak of screaming the speech provoked among the multitude—until the people's god once again, more sternly this time, commanded silence. Once he was perceived as being serious on that point, a deathlike hush fell over the assemblage.

With relative quiet established, Vilkata in his smooth, deep voice at first complimented the mass of his followers on the zeal they had so recently displayed in hunting down and killing anyone suspected of still adhering to the cause of the old royal family. But in the next breath the Dark King sounded a different note, saying that the time for such random slaughter had now passed—all the citizens of Sarykam were to be considered valuable assets in his cause, except, of course, for any unregenerate scoundrels who proved unwilling to serve.

Turning from side to side upon his balcony, waving both arms to acknowledge the renewed cheering of his worshippers, Vilkata from time to time revealed the dark hilt of a Sword at his side.

Now the speaker let his hand rest on that dark hilt. The crowd roared anew. Amintor, watching, nervously continued to assume that this was the Mindsword.

The Baron knew a chill of fear. *If he should draw Skulltwister again right now, I'm lost. . . .*

But Coinspinner, by whatever means, was evidently still doing an adequate job of looking after its owner; or else some other tremendous power was on the Baron's side. For though Vilkata's hand stayed resting on the dark hilt, he did not draw his Blade.

The Baron, forcing himself to relax again, mused that Coinspinner might very well have brought him here for the very purpose of becoming the Dark King's partner; what he had told the fanatics earlier had contained more than a grain of truth. The two men had in fact worked together in the past.

And the Sword of Chance seemed to confirm this idea as soon as Amintor tested it. The magic-laden tip of Coinspinner twitched decisively in the direction of Vilkata on his distant balcony.

Granted this seeming encouragement, trying to put thoughts of Skulltwister out of his mind, Amintor began to use his bulk to work his way in that direction.

Meanwhile Vilkata, even as he stood looking out over the adoring throng, found himself obsessed by the idea that every one of these folk now offering him such frenzied adoration would very shortly be starting to come out of the Mindsword-fog. A few of them—and the thought was enough to give him chills—might be already faking their devotion. The very first defections, he surmised, had occurred already. They would have begun within a few hours of Skulltwister's smashing, an event now some eight hours in the past.

Perhaps the most urgent problem that he faced was that there were very few humans whom he could even begin to trust on any basis other than enslavement—and, at the moment, none of those people were within a hundred kilometers. Demons were useful in many ways, sometimes invaluable, but that race certainly had its limitations.

The Baron, having managed to consult his own Sword once again as he kept pushing his way through the crowd—his actions with that formidable weapon earned him a few suspicious looks from people around him —persevered in his bold effort to approach the Dark King.

The closer Amintor got to the balcony, the more his progress was disputed. Trying to elbow one's way through a throng of jealous worshippers was inherently dangerous. A murmur went up, then an outcry, at last enough of a disturbance to attract the attention of the Eyeless One upon his balcony. The Baron gestured with his free hand, and called out. A guardian demon, watchful, came buzzing overhead.

Vilkata's demonic vision was evidently acute, for a moment later he had recognized Amintor and was shouting orders for the crowd to make way; and once the Master's will was made known to the crowd, they instantly complied. Very quickly the Baron was pushed and drawn into the palace, then, after some further delay marked by arguments among converts, he was conducted to Vilkata's side.

It was unnecessary for Amintor to climb all the way to the balcony, for Vilkata in his eagerness had come down from it to meet him in an intermediate room. On first coming into each other's presence, the two men hailed and greeted each other warily, though with considerable show of good fellowship and enthusiasm.

Vilkata at once felt confident that Amintor was not under the Mindsword's influence; certainly the Baron's manner, while respectful, was vastly different from the adoring attitude of those by whom the two men were surrounded.

The Baron, as if he could deduce what thoughts were running through the Dark King's mind, stated the fact explicitly. "I am here by my own decision, Majesty."

"I am glad to hear it . . . some years have passed since we have seen each other. You look healthy and prosperous."

"Indeed, too many years, Your Majesty."

Vilkata's eyeless gaze fell to the black hilt at the other's side, which Amintor was making no effort to conceal. "What brings you to Tasavalta, and to this city, Baron, at this auspicious time?"

"With your permission?" Amintor—taking care to move his hand very slowly and cautiously—drew Coinspinner, just enough to let the Eyeless One have a good look at the hilt.

The pale brows above the empty sockets rose. "Aha! So the Sword of Chance has counseled you to come this way—I take it that your arrival in the city was quite recent?"

"Shortly before dawn, Majesty." Amintor was wincing involuntarily, making a not entirely successful effort to ignore the close proximity of the Dark King's demons.

The Dark King smiled in amusement, then scowled fiercely. "Do they bother you, my little pets? Hey there, Arridu, Pitmedden—all the rest of you—stand back a little! Give this, my partner, room to breathe."

At once the noisome cloud of demons, their looming presence, became, gratefully, less obtrusive.

Amintor raised a not completely steady hand to wipe his forehead. "My thanks," he said sincerely, "and my apologies for any inconvenience. But such creatures inevitably make me feel a little sickish." He did not mention the other side of his concern, which was not directly for his own personal welfare, rather that one of the pets out of sheer exuberant malignity would attempt to play some prank upon him, and Coinspinner, active at his side, would somehow blot the foul thing out of existence in a twinkling. Which would not endear the Baron to the Dark King.

Vilkata shrugged, dismissing the subject of his pets and guardians. He stood waiting, evidently considering something very thoughtfully.

The Baron seized what seemed to be an opportunity. "Your Majesty, I have never been one to hide my intentions in clouds of rhetoric. With all respect, I propose that you and I form a partnership—you, of course, to be the senior."

The Dark King did not appear to be at all surprised by the offer. Better, from Amintor's point of view, he was immediately receptive to the plan, spreading his arms wide in a slow gesture, as if to say: It is accomplished! Not bothering with any coy pretense of reluctance. He confessed that he stood in need of relatively trustworthy human assistance.

Not that the Dark King gave the impression of begging for help. Far from it. Vilkata's willingness to take a partner was surely the confident seizing of an opportunity, not an act of desperation. A sixth sense warned Amintor that something in the situation remained unexplained. "But, Majesty, if you have the Mindsword, surely recruiting people to serve you is no problem?"

All human onlookers, prodded by demons, had withdrawn to a distance of a room or two. Vilkata, taking the Baron by the arm familiarly, began to stroll with him along a marble hallway. Their boots clopped almost in unison, drawing rich echoes from the stone.

The Dark King said quietly: "Since we are partners now, I'll keep no secrets from you. Alas, I have it no longer."

"The Mindsword? Ah!" Amintor stopped in his tracks.

"The fact is that no one does." And Vilkata related in a few terse words the basic facts of his skirmish in the armory—leaving out, of course, the great fact of the abject terror he had experienced.

He concluded: "At this moment I am in possession of perhaps a thousand enthusiastic human converts, for a few days more—perhaps for no longer than a few hours, in some cases. You know, Baron, how these things work."

"Indeed, I have some passing acquaintance with the effects of all the Swords. And your demons? To what degree, if I may ask, will your control of them be altered?"

The Dark King shrugged, then explained that it was not the fact that his demons would soon be free of Skulltwister's spells that worried him the most. Vilkata had been dealing with demons almost all of his long life, and he considered himself magician enough to handle his present crew, even without the Mindsword in hand to set the ultimate seal on his authority.

But controlling people was in many ways more difficult.

Amintor nodded. Then he asked: "If Skulltwister has been smashed, Your Majesty, then what Sword is it that you now wear at your side?"

Vilkata smiled faintly. "Another reason we may hope for ultimate success." And he allowed the Baron to see the small white hammer on the hilt, and gave some indication of how he had so recently come into possession of Shieldbreaker.

Now Amintor could understand the confidence.

When some minor details of the partnership had been concluded by mutual agreement, the Dark King—naturally confirmed in his expectation to be senior partner—now in effect getting his hands on Coinspinner, began to consider out loud whether it might be better to smash it right away.

When the suggestion was made, Amintor was horrified.

The Dark King yielded the point. He admitted that it seemed preferable, almost essential, at this stage of affairs, to get all the help the Sword of Chance was capable of giving. For one thing, it could be an invaluable help in finding the other Swords and eventually getting them all out of circulation. Not to mention Coinspinner's usefulness for other purposes as well—for example, in finally disposing of Prince Mark.

The partners quickly agreed that Coinspinner's first assigned task ought to be tracking down Prince Stephen—or whoever else the lonely warrior in the armory might possibly have been.

Amintor, struck by what he considered inspiration, drew a deep breath and announced that he was presenting Coinspinner freely to his new senior partner as a gift. With a dramatic gesture he actually unbuckled the swordbelt and held it out.

Vilkata was immediately wary of such generosity; the hideously smooth, pale face, eyeless but very far from blind, pressed a silent and suspicious query.

The Baron was smoothly reassuring, and disarmingly frank. "In the first place, Your Majesty, I could not, even supposing that I wanted to, use this weapon against you, armed as you now are. And in the second place, the Sword of Chance has been with me now for many months; as you know at least as well as I, there's no telling when it might fly away of its own accord. Therefore it seems to me that the best use I can make of it right now is to cement our bargain."

And he handed over the sheathed weapon.

He was right, suspicion had not been allayed. Vilkata, reaching out as if to accept the great gift, gave it only a symbolic touch, then pushed the Sword of Chance right back to the giver.

Both partners considered themselves to be in a position of great strength, armed with Shieldbreaker and soon to have available Amintor's army, which was still offstage—now Amintor had to tell his new partner about that asset as well.

Just like the old days, Vilkata commented, smiling. Amintor agreed. The old days when they had sometimes worked together.

Neither man chose to remind the other that in the old days the relationship had sometimes been far from smooth.

12

T HE partnership agreement was soon concluded with a formal oath, a
vow of mutual loyalty rather hastily and mechanically recited by both
parties, and solemnized by the sacrifice of the small child of a servant,
willingly donated by its convert parent. The formalities being thus concluded, the Dark King called his new colleague into a private conference,
inviting him to breakfast on the least damaged of the palace's rooftop
terraces. The Baron, still faintly belching the street vendor's fried bread
and broiled fish, accepted automatically.

No more than half an hour after Amintor had entered the palace, the
two men, quite alone except for the ubiquitous demon Pitmedden, were
comfortably seated under a summery arbor of grapevines, on an architec-
tural elevation which gave them a view of the ocean beyond the red
rooftops of Sarykam. It seemed plain now that the surrounding city was
not going to burn after all, in any wholesale way, though here and there a
diminishing column of smoke still rose from among the roofs.

The Dark King gave orders to his guardian demons, and to his new
human aides, that he and his new colleague were not to be disturbed at
their conference, save for the most serious emergency.

Vilkata had also seen to it that the convert servants waiting on table
were magically rendered deaf, in a selective fashion, that they might hear
table orders and yet learn nothing of importance—just in case they survived long enough to be deconverted.

These details out of the way, Vilkata settled himself in his chair at the
head of the table. "Now, Baron. Tell me about this army you claim to
have. Where is it now, and how strong?"

"No mere claim, Majesty." Amintor began to explain in circumstantial
detail about the current disposition of his forces, just where and how his
people were encamped, in certain well-watered meadows not far outside
the borders of Tasavalta. There were some five thousand fighting men,
plus auxiliary magicians, and several hundred flying reptiles of diverse
sizes and subspecies.

Vilkata did not appear to be entirely convinced. Amintor was aware that his former associate cultivated an attitude of rarely approving anything enthusiastically, of never really trusting anything that he was told. The Dark King said: "Such a force must have been difficult for any individual, no matter how wealthy and talented, to raise—and it must be hard to maintain in the field."

"Oh, quite impossible, Your Majesty—except for this." And the Baron tapped the black hilt of Coinspinner, now so luckily restored to his side.

"Of course." The Dark King went on to wax somewhat enthusiastic about all he was going to be able to achieve, in the way of further conquests, with a reasonably reliable army at his disposal. "With Shieldbreaker here, and Coinspinner now as well, I think we may say conservatively that we have good grounds for optimism."

"Indeed we do." And Amintor raised his fruit juice in something like a toast. Suddenly he had to struggle to keep from yawning. He had spent a long night in the saddle, and was now well into what promised to be a long and busy day.

Not that Vilkata was openly discussing all his assets. He continued to keep secret one he considered among the most important—the Old World spacecraft he had ridden from the Moon and now had stowed and waiting in a certain cave little more than an hour's ride south from Sarykam along the coast.

Amintor, of course, did not suspect anything of the kind. But in the privacy of his own thoughts he was congratulating himself on his success in keeping a certain secret of his own.

Having indulged briefly in mutual congratulations, the partners turned urgently to planning.

Vilkata seemed to consider seriously the possibility of leaving Amintor in charge in the city while he himself took personal command of the pursuit of Mark's young cub, Prince Stephen. It was important that the enemy not be allowed to retain Sightblinder.

His junior partner inquired: "This lone opponent you faced down in the armory—that must have been Mark's offspring Stephen, hey?"

"So it seems."

The two men were casting back in their respective memories, calculating how old Mark's younger son must be by now. The result was not complimentary to the Dark King's image as a conqueror. "A mere stripling—you are sure that he's the one?"

All the evidence pointed that way. Karel, still trembling with a convert's emotions, almost weeping, was called in to testify again about the current whereabouts, as far as they were known, of the members of the Tasavaltan royal family. Yes, all the available evidence indicated that the Dark King's anonymous opponent in the armory must have been young Prince Stephen.

Arridu—who was still safely under the Mindsword's influence, the Dark King was sure—was also called in for consultation. This time, on joining the two men, the demon took for himself the image of an elderly and grave enchantress.

Arridu stoutly denied that anyone answering the description of young Prince Stephen had been near when the demon picked up Shieldbreaker. There had been only a few inconsequential citizens of the neighborhood —"and, of course, the person of Your Glorious Majesty."

There was a little silence before the Dark King reacted. *"You thought I was there? I assure you I was not."*

A complete explanation of the powers of Sightblinder, followed by lengthy persuasion, was needed to convince Arridu that his glorious Master had certainly not been on the scene when the Sword of Force was captured.

The Dark King rubbed his temples, and said for the fourth time: "I tell you, you did not see me—you saw an image cast by the Sword of Stealth."

Amintor interrupted to point out that, whatever images had been seen, Stephen's presence at the demolished house of his grandparents seemed to be confirmed by the fact that the demon's banishment had been effected at that place—only the Emperor's children, and, apparently, grandchildren, could hurl away demons with such authority. And it appeared highly unlikely that Mark himself had been there.

Another problem loomed, seeming at least equally as pressing as the search for Sightblinder. Within twenty-four hours Amintor, assuming he was still present, would be the only human being within a hundred kilometers who was not the Dark King's bitter enemy.

Vilkata, toying with the black hilt of Shieldbreaker at his side, cast a sardonic eye at the figure of the elder convert standing patiently beside the table. "How soon will you become my enemy again, old Karel? Another three or four hours perhaps, before your faith begins to weaken? Another entire day, before you are completely apostate?"

The stout old man was shaken, hurt, insulted. "Never, Master! I had rather die first. And I refuse to believe that our people will turn on you, now that it has finally been given to them to know the truth."

"Your confidence is touching," the Dark King remarked drily. "See that you do die before you waver—I will make sure of that—but it occurs to me that I will have another mission for you to accomplish before your loyalty begins to flag."

In fact, as Amintor now remarked, the two of them and Vilkata's thousand or so converts were already surrounded by swarming enemies —all of Tasavalta who had managed to remain out of the Mindsword's range before that weapon was destroyed. These people would soon recover from the effects of the lightning attack and begin again to be effectively organized. Moreover, the great majority of the converts, however fanatical in the Dark King's cause they might be at this moment, were, within a matter of a day or so, going to become his bitterest enemies of all.

After brief discussion King and Baron had to agree that Amintor would almost certainly find it impossible to hold the city without Coinspinner. The Baron's army was still more than a hundred kilometers away and could not possibly arrive in Sarykam before the majority of the converts relapsed. Add to this the difficulty that Amintor had no skill in the control of demons. If the Dark King were to proclaim this man his regent in command of Sarykam, surely what remained of the city's population, hostages or not, would revolt and murder him long before Amintor's own force could reach the city.

On the other hand, if Amintor were allowed to keep Coinspinner, he would probably succeed at holding the city or at practically any other task—the Sword of Chance could work miracles of good luck. But then Coinspinner would not be available to help run down the escaping Prince.

Arridu or other demons could not very well be sent in pursuit of Stephen, because Stephen had already demonstrated his power of exiling their kind. Of course, if Arridu were given the loan of Coinspinner for the task, then unlucky things might be expected to start happening to Stephen at once, to arrest his flight or at least slow him down.

Vilkata soon came to one firm decision: that he himself had better stay in Sarykam. With Shieldbreaker in hand, and his demons and a large number of hostages all at his disposal, he felt confident of being able to maintain his grip upon the capital. Baron Amintor would be allowed to retain the Sword of Chance, and to him would go the job of running down the Princeling.

Amintor agreed that this was probably the best way to manage things. Privately he was well pleased with this arrangement, because it allowed him to keep the Sword of Chance. His intention, as soon as he should be alone again, was to consult Coinspinner once more, with an exclusive view to his own self-interest.

Still mulling over the problem of how best to achieve his own advantage, the Dark King nibbled absently at his elaborate breakfast while he continued his conference with the Baron. Meanwhile the selectively deafened palace servants, naturally all converts desperate to please, plied their god and his new second-in-command with hot tea, fruit juices, and the finest viands from the palace cellars. There was also some fine wine on the table, but both men sipped it only sparingly.

When the Baron got to his feet to stretch and stroll about the vine-shaded terrace, he found himself overlooking one of the palace courtyards into which the thousand or more hostages had been crammed. The murmurous voices of these victims rose; Amintor could hear some of them still singing the hymn to their new god. Well, in a day or two, that at least was going to change rather drastically.

All exits from these courtyards had been blocked off—some magical provision for sanitation had probably been made—and above each of the enclosed spaces a minor demon crouched like a stone gargoyle, sleepy-eyed but watchful.

Staring at the table before him, Vilkata remarked almost wistfully that this would probably be the last peaceful meal either of them would be able to enjoy for a while. The burdens of leadership were immense.

"Immense!" Amintor agreed, matching his senior partner's mood.

They toasted each other and their joint enterprise, sipping some of Prince Mark's fine wine.

During this time old Karel was kept in silent attendance, like one of the table-servants—except that his hearing was left intact.

"What are we to do with this one?" the Baron asked, after a while.

The Eyeless One smiled faintly. "Something special, I think—there's no great hurry, we have many hours yet before his faith could possibly begin to waver. Perhaps he should go with you on your search. With Coinspinner at your side, that should not take you many hours."

Amintor nodded. And yawned. He had been in the saddle all night, and his first breakfast had not entirely agreed with him. He fought against yawning and remarked that he wanted to get a couple of hours' sleep before setting out to hunt the enemy who seemed still to be equipped with Sightblinder. He was far too experienced a campaigner not to prepare methodically, even when time was pressing.

"Anyway, there's no great hurry. He'll not be making very good time out of the city."

The Dark King looked a question.

Amintor smiled faintly and tapped the dark hilt of the Sword of Chance.

"Oh. But of course."

When Vilkata, a moment later, wanted to know whether the Baron had yet formed any plans for the search, Amintor pushed back his chair from the table and drew and consulted his Sword. Coinspinner gave him a northwesterly direction in which to begin his search for Sightblinder and the youth who was presumably still carrying it.

Amintor would have liked to consult the Sword on another matter—what direction his army should take, on its forthcoming march to Sarykam—but could not think of a way to frame the question so Coinspinner would answer it.

Vilkata, when informed of this difficulty, only shrugged. "Actually there are several questions I would like to put to the Sword, but I cannot think of any way to do so." Of course, it was hopeless to try to obtain guidance, beyond the indication of some physical direction, from the Sword of Chance. In that respect the weapon shared largely the same virtues and limitations as its fellow Sword, the late lamented Wayfinder.

The Dark King frowned when Amintor, now yawning helplessly, repeated his suggestion that he really ought to get some rest before starting after Stephen. Still, the fact that Amintor, no longer young, had been up all night could not be ignored.

"I have a better idea," his senior partner stated.

He, Vilkata, would treat his junior partner to a magical stimulus; privately Vilkata thought that the spell would probably wear the old man out in a few days, but ought to spur his aging body to two or three days of quasi-youthful vigor.

The administration of a powerful wake-up spell was simple as child's play for a magician of the Dark King's caliber. The business was conducted with little ceremony, and with no need for additional sacrifice, right at the breakfast table. Vilkata gave his subject no information about possible long-term effects, but Amintor wondered privately if this stimulation was good for his no-longer-youthful heart.

While the conqueror of Sarykam and his new partner continued their business on the palace roof, Prince Stephen was awakening—the feeling was more like that of regaining consciousness after an injury—under a hedge in the garden of Ben of Purkinje's house, the heat of midday sunlight on his back. He had not rolled over, indeed he had hardly moved a muscle, in the course of his badly-needed sleep.

Now, slowly, he did turn over, and presently sat up. Stretching stiffened joints and muscles, he looked for, and soon found, some water to drink—there was a garden fountain still burbling merrily, as if the peaceful world had not turned upside down.

Close around him birds sang, and a squirrel climbed a tree in summer foliage. Although this grander house, like his grandparents' cottage, had been smashed, the world was still here, it still had peaceful parts, and he was in it. Remembering last night's events, Stephen felt confident that the Mindsword must have been truly destroyed. And as for Shieldbreaker, perhaps the enemy really did not have it yet. Maybe in his swelling anger he'd hurled that demon to a year's distance, or two years', as his father had. That would at least give people who were demons' enemies time to prepare.

Casting an eye at the elevation of the sun behind a barrier of leaves, the young Prince knew a lesser twinge of guilt for having slept so long, and determined that if possible he would not rest again until he had reached his parents.

Also, he was ravenously hungry. He realized now that he hadn't even eaten very much yesterday, during his long work session in the armory.

Stephen understood it would be necessary to provide himself with transportation before he went outside the city walls, and also to acquire some provisions for the journey.

Trusting in Sightblinder's power, knowing that unless he should run directly into Shieldbreaker in the enemy's hands he had little to worry about, the young Prince had no difficulty in moving freely about the streets to obtain what he needed.

Back in the street, he appropriated a fine riding-beast from a joy-screaming convert who could not get himself out of the saddle quickly enough once Stephen, no doubt perceived as the great Dark King himself, had indicated an interest in the animal.

After this acquisition—while the former owner accommodatingly held his new mount for him in the street—Stephen entered shops untended in the city's chaos, where he helped himself to some food and a water-skin. He felt in his pocket for coins to leave in payment, realized he had no money, and decided that in the circumstances it did not matter. Coming out of the last shop, he filled the skin with water at a public fountain.

Meanwhile he continued to observe the condition of the city around him, and his mind raced in an effort to assess the situation clearly.

Though still nagged by the minor physical injuries he had sustained in his first skirmish with a demon, the young Prince had been recovering mentally ever since he had been separated from Shieldbreaker.

Stephen remembered from his father's teaching that the effect of the Mindsword dissipated only gradually. The young Prince realized that, even if his belief that the Mindsword had been demolished was correct, all of the humans recently brought under its influence would probably remain in that hideous condition for at least a day, more likely several days to come. In some cases, where the person was naturally susceptible, the madness might persist much longer or even become permanent.

Remembering last night's confrontation in the armory, he felt sure now that at least no one need ever again fear falling under the Mindsword's control. He was sure now that Skulltwister was gone; and whatever else might happen, he would feel proud to the end of his days that his hand had dealt the blow of its destruction.

Before Stephen could travel more than a few blocks from the house of Ben of Purkinje, his riding-beast pulled up lame.

Bad luck, he thought, bad luck. Well, it should be easy enough to obtain another animal.

As Stephen got down from the saddle, he stepped accidentally upon a pebble in the street, twisting his ankle painfully.

Meanwhile, the roof-top conference, where Amintor sat thinking about Stephen and toying with the hilt of the Sword of Chance, was not yet over. The two partners still sat at the table, old Karel standing beside them, the elder's helpless eyes fixed with an expression of seeming contentment upon something in the far distance.

Vilkata was saying that it was imperative that Amintor, even before beginning his search for Stephen, dispatch marching orders to his army.

"My swiftest demon will convey them—I presume you have some capable wizard in your camp? At least one who can hold intelligent converse with a demon without retching or fainting?"

The junior partner assented meekly. "I am served by several who are more than merely capable, Majesty—though, of course, none of them approach your stature."

The Baron went on to assure his partner that his army was waiting for orders, that it was ready to march, to fight lustily, to conquer, in whatever cause he might choose to assign it. The five thousand or so fighting men and male and female enchanters, and those commanding their associated beasts of war, were purely mercenaries.

The need to continue to feed, maintain, and inspire this army provided a strong argument that Amintor ought to be allowed to retain the Sword of Chance.

A force of only five thousand men would be ineffective if scattered around the countryside. Both men agreed that Amintor's army, or the bulk of it, ought to stay together and march to Sarykam as quickly as it could—doubtless it would prove necessary for the men to fight their way in across the Tasavaltan frontier. At the moment there were no large Tasavaltan units known to be in position to block such an invasion, but certainly spirited resistance could be expected, especially after word reached the frontier patrols of the disaster at Sarykam. Therefore the success of the invasion could not be automatically guaranteed.

Vilkata spoke of being ready to employ his demons more energetically and of devising further schemes to get as much use as possible out of his converts before their usefulness should turn to treachery. At the proper moment he would dispatch such a ground-air force to join with the rein-forcements soon to be approaching in the form of Baron Amintor's army.

And Amintor voiced his approval of Vilkata's gathering thousands of hostages.

Within a matter of a few minutes, the new partners had dispatched a demonic messenger carrying a handwritten and personally identified note from Amintor, complete with personal token, to the experienced officer the Baron had left in command of his five thousand or so men when he himself had gone following Coinspinner off to Sarykam. Acknowledgment of the message could be expected within the hour, if all went well.

Amintor was gone to prepare for his Sword-hunt. The Dark King, still seated at the table, with crushed husks of fruit around him, turned his eyeless countenance up to Karel, who still stood by faithfully. "Well, old man?"

"Sire?"

"Tell me something—profound—about the Swords. You are still loyal to me, for a little while as yet, and you know as much or more than any human about this handiwork of Vulcan. I am interested in how you foresee the course of the Great Game."

Karel hesitated. Then, gazing into the distance, his voice grown vaguer and softer than ever, he stated that anyone keeping track of such things must realize that if this recent rate of Sword-destruction should persist, the time was fast approaching when a majority of the gods' weapons would have perished from the Earth.

Karel noted also that the balance between destroyed and active Swords was now approaching the point of even numbers. Townsaver, Doomgiver, Dragonslicer, Wayfinder, and the Mindsword all were gone. But there still endured Stonecutter, Woundhealer, Shieldbreaker, Coinspinner, Farslayer, Soulcutter, and Sightblinder to tempt and afflict humanity.

Vilkata in turn revealed to the helpless Karel his plan ultimately to gather all the remaining Swords, acquiring them by one means or another, one by one, and as soon as possible destroy them, retaining only Shieldbreaker, the maximum weapon, for himself.

"Destroy them all," the uncle of Princess Kristin muttered. "Destroy the Swords."

"Yes, old man. I tell you it seems impossible to impose true order on the world as long as they exist."

Vilkata's long-range plan, on his return from the Moon, had been to do his best to conquer and rule the world with one Sword—preferably the Mindsword, which he had then possessed. But now, with a smile of satisfaction, he said to Karel that it was probably just as well things had worked out as they had. Shieldbreaker was superior to Skulltwister. Because, among other things, having the Sword of Force made possible a systematic attempt to annihilate the rest of the output of Vulcan's forge.

13

Aᴍɪɴᴛᴏʀ, energized by the powerful stay-awake magic so efficiently administered by his senior partner, paced the alley and yard behind the palace stables in a swift restless limp, barking impatiently at nearby converts, damning their clumsiness, demanding they bring him a totally acceptable mount—he'd already rejected two riding-beasts as looking spiritless. In some ways the stay-awake spell had made the Baron feel twenty years younger, but in other ways he had retained his age; his joints still ached, and he found himself puffing when he began to pace too rapidly.

It was now around midday, the sun as close as it was going to get to overhead, and the Baron had not slept for approximately twenty-four hours. He could remember this fact clearly, but the lack of sleep seemed to carry no mental or physical impact. At the moment weariness and rest were among the farthest things from his mind.

Foremost in his thoughts at the moment was the impression that the Dark King's convert and demon forces, despite their relatively small numbers, were tightening his grip on the city with fair efficiency. From where the Baron paced, he could both see and hear the hundreds of hostages crammed into one of the sealed-off courtyards nearby. More prison-voices came floating up out of the heavily barred ground-level windows behind which a dungeon had been improvised. More hostages were constantly being brought in, and Amintor wondered vaguely where Vilkata thought he was going to put them all.

At this moment old Karel, who had been detailed to accompany Amintor on the hunt for Stephen, came stalking out of the palace to talk to the Baron while they both waited for the routine stable preparations to be completed. Amintor was eager to bring Karel with him on the search for Prince Stephen. Certainly the old wizard, Princess Kristin's uncle, was well acquainted with Prince Stephen and with the city. Also he probably knew as much about Sword-magic as anyone in the world— except, of course, the inimitable Master. It would be a pity to waste that knowledge. The Baron thought that in the remaining hours of the old man's life, before Karel's conversion began to wear off and it became necessary to dispose of him, his help could be invaluable.

Now a fresh sound of hooves echoed sharply from the walls of stone enclosing the stable-yard. With glad cries a lackey announced that the Baron's own riding-beast had just been located, and now it was being brought back to him.

Amintor, a vein swelling in his forehead, waved away this gracious present with an oath, startling and upsetting the convert who'd hoped ardently to be helpful to one so exalted as the Master's partner. The Baron, hand on Swordhilt, shouted to the convert lackeys that he wanted a fresh animal, not one already run half to death. Surely the Tasavaltan stables offered a number of good choices?

Attendants scurried to satisfy his demands.

Now Amintor and Karel both flinched, as there came an unwelcome swirling of nauseating presences about their heads; both were well aware that the Dark King had assigned a pair of demons to accompany them on their search. The announced purpose of having the creatures on the search for Prince Stephen was to provide a swift means of communication with Vilkata; but Amintor had no doubt that they were also under orders to keep an eye on him for their Master. There appeared to be no good way for the men to get rid of the unwelcome creatures.

At least, Amintor supposed, the foul things ought to be constrained to obey his orders, or most of his orders, and he could keep them from hanging over him like poison mist. "Take some approximation of human form!" he snapped.

In a moment the poisonous-looking mist had coalesced into shapes of solid appearance. The foul fiends now appeared as a rather ugly man-servant and his wife, standing beside the humans in the stableyard. The Baron was relieved to find that they obeyed him.

Now the last members of the search party arrived—an escort of human converts armed mundanely. These were a squad of regular Tasavaltan soldiers, augmented by a few civilian volunteers. Mounts were soon provided in sufficient number—even for the demons, though they certainly could have kept up on foot—and all was at last in readiness.

The search party, the Baron leading with Coinspinner in hand and vibrating, cantered out through one of the great gates of the palace.

Stephen, meanwhile, had been unable to make any headway at all in his effort to return Sightblinder to his parents. A series of unlucky happenings had prevented the young Prince from even leaving the neighborhood of Ben's house.

The bad luck had been so pervasive that the fugitive had already begun to suspect strongly that the Sword of Chance must be in action against him. The second mount obtained by Stephen had run away, and the third had also been disabled before it could be ridden any meaningful distance. Fortunately he himself had suffered no additional injury; evidently whatever individual enemy was being served by Coinspinner did not want the young Prince dead, or seriously hurt—the idea, simply and ominously, must be to keep him where he was.

Exhaustion soon set in, and Stephen slept again, once more lightly concealed among the bushes of Ben's garden, stretched out upon the flat of Sightblinder's blade.

Stephen awakened from this second sleep to find that his most recently lamed riding-beast was nuzzling at the back of his neck. He turned over and began a mumbled protest, then suddenly pushed the animal's head aside and sat up straight. Ten meters away, a small band of mounted men—two of them looked to be more or less than men— had come riding into the extensive walled garden of Ben's house. They were halted now, ten meters away, shifting uneasily in their saddles and looking at the young Prince with expressions he could not immediately interpret.

In the next moment Stephen realized that one of the mounted men was Karel. Another of them, who looked as old as the Tasavaltan wizard, held a Sword half-drawn from the scabbard at his side. *Coinspinner,* the young Prince realized suddenly, his perception sharpened by the magic of his own Sword. He could only hope that the Sword of Chance, powerful as it was, could not recognize Sightblinder as an opposing factor, and would not be able to deal with it effectively.

Amintor and those with him, led to this spot by the Sword of Chance, had reined in sharply on catching sight of the figure among the bushes. Looking toward Stephen, the members of the search party saw—never doubted they were seeing—the Dark King himself, Vilkata, now rising from an inexplicable prone position to his feet, then swinging himself up into the saddle of a restive griffin.

The pursuers, gazing at a collective image of Vilkata—whom they visualized as holding in his hand the Sword of Force—were taken aback, perturbed, to see that the Master had evidently got ahead of them somehow to this unlikely place, and even gave the impression that he had been waiting for them.

"Master?" Karel called tentatively.

The young Prince experienced a moment or two of hideous fright before that word reassured him, informed him of exactly who his discoverers thought he was.

More than one of the searchers were thinking it odd that Vilkata, with a whole palace and its people now at his disposal, had chosen to come into an enemy's garden and lie down alone under a hedge—but still it did not occur to any of them to doubt for an instant that they were really looking at Vilkata.

Amintor, wishing to hold converse with his senior partner, moved as if to urge his riding-beast a little closer.

But instantly, to his amazement, the Baron's own Sword, twitching and tugging in his hand, warned him sternly not to advance.

Warily Amintor reined in his mount. Then he began, from a respectful distance, to issue a hopeful report on the progress of the pursuit of Stephen, with some additional remarks on the gathering of hostages.

In the eyes of those hunting him Stephen's lamed riding-beast still appeared to be a saddled demon or griffin; but now the animal moved uneasily, and the lad hopped down from the saddle briskly before he could be thrown. It seemed to the beholders that their Master was now minded to stay with them for some serious discussion.

Meanwhile the young Prince was doing his best to think what his next move should be. He understood with a pang that Karel was still under Skulltwister's spell. Stephen had heard of the adventurer Baron Amintor, though never actually laid eyes on him before and, aided by Sightblinder's enhanced perception, he thought he recognized the Baron now. This identification was confirmed when Stephen heard Karel address the scoundrel by name, in tones of respect that Stephen found sickening.

When Amintor momentarily urged his mount forward, Stephen made ready to stab the man as soon as he came close enough—after making as sure as possible that this enemy wasn't armed with Shieldbreaker.

For a moment Stephen hovered on the brink of swirling away the two demonic members of the search party—but he held back, fearing to reveal his own identity and accomplish nothing. It would be better, much better, to kill the Baron if he could . . . and there was Karel. If only he could find some way to set the powerful wizard free. . . .

Of course, as Stephen fully realized, great caution was necessary in opposing, let along trying to kill, anyone who was holding Coinspinner. Until now, the bad luck inflicted upon him by the Sword of Chance had been minimal, a mere holding action sufficient to prevent his escape. One of the facts that had been drilled into the young Prince during his lifelong education in the matter of Swords was that killing someone armed with the Sword of Chance was well-nigh impossible, and trying to do so was a good way to attain an early end oneself.

Meanwhile Coinspinner in the hunter's hand was continuing to behave erratically. That weapon was now signalling its owner to keep back, remove himself to an even greater distance from the dangerous illusion that he faced all unaware. The rest of Amintor's party started uncertainly to move with him.

Stephen called: "What are you doing?"

The Baron, hearing the words in the Dark King's commanding voice, hesitated briefly. But then the obvious explanation for his own Sword's peculiar behavior occurred to him.

He replied as calmly as he could. "Of course Your Majesty is armed with Shieldbreaker—I suppose that's why Coinspinner here is giving me erratic signals." Patting his black hilt, Amintor peered more closely at the figure before him. Still, no suspicion that he was not looking at Vilkata found room in his thoughts.

The young Prince was silent, thinking furiously of what he ought to say and do. He was afraid, but not so much of men or demons as of failure, of losing another Sword as he had lost Shieldbreaker. . . .

The guilt of that loss now struck Stephen with renewed force. Now he knew beyond any doubt that Vilkata—who was, fortunately, not here—must indeed have been given Shieldbreaker by the demon.

The Baron meanwhile had begun to deliver a kind of non-report, in respectful tones, from the back of his riding-beast, and from a timid, rather inconvenient distance.

Stephen, listening, soon had confirmation, if any were needed, that he himself was being eagerly sought by the enemy.

But he could see that Coinspinner was even now urging its owner to retreat. Why—?

And then, in a flash of revelation, Stephen understood.

"Baron!" He tried to make his voice that of a tyrant who tolerated nothing less than instant obedience—he could only trust that Sightblinder would help him to succeed. "You will hand over Coinspinner to me. Now."

Amintor's mouth fell open at this belated acceptance of his earlier gift, even as the Sword of Chance redoubled its signals advising him to beat a swift retreat—but the Baron, totally convinced that he was confronted by Vilkata with Shieldbreaker, this once did not take his own Sword's advice.

He had planned no specific treachery against Vilkata—as yet there had hardly been an opportunity to do so. And now it might well be that he was doomed. The Baron concealed his own rage and desperation behind a smile. It would be useless to disarm himself and try to leap upon the Dark King—one of the fanatical converts watching jealously would skewer him in an instant, or a demon's claws would find his flesh. . . .

As for the Dark King's demand, the Baron had no choice but to comply, swallowing his own anger, for the time being, as best he could. With shaking fingers Amintor began to unbuckle his swordbelt. Then he dismounted and carried the treasure to his lord.

Feeling the double burden of Sword-magic once more come upon him as he did so, Stephen grasped the black hilt of the Sword of Chance, letting sheath and belt fall free. He needed guidance, required all the help that he could get. His brain once more buzzing and swirling with the psychic burden of two Swords, he decided uncertainly that he ought to kill this man—though it was going to be hard to do that in cold blood.

He was given an even better reason to hold back. The Sword of Chance itself, as soon as the young Prince began to raise the heavy steel to deliver a killing blow, tugged at Stephen's arm, unambiguously directing him to let Amintor live.

Obeying this tugging indication by the Gods' Counselor, the young Prince pondered what he ought to do with the Baron and his unpleasant cohort, if he was not to endeavor to wipe them out.

Roughly he demanded of their leader: "So, you have not found the young Prince yet?"

The shaken Amintor had rejoined his party and was climbing back into his saddle. "No, sire. We have hardly started—"

"Never mind. Abandon that pursuit. I have new orders for you."

Stephen had the satisfaction of seeing Baron Amintor's assurance crack momentarily, this elder warrior blink at him in astonishment and poorly concealed fear. After a moment the Baron ventured: "But Majesty, what of the Sword the young Prince Stephen still carries?"

"Do not dispute my orders!"

"Of course, you are the senior partner. But—" Then Amintor quailed. "What are the new orders?"

Again imagination flagged, and Stephen was momentarily stuck. Then inspiration flashed again. "What would you expect them to be? Use your head, man!"

"I—I— to rejoin my army. To see that my forces reach and occupy Sarykam as swiftly as possible."

"Clever. Good thinking, Baron. Would you like me to provide demonic transportation for you?"

The Baron declined that offer.

"One more thing, Baron. The wizard Karel will stay here with me."

"As you wish, sir. Of course."

Karel, delighted to be allowed to serve his new god directly, stood worshipfully beside the image of his Master, while Amintor and his remaining escort rode out of the garden and out of sight, starting on the new mission.

Back in the palace, the Dark King was pondering intensely his problems and his opportunities. He understood that Arridu, as well as his squadron of lesser demons, were likely to remain under the Mindsword's lingering influence for only a few more hours at most. His only prudent course from now on would be to assume that all his demons had thrown off Skulltwister's yoke.

Fortunately for himself, Vilkata had never been forced to depend entirely on the Mindsword when dealing with Arridu's race. He had taken care to establish an independent magical control over his demonic cadre. Even after the Mindsword's influence had faded, the vicious creatures would still be constrained to serve him, as many another mighty member of their race had been in the past.

The Dark King thought that, of course, the difference between demons in an ordinary tamed condition and those under the Mindsword's bondage was that in the former case it was not totally unthinkable that the foul creatures should turn treacherous. In fact it was almost certain that, sooner or later, one of Arridu's strength would make the attempt to do so.

Vilkata's thin lips smiled faintly. He, the Dark King, if anyone, knew how to manage demons.

And he judged that an opportunity had now arrived for him to satisfy at least in part his curiosity about the Swords.

The fact was that Arridu, until very recently a stranger to the Swords, was still not totally convinced of just how incomparably strong those weapons were. In fact Arridu, going along with his Master's wish to rid the world of most of them, announced that he could manage that.

"You? Are you saying that you by your own powers can break a Sword that was forged by the gods themselves?"

Arridu, projecting an image of serene power, was quietly self-assured. "I see no gods about me now."

"They have been vanquished. Exterminated."

"But I have not." Truly it seemed that the great demon did not believe that any mere artifact of metal and magic, whether forged by a god or not, could resist his strength.

The Dark King, staring at his most powerful vassal, nodded slowly. He was in a mood to accept this challenge. He thought he could be certain of the outcome.

Vilkata considered that there had always been difficulties, certainly, in the way of any plan to destroy all the Swords. Not the least of these obstacles being that the only known means of permanently eliminating any Sword, the only method by which any had yet been demolished, was by bringing the Blade of lesser strength into violent opposition with Shieldbreaker.

At least that was the consensus of knowledgeable opinion. Vilkata, wavering somewhat in his assurance, questioned on the point by the confident demon, had to admit that he wasn't at all sure how often Sword-smashing had seriously been *tried*.

Descending into the airy cellars of the Tasavaltan armory to try it now, Vilkata gave Arridu full permission, nay, commanded him, to do his best to obliterate or at least damage Stonecutter. To swing a heavy blacksmith's hammer right at the keen edge, with superhuman strength.

For the purpose of this test, Vilkata ordered the Sword of Siege to be set up in a vise on a handy workbench, under an Old World light. Arridu selected a hammer, the biggest and hardest available from the armorers' shop in an adjoining room, and, after warning his Master to take cover, wielded the tool with all his strength.

This effort produced impressive pyrotechnics, a stunning blast and a ruined hammer, but no detectable damage to the Sword.

Arridu in baffled rage, and his Master in restored confidence, inspected the result carefully. Not the finest chip or nick marred even the very thinnest edge of Blade.

"Let it stay there, in the clamps." And Vilkata raised Shieldbreaker, whose muttering drumbeat swelled. In another moment, Stonecutter had perished, in a blast whose flying fragments left the Dark King totally unscathed.

In the course of their subsequent discussion about the surviving Swords, Arridu calmly assured his master that he knew where the Tyrant's Blade was to be found.

Vilkata became very still, staring at the great demon, who had now assumed the likeness of an elder sorceress. Pitmedden buzzed like a great fly beside the wizard's head. Vilkata demanded: "Soulcutter? Do you know what you are saying?"

"Oh, indeed, Master, indeed I do. Now that you have taught me about the Swords, Master, I can understand certain events on the Moon which for the past twenty years have puzzled me."

"And what events were these?"

"Those surrounding the visit, to a site near our place of imprisonment, of a man whom I can now identify. It was he who is called the Emperor, and he brought with him a certain object, and he caused that object to be there buried, deep, deep in lunar rock, where once volcanoes flowed; and he sealed the burial with mighty spells and other sealings."

Vilkata demanded more details, and Arridu was ready to provide them. Though, of course, the demon could not answer every question, Soulcutter, it indeed appeared, had somehow been carried to the Moon. Piecing together what Arridu now told him with certain facts he had long known, Vilkata decided that the deadly toy must have been put away there by the Emperor some twenty years ago.

Still Vilkata had scarcely moved since Arridu's claim, and promise, first fell upon his ears. The human wizard mused: "Aye, that would have been like him—the Great Clown, the matchless hypocrite. Saving Despair to use it, for his own advantage, later." Vilkata chewed his pale lower lip.

The speech of the elegant, gray-haired lady's image was soft, utterly reassuring. "And I know where it is, great Master. Say the word, and that weapon shall be yours."

The Dark King thought for some time. Suspiciously he at last replied: "When the time comes, you will return there with me and show me where that Sword is buried, and help me remove such obstacles as may keep me from it; but it will be my hand alone that takes control of that Sword, or any other we may find."

"It is easy to see, great Lord, how that Sword might be of inestimable value to your cause."

"Indeed."

* * *

Whenever the Dark King perceived the Sword of Despair, in reality or in imagination, the symbolism of his special vision presented that weapon to him as a narrow pillar of darkness, radiating tendrils of negation, stifling light and movement, hope and purpose, everywhere nearby. So, in his mind's eye, he visualized Soulcutter now. . . .

Yes, that Sword was what he needed to set in motion the perfect plan for domination.

It would, of course, be folly *for anyone not armed as well with Shieldbreaker* to simply draw Soulcutter, thus exposing oneself to its deadly, corrosive power, along with all other humans, beasts, and demons within a long bowshot. But Vilkata *was* armed with the protective Sword of Force. He could walk unharmed, untouched, amid despairing armies.

And there would, of course, be other ways to use the Sword of Despair intelligently. For example, to arrange for it to be unsheathed in the midst of an enemy army. For example, give Soulcutter to Mark or his associates, to some person among them who could be fooled or persuaded into drawing Despair at the right moment. . . .

Oh yes, the tactical details would all have to be calculated very carefully. But the Dark King had no doubt at all that he could manage them.

An hour after Vilkata had dismissed Arridu from his presence, another conference took place, this one between Arridu and Amintor. It happened in the latter's tent, while the Baron was resting, somewhere well outside the city, after the first few hours of the wild-goose chase he had been sent on by Stephen.

Outside, around the tent, Amintor's escort, all unaware of his visitor's arrival, were going on about the routine chores of camp. The Baron felt seriously sickened by the close presence of this thing which had intruded its presence upon him.

The demon, becoming aware of this reaction, caused itself to be perceived as having withdrawn to a somewhat more comfortable distance—the tent having apparently elongated itself rather strangely. Also, Arridu took the non-threatening appearance of a simple peasant, some prosperous small farmer who might have come to discuss the sale of an allotment of potatoes.

"Thank you." Amintor wiped sweat from his forehead, not bothering to try to conceal the action, or the discomfort which had caused it.

The gray-stubbled peasant, sitting easily on a camp stool with fingers interlaced across his ample paunch, remarked that he, Amintor, had never been a slave of the Mindsword.

"True. While you, of course . . ."

"I have been subject to such enthrallment, but for the past few hours I have been free. The weapon called Skulltwister has been smashed—doubtless it could not have held me much longer in any case."

The Baron moistened his lips and tried to appear comfortable. "He has, of course, instructed you to say that you are now free. To try my loyalty."

"No. You know the Mindsword's spells must fade with time. And I can prove what I say." The peasant-demon, settling itself in as if for a leisured talk, went on to inform the man of how he, the Baron, had just allowed Sightblinder in young Prince Stephen's hands to make a fool of him. "But I have not mentioned your failure to the great fool, who thinks I am still bound to him by a broken Sword."

The Baron, staring at the lifeless gray eyes of his informant, felt a chill as the conviction grew in him that for once a demon was telling him the truth: He had indeed been fooled by the Sword of Stealth in the hands of the Tasavaltan princeling.

The demon, as if it could read his mind, nodded slightly. "Your partnership with the Dark King—such as it was—is already ruined. Therefore, Baron, you had better seek to make some other arrangement for your own survival as soon as possible."

Arridu, originally somewhat contemptuous of the Swords, had been forced to concede that they must be respected. To cope with the Sword of Force he needed a human ally, or tool—someone with the nerve and knowledge necessary to wrestle Shieldbreaker away from Vilkata. Ideally, this human helper would be a non-magician, who could be dealt with more reasonably thereafter.

The Baron seemed an eminently suitable choice. The man possessed both nerve and knowledge, and would therefore be worth some effort at persuasion. Amintor was somewhat physically decrepit compared to the magician, the much greater age of the latter having been more than compensated for by magic. But in this wrestling bodily strength was not a requirement.

Amintor, listening to the demon's proposal without yet committing himself, appreciated the skill and daring with which the plan had been made. At the same time, he felt extremely reluctant to agree to anything of the kind without what he considered some enforceable guarantee of his role in the new partnership to follow. Second place in any partnership was generally good enough for him; he was not a man who really wanted to be supreme dictator.

And—wasn't there some relevant old proverb? If not, there ought to be. Only a lunatic, the Baron thought to himself, would ever willingly become a demon's partner.

The question was whether he, Amintor, really had any choice.

"Then I am with you," he said at last, trying to make the agreement sound hearty and whole-hearted.

The tent restored itself to normal interior dimensions as the peasant got to his feet, his small eyes twinkling. "Of course you are," the demon said reassuringly.

"When do we strike?"

"That has yet to be decided. Probably the next time you and the Dark King are together. But let the coming-together be his suggestion and not yours."

Arridu agreed with the Baron that Amintor at this point had best go on trying to rejoin his army.

When the thing was gone, Amintor once more stretched out, shakily this time, to try to get some rest. He wondered whether Vilkata's wide-awake spell was going to keep him from sleeping altogether.

Dozing, or trying to doze, the Baron also considered privately whether it was yet utterly hopeless for him to make a deal with Prince Mark and his royal wife, or with Stephen if and when he encountered the lad again. Amintor was quite ready to ally himself with Tasavalta, for the time being at least, if other choices seemed unsatisfactory. And the Tasavaltans, their capital in enemy hands, were in no condition to be too choosy about their allies.

Darkness was falling outside his tent. His minor demons and his hapless converts went about routine activities. If only he could sleep.

14

THE compact realm of Tasavalta lay for the most part green and beautiful, in sunny early afternoon, some twelve hours after Vilkata's surprise attack on the capital, Sarykam—and approximately two hours after Stephen had confronted Baron Amintor and relieved him of the Sword of Chance.

Ben of Purkinje—massive, heavily muscled, scarred, graying and ugly Ben, who was a couple of years older than the Prince and looked a little older still—and Prince Mark, companions since their early youth, had ridden together out of the village of Voronina before dawn, feeling the urgent need of a scouting expedition in the direction of the city.

Mark was wearing Woundhealer at his right side, and at his left, just in case of untoward encounters, a mundane sword of comparable size and weight, an efficient killing tool.

Captain Miyagi and his small company of soldiers had remained in the village with Princess Kristin, as had the beastmaster and his trained animals, with the exception of one day-flying bird-messenger that went with Mark. In expectation that Vilkata's invading forces would soon renew and extend their assault, the understanding was that the Princess would, at some time during the day, move her field headquarters to a different village. If all went well, her husband, having completed his reconnaissance for the time being, would soon join her there.

Mark and Ben, long familiar with each other's thoughts, had little to say as they cantered toward Sarykam. The morning was well advanced by the time they came in sight of the city's familiar walls.

At this point the pair encountered a handful of people, good Tasavaltan citizens, but now with the look of refugees about them, carrying homemade bundles and wearing expressions of bewilderment. One couple pushed a laden cart built to be hauled by animals. All of these people recognized the Prince on sight, and most of them knew Ben as well. All told at length of the devastation in the capital, and several were eye-witnesses of Vilkata's demons taking hostages by the hundred.

One man had heard a rumor that the Mindsword had been destroyed, but that all the weapons in the armory were captured by the foe. Another rumor was that Vilkata had been slain; and there were less happy rumors concerning things that might have happened to Prince Stephen. The father of the young Prince, well aware of the unreliability of tales in wartime, managed to hear these last without giving any overt sign of great dismay.

Leaving the refugees to settle their concerns of food and shelter for the coming night, Ben and Mark moved on a little way. They were considering whether to approach the city more closely, when in a suburban street one of the death squads dispatched by Vilkata against Mark, half a dozen Tasavaltan converts sent out as assassins, recognized the pair and attacked, shrieking their glorious Master's name.

Some of these men were literally frothing at the mouth with the violence of their hatred, with their joy at the prospect of killing and dying for the Dark King.

Ben had only a moment's warning, but that was all he needed. He met his attackers with considerable skill and overwhelming strength. Knowing that Woundhealer was available, in his partner's hand, made it possible also to fight with an unusual recklessness.

Mark, standing back-to-back with his huge ally, engaged in peculiar Swordplay—every time he thrust home with Woundhealer, or even nicked one of his attackers, the bright steel of his Sword brought swift healing, recovery, to the Mindsword's victims.

First one attacker then another, bloodlessly slashed or neatly skewered, staggered back, dropping weapons, moments later crying out in horror at their own behavior.

The first men so efficiently de-converted were in moments hurling themselves upon their former comrades, grabbing at sword-arms, trying desperately to stop those still under Skulltwister's spell from pressing the attack. The odds in the fight had soon shifted dramatically.

Those injured soon received Woundhealer's swift, sharp blessing, some of them two or three times before the fighting stopped.

In a minute the skirmish was over. After a last round of healing, wiping away whatever wounds Mark and Ben and their opponents had incurred in the deadly business, the Prince, breathing heavily, sat down on a curb to rest. Ben, gasping even more loudly, had slumped beside him.

"I am going," Mark said presently, "back to rejoin the Princess. There will be decisions to be made, and I must learn what reports have come in from around the country. Will you come with me, or scout some more? I leave it up to you."

Ben thought it over for a few more gasps. "I will stay here, or move closer in, toward the palace, and learn what more I can learn. Send me a messenger-bird or two when you can."

Mark nodded. The Prince took Woundhealer with him when he departed to rejoin Kristin. But he left with Ben a freshly acquired squad of de-converted Tasavaltan soldiers to aid him in scouting out the city and trying to establish an organized resistance.

Ben ordered his de-converted squad back into the city, where, without his easily identifiable presence, they could pretend to be still carrying out Vilkata's orders. A tentative plan was made for rendezvous.

Ben himself waited alone for a few hours, indoors in an abandoned suburban house, till darkness fell—then he cautiously advanced, passing inside the city walls without trouble, through an abandoned gate. He was increasingly consumed with the urgent need to find out what had happened to his home, and to his wife and daughter.

It was no secret that Ben had been on poor terms for years with his wife, Barbara, and in fact months had passed since his last visit to his home—or house—in Sarykam. But since the horrible news last midnight, he'd discovered that this degree of estrangement gave no immunity from fear and grief. For years he'd not seen much of his and Barbara's only child, their grown-up daughter Beth, but now he knew beyond any doubt that Beth's fate was still of great importance to him.

It had also crossed his mind that young Prince Stephen, supposing he had somehow escaped the palace, might have come to Ben's house looking for help.

From a block away, Ben saw the ruin of his own dwelling—the upper floor completely gone—without surprise. He knew, without particularly worrying about the fact, that it was extremely dangerous for him to be here in the city, especially in the vicinity of his old house. He did not doubt that the destruction which had claimed this building and much of its immediate surroundings had been meant for him primarily.

Meanwhile, the afternoon had worn on for Kristin, in another little village much like Voronina, but with a different name, and closer than sixty kilometers to the capital, lying outwardly tranquil under a complacent sun.

In this new village Kristin had relocated herself and, thus, the royal headquarters. By midafternoon she was waiting anxiously for, among other things, her husband to rejoin her.

Kristin had not been brought up in a farmer's house—far from it. But she had learned long ago to put up with much worse, when necessary. Today, like most of the village women, she was wearing trousers and loose shirt of homespun.

The owl which had brought the royal couple their first word of the disaster in Sarykam had come with her to this village and was even now sleeping the remainder of the day away in one of the barns, a bulky alien presence making the pigeons nervous. The Master of Beasts, considering that he had done everything useful that he could do for the moment, was catching a nap there too.

The central village square, enclosed on four sides by rows of little houses, was quiet except for the usual domestic noises of fowl and other farmyard animals, including a barking dog or two.

Surrounding the small settlement, which consisted of no more than a score of houses, were fields now lush with summer crops, demarcated by hedgerows. A range of coastal mountains loomed blue in the distance. The people, like most of their compatriots more or less accustomed to the occasional presence of Prince and Princess, were today for the most part going about their usual affairs, though with uneasy faces and many pauses to search the sky.

Mark, about an hour after leaving Ben, came riding into the village, returning about on schedule from his reconnaissance.

His wife made no great demonstration at Mark's appearance, but to anyone watching her closely, her sudden relief was intense and obvious.

Mark agreed with his wife's suggestion that he get some rest now, while he had the chance. He'd been up since the alarm was sounded, since very early that morning.

For the last few nights, back in Voronina, he had shared with his Princess the tiny spare room—perhaps the only such chamber in Voronina—of a prosperous yeoman's house. This new village was even smaller, and Mark guessed there would be no spare rooms available.

When the Prince had seen to it that his mount was stabled, and heard such reports as had come in during his absence—they seemed of little importance—he lay down in the shade of a tree. The Prince felt comfortingly at home among these country smells and sounds and people. He had grown up in a small village not that much different from this one, and at no enormous distance either, though the home of his birth had not been Tasavaltan.

An hour later, after a sleep troubled by strange dreams, Mark was up again, standing near the middle of the small village plaza, anxiously scanning the afternoon skies, hoping for another winged messenger. Even more bad news—provided it was not too bad—would be, in a way, some relief.

For both husband and wife this waiting, with no knowledge of what the limits of the ordeal were going to be, gave promise of becoming a supreme test of patience. The hours since the first word of the attack had seemed endless, a desert of time to be got through in which it seemed impossible to do anything useful, or anything at all but wait.

As the afternoon wore on, with shadows lengthening, it became impossible for Mark, and Kristin too, to sit without doing anything. While continuing a desultory conversation, the royal couple were soon at weapons' practice, sharing a single battle-hatchet for the purpose. The sound of the thick blade's impact on the trunk of a dead tree echoed repeatedly from the flat house-fronts of mud brick and wood. Soon some of the simpler villagers came to stand gawking in the background. Soon Captain Miyagi came to join the onlookers.

Those who had stopped to silently judge the skill of Prince and Princess, some of them with expert eyes, were favorably impressed. The arm drawn back—swiftly, not giving an enemy a chance to dodge—and then snapped forward. *Thunk!*

First Mark's long powerful legs (next turn, Kristin's, somewhat shorter) strode restlessly toward the target and back again, his (or her) right arm swinging the recovered weapon in a practiced hand.

This time it was Prince Mark who spun around and threw. Again the sharp blade thudded home. Small chips flew from where previous cuts were intersected. Mark's aim was good, mechanically good. Another day or two of waiting, he thought, and the target tree was going to be chewed away to nothing. But no, they would have to relocate once more to another village before that much time had passed.

And every few moments he raised his head, as did his Princess, to scan the skies, on watch for an attack by demons or flying reptiles, but particularly for more news.

One of the problems reviewed by the royal couple while practicing with physical weapons was that of how to obtain the best possible magical help, and as soon as possible. If only Adrian were finished with his studies and were here . . . but in fact Adrian was not ready, and not here, and it was not possible that he could be of help just now. Thank Ardneh, the older son at least had not been taken by surprise, as the younger must have been, in Sarykam.

Karel, too, was ominously out of communication, like everyone else the royal couple had left behind them in the supposed safety of their capital.

At least General Rostov, traveling in another province at the time of Vilkata's attack, had now checked in, sending a messenger with some reassuring word about mobilization there.

Kristin and Mark by now had convincing evidence that Vilkata was the author of this latest disaster. The plenitude of demons in the assault had suggested as much. Refugees' information, such as Mark had now heard first hand, provided more solid evidence. It was true, then: The Dark King had returned to the attack, bringing with him the Mindsword which had been in his possession two years ago when he was hurled away. The Prince could remember all too well the horrible events of two years past, on the night of Vilkata's previous attack, which had resulted in the Dark King's banishment and also Kristin's injury.

In the hours since the first news of the disaster had reached the Prince and Princess, the couple had endeavored to keep up each other's hopes regarding their younger son, still unaccounted for in Sarykam. Their best grounds for optimism lay in the facts that Stephen was more often than not level-headed and responsible for his age—and that he had been granted access to the Swords.

The mother and father of Prince Stephen, once more scanning the skies together waiting, hoping, for the next messenger-bird to appear in the sunset skies, repeatedly assured each other how good it was that they had given their young son that much of a chance.

Holding frequent, almost continuous consultation with his Princess, Mark, since the news had arrived, had been making plans—most of them, so far, necessarily only tentative. Which way would Vilkata move now? Was a fresh assault to be expected upon some other part of the realm?

He was also trying to lay the groundwork for effective countermeasures, as more reports about Vilkata's assault, each in itself fragmentary, reached him. But there was as yet almost nothing he could do, beyond sending warning to everyone with whom he was able to communicate by messenger, that the Mindsword was in the city and the place must therefore be avoided.

Mark most especially wondered what had happened to the Swords in his armory.

It began to be possible for Mark to believe the rumor he had heard concerning the Mindsword. Though Skulltwister had undoubtedly been present last night in the capital, Vilkata was no longer pressing his attack with the enthusiasm that might have been expected had the Blade of Glory been still available. Of course, the Prince dared not disregard the possibility that the horror could be reimposed at any moment.

And Mark's and Kristin's worries continued unabated regarding Stephen, as well as Mark's parents, Jord and Mala, who had been the only other members of his immediate family in Sarykam at the time of the latest attack.

15

MOMENTS after Stephen had shouted his last order at them, Amintor and his search party had departed from the walled garden in the middle of the ravaged city, leaving the young Prince alone with the still-befuddled wizard, Karel.

Stephen, still enduring the renewed burden of a Sword in each hand, stood staring with perplexity at his Great-Uncle, who gazed back at him —rather, at a spot just over Stephen's head—with all the solemnity of confident worship. The young Prince was about to appeal to Coinspinner for help in dealing with this problem when the Sword of Chance suddenly twitched of its own accord. Then it tugged again, the direction unmistakable. It was guiding Stephen to one of the side gates in the garden wall.

Both hands still filled with black-hilted magic, Stephen stepped unsteadily along the indicated course and leaned on the gate to open it. Looking out into an alley, he saw two people half a dozen meters away, both of them frozen in watchful attitudes. Their faces, turned toward him, were studies in controlled fear. Immediately Stephen recognized his cousin Zoltan, a sturdy, brown-haired young man of twenty-four, and the Lady Yambu, a gray but relatively youthful fifty-three. Both were armed and on foot, wearing common pilgrim gray.

Over the past several years Yambu and Zoltan had developed a relationship resembling that of mother and son. They had been out of Tasavalta a great deal, often traveling together on one pilgrimage or another. Meanwhile they had remained on close and friendly terms with Prince Mark and the rest of Mark's family, and it was not surprising that both of them had been in the vicinity of Sarykam when Vilkata's latest attack fell upon the city.

Karel, now doubly deluded, trying to be watchful and protective of his great Master, had followed Stephen to the gate, and was frowning out over his shoulder.

The four people held their tableau for a long, silent moment in which Sightblinder helped assure Stephen that neither his cousin nor the lady were Mindsword-converts. But the lad quickly realized that they might well be seeing him as Vilkata and trying to play the role of faithful slaves.

Actually Yambu's first look at Stephen had shown her the image of the Emperor; but then that form shifted, back and forth, in swift alternation with Vilkata's. At the same time, Sightblinder's magic held her enthralled, prevented her from realizing the scope of its deception. Understanding little more than the fact that something magical and out of the ordinary was taking place, she glared back proudly at the latest image of the Emperor, and stubbornly refused to speak.

Zoltan was seeing the Dark King too, but interspersed with fleeting glimpses of a certain mermaid, a creature of importance in his past. Stephen's cousin, quietly stunned, like Lady Yambu remained silent for the moment.

Stephen, naturally enough, was first to recover from his surprise. Fiercely he ordered Karel to go and stand guard at the other end of the garden, the far side of the grounds surrounding Ben's ruined house—then the young Prince put aside Sightblinder long enough to joyfully disillusion his newly-arrived friends.

Before the three could do more than begin to exchange greetings, the elder wizard was coming back from the other end of the garden. Karel, obviously reluctant to leave his Master in what he perceived as a situation of potential danger, came near disobeying orders, and returned so swiftly that Stephen barely had time to grab up Sightblinder again.

As he rejoined the small group, Karel looked suspiciously and anxiously at Stephen's companions, and to his Master openly expressed his doubts that these people were really true faithful converts like himself.

The young Prince hesitated. He did not dare reveal his true identity to Karel lest the old man try to kill him, as the armorer had done—and Karel was vastly more formidable.

After some argument he persuaded the old man to move away again, long enough for a hasty, whispered conversation to take place concerning him. It was obvious that much craft and energy would have to go into the job of managing the old wizard until he recovered from the Mindsword's lingering influence. There was no known way, as far as any of his three friends knew, to hasten the recovery.

It was Yambu who came up with what seemed a good suggestion. Stephen, speaking in Vilkata's name, ordered Karel to mix himself a strong sleeping potion and drink it. "Something that will make you sleep for twenty-four hours."

Karel, though frowning, was unable to resist obeying a direct and

forceful command from his Great Lord. Stephen's Great-Uncle mixed
the potion as commanded, dutifully conjuring up the necessary materials,
along with a crystal cup, apparently out of nothing.

Having quaffed the draught, the elder, his eyelids already sagging, was
put to sleep in a sheltered place under one of the broken walls of Ben's
house, in what his friends hoped would be safety, until he should waken,
they hoped, in his right mind.

"Will he be all right there?" Stephen asked, leaning against a half-
ruined wall. He was feeling an immense relief at having someone he
could talk to.

Yambu shrugged. "We can only hope so. What else could we do with
him?"

Half a minute later, Stephen, with a profound sigh of relief, gave his
two Swords temporarily into the care of his two friends, and sat down to
rest his psyche and his body alike.

There was no question in his mind about one thing: He had been
simply unable to deal any longer with the pressure of carrying two
Swords. If he hadn't lost Shieldbreaker, he might have been forced to
abandon it—to hide it on the slim chance he, or someone, could retrieve
it before the Dark King's magic succeeded in discovering the now-own-
erless Sword.

Dusk was deepening, and the three were busy comparing notes on
recent events, when there came another movement at the garden gate, a
cautious opening. The young Prince grabbed up Sightblinder again, then
relaxed when the massive figure of Ben of Purkinje came into view.
Stephen realized that Coinspinner was still at work for him, bringing him
further reinforcement.

Ben, cautiously entering the garden of his own ruined house and coming in sight of the occupants, stopped in his tracks as if he had sustained
some heavy blow. He saw Stephen's image transformed into that of a
red-haired young woman, tall and strong, and for a soul-shaking moment
it was possible for the huge man to believe that his long-lost Ariane was
not dead after all.

It was not the first time that the Sword of Stealth had played him such
a cruel trick, and in another moment or two he was able to greet his
friends in a normal voice.

Karel had obeyed to the letter the command of his Master (as he
thought) to put himself to sleep for a full day; but his need to protect and
serve that Master actively soon brought the old man to his feet, sleep-

walking. Unnoticed by his three friends, now deep in conversation at a little distance, the elder wizard, obviously in the grip of some purpose which transcended sleep, walked out of the garden by another exit, and away.

Meanwhile, the young Prince was congratulating himself and entertaining his new gathering of friends with the story of how he had swindled Baron Amintor out of the Sword Coinspinner, and had effectively gotten rid of Amintor and his search party—at least for the time being.

Coinspinner had not failed to provide the little band with food. A root cellar under Ben's house, and a small icehouse in his garden, had both been spared demonic vandalism.

But hours were passing and there was only limited time for self-congratulation. Stephen and his friends, finding themselves fortuitously armed with two Swords, now had to determine the best way to put Coinspinner and Sightblinder to work.

Zoltan opened the serious conference by suggesting that they carry the pair of god-forged weapons to Stephen's royal parents as quickly and by as direct a route as possible—Ben ought to know where Mark and Kristin were most likely to be found.

But Ben was already shaking his head. He had ominous and urgent news to relate, eyewitness reports of Vilkata's hostage-taking.

This seemed important enough to compel a change of plan.

Stephen and his friends, still benefitting from Coinspinner's untiring influence, had not got much further with their talk when a messenger reached them from the Prince and Princess—a night-flying scout, a great owl dispatched from village headquarters, discovered their whereabouts in the city.

While the bird rested and ate, Ben took the opportunity to indite a short message laden with good news, written in code and addressed to Stephen's parents. The note informed Kristin and Mark that their son had been located, that Sightblinder and Coinspinner were available, and that the destruction of the Mindsword had now been definitely confirmed.

Soon the messenger, somewhat rested, was urged on its way. Still, there could be no thought of merely waiting now for orders from Mark and Kristin. The need was urgent to do something about the hostage situation, and orders sent from headquarters might never get through.

But everyone in the garden needed a rest before undertaking any substantial tasks. Stephen in particular was grimy and bleary-eyed from digging in the ruins of his grandparents' house and had suffered burned fingers on both hands in the effort to save their lives; his legs and ankles were scratched from climbing through the rubble, his right shoulder had been wrenched by last night's Swordplay, and then Coinspinner, before coming into Stephen's possession, had twisted his ankle, enough to keep him from walking easily or far.

The lad had put in rather more than a full day's hard work in the armory even before the attack fell on the palace, and had enjoyed only brief periods of real rest since then.

Now and then pangs of guilt still assailed Stephen over the fact that he had lost one of the Swords, perhaps the most important, to the enemy. But each time he forced himself to try to think the matter through clearly and logically, telling himself that he had done the best he could manage at the time.

In the hours before dawn—the messenger had been perilously delayed en route—Prince Mark and Princess Kristin received the happy news of Stephen's safety and confirmation of the Mindsword's destruction.

Prince and Princess happened to be awake when the good news arrived because people from an outlying farm had come to the village shouting, pleading, seeking Woundhealer's blessing on a scalded child. This victim was no casualty of Vilkata's attack, but only of domestic accident, a broken table-leg, a falling pot. Even in the midst of war, the other terrors of life went on.

While Mark and the cavalry remained suspiciously on guard against some trickery, Kristin drew the Sword of Love. As always with Woundhealer, the healing was swiftly and easily accomplished.

The child, relieved of pain, shock, and disfigurement, contentedly fell asleep. The grateful parents could not be as easily sent away. In fervent voices the man, named Bodker, and his wife Alta, praised and blessed the Prince and Princess, and the Sword the royal couple had brought among their people.

Kristin, more at ease than her husband in such situations, walked with the parents outside the cottage. Left alone again for the moment, Mark stared with a bitter smile at the Sword of Healing in his hand—one Sword which was never going to do the least harm to any of his enemies. Still, he had come to know the Sword of Love too well not to appreciate the ways in which it could be useful to the fighting man.

With enemy reptiles and demons tending to dominate the sky, flying messengers could now afford the Prince only an intermittent and indirect contact with his son. Messages could be exchanged, some co-ordinated plan of action could be at least outlined. A messenger approaching Stephen and his friends could be as confused by Sightblinder as any human or demonic enemy—but, of course, Coinspinner could help to straighten matters out.

Mark had to assume that Vilkata, with a thousand fanatically helpful converts to call upon, would soon learn to what village his archenemies, the Prince and Princess of Tasavalta, had gone, and when and why. Then —if the Mindsword still existed—the Dark King would soon be marching after them, doing his best to create an avalanche of new converts on the way.

But no such attack seemed to have been launched. Another indication, if any were still needed, that Skulltwister had actually been smashed.

Still, Mark and Kristin warily decided to continue moving their headquarters repeatedly, perhaps several times a day, keeping in touch with their key people by means of galloping couriers and a small band of flying messengers. Even now, in the village currently occupied by the royal couple, someone was getting the riding-beasts ready for the next relocation.

Meanwhile, with hard information gained, more orders could be dispatched to all the outlying districts of Tasavalta and to any reliable allies in the region. Mark's new confidence that the Mindsword had been destroyed rendered a general assault with an army on Vilkata's forces feasible again. Mark and his Princess were both busy, full time, sending reassurance to their people and marshalling troops.

16

WITH dawn, squadrons of flying reptiles, precursors of Amintor's advancing army, patrolled the sky over and around the city, making further Tasavaltan communication by flying messengers, at least temporarily, almost impossible. More couriers, and fighting birds to escort them, were being summoned from the more distant provinces.

Dawn found Karel still walking in his sleep, a man moving with the dazed sense of some unknown, urgent task to be accomplished—the elder wizard was wandering on an erratic course that had already taken him out of Sarykam. Twice minor demons tried to interfere with him, and twice he blasted them magically out of his path, even without becoming fully aware of his surroundings.

With the passing hours, the hold upon him of the vanished Mindsword was decaying, and the old man struggled internally to regain control over his own soul.

At first light, Yambu made her way across the grounds of Ben's ruined house, looked at the place where Karel had been put to sleep, and discovered that he was missing.

There were no signs of violence, nor did it appear that the wizard had taken anything with him, even food or water.

The lady reported her discovery to her friends, but there was nothing any of them could do about Karel now. Rather, it was necessary for the four remaining, having restored themselves with food and rest, to take action quickly to help the many hostages Vilkata had now crammed into the courtyards and cellars of the palace. Ominous sounds from the city streets, drifting in over the garden wall to Coinspinner's charmed redoubt, confirmed that more victims were being added hourly to the total.

There could be little doubt that the Dark King's prisoners were in urgent peril of being slaughtered within the next few hours. Such an atrocity was only to be expected, given Vilkata's nature and the situation in which he now found himself.

Stephen and his three friends all agreed that the most effective action would be direct, getting in among the hostages with Sightblinder and Coinspinner. It was entirely possible, even likely, that the rescuers, in following such a course, would find themselves facing Shieldbreaker—but the risk had to be accepted.

Naturally the organization of the rescue operation would have been much easier could it have been postponed for even one more day. Now it would be more difficult because of the necessity to save some all-too-willing victims; but in another day the great majority of Vilkata's converts would be emerging naturally from the mental fog generated by the Mind-sword. Hour by hour, even minute by minute, they would experience first doubts, then confusion, then a full readiness to rebel against the man who had so briefly made himself their Master.

But of course it was not possible to wait that long. The Dark King, anticipating just such a mass reversion, would be planning already to slaughter those he had confined—or to have them massacre each other, or be devoured by demons—before they could regain their senses.

Before pushing open the garden gate and launching their attack upon the palace, Stephen and his companions had to decide, of course in consultation with Coinspinner, which of them was going to carry each Sword in among the hostages.

"Who shall carry this?" The Silver Queen, addressing one Sword, raised high the other.

The tip of the Sword of Chance twitched, tugged decisively. The task of wielding Sightblinder in combat had fallen to Zoltan. The young man gripped thoughtfully the black hilt marked with the symbol of an eye, and in the perception of his comrades he vanished, was transformed into a series of images compounded of their own hate and fear and love.

"And this?" Yambu, like a priestess, held aloft the very Sword that was being questioned.

Coinspinner's magic weighed straight down upon her; and thus remained in Yambu's hands.

There were a few tactical questions to be settled. Ben, mundanely armed, undertook the job of bodyguard to the now-Swordless Stephen. The young Prince's chief responsibility would, of course, be the exercise of his unique power; when the fighting started, he would banish as many demons as he could, to as great a distance as possible.

A minute later, Ben yanked open the door leading to the street. Stephen and his friends, doubly Sword-armed, marched out of the walled garden and toward the palace. They anticipated that on their arrival their work would be for the most part indoors and in enclosed courtyards; therefore they made no attempt to equip themselves with riding-beasts, which under the circumstances seemed more of a complication than an advantage.

Still the unconverted population of Sarykam had not totally evacuated the city, though by now a high proportion had fled. Many old people remained, and a scattering of others, some simply unwilling to be driven from their homes, had been hiding from the hostage-taking demons. Zoltan, advancing with Sightblinder, had not walked two blocks before he began to attract a following crowd of Vilkata-converts, some no doubt genuine, some playing the role, all deceived into believing they were following their all-important Master. Among them a few confused individuals, who beheld in Zoltan an image of some dearly beloved child or spouse or parent riding toward them, hastened to give thanks for that person's survival.

In a loud voice Zoltan introduced his three original companions as his faithful servants; then all four began to tell the swelling crowd that an impostor, a false Master, now sat in the palace.

More than once while walking the modest distance to the palace—and later, coming at him in the jammed interior courtyards—total strangers, deceived by the Sword of Stealth into the conviction that Zoltan was someone they loved, still accosted the young man with maudlin apologies, self-accusations regarding old and unknown mistreatment. Again and again his ears rang with tearful pleas that he—or she—come home with them at last.

Less visible, or audible, were an equal number of people who fled from his path in total terror.

Coinspinner, in the hands of the Silver Queen, unobtrusively set the raiders' course. The marching crowd, urged on by Zoltan's shouts, soon swelled into an angry horde. A figure appearing to be, in the eyes of hundreds of onlookers, the Dark King himself, accompanied by a rapidly growing entourage whose purpose was uncertain, pushed through the outer gates and entered the palace grounds.

That company went in unopposed, unchallenged by human or demonic guard, through one of the main doorways of the palace itself.

Complicated, conflicting reactions by the hostages themselves surrounded Zoltan and his close escort when he carried Sightblinder in among them. A roar went up from a thousand human voices, and what had been a passive crowd of captives was transformed in a moment into an utterly chaotic mob.

Eagerly the four invaders began their inside work, shouting into the cellars and improvised dungeons, freeing hostages with sharp commands in Vilkata's name. Even as Stephen and his band began their rescue operation in the palace, the most recently rounded-up contingent of genuine hostages, a scant few, were still being penned up with the others in the inner courtyards. Those interior rooms of the huge building which were most suitable for the purpose had already been filled far beyond their normal capacity. Up till the hour of the raid, in an effort to forestall, or weaken, the inevitable Tasavaltan counterattack, the Dark King had continued to cram more hostages into the courtyards and cellars of the palace, an indiscriminate gathering of whatever men, women, and children could be rounded up by his remaining human converts and his demons.

Aside from elderly folk, or those who had been injured or crippled after Woundhealer ceased to be available, practically everyone who was not a hostage or a direct combatant on one side or the other had by now fled the capital.

Doors and gates were opened in blind obedience, convert guards were trampled, demons hurled away by Stephen, who stood chanting steadily, pointing at one inhuman form after another. Lady Yambu continuously consulted Coinspinner, trying her best to interpret the results and convey them to her comrades amid the din.

In moments, a mass escape was under way.

On the theory that the prisoners most remote from freedom should be released first, or, in any case, must not be forgotten, Zoltan, almost as familiar as Stephen with the palace, urged his comrades to the lower depths, where they found some doors still locked. With shouted commands the raiding party dug people out of cells and an improvised torture-room, then moved above-ground again to visit one courtyard after another.

It was plain from their behavior that demons and converts saw Zoltan as their god, the Dark King, the ultimate object of both love and fear, whereas the non-converts among the prisoners beheld Vilkata as an object of stark terror. Many feared some kind of sadistic trap when he told them they were free, but few dared to let the opportunity slip by.

At the hour when the emptying of the palace began, Baron Amintor was still riding away from the city, heading generally northwest at a steady pace—reversing the route of his entry little more than a day earlier. He was taking his handful of convert troops to attempt a linkup with his own advancing army.

The Baron—still agitated and energetic as a result of the no-sleep spell —was furiously regretting the loss of Coinspinner and making his own private plans to regain control of the situation, when the great demon Arridu came dropping down out of the sky to visit him for a second time.

The little group of riders halted. Arridu, taking the form of a mounted warrior in black, at once informed Amintor that a strong effort to free the hostages in Sarykam was even now in progress by a small band of Vilkata's enemies armed with Sightblinder and Coinspinner.

The demon added: "I would, of course, have rushed to help our glorious Master—but, alas, one of the attackers would see to it that I was swiftly banished, were I there."

The Baron drew a little aside with his illustrious visitor to talk while his mounted escort waited uncomfortably at a little distance, out of earshot.

Eager to hear details of the attack on the palace, Amintor demanded: "And Vilkata? Does he come to meet these raiders with the Sword of Force?"

A smile showed under the black warrior's helmet-visor. "We must expect that will soon happen."

So far, Coinspinner's luck appeared to be sustaining the rescue party in excellent fashion. The Dark King himself, and the great Trump-Sword he carried, still had not taken the field against them.

Until now, Zoltan and his small band of companions had ravaged and emptied the familiar cellars and the prison-courtyards with impunity. Everywhere their orders for a general release of prisoners, shouted in the Master's name, were being accepted as genuine and obeyed.

When some hundreds of people who were still under the Mindsword's spell, guards and prisoners both, came swarming round Zoltan in bewilderment, he ordered them firmly, in the Dark King's name, to return to their homes and their old loyalties, and honor the Prince and Princess of Tasavalta.

The confusion precipitated by the attack among the demons and converts guarding the palace had quickly escalated into total chaos—perhaps it was only chance that some of the Dark King's loyal creatures, discovering him in a high tower, stammered out the story of what they had just seen. They were positive that he, the Dark King himself, had given and was still giving puzzling and contradictory orders for a general release of hostages.

Vilkata, recalled by this alarm from a certain magical enterprise which had distracted him, recognized that some enemy armed with Sightblinder must be attacking—but he had been more than half expecting some such move for hours, and thought himself ready to meet it.

The Dark King looked forward, with the gleeful anticipation of impending triumph, to holding Shieldbreaker in one hand and Soulcutter in the other—and then walking among these Tasavaltans and enjoying watching what became of them.

But the Sword of Despair was not available just yet, and the joy of wielding Soulcutter against his enemies was going to have to be postponed for just a little while.

Scrambling up a ladder to the tower's roof, the Dark King brought into action his secret weapon, a griffin he had recently obtained, and leapt into the saddle already secured to the magical hybrid's back. The great lion's head turned on its long neck, looking back for orders; the vast wings spread, the gigantic eagle-talons scratched at stone in an eagerness to taste soft human flesh.

In moments Vilkata was airborne, hovering over the most central courtyard—the point of riding a griffin rather than a demon was, of course, to render himself immune to being swirled away to the Moon again by Mark or his misbegotten offspring.

The Dark King was holding Shieldbreaker drawn and ready, and in his demonic vision Sightblinder below was no more than a silvery twinkle in the hands of one he recognized as a scorned enemy. And Coinspinner was there too, in the hands of another he had long hated! Today there were prospects for good hunting with the Sword of Force!

In the blink of an eye, Vilkata and his magic mount were hurtling down upon the raiders, ready to put a stop to their daring raid and to their lives as well.

Mass confusion was compounded, with rival Masters issuing contradictory orders. Even when Vilkata was present with the Sword of Force, Zoltan with Sightblinder could still deceive everyone else. To that extent another Sword could indirectly be effective against a leader armed with Shieldbreaker.

The difficulty on the Tasavaltan side was that Stephen and his friends were at times uncertain as to which figure was Zoltan and which Vilkata.

Zoltan was bellowing commands for all that he was worth. *"He* is the impostor, I tell you! But be careful, he carries the Sword of Force. You men, disarm yourselves and seize him."

But there was no use trying to disarm a man flying overhead and out of reach.

Vilkata, gripping his own Sword firmly, swept low over the field astride his griffin, seeing very clearly the doomed impostor issuing orders in his name. With a howl of glee, the Dark King smashed Sightblinder from Zoltan's hands. The magic Sword of Stealth was transformed into a shower of dead and deadly splinters, and Zoltan fell.

Once more the palace echoed with the violent explosion of a ruined Sword—but in the next instant the Dark King came near falling from his saddle.

His griffin-mount, understanding that something had gone wrong, landed abruptly. Vilkata clutched at the sockets where his eyes had been.

He was freshly blinded, his grip on triumph shaken.

Young Prince Stephen had just hurled into distant exile the latest demon to appear before him—it was Pitmedden, who had been providing Vilkata with his only vision of the surrounding world.

17

AT the moment Sightblinder was destroyed the great majority of the thousands of hostages were already free, and the remnants of the captive horde were streaming swiftly out of the palace through its many exits, spreading away across the grounds, escaping the Dark King's malevolence in dribbles and gouts of flight and panic.

Among those last to leave the palace were a number of people who fled unwillingly, converts still stubbornly clinging to their conversion; they were now in headlong flight only because they had heard their god, Vilkata himself, order them to do so.

Converted and unconverted alike departed unmolested. Stephen had for the time being banished all of their demonic gaolers, and the human converts Vilkata had assigned as guards were chaotically bewildered and demoralized. Thrown into a panic by their Master's misfortune, those near Vilkata were desperately intent on shielding him from further harm. They were frenzied by his blindness, a deprivation of external help against which the Sword of Force had done nothing to protect him.

Adding to the confusion in the courtyard, the Dark King's griffin-mount, prowling near him on the ground, slashed with lion-claws at the faithful who would still have helped their Master, and bared fangs large as human hands, keeping friends and foes alike at bay.

Vilkata in the courtyard had for a little while remained astride his plunging griffin, though unwilling to trust it airborne when he could not see; soon he had slid from the creature's back. Now, on foot, with Shield-breaker still firmly in his hand, and guarded from unarmed attack by the griffin and a circle of fanatical human converts, he was prohibitively dangerous for either friend or foe to approach.

Cursing and raging, the Dark King had no demons to bring him quick reports; and still he dared not attempt to fly, to pursue his enemies and their remaining Sword, until one of the creatures should return to provide him with sight. He called out repeatedly to his human bodyguards, urging them to protect him.

Coinspinner was still in the hands of the Silver Queen, but the Sword of Chance would of course be ineffective in any direct action against the man who still brandished Shieldbreaker.

When Yambu, with Ben looking on, questioned the Sword as to how best to defeat their enemy, Coinspinner unmistakably urged her toward the nearest exit from the courtyard.

Meanwhile, Stephen had been separated from his friends and lacked any magical guidance. But he saw that there was no way to attack Vilkata at present, and he too moved quickly to get himself out of the courtyard and away from the palace before the Dark King could recover his sight. More reptiles, and perhaps more griffins, were coming to sweep the place clear of potential enemies.

In the rush to get away, the young Prince left the palace by a different exit from Yambu and Ben. Neither party paid much attention to this fact at the time.

Vilkata was enraged by the awareness that some of his enemies must be getting away—but he was savagely pleased at having achieved the destruction of Sightblinder. That meant there was now one less Sword-prize in the world for which his many rivals and enemies might contend; and his own ultimate goal of dominating the world with a single Sword was further advanced by the same amount.

The Dark King's pleasure was increased on hearing confirmation from his converts that Zoltan, cousin to the accursed Tasavaltan royalty, was undoubtedly dead.

Yambu and Ben, trotting away from the palace at a good pace for folk no longer young, heeding Coinspinner's urging though they scarcely needed it, looked about them as they ran in an effort to locate Stephen, but without success.

And naturally no messenger-birds were available just now; the report to Kristin and Mark would have to wait.

The Silver Queen and her massive escort paused to catch their breath after a few blocks. Ben seized the opportunity to borrow Coinspinner from Lady Yambu. The Sword of Chance assured him that he should remain with her to reach whatever was his most important goal.

Stephen, running in a different direction, had escaped from the palace with his life and little else. He found himself once again moving through almost-deserted streets, still separated from his friends.

This separation was not necessarily any worse than inconvenient. Before launching their raid on the palace, the methodical veterans had designated a point of rendezvous for survivors, if their attempt to free the hostages should somehow miscarry.

Stephen went to the appointed spot—an intersection otherwise of no particular significance—and waited, under cover, for a quarter of an hour. When none of his comrades showed up, he comforted himself with the hope that they had probably survived anyway; and he decided that he had better move along, keeping a wary eye out for flying reptiles.

Mourning the death of Zoltan, but believing that his cousin had not died in vain, the young Prince started to make his way out into the countryside, where he hoped to be able to locate his parents.

It was late in the day before Prince Mark and Princess Kristin learned, from a winged scout fortunate enough to survive the leather-winged predators, of the attack on the palace by their people armed with two Swords, and the general success of that endeavor, despite the death of Zoltan.

The bird could give its master and its mistress no news of Stephen—or of Yambu or Ben—and Kristin and Mark were once more uncertain of their son's fate, and of the current whereabouts of the Sword of Chance.

The day wore on, and their knowledge of the situation improved minimally as more bits of information came in.

Mark, even before the attack on Sarykam, had heard some rumors concerning the independent army of mercenaries being organized in a neighboring territory by his old foe Baron Amintor.

To Kristin he muttered: "Wouldn't have expected him to have a great deal of success, at this stage of the game; but he appears to have been successful."

Amintor had been too distant from the palace to be caught up in the struggle to free the hostages, or in its aftermath. But his new partner, Arridu, was prompt at bringing him news, including that of Sightblinder's destruction. The Baron smiled grimly to hear of such a serious setback for the Dark King.

Shortly after the Baron had received word and Arridu had once more taken himself away, Amintor succeeded in making contact with the most advanced scouting unit of his own mercenary army, a fast-moving cavalry patrol. One of this party's scouting reptiles spotted him and guided him to the meeting.

To the Baron's considerable relief, his second-in-command rode out to meet him. Amalthea was perhaps twenty years his junior, tall, dark, and slender, an attractive woman and a skilled magician as well as an effective warrior—a rare combination and one that suited Amintor perfectly. He understood very well that only the power of Coinspinner had made it possible for a man of his own age and condition to recruit a junior partner who was so eminently satisfactory in so many important ways.

Amintor felt a fierce joy when he beheld Amalthea cantering toward him, followed immediately by a pang of regret as he realized how likely it was, given his loss of the Sword of Chance, that she would not be with him much longer.

Still, for the time being, their relationship remained secure, as far as he could tell. Amalthea welcomed her leader in a warm though not greatly demonstrative fashion. She favored him with a simple kiss, while the picked mercenaries of the cavalry patrol looked on impassively.

Then Amalthea drew back a little. "Is there something wrong with you?" she asked sharply.

No doubt, he thought, her magician's sense detected Vilkata's stay-awake treatment. "A spell—one more spell, more or less . . ." The Baron shrugged. He was still breathing heavily from the excitement, the exertion, brought on by Vilkata's magic.

"What kind of spell? And where is Coinspinner?"

"As for the spell, I tell you it is nothing of importance. Only a few words from our glorious leader, with the object of helping me keep awake. And Coinspinner has taken itself away." That last explanation was near enough to the truth, the Baron thought, to serve the purpose. "You've brought what I asked for?"

"Of course." Amalthea nodded. But had the woman hesitated fractionally before replying?

Leading Amintor to a little distance, just out of sight of their troops, Amalthea opened a large bundle of magical equipment and brought out a certain package—she had taken care that the soldiers not know that she was carrying it—and showed Amintor the Sword she had been taking care of for him.

It was another of Coinspinner's gifts, of course.

Her eyes studied her elderly leader with concern as he unwrapped the weapon and looked it over.

The concentric rings of a target made up the stark white symbol on this particular black hilt. Farslayer. He nodded silently, knowing that he was going to need all the help that he could get.

Having inspected the Sword of Vengeance, the Baron sheathed it again and handed it back to Amalthea.

"And what am I to do with this?" she asked him sharply.

"You are going to have to use it." He smiled at her in the way—if he could remember—that a young man would.

The woman only stared at him in silence, trying to fathom his plan, and perhaps his worth. Then she paused to do a little magic, seeing to it as best she could that they were not being spied upon.

Amintor added: "Use it when I am not with you. But at a time and in a way that I command."

"Of course," Amalthea responded, calm and business-like. "When and where?"

The Baron explained. The Sword of Vengeance was a marvelous threat, but its actual use was not without strong disadvantages. Chief among these was the tendency of the victim to be among friends when he was so helplessly skewered, and the concomitant tendency of the bereaved friends to retaliate in kind, when they found themselves so providentially provided with the means as well as motive.

Amintor, considering the matter coolly, as was his wont, thought it would certainly be satisfying to at last rid himself permanently of Mark, who had caused him so much trouble in the past, and continued to do so now. But Amintor was at the same time very reluctant to give Mark's friends a return shot at himself.

Anyway, Amintor did not consider Mark his most immediately pressing danger.

He had barely finished his explanations, given explicit orders, and made sure that Farslayer was again securely hidden, when Vilkata's demonic messenger—not Arridu this time—arrived to bid him hold himself ready for a conference. The Dark King, griffin-mounted, was on his way.

Some of the demons so recently banished by Stephen from inside the palace had been able to return relatively quickly to the Dark King's service. Within an hour of his blinding, Vilkata had regained the ability to see and had jumped back into the saddle on his griffin's back.

Before implementing the next step of his overall plan, which would involve going to the Moon, Vilkata wanted to settle matters between himself and Amintor.

When the two men met, in a small patch of summer forest, Amalthea retreated with her cavalry patrol, leaving Vilkata and Amintor alone except for certain members of the former's escort.

The Dark King sarcastically demanded of the Baron what assurances the latter needed to be convinced that he now faced the genuine Dark King.

Amintor tried to sound conciliatory.

The senior partner, in a black humor, waved Shieldbreaker, and shouted that Sightblinder had now been blasted into fragments, damn it!

Then the Eyeless One, still brandishing the Sword of Force, angrily demanded of his junior partner: "What is the matter with you?" Under the circumstances, this could be only interpreted as rhetorical abuse. It was quite obvious that there were serious difficulties between them.

"Oh, Great King," Amintor murmured, as if in an excess of self-re-proach and fear, "pardon me!" And he moved clumsily as if to fall to his knees before his Master—a maneuver that brought him physically closer to his senior partner, by the two steps the Baron judged were essential.

From that position, crouching as if about to kneel, the Baron hurled his aging body forward, in a desperate effort to wrestle Shieldbreaker from its possessor. For once he would stake everything upon one move— because at this exact moment, if Amalthea were faithful, Farslayer should be coming to strike down his foe. If Vilkata dropped Shield-breaker, he would die, and if he held the Sword, Amintor would wrest it from him.

There came a whistle and a ringing in the air, a flash of silver. The Dark King, Shieldbreaker still held high in his right hand, his counte-nance betraying no surprise, had withdrawn from his unarmed assailant by a single step.

At Vilkata's feet the Baron lay dead, instantaneously transfixed by a bright Blade. Amintor's body still twitched, fingers closing spasmodically as if to grasp some prize, but his eyes stared lifelessly. He had been slain by Farslayer, flying at him from some unseen hand.

Only a moment passed before Amalthea appeared, emerging from summer greenery some meters behind the Dark King, walking slowly forward among the trees. Her manner was demure and subservient to Vilkata, who was not at all surprised to see her. Obviously they had met before. A look of understanding passed between them. The enchantress had decided she would be better off serving the Dark King directly.

An instant later Arridu appeared too, materializing out of thin air, smoothly assuring his Great Master that had the Sword of Vengeance not killed the traitor, he would have done so.

"It appears you both were right," the Dark King complimented his two assistants. "The fool was planning treachery all along."

In the next moment, brushing aside the congratulations of his aides upon his cleverness, the Dark King, laughing triumphantly over Amintor's skewered corpse, planted a boot on the Baron's chest, and plucked forth the Sword of Vengeance from the Baron's heart.

For a long moment Vilkata found himself brandishing two Swords, Farslayer and Shieldbreaker, at the same time, a rare experience even for him. His demonic vision suddenly began to play tricks on him. . . .

Or rather, he thought in a flash of insight, he was forcibly reminded of something he should always have kept in mind, but tended to forget—that his self-chosen mode of perception had always been playing tricks.

Whatever its exact provenance, this particular vision was unsettling.

From somewhere there came into his view unbidden an odd glimpse of a small room, stone-walled and cramped, containing a torture-rack and little else, the rack complete with anonymous, screaming victim. And this made the Dark King suddenly feel better—he could get used to this business of the two Swords.

Vilkata was not afraid of casting the Sword of Vengeance in among Mark's vengeful friends—not as long as he, Vilkata, had Shieldbreaker in hand to fend off the likely riposte.

Holding the black hilt of Farslayer at arm's length in both hands, spinning his body gracefully, the Dark King chanted the old rhyme: "For thy heart, for thy heart, who hast wronged me—"

In a blur and a flash, Farslayer was gone, howling away into the distance, from the moment of its launching become invisible with its own speed.

As soon as he had thrown the Sword, Vilkata felt confident (though, as always, there remained a shade of nagging, suspicious doubt) that he'd killed Mark. Only Shieldbreaker could have protected the Prince, and the Sword of Force was still here at his own side.

Hastily he drew his protection, held it ready, smiling as he awaited the counterblow from Prince Mark's grieving friends.

The Prince of Tasavalta was on his riding-beast, leading a growing force of mounted troops and infantry toward Sarykam to reclaim his capital, when the Sword of Vengeance came for him.

Mark was granted no more than a moment of warning.

Only the Prince himself, and a few people who were closest to him, saw or heard Farslayer flying toward him.

It was Kristin, as so often watchfully protective at the Prince's side, who in a flash drew Woundhealer from where it was kept ready, belted at her own waist.

Vilkata's gift came bursting through whatever magical defenses Mark had in place—Karel, recovered now from Mindsword-magic but still at a distance, had seen to it that those barriers had become considerable, though intended only against weaker attacks than this. Neither the Prince nor his chief magician would have wasted time and energy trying to build defenses against this weapon.

The shock of Farslayer's impact knocked Mark clean out of his saddle, impaling him bloodily. No voluntary cry broke from his lips, only the mechanical grunt of air out-driven by the impact of Farslayer's hilt against his chest.

Kristin was no more than an eyeblink later with Woundhealer, which she plunged right into her husband's heart, then did her best to catch his falling body before it struck the ground.

Then, for a few terrible moments, Mark endured having the Sword of Vengeance stuck right in through his breastbone, next to the Sword of Love, the two Blades crossing, clashing, somewhere near the center of his body. His eyes were open, his face working, as if he were struggling to endure, to understand.

The Princess, shifting her grip to the other hilt, pulled Farslayer from Mark's body and cast it blindly aside.

A swarm of supporters, crying out their shock and rage, at once gathered round the fallen Prince. Meanwhile, the peasant Bodker, grateful and fanatically devoted to the man who had healed his child, and neither knowing nor caring whether Vilkata possessed Shieldbreaker—perhaps possessing little knowledge of any Swords—grabbed up Farslayer and hurled it angrily, muttering his clumsy prayer that it should slay whoever had just tried to kill the Prince. . . .

The Dark King was still waiting alertly, Shieldbreaker pounding and drumming in his hand, when Bodker's gift arrived; after a startled moment of noise and glare and flying fragments, Vilkata of course remained unscratched.

Again there had been the Sword-shattering blast—again the lethal spray of fragments of ensorcelled metal.

Nearby demons screamed in pain; their lives, being elsewhere, of course, were safe.

Meanwhile the Dark King endured a split second in which he feared that his defense had failed him—but after that split second he laughed wholeheartedly at this evidence of what he saw as his own continuing invincibility.

18

THE two veterans, Ben of Purkinje and the Silver Queen, were making their way in near-silence south along the coast, the east wind from the sea whipping their graying hair. Yambu rode with an almost unconscious queenly dignity, most of the time holding the reins in her left hand, carrying Coinspinner unsheathed in her right. Her wiry arm drooped with the Sword's weight, but her grip on the black hilt held steady, sensitive to its least vibration. The lady's eyes continually scanned the road ahead. Her giant escort, grim-faced and for the moment no more than mundanely armed, kept his large and powerful mount close behind hers.

Since leaving the city behind them, the Silver Queen's companion had twice asked for and been loaned the Sword from her. Twice he had tested Coinspinner's powers with questions containing obscure allusions, phrases that would have been hard to understand even had the wind not whirled the words away so quickly.

Twice the result had evidently been affirmative, for Ben each time gave back the Sword and followed the lady on in silence. It was evident that the Sword of Chance had recommended these two people to each other.

The Dark King now had adopted Amalthea as his chief human aide—or at least had promised her that status—and meant to leave her in control of his army, formerly Amintor's.

Meanwhile he, Vilkata, had other things to do. He told his new assistant no details of his own immediate plans, only that he was going away for a day or two and that she should save what she could of the army which had been Amintor's. Doubtless that would require a temporary—only temporary—retreat from Tasavalta. But the army would be useful when the Dark King came back to renew his attack with overwhelming force, and it was important that as much of it as possible be preserved.

One of Vilkata's first acts on arriving back on Earth from his two-year exile had been to order his demons to conceal his spacecraft in a seashore cave only a few hours' hike south of Sarykam. The Dark King had considered it prudent to keep this equipment standing by in case some sudden need for it arose. Riding on his griffin now, he was able to reach the site in minutes.

Vilkata, on his way to the cave in which the spacecraft lay hidden, consoled himself, in conversation with Pitmedden, that in the freeing of his hostages he had suffered only a temporary setback. He had driven his enemies from the field in their most recent skirmish, and with his own hand had cut down a nephew of Prince Mark.

But of course those achievements fell far short of total victory. The complete conquest of the realm of Tasavalta, let alone that of the entire world, seemed as remote as ever.

Given Soulcutter and Shieldbreaker both in hand, of course, he would possess the means to rout his enemies for good and all. Arridu whispered, and the great prize beckoned. Thinking he now had a priceless opportunity to obtain the Sword of Despair, the Dark King with his demonic vision eagerly scanned the darkness ahead for the seashore cave.

Ben and Lady Yambu were being guided by the Sword of Chance in the same direction that Vilkata had chosen for his flight. As they rode, they saw him go soaring, streaking overhead, traversing the daylight sky at a much swifter pace.

Coinspinner had provided the Silver Queen and her partner with excellent riding-beasts for this journey—a circumstance which suggested either that speed was important in their journey or that their destination lay at no great distance. Before leaving the city, the pair had come upon a pair of animals, untended, providentially abandoned in the middle of an otherwise deserted street, saddled, well-rested, and fed. Then the Sword, buzzing and twitching in the lady's hand from time to time, led them on a brisk ride out of Sarykam.

After Ben's latest trial with the Sword, the lady confronted him. "Are you asking for something else, big man, apart from some immediate tactical success?"

"And if I am?"

"No harm in it—I was only curious. As we left the square back there, I put a personal question to the Sword myself." After a moment the lady added: "Since we are in retreat already—what I really want, apart from seeing these damned demons and their human lovers crushed, is once more to confront my husband."

Ben was frowning. "Your husband, lady? I thought—"

"Call him my former husband, then. You know who I mean, however you prefer to name him. The so-elusive and mysterious Emperor. The older I grow, the more I am convinced that that confrontation is what I want—nay, what I need—above all else. There are answers I must have, and nowhere else to turn for them."

Before another hour had passed, while, under the Sword's guidance, still heading south along the coast, they had passed several encampments of refugees from the city, and were a dozen kilometers from the capital.

Soon afterward all signs of settlement dropped out of sight. The coastline here was rocky and inhospitable, with few harbors or real beaches. The stony earth held little soil for farming or even grazing, nor were these shallow, tide-riven coastal waters hospitable to fishing boats. Nevertheless, the only indication of the presence of human life was two or three of these craft several hundred meters off shore.

Atop a deserted-looking stretch of cliff, no different in its general appearance from the regions immediately to north or south, they discovered an entrance to a large cave, a gaping hole in the ground at least as big a small house—no particular surprise in this area, though neither traveler had ever seen this particular cave before.

When Ben and the Silver Queen concentrated their attention on the opening, certain strange sounds and dim lights were faintly perceptible from the darkness deep within the cave.

But Coinspinner was silently tugging its clients in a different direction. Away from the discovered entrance, and down the cliffside, guiding their riding-beasts along an unmarked path which led them to another opening in the rock, right at sea level, quite likely a second entrance to the same cave. Whereas the upper opening was fairly plain on the top surface of a low cliff, the lower was inconspicuous, almost invisible until you were right on it.

Ben dismounted and advanced a few paces, to stand squinting in sunlight, peering into dimness. This lower entrance was awash, at least at the current stage of the tide. Waves continually splashed and roared into the space that had been carved from solid rock by their ancestors over a myriad of years.

The Sword of Chance bade the seekers wade into the cave; the low entrance made it necessary for them to leave their riding-beasts outside.

Some strange inhuman sound, a heavy shifting of great weight upon clawed feet, came out of the darkness ahead, raising visions of deadly monsters in Ben's mind. "Dragon!" he whispered sharply, backing into a retreat.

Yambu's hand was on his arm. "No, a griffin, I can see its wings." Her eyes were evidently better than Ben's in darkness. A leonine growl confirmed her identification. "It must be the creature Vilkata rode—remember, we saw him pass us in the sky."

Ben relaxed a trifle. "What now? The Sword has led us to this thing—are we supposed to climb upon its . . ."

Ben's voice trailed off. A premonitory wave of nausea, a seeming tilting of the watery shingle beneath his feet, warned him at last that the griffin was not the only guardian of this entryway.

Yambu was experiencing the same sensations, and her hand gripped hard at Ben's arm. But the demon had scarcely appeared, a luminous form in warrior's shape drifting in the cave entrance, when the Sword of Chance went into action in defense of its human bearer.

Ben's heartfelt prayer was answered almost before it could take shape in his mind: Coinspinner could as easily visit catastrophe upon a demon as on a human or a beast. The thing had no more than confronted them when its image froze. Ben understood in a moment that some horrible accident had just happened to that demon's life-object, however remote in space that object might be from the manifestation he confronted.

. . . *the thing's eyes stared into some terrible distance, where its hidden life was being menaced . . . no time for it to reach the spot, to try to defend itself . . .*

The blank expression in the doomed demon's countenance turned into one of tremendous shock. In the next moment the image had crumpled, then evaporated, and the watching humans knew it must be dead.

The griffin, indifferent to their presence, mumbled a sleepy lion-roar and seemed to be crouching, turning round, dog-like, as if preparing to go to sleep.

The Dark King, observing these events from a place of concealment within the cave, understood perfectly well what had just happened. Vilkata, gnashing his teeth at being so inconveniently deprived of one more demon, was fully alerted to the fact that his enemies were on his trail—and that they must have the Sword of Chance still with them.

Vilkata found the situation quite to his satisfaction. Now, with Pitmedden as usual providing him his sight, in this case letting him see around a corner, he waited in ambush, clutching his Sword, behind one of the gnarled rock formations in the inner darkness of the cave.

In this part the cave was deep and dark enough to keep out most of the sunlight. Some Old World lighting glowing indirectly out of the parked space vehicle provided a partial illumination.

Though Ben and Yambu had so far been given no direct evidence that Vilkata was here, the presence of the griffin and at least one demon certainly made his presence likely. They had to operate on the assumption that the Dark King was still armed with the Sword of Force, and that he might well have more demons with him, as well as a bodyguard of human converts.

Ben, now advancing into the cave, climbing wet rock past the somnolent griffin, warily got ready to throw down at a moment's notice any mundane weapon he was holding. Perhaps he did thus far disarm himself.

He and the Silver Queen were both experienced in Sword-matters, and with a minimum of words and gestures made their arrangements for mutual defense. It was decided between them that Ben would hold their Sword and lead the way.

But Vilkata jumped out of ambush and struck, before Ben, being led by Coinspinner and still trusting in the guidance of that Sword, could throw it down.

When the Dark King, a lunging shape not instantly identifiable, came jumping out from behind a rock, Ben raised the Sword of Chance instinctively, just as Vilkata had raised his weapon in the armory under the palace.

Shieldbreaker emitted a barrage of drumming sounds. In the next instant, with a violent crash whose visual component lit the cave, Coinspinner had been destroyed.

Flying fragments of the broken Sword stabbed into Ben's head, sent him slipping, sliding, finally tumbling, down a little slope. But the huge man was not immediately disabled, and for the moment could disregard the fact that he was hurt. An instant after the blast, Ben, bleeding from his face and scalp but again on his feet and now unarmed, charged uphill at Vilkata, who was still holding Shieldbreaker.

The Silver Queen, considerably more distant from the blast, had also been injured by stray bits of Sword, but not severely, though momentarily stunned by the concussion.

Seeing the energy with which Ben was coming after him, the Dark King muttered blasphemies, angered that his latest victim should retain such strength—and was coming unarmed.

Vilkata considered hastily whether to retreat, or stay and fight. He was unsure of just what powers or what people were here arrayed against him, and he had no intention of throwing down his own invaluable Sword —that would mean assuming some risk, however small, of not getting it back. Having come to depend upon the matchless, Sword-smashing power of Shieldbreaker in his own hand, the Dark King had no intention of giving it up.

Briefly Vilkata considered trying to deal with the still-advancing Ben by means of some lesser magic, or by hurling rocks. But common magic worked poorly when, as now, fighting blades were drawn. And the Dark King was determined not to be delayed in his trip to the Moon. Rather than deal personally with Ben and Lady Yambu, Vilkata snapped a few terse words to another of his lesser demons and turned away. The thing shrilled an obedient acknowledgment of its Master's command.

The Dark King, with Pitmedden and one other minor demon still clinging to him like tendrils of evil smog, darted to the open hatch of the waiting Old World spacecraft and jumped in. The hatch closed with a soft thud behind him and the spacecraft almost immediately whirled aloft, to go rushing in near silence out of the cave through its upper aperture.

Ben and Lady Yambu, recoiling from this demonstration of the powers of Old World machinery, found themselves still free to move about. Though certain ominous and unfamiliar sensations in his head were now giving the man to understand that he had sustained some serious injury in the latest Sword-explosion.

Warrior-fashion, he did his best to shake off the difficulty.

Yambu and Ben were now closer to the cave's upper entrance than the lower aperture, and moved out of it to stand on the rocks atop the cliff.

Once in the open air again, Ben stood swaying, his head back, mouth gaping upward—he had come out of the cave just in time to get a last glimpse of the Old World shuttle bearing the Dark King before it disappeared at a tremendous distance overhead.

The Silver Queen had followed Ben out of the cave and stood beside him.

Only briefly were the two humans allowed to hope that Vilkata, in his haste to leave, might have decided to ignore them. Scarcely had they time to draw a deep breath before the demon who had been appointed their executioner was with them, making its presence known in the form of a vague, half-human shape.

But before the demon could begin to toy with its all-but-helpless victims, the whispering sound of the spacecraft's passage through the lower air, which had faded only moments earlier, returned. Ben, looking up, saw that the near-spherical shape had reappeared in the sky and was descending rapidly.

Silently and swiftly, emitting no great glare of light, this vehicle approached the upper entrance to the cave, where the two people and the demon who confronted it were standing.

The spacecraft, hard metal scrunching solidly on rock, touched down very near them.

The onlooking demon gaped, as surprised as Ben and Yambu, and perhaps almost as frightened. The clear, glassy surfaces of the Old World vehicle had been turned opaque, and no one could see into it from outside.

The lights inside it dimmed or went out, and a hatch opened.

The head emerging was certainly not Vilkata's. Nor was it even human —or demonic.

The three onlookers watched with utter astonishment as the rest of the emerging form came into view—a figure, despite its size, speedily, grace-fully unfolding through the open hatchway, then elongating to its full height of some six meters. A body standing on two almost man-like legs, all clad in glowing fur, a face and body neither quite human or quite animal in aspect, though obviously male.

"Hail, Lord Draffut!" Ben breathed fervently. The utterance sounded like a prayer.

Yambu and the demon were equally quick to recognize Draffut, the famous Beastlord, a being everywhere believed by common folk to be-long to the pantheon of gods. What stunned Ben even more than the fact of Draffut's arrival was that of his god-like size and evident power. Ben had heard the appearance of the Lord of Beasts, in recent years, very differently described.

Draffut had no sooner unlimbered his gigantic form from the space-craft than he growled out a challenge to the stunned demon watching.

Whatever followed between the two beings on the level of magic, in the way of an exchange of threats, even of direct blows, Ben failed to perceive the interaction at all. All he could be sure of was that a moment after the Lord of Beasts confronted the demon, Vilkata's creature had fled, or had been driven from the field.

Now that an oasis of safety had been established, at least temporarily, Draffut greeted Yambu and Ben as old acquaintances, even as friends.

Ben was just starting to reply, when, to his surprise, the throbbing which had been put inside his head by Coinspinner's dying blast rose up and wiped away the world.

When the huge man recovered his wits, he found himself being held, supported like a baby in Draffut's gigantic hands, while Lady Yambu stared at him with concern. Brusquely Ben asserted a warrior's contempt for his own wounds, announced that he was fine, and climbed out of the Beastlord's grip to stand, somewhat shakily, on his own two feet. Blood from his scalp injury was still coming down his face in an occasional thin trickle, and he brushed at it impatiently.

"A long time since we've met, Master Draffut." Ben was too knowledgeable to speak to this creature before him as to a god.

"Many years, Ben of Purkinje." Draffut was half-kneeling now, a position which brought his huge head closer to a level with those of his companions. The great voice was as soft as it was deep.

Ben, his head suddenly once more awhirl, spoke again before he'd taken careful measure of his words. "I remember that we were in a battle together, you and I and a thousand others, and you . . ."

The vast eyes, of shifting colors, stared at him. He thought the inner radiance of the white fur dimmed momentarily. Draffut said: "I killed a man that day. The act was unintentional, but yes, I killed."

That hadn't been Ben's key memory of Draffut's part in the battle, but he couldn't deny that it had happened. Ben did his best to reassure the luminous giant. "Killing is a part of any war."

Draffut only shook his head.

"I had heard . . ." The huge man began, then hesitated.

The Beastlord nodded. "That I had changed. Had been diminished, as a result of what happened to me on that day of war."

"Yes."

"And what you heard was true, for I was changed indeed. Once more, as in my early youth, I ran about the world on four legs, and was content to be again a dog, the form in which I was created. But I have a friend who was not content that I should remain so."

It was Yambu who brought the discussion back to a practical level: "We owe you our lives, Master Draffut. Where have you come from in that Old World device, and why are you here now?"

"I have been sent here, from the Moon, with instructions to bring two people back."

Yambu had never been timid, and now, at her time of life and with her experience, there were very few things that really frightened her. Still she felt a qualm at the thought of embarking upon the shuttle-voyage Draffut was proposing.

Coinspinner was no longer available to provide guidance, but her doubts were thrust aside when Draffut promised the Silver Queen that he could bring her face to face with the Emperor at last.

"You hesitate, great lady. But you are wanted there." And Draffut looked up into the sky—to human eyes the Moon, today risen in early daylight, was now, near midday, quite invisible.

She could not doubt that this gigantic being was telling her the truth. "He himself has said this to you? He mentioned me?"

"Indeed, great lady, the chief reason I am here is that the Emperor has asked me to bring you to him."

Young Prince Stephen, halfway through a journey to the village where he thought his parents most likely to be found, had taken shelter in a small shady grove, trying to keep out of sight of patrolling reptiles in the sky.

Stephen, who had closed his eyes in weariness, was almost entirely sure that he was dreaming when he opened them at a small sound, to behold his famous grandfather, now sitting quite near him on a fallen tree, and nodding to him in familiar greeting. Stephen recognized the Emperor at once, despite the fact that the Emperor now looked a little younger than his son Prince Mark.

Today Stephen's grandfather, a surprisingly ordinary-looking man clad all in gray, had not chosen to put on one of his famous masks, or play the clown. Instead he appeared in the boy's dream—if dream it was—as armed with many Swords. The familiar figure was carrying them all glittering and gleaming, the bright Blades clashing together harmlessly, in a kind of crude gardener's bag. He opened that container to let the young lad look inside.

But soon the Emperor covered up the Swords again and put aside the bag.

Then he said, as if this were his point in making the display: "They're not really all *that* important, you know."

"What's more important than Swords, Grandfather?"

"A number of things—for example, that you and I have a talk every now and then."

"Really?"

"Yes. Oh, yes. And now seemed like a good time."

Stephen sat up, shifting his position. He now had the feeling that he was wide awake. "I'm trying to find my parents."

His companion nodded. "I know you are. I expect you'll manage to locate them all right. Tell your father that he and I must have a talk again sometime."

"I'll tell him." Stephen blinked. "And I know he wants to talk to you. He spends a lot of time trying to find you."

"Your father worries a great deal, unnecessarily. You might tell him I said that."

They chatted for a few minutes more—about nothing out of the ordinary, as Stephen remembered later—before the Emperor got to his feet and slung his bag—had it really contained Swords?—over his shoulder.

Taking these actions as signals of departure, Stephen said politely: "Good luck, Grandfather, safe journeying—Ardneh be with you."

"Thank you." The man's reply was solemn. "And with you as well."

"I'll see you again, won't I?"

"Oh yes. It might be a while, but we'll meet again. Never worry about that."

Ben and the Lady Yambu, standing with Draffut just outside the seaside cave, looked at each other. Both of the humans at the moment were feeling sharply the lack of the Sword of Chance. But Coinspinner was gone, and that was that.

Following the guidance of the revitalized Draffut, the two humans boarded the Old World spacecraft without argument or serious hesitation, despite the utter strangeness of the device.

Draffut communicated in some way with the machinery. Moments later, the craft and its three occupants were being borne upward at a speed achievable only by Old World technology.

For the first hour or so of the flight, Ben lay on one of the strange beds and briefly slept. When he awoke, the bleeding from his head wound had entirely stopped, but he still felt pain and occasional disorientation. As their hours in space lengthened into a full day, the two human passengers occupied themselves alternately resting and moving about inside the glass-and-metal vehicle, watching the Earth recede and the Moon grow ever larger. It was indeed a mind-bending experience.

Not counting small latrine-bathrooms and a galley, there were three habitable chambers inside the shuttle, which was easily the size of a small house—the largest cabin was capacious enough to house without undue hardship the six-meter length of Draffut as well as the two humans. Particularly as Draffut soon manifested the ability to double his body into a relatively small space with no apparent lack of comfort. The humans now discovered that the movable interior partitions of the craft could be repositioned to provide one long, narrow chamber in which the Beastlord was able to accommodate himself at full length.

The passengers experienced no fierce acceleration even though the Earth seemed to be falling away at breathtaking speed; and the human passengers speculated as to whether the speed and ease of the journey were due to magic or *technology*. "Up" and "down" remained, respectively, the directions of the shuttle's overhead and of its deck; but the sky outside, and the Earth visibly embedded in it, assumed alarming and upsetting positions.

Ben's wounds, though bandaged by the Silver Queen with Old World medical materials on board, still bothered him, and her own minor injuries still pained. Draffut several times administered such healing as he was able to perform by the laying on of his huge hands, and Yambu was greatly helped. Each treatment made Ben feel a little better, though the benefit was only temporary. The Beastlord grumbled that his healing power was not what it once had been, and solemnly promised a more efficacious therapy once they reached the Moon.

Ben dozed repeatedly and dreamed. The cumulative weariness of a hard life seemed to have caught up with him, and he welcomed the chance afforded by these comfortable quarters to catch up on sleep, and also on food, which proved to be plentifully available in several acceptable forms. Draffut showed both human passengers how to control the Old World equipment concerned with health, safety, and comfort.

There was talk of Swords, and of the prospects in the war now raging, among the three now traveling so swiftly together to the Moon.

For their own satisfaction—Ben's in particular—they brought up to date the inventory of Swords as well as they were able.

Yambu had for some years been making an effort to keep track of the Twelve Swords—Draffut announced that he had been doing so too, and now gave his companions his current reckoning in the matter.

After Coinspinner's recent ruining, only Farslayer, Soulcutter, Shieldbreaker, and Woundhealer still survived—and Draffut was not at all sure about the first of those. One by one, over the past forty years or so, all the rest of the output of Vulcan's forge had been reduced to bits of black wood and dull metal, the nothingness of dissipated magic.

The Sword of Despair, said Draffut, was really the one to worry about. The Emperor had told him that.

It was Yambu who theorized that a few of the Swords, including Soulcutter, had shared an interesting property—the Tyrant's Blade never discriminated among individuals. In effect, Soulcutter didn't care who anyone was.

Neither did Woundhealer.

Nor had the Mindsword, before it was destroyed, ever distinguished one person from another—apart from singling out its current owner as the supreme object of devotion.

Back on Earth, Stephen had not traveled far from the grove in which he met the Emperor when, to his great joy, he encountered a recovered Karel, whose own magical search had led him to the young Prince. From that point on, under the great wizard's protection, Stephen had nothing to fear from flying reptiles, nor could his reunion with his parents be delayed much longer.

Woundhealer had restored Mark to full health almost instantly upon its application, and now only a nearly-invisible white scar marked the place where Farslayer had come ravening into his flesh.

Prince and Princess together had continued their advance upon Sarykam, recruiting more armed troops readily from the villages, where a number of trained militia were available. Scouts reported that what had been Baron Amintor's army, now commanded by a woman named Amalthea, was trying to reverse course and withdraw from Tasavalta.

And with the loss of Coinspinner's luck, the army gave signs that, lacking some triumphant stroke by the Dark King personally, it would soon break up in internal conflicts.

Coming out from the capital to join Prince Mark were a number of deconverted soldiers, along with the bulk of the general population. With every passing hour, more converts now recovered spontaneously from the Mindsword's hideous spell.

With these and other forces rapidly becoming available, the country moving toward full mobilization, the Prince acted swiftly to harry and punish the force of mercenaries as it strove to withdraw from Tasavalta. General Rostov, and the local leaders elsewhere, had not waited for Mark's direct leadership before organizing and taking action.

The mercenary force was in retreat, threatened with disintegration, united now only for self-defense.

Less than two days after departing the coast of Tasavalta, the three passengers in the space shuttle were preparing for a landing on the Moon.

The lifeless-looking desert globe first became frighteningly large, then ceased to be an object in the sky at all, and was transformed into a world reassuringly below their feet. Draffut, the experienced traveler, meanwhile pointed out certain sights of interest—including the place from which Vilkata had rescued the demons—as they approached, and indicated at least roughly what territory lay definitely within the Emperor's domain.

Yambu gritted her teeth, doing what she could to get ready for a confrontation with that impossible man, who had once been her husband.

The Beastlord also explained, to a pair of human beings too awed and bewildered to understand him very well, how he himself had come to be restored to power and majesty by immersion in what he called the Lake of Life—that had been the Emperor's doing, of course. Draffut told his questioners that he expected they would have the chance to see the Lake of Life for themselves.

Yambu and Ben had both heard of the ancient, legendary Lake of Life, which supposedly had existed at some unknown location on the Earth.

Draffut assured his human listeners that the lunar Lake was a duplicate of the legendary one.

Below the travelers, a smooth area of the Moon's surface that looked like pavement grew and grew.

Ben, long past astonishment, observed some kind of giant hatch or window in that surface yawn open to receive their vehicle.

And then, fairly abruptly and without fanfare, the voyage ended in an intact base or spaceport built securely under the lunar surface.

Back on Earth, at about the same time that their friends' spacecraft reached the Moon, Prince Mark and Princess Kristin were joyfully reunited with their son and the old wizard who was Kristin's uncle.

Moments later, while Stephen enjoyed the benefits of Woundhealer, he passed on to Kristin and Mark the most recent intelligence regarding the conditions in Sarykam, and what had happened to him in the course of his journey since leaving the city. Naturally the youth included his most recent information about Ben and Yambu—and Zoltan.

As a kind of afterthought, Stephen told his parents about his encounter with the Emperor—adding his continued uncertainty as to whether that meeting might have happened only in a dream.

Mark acknowledged his son's information about that talk with a nod, but made almost no comment on the matter. Everyone, it seemed, got to talk to the Emperor sooner or later—everyone but him, the Emperor's son. And what good did it all do, anyway, all these vague signs of encouragement and advice from the imperial Great Clown?

No one at the royal headquarters as yet had any certain knowledge of Coinspinner's destruction, or Farslayer's. Through Karel's art the Prince was soon given warning that the Dark King was coming back with Soulcutter and more demons from the Moon.

19

WHEN Ben's mind grew clear again, he found himself standing, leaning against the wall, in a long hallway with several distant branches
and many doors. The passage was three or four meters broad and considerably higher, smoothly carved from rock, and lighted by peculiar Old
World lamps—a strange place, a very strange place indeed.

He was unarmed and still wearing the clothes in which he'd come from
Earth.

Most unsettling at the moment was the fact that he could not remember just how he'd been separated from his two companions. He knew his
parting from Draffut and Lady Yambu must have taken place—somehow
—soon after their arrival on the Moon; but he could no longer recall the
circumstances.

The big man distinctly remembered the blasting of Coinspinner into
little pieces against the edge of Shieldbreaker back in the seaside cave—
and then the menacing demon, and Draffut's timely arrival. But the details of his journey to the Moon were hazy. He realized that his head
injury must be producing some serious effects.

However he had come to be here, here he was, standing more than
half weightless in this strange lunar corridor, with his companions nowhere in sight, listening to a droning, unearthly background murmur, as
of Old World machinery. . . .

He thought that perhaps, buried deep in the sound, he could hear
someone calling. Calling his name.

Ben found that he could walk—a little unsteadily, but he could certainly walk. Getting about here was quite easy because of the lack of
weight. On he went, sampling the doorways in the long hall, discovering
more rooms and tunnels, trying to find some clue as to how he might
rejoin Draffut and the Silver Queen—and trying also to accustom himself to the strange lunar environment. Yes, he was on the Moon. That
was hard to believe, but in his time he'd seen a few other things that were
almost impossible, and he had managed to deal with them.

* * *

Vilkata, on returning to the Moon, at a landing place far from Draffut's, had quickly noticed that the mysterious subsurface being, or entity, which he and his demons had previously observed, was now detectably more active than it had been a few days ago.

That was interesting; but just now the Dark King had little time to spare for odd phenomena. He had come here with the fixed purpose of obtaining Soulcutter, and he immediately bent all his efforts toward that goal.

When his attention was caught by the unexpected presence of more demons, fresh exiles from the Earth now gibbering and squealing in the airless lunar distance, he did the best he could, in passing, to gather these hapless creatures under his control. They would be useful, though not essential, when he made his last return to Earth, there to stake everything on one climactic effort to win the ultimate game of power.

Ben still continued his wandering in corridors of stone and Old World glass, trying to read the symbols of unknown languages carved into the stone walls.

Entering a room containing certain objects that struck him as hearteningly familiar, Ben decided he had found what must be a branch of the White Temple. The man-sized carved images of Ardneh, cubistic and vaguely mechanical, and of Draffut, were both eminently recognizable. Ben had never been one for much Temple-going, whether White, Red, or Blue. But under his current circumstances the familiarity of this room's contents seemed benign and reassuring.

At the next door, Ben came upon what looked like a peculiar kind of library. At least part of the extensive chamber was devoted to that purpose, for, besides the incomprehensible Old World machines, there were real books and papers, maps and drawings, spread across many shelves and over tables. The visitor leafed through a few of the papers and bound volumes, discovering several different languages, but none that he could understand.

One book, occupying a place of prominence upon an incongruous hand-carved reading stand, drew Ben's particular attention. The thick volume was printed in the common language that he understood, and the pages lay open at the place where in the ancient scripture the words said: *Ardneh, who rides the elephant, who wields the lightning, who rends fortifications as the rushing passage of time consumes cheap cloth . . .*

* * *

Ben looked up at a slight sound, to discover that he was no longer alone. The Emperor had come in and was standing near the doorway through which Ben had entered.

"Hello," said Ben simply, feeling no fear, but a certain awkwardness. He'd met this man before and, though that meeting had been years ago, had no trouble recognizing him at first glance.

"Hello," replied the Emperor, in his unassertive voice. "I thought you'd probably soon find the library."

Ben nodded gravely and looked around. He could feel the latest trickle of blood from his head wound drying on his face, but for the moment he was experiencing no pain or dizziness. "I've also discovered one of the few books in it that I can read."

The other looked sympathetic, and Ben thought he might be about to offer medical assistance. But instead the Emperor asked: "Is there anything in particular you'd like translated?"

"I don't suppose so. I . . . yes." Ben nodded decisively. "Not these books, though. There were some words on the wall, out in the corridor—"

The Emperor was nodding. Then, in the manner of one preparing to convey information, he turned away, with a jerk of his head to indicate that Ben should come with him.

Two minutes later, the two men were standing in the branch of corridor where characters in Old World script were carved or painted on the wall:

AUTOMATIC RESTORATION DIRECTOR 2
NATIONAL EXECUTIVE HEADQUARTERS
REDUNDANT SYSTEM

A word-for-word translation of this legend left Ben little better informed than he had been; and the Emperor offered further explanation.

"The first letters of the words in the first two lines form an acronym— ARDNEH. You see, Ardneh, the Earthly entity destroyed so long ago, was a machine. A thinking machine of sorts, what the Old World folk called a computer.

"Doing the job for which it had been constructed, Ardneh cast a Change upon that world, and saved the world when war threatened to destroy it. A Change that cancelled the effectiveness of much of the Old World's *technology*, and, at the same time, brought back magic. What had been nuclear explosions became demons. . . ."

Ben said: "The truth behind the story that the Scriptures tell."

The Emperor nodded.

Ben felt light on his feet, light in his head. But not bad. It was perfectly easy to stand here. "But Ardneh, whatever he really was, existed on Earth. And was destroyed there, two thousand years ago, along with the demon Orcus."

The Emperor's hand—how human, how ordinary it appeared—reached up on the wall to tap a finger on the last two words of the inscription. He repeated their translation. " 'Redundant system.' Meaning another Ardneh. One might say *Ardneh Two.*" He spoke two words in the old language. "The reason why the Change endures, and magic works, long after Ardneh on the Earth was done to death."

"Ardneh-tu?" Ben repeated unfamiliar syllables.

"Yes. Would you like to meet him?"

Minutes later, at the entrance to yet another chamber carved from deep and ancient lunar rock, the Emperor stepped back, allowing Ben to go in alone.

He noted with little surprise that Yambu was already there, and looked up at Ben's entrance. But before Ben could speak to her, a box of metal, large as a man but built into a wall, greeted him with words of welcome.

Ben stared back at the box, and was reminded of the White Temple's carven image. He asked it: "You are Ardneh-tu?"

"I am." The voice from the box was bland, human and yet unfeeling.

The two humans and the machine were confronting each other in a strangely-lighted room, densely occupied by metal boxes, cabinets, and consoles of unknown materials. There were chests of tools, long cables like multiheaded snakes, interlocking nests of metal and glass.

It was Yambu's turn to ask a question; evidently she and the machine had begun a dialogue before Ben's arrival. Now the Silver Queen, in the manner of one continuing some earlier discussion, asked Ardneh-tu: "Then the Emperor is your creation?"

"No. It would be closer to the truth to say that I am his work. And so are you. All humanity."

Yambu questioned Ardneh-tu sharply: "But you told me that people of the Old World made you."

"That is true."

The lady looked helplessly to Ben, but he could only gesture vaguely with his huge hands, signalling his own hopeless lack of comprehension.

Yambu turned back to the box that spoke. "Then I do not understand."

"Humans are not fully equipped to understand. It is not required of them."

The Dark King, totally ignoring all presence on the Moon save for his own and those of his demonic escort, had been making his way, overcoming one magical barrier after another, to the crevice in deep rock where, according to Arridu's story, Soulcutter had been hidden by the Emperor some twenty years ago.

For once, it appeared, Arridu, even without compulsion, had told the truth.

The Sword of Despair was encapsulated even as the great demon had described it, almost as the demons themselves had earlier been sealed in, embedded in a block of some solid crystalline material, and that, in turn, sunk deep in black volcanic rock.

Around the intruding wizard the rock for half a kilometer in every direction was shaking, breaking, shattering—the demons who were aiding him groaned and labored and cried out in their travail.

Extremely powerful magic was necessary to retrieve the Sword of Despair—a great price, of course, had to be paid to undo the Emperor's sealing. But to a man who had willingly steeled himself to sacrifice his own eyes, no price was too great that still left him able to hate, to strike his enemies.

The job of extracting Soulcutter from the Emperor's sealing required many hours, extreme exertion, and no little pain, even for a sorcerer of the Dark King's power. But eventually, by dint of determined and ruthless effort, the magical procedures were completed and Vilkata was able to draw forth the sheathed Sword—and at that moment he collapsed, overtaken by some disaster against which Shieldbreaker had been able to afford him no protection.

The collapse was not physical, and it was accompanied by no dramatic show, but it was certain, and effectively complete. But the Dark King still stood tall, even as he allowed Arridu to strip him of both his Swords.

The demon standing in warrior form held the gods' sheathed weapons negligently, both hilts clasped in one huge hand, as if he were as far beyond the power of their double magic as they were beyond mere ordinary steel.

Vilkata meanwhile continued to hold up his two empty hands, their fingers still half-clenched as if around black hilts. He gave no sign of understanding that the gods' weapons had been taken from him. He turned his eyeless gaze from one hand to the other, seeing only what he wanted to see there—because Pitmedden had been driven insane too.

"Arridu!" The Dark King's command still crackled with authority.

"Yes, great Master?" The demon's voice this time was thick with mockery.

But Vilkata did not notice. "I want to get back to Earth as quickly as possible. Do you think the spacecraft or on a demon-ride . . . ?"

"Which would be swifter? Why, the great Master must decide that for himself—but is not the Master forgetting something?"

A light frown creased the eyeless face. "Forgetting—what?"

"Why, Unsurpassable Lord, that Your Lordship's greatest enemy is even now your prisoner. And that the torture chamber awaits your pleasure."

"I—yes, of course." And Vilkata, turning in the indicated direction, saw to his delight that all was indeed as the demon had said. There, in the small, cramped room was the rack in readiness, the thumbscrews waiting, the small brazier where a fire of magical intensity heated sharp slivers of poisoned metal—a whole array of delights for the connoisseur of torment.

Only the victim was missing; and that lack, of course, could soon be remedied.

The great demon watched with amusement as the blind man approached the rack. Vilkata set aside, for the moment, his imaginary Swords, and began the task of fastening himself upon it. The ankles were easy, the left wrist a trifle more difficult. The right hand of course would have been impossible—but then it was necessary for the torturer to keep at least one hand free to work with.

Looking on, listening critically to Vilkata's first scream of mingled agony and triumph, the great demon toyed with the hilt of Shieldbreaker and murmured: "Even the Sword of Force could not save you. Because it was no weapon which brought thee to this sorry state—only thine own will. Thy pledge so freely given was accepted, the bargain kept. Still art thou able to hate, to strike at thy enemies—that thy blows should actually hurt them was not guaranteed."

The Dark King, slowly, sadistically rending his own flesh, was now muttering disjointed phrases, cries of triumph mingling, alternating, with groans of pain.

Arridu, savoring this suffering, bent a little close to hear better.

In the intervals when Vilkata was capable of speech, he spoke of future plans. When Earth was conquered he would command his demons to carry him off into space, there to complete his glorious conquest of the Sun. . . .

* * *

A few hours later Arridu, contemptuous of any human resistance which might face him when he arrived, completed his own swift return to Earth.

He brought with him two Swords, Shieldbreaker and Soulcutter. And he was well aware that on Earth, in the hands of his enemies, only one Sword, Woundhealer, still remained intact.

Arridu knew the bearer of the Sword of Love and sought him out at once.

The last duel took place in full daylight, upon a grassy summer hill not far from Sarykam, and it was fought between Arridu, carrying both Soulcutter and Shieldbreaker drawn, and Prince Mark of Tasavalta, armed only with the Sword of Love. Other loyal humans stood by ready to help Mark—until the arrival of Soulcutter cast all who were within arrowshot into a deep and paralyzing despair.

Mark, holding Woundhealer embedded in his own heart, was unaffected by the Sword of Despair. And the Prince had no thought, in this climactic confrontation, of simply banishing his tremendous foe.

"Should I do so, he will only come back, sooner or later, to attack me. Or worse, to ravage the rest of the world. Let the matter between us be fought out here and now."

Prince Mark, when the subject of the Sword of Despair had lately been raised in discussion, or when it had come up in his own thoughts, would recall a brief meeting he had about five years ago with his true father. At that time the Emperor had denied possessing Soulcutter, even though Mark had earlier seen him pick up that Sword from a field of battle. And whenever Mark's father made a flat statement like that, Mark had never known it to be wrong.

And now Mark faced a nice, practical, tactical question: How should an unarmed opponent—like himself, for one armed only with Woundhealer was effectively unarmed—how should such a one attempt to fight an enemy who held Shieldbreaker *and* the Sword of Despair?

And Mark thought he knew; his recent experience with Farslayer had helped him acquire the knowledge.

It could be assumed, or gambled, though no one could claim solid proof, that Woundhealer would save the mind as well as the body from ongoing damage—or repair the damage as fast as it was inflicted.

Mark, his left hand still clamping the hilt of Woundhealer hard against his own ribs, feeling the transcendent giddiness of the Sword of Love buried in his own heart, leapt in to wrestle with only his right hand.

Arridu immediately dropped Shieldbreaker—and was at once seized, staggered as he had dared to hope he would not be, by the mortal power of unsheathed Soulcutter still in his other hand. The impact of Despair was strong enough to stun the demon momentarily, send him reeling back. Soulcutter slipped from his weakened grip.

Mark, still holding himself transfixed with the Sword of Love, grabbed up the discarded Sword of Force and struck at the nearest vital target, smashing Soulcutter to bits as the Sword of Despair lay on the ground.

Its poisoned fragments stung him harmlessly. *At least, at last, if all our struggles achieve nothing else, that damned thing is gone.* . . .

Now the great demon, stunned and terrified by the loss of two Swords, turned to flee. And Mark, determined that Arridu should not escape, hurled Shieldbreaker after him . . . he saw to his horror the demon's figure twisting in mid-air, saw the gigantic warrior's hand reach out to seize the spinning hilt of the Sword of Force. Screaming with new triumph, howling like a whirlwind, the enormous demon fell upon him.

Mark started to draw from his own breast the only Sword he had, meaning to meet the last attack full on.

His effort came too late. Shieldbreaker and Woundhealer were smashed together, inside a human heart.

20

Ben of Purkinje and Lady Yambu walked out of Ardneh-tu's lunar dwelling place together, having been told by that ancient intelligence that they would each find what they were seeking on the shores of the Lake of Life.

The path on which Ardneh-tu had directed them lay through the little spaceport. As the Silver Queen and Ben traversed that chamber with slow, almost bounding lunar strides, both humans glanced once more in passing at the Old World spacecraft which had brought them to the Moon.

"All right with me," said Ben, "if I never have to ride in one of those things again."

Actually the huge man had little thought or feeling one way or the other about getting back to Earth. He was rather surprised that the question seemed so abstract, did not seem to concern him. But so it was.

Nor, he decided, was this attitude entirely the result of his head wound, because the Silver Queen, whose injuries had been much lighter than his, muttered some vague agreement with Ben's remark—her thoughts continued to be concentrated upon her promised opportunity to see her husband again, a chance to demand some answers from him.

Yambu and Ben, still following their respective directions given by Ardneh-tu, soon came to another temporary parting of the ways. Neither was concerned; all sense of danger had imperceptibly receded; and Ardneh-tu had assured them that they would be safe if they went where he had directed them.

Ben could smell the fecund moisture of the Lake of Life for some time before actually entering the great cave in which it lay. The impression on entering was far from cave-like—a crystal ceiling, startlingly distant, was lighted by refracted sunlight. Ben remembered Draffut's mentioning that the slow lunar sunrise would soon take place in this region of the lunar surface.

* * *

On hearing his goal described as a lake, Ben had envisioned some kind of underground pool; but the reality surprised him, even though the Lake itself was not yet in sight. He was standing on one edge of a vast columned space whose glowing overhead suggested an Earthly sky and whose floor sloped down toward a mass of bright vegetation, concealing whatever might lie beyond—presumably including the Lake of Life itself.

He had not advanced much farther when he stopped suddenly in his tracks. All he could think was: *Sightblinder cannot be here. The Sword of Stealth has been destroyed. What I see now must be an image cast by some other magic.*

Or else—

Perhaps fifty meters from where he stood, on the far side of the visible space, in the garden area where the light was brightest, Ben saw Ariane, the red-haired love of his long-vanished youth.

Birds rose in alarm from among the nearer trees as he went bounding and stumbling forward, all else forgotten.

The young woman—to all appearances still unchanged from when Ben had last seen her more than twenty years ago—was dressed in simple but attractive clothing. When he first saw her, she was busy about some routine task—some kind of gardening, troweling rich black and very Earthy-looking soil.

At the sound of Ben's voice, Ariane looked up. His last doubt vanished —it was she. Joy came to her face, but no enormous surprise. In a moment she was running to greet Ben happily, as if she had been expecting him.

For a long, cold moment, the thought of Sightblinder's illusions returned to torment Ben's mind. But he knew, if he knew anything, that that Sword had been destroyed.

Then the moment of renewed doubt was past. Ben clutched the young woman's large, strong body to him, swept her off her feet. This was no illusion. No. His knees had felt weak as she came running toward him, but now his whole body felt strong again.

A minute later, he and Ariane were seated side by side, on the fallen bole of some odd tree or giant fern, quite near the spot where she had been gardening. The whole garden, smelling of damp earth and life, seemed a fascinating mixture of the controlled and the natural.

And peaceful. In a dazed way Ben became aware that this lunar environment, so strange and changeable, sometimes so antagonistic, had in the last few minutes, even apart from the miraculous presence of Ariane, grown astonishingly friendly.

Even the gravity now seemed more like that of his homeworld—he wondered if that meant that he was weakening. But at the moment illness and injury were the farthest things from Ben's thoughts.

It required recurrent mental effort to reassure himself that he was really still on the Moon, and not somewhere beside one of the warm seas of his own world. There were green things, some plain, some exotic, spiked with a profusion of multicolored flowers, growing on three sides of where he sat. And in the middle distance beyond the thickest greenery, where the distant crystal cave-walls were no longer visible, a bright mist suggested almost irresistibly that gray sky, and not a cave-roof, lay beyond.

Here and there among the nearby shrubbery, several fountains played —Ben had not noticed them before. The statuary in at least one of them was slowly shifting shape, as if on the verge of bursting into life—and it was into this rippling, unquiet basin that Ariane dipped a crystal cup, then brought it to Ben, saying: "Here, drink this."

Until that moment Ben had not been conscious of thirst, but having brought the cup to his lips he drank deep. It was, he thought, the best drink he'd ever had.

Feeling refreshed, seeing and hearing everything more clearly, he cocked his head a little on one side. "You know, I hear something that sounds like surf, big waves. Or I think I do."

Ariane glanced back over her shoulder. "Yes, there are waves. It's the Lake of Life just over there. The people of the Old World made it. They made a smaller one on Earth, too—or so Draffut tells me. But that was destroyed two thousand years ago."

"I thought that Lake was only legend."

The waves of red hair bobbed. "Legend, yes. But also as real as Draffut is. He says it was immersion in the Lake on Earth that first made him something more than a dog."

"I think I could use some of it myself." Though at the moment he really felt quite well.

Ariane's green eyes twinkled. "You don't really need it any more— anyway, you've just had some."

Ben nodded slowly, as if on some level he was beginning to understand. What little he could see of this lake through the screen of vegetation, no more than a small glimpse here and there, suggested that it might stretch on for kilometers—or was that only an effect of mist and light? Certainly the forest of growth on this shore was diverse and fertile beyond anything Ben had ever experienced or even imagined.

* * *

Ariane had put a hand on his shoulder and was looking him in the face —as if she were looking at a young man, in a way that stirred his blood. Then she smiled and asked him: "Tell me how you came here?"

In a few moments, after a false start or two, Ben was relating the tale of how Coinspinner had been blasted out of his hand in the coastal cave near Sarykam. He added the comment that there must now be very few Swords left on Earth or anywhere else, though he had no up-to-date certainty about numbers.

Ben also expressed his worries about Shieldbreaker and Soulcutter, and how Prince Mark and the rest of Tasavalta were going to deal with them.

But Ariane did not seem at all perturbed. She assured the man she loved that he had done all he could do. He didn't have to worry about such matters anymore.

He protested. "If Mark—"

"You've done all that you can do for Mark."

"I suppose you're right." Ben put his face down in his hands and rubbed his eyes. Then he looked up again. Ariane was still sitting right beside him.

"Are you really here?" he whispered hoarsely. "Am I?"

"I'm really here. And so are you." And the young woman, garbed simply but richly in garments whose shapes showed her strong body to advantage, whose colors harmonized with her red hair, continued to sit close beside the huge man, looking at him lovingly. It was a restful attitude. There was no hurry about anything.

"Ben?" As if she were wondering—not worried, only curious—why he remained silent.

"Ariane? It's really you?"

"Yes, foolish man, are you still worried? Of course it's me." Strong pale fingers pinched his arm.

He rubbed the pinched spot absently. "But how did you get here? On the Moon? And when?"

"You're here, aren't you?" She made it sound like an eminently practical answer. "Well, I've been here, with my father, almost since I last saw you."

Absently he rubbed at his forehead, where his fingers could no longer discover any sweat, or blood. Or wound. He asked: "You mean with the Emperor? Since when?"

"I've just told you. Yes, the man you call the Emperor's my father— but you knew that. Actually, to me it doesn't seem very long since you and I were parted. We were trying to steal some treasure, as I recall. All in a worthy cause, of course." She smiled as at some memory of childhood pranks. She stroked Ben's head, the back of his neck. If there was a little soreness still, pain had receded so far as to be faintly enjoyable, little more than a memory, as happened when a wound or a sprain was almost healed.

He asked: "Just you and your father live here?"

Ariane's laughter tinkled; a delicate sound to come from a body so big and strong. "*No,* Foolish One. There are others. A great many other people. You'll meet them. Some you already know."

"Really?"

He wanted to ask who else was here that he might know, but instead closed his eyes. Whether magic was involved in what Ariane—and her father—were doing for him, or *technology,* or some sweet drug in the drink she'd given him, or what, Ben was being slowly overwhelmed by a sense of blissful tiredness and relaxation. In a little while, he felt sure, he was going to fall asleep. Now there would be time and security in which to sleep.

Ben felt a momentary regression toward childhood. How strange. But he was certain there was no danger, now, in such abandonment. Opening his eyes again, Ben told his love: "I wish I had a father like yours."

She nodded soberly, as at some reasonable request. "He'll be glad to be your father if you want."

Ben thought about it. The last time he had seen the Emperor, the Emperor had looked younger than Ben. Ben started a chuckle but it quickly faded.

Then something occurred to him, to his renascent adult self. An item of information that should be passed along. "Your mother's here," he told Ariane. "Lady Yambu came with me in the shuttle, from—from the Earth."

The green eyes of his beloved opened wide with eagerness; a delicious little personal trait that Ben realized he had forgotten until this moment. She said: "I want to see my mother—but there's no hurry. Right now I just want to be with you."

Ariane, Ariane. Yes, it had to be twenty years, Ben thought—really a little more than twenty—since he had seen this young woman or touched her hand. But he remembered perfectly how her hand felt, solid and warm and somewhat roughened by active use. It felt just like this.

So many seasons, so many events and people had come and gone that he was finding it difficult to be accurate about the reckoning.

"As I remember the way things were so long ago—you loved me then. You really did."

"I really did. I really do." And at this point the red-haired young woman kissed this man who loved her. Then she got up from her seat and her fingers became busy, rubbing her fingers over the now-painless spot on Ben's head where he'd been wounded, then splashing him gently with more water from the fountain.

It was all delightful. Perfect. But Ben's lingering sense of mundane reality, though fading by the moment, was still strong enough to be offended by this situation. "I was a young man then, when last we met. I'm getting to be an old man now. My wife and my daughter may both be dead, for all I know. They were taken hostage, I think. . . ."

"I know." But here, now, no one's death seemed to be of any great concern. Everyone had some difficulties along that line, but they were temporary. And Ben's beloved, as young and beautiful as memory would have her, put a hand on his arm. Her touch was very real. She only smiled, faintly, as if there was something, some delightful secret, that she was going to explain to him, sooner or later, when she got around to it. But there was no hurry. Ben understood, without having it spelled out for him, that there was going to be plenty of time for explanations. All the time that anyone could want.

A little later, Ben became aware of other people, moving, strolling, at some distance along the shore of the Lake of Life. He could hear other voices from time to time, though their words were indistinguishable. "Who's that—?"

And at the same time, in a secluded cove not very distant along the shore of this Lake of Life, the Silver Queen, Ariane's mother, was being reunited with her husband.

There was a black-brown curve of sandy beach, lapped by occasional waves, and out beyond the gentle surf the surface of the water in the Lake vanished into a shimmering, indeterminate distance. When the Lady Yambu came upon the Emperor in this spot he was also gardening, driving with his right foot to thrust his shovel firmly and unhurriedly into the black rich soil, getting ready to plant something new in the superfertile soil beside the Lake.

Gladly he paused in his work, wiped a trace of sweat from his forehead, leaned with muscular forearms crossed upon the handle of his shovel, and welcomed his caller with the calm of a loving husband who has perhaps been separated from his wife for a few hours.

In fact he moved at once to kiss Yambu, but she was still wary, and put him off.

The Emperor shrugged, stepped back and did not press the matter. He had all the time there was, and he could wait.

Husband and wife soon found several things that both of them were eager to talk about. One of the first such topics was their daughter.

Another was the fact that the Emperor really wanted the help of the Silver Queen in cultivating the new garden he was planning on this section of the Lake's shore.

"Are you telling me that you've brought me here simply to help you tend a garden?"

This led the discussion to another item: some explanation for the fact that the two of them, despite an obvious mutual attraction, had frequently argued and quarreled.

And Yambu (she was now sitting on a beach-side boulder, the rock's surface mottled with some ever-moving design of life, while her husband still leaned on his spade; and now she noticed, with a feeling of merely confirming what was right and proper, that her long hair when the breeze stirred it before her eyes was no longer gray but jetty black) said to her husband: "It seems to me, looking back on it, that we never got along at all when we were married. And yet, I doubt that I would ever consider marrying anyone else."

He almost frowned. "If I have anything to say about it you'd better not consider that."

"You're jealous." She said it unbelievingly.

"I am."

Her anger rose up. "But of course it's quite all right for you to be promiscuous, because you are . . ." Yambu stopped uncertainly.

"A man? You know me better than to think I would make that excuse."

"You father children everywhere."

"I give them life. It is not behavior I can recommend to every man."

"But, of course, for *you*—"

"Yes. For me."

Yambu shook her head as if to clear it. She meant to come back to argue that point later. "Speaking of your children, do you know your son Prince Mark for years has spent a great deal of time and worry trying to locate you? Even to the neglect of his own family?"

"I know."

"Well?" Impatience flared. "The poor man wants to know who you are, beyond a name, an image. And so do I."

Her companion raised an eyebrow. "You have been my wife for all these years, you've borne my child—and you don't know?"

"If I had lived with you for all these years, perhaps I could comprehend the situation. As matters stand, I want you to tell me."

The Emperor was no longer leaning on his shovel; his shovel had somehow disappeared. His face seemed plainer, more distinct, than any man's face should be. He said, in a voice not grown louder, but much changed: "Some long ago have called me the Sabbath, or the Covenant—some have called me Wisdom. Some lately have said that I am the Program of Creation."

A long moment passed before the Silver Queen persisted: "And you—? I want you to tell me what you are."

He—plainly her husband once again—stretched out his hand to her. "Come live with me. And argue with me again, and learn. I am the Truth."

Under a balmy Earthly sky a Tasavaltan celebration was just getting under way. And people were considering the result of the last Swordcombat. Arridu was dead, obliterated in the explosion of Shieldbreaker's deadly fragments—and only Woundhealer, of all the Twelve Swords, still survived.

It was Stephen's older brother Adrian, come home from his distant studies as quickly as he could, but just too late to join the fight, who at length deduced and announced an explanation—how Shieldbreaker, once in Mark's heart, had become the Prince's and not the demon's weapon—and how the blast of its destruction, edge to edge against the one Sword it could not break, had slain the demon at close range.

The victorious Prince Mark, his family, and all who stood by them were aware that Ben of Purkinje and Lady Yambu had somehow left them, but they were not unduly worried about either missing person.

Mark had his wife and his children safe, and for the time being he was content.

And it was Stephen, marveling, who discovered, at some distance from the field of combat, the charred, cracked, useless hilt of what had once been the Sword of Force. In the boy's hand the black wood was now suddenly sprouting a green shoot.

Stephen went running to show the marvel to his father.

THE END